The Age of Serpents and Scorpions

US edition first published in 2026
by The Black Spring Press Group
London, United Kingdom

Printed in Canada

Cover and interior design by Edwin Smet
Cover art by Alice Lockhart

ISBN 978-1-915406-92-7

This is a work of fiction. Names, characters, places, and
events are either products of the author's mind or are used in
a fictional way. Any likeness to real people, living or dead, or
actual events is totally by chance. It is up to the reader to decide
if the Biblical characters are as represented here.

BLACKSPRINGPRESSGROUP.COM

The Age of Serpents and Scorpions

Tom Cladis

THE **BLACK SPRING**
PRESS GROUP

Dedication

Dedicated to my heartbeats, Doria, Elleni, Cassiane, and Mariah; to my son-in-loves, Will and Philipp; to all the open-minded "rule" changers who refuse to drop anchor;
and to my grandsons, Flynn and Liam, and the next generation of free-thinkers who see the world not as it is, but as it should be.

"Watch, therefore, for you don't know the day nor the hour in which the Son of Man is coming."

—Matthew 25:13

Part One

In 1884, *Scientific American*, America's oldest continuously published magazine, joined the debate initiated 174 years earlier by philosopher George Berkeley when it addressed the question, "If a tree were to fall on an uninhabited island, would there be any sound?"

The venerable magazine concluded, "Sound is a vibration, transmitted to our senses through the mechanism of the ear, and recognized as sound only at our nerve centers. The falling of the tree or any other disturbance will produce vibration of the air. If there be no ears to hear, there will be no sound."

Accordingly, there was no sound when a woman's voice in southeast Denver worried, "It's amazing how focused he is, and how clearly he sees things."

A man's voice answered, "That's what happens when you break out of the self-imposed prison of Can't/Won't. There are no walls to obstruct your view."

"They're coming for him."

"Yes."

"I'm afraid for him."

"Don't be. The wise man prays not for safety from the storm, but for deliverance from fear, lest he breathe life into what is feared. He's on the right path."

Nor was there a sound when, minutes later, a rifle shot killed Roland Thomas in the Wet Mountains, just east of Westcliffe, the historic county seat of Custer County in southeast Colorado.

Part Two

I

George Rivers bounded up the steps in front of Benjamin Franklin High School, two at a time. He was late. He'd blame it on the traffic. Who was he kidding? He simply hadn't allowed enough time to get there. He pulled on the door. Locked. "Perfect," he groaned. A sign next to the door said to push the buzzer to gain entrance, then to proceed to the main office to check in. Sign of the times. He pushed the button.

A disinterested voice came across the intercom. "May I help you?"

"Yes," he answered. "George Rivers to see Mrs. Keeler."

After a pause best described as pregnant, a buzzer sounded. This time the door yielded to his ministrations, and he hurried to the main office where he showed his driver's license, signed in, wrote his name on a nametag, and stuck it to his shirt.

"Room 417," the receptionist rotely directed. "Take the stairway on the left to the fourth floor, then turn right." She looked at her watch. 3:05. "You're late."

As if he needed reminding. George rounded the corner to his left and, again, raced up the stairs by twos. By the time he burst into Room 417 and breathlessly introduced himself to his son's teacher, beads of perspiration had formed on his brow.

"I'm sorry I'm late," he apologized.

Ruth Keeler laughed off his apology. "I see you met Brandy at the front desk!" she smiled disarmingly. "You're fine. Can I offer you some water?"

"That would be nice, thank you!"

The teacher retrieved a small bottle of water from the mini-fridge behind her desk, then suggested they sit in two of the students' seats at the front of the classroom. As George savored the water, Mrs. Keeler began.

"Thank you, Mr. Rivers, for taking the time to meet with me."

"Of course," George replied. "Has Jimmy done something wrong? I know his grades are pretty good."

"Jimmy's a wonderful student," she reassured him. "The reason I asked you here is more of a personal nature."

"I don't understand."

"First of all, I know it's been almost six years since you lost your wife, and I am so sorry for your loss."

"Thank you," George said in a low voice.

"Is Jimmy currently seeing anyone to help him move on?" she continued.

"He is. Why?"

"Well, don't get me wrong. As I said, he is one of my top students, and he gets along very cordially with his classmates. It's just that seventeen-year-old boys should be more than cordial with their peers."

George considered the well-meaning teacher's words carefully. "He's been through a lot," he sighed.

"I know he has, Mr. Rivers. To lose his mother at such an early age under such tragic circumstances is almost unfathomable. It's good to know he still has a professional to talk to – and I know that healing is a process and that it's different for everyone, but I'm getting the feeling he's not entirely open to it."

"I'm sorry. I'm not sure I'm following you."

"Did you ever read the book or see the movie, *The French Lieutenant's Woman*?"

"Yes, a long time ago. Maybe twenty or thirty years ago."

"You may recall that Sarah Woodruff had an affair with a French naval officer named Varguennes, who abandoned her. And she spends her time at the Cobb, a pier jutting out to sea, staring at its vastness, hoping to see Varguennes somehow emerge from the emptiness to swoop her back into his arms and carry her away.

"Of course, Varguennes never returns and she would have been left to pine for him for the remainder of her days were it not for the attention of Charles Smithson, whose curiosity evolved into love. And Sarah finally left the Cobb.

"Mr. Rivers, Jimmy is at the Cobb right now, still pining for his French lieutenant, his Mother. He refuses to engage beyond politeness. He has removed himself from the life around him. Just like Sarah, he is not living."

George Rivers shook his head in frustration. "I have tried everything. He's been seeing a therapist three times a week since his mother was killed. We go to church. I've tried to get him involved in sports and music, but he's just not interested. When we're together, he seems like he's healing, like he's getting better, but he has such separation anxiety.

"I don't think he's ever really accepted that his Mother is not coming back. His therapist says the same thing – even after six years, the minute he broaches the subject of his Mother's death, he completely shuts him out. I'm really at a loss for what to do next."

Mrs. Keeler gently placed her hand on George's forearm. She could tell he, too, was in a lot of pain – mostly, from the suffering he saw in his son that he could do nothing about.

"Has Jimmy ever mentioned a girl named Sasha?" she asked.

George thought for a moment. "No, not that I can recall. Should he have?"

"She's a lovely young girl in his class. I only ask because I've noticed that she has taken an interest in him, and he seems to be responding to her a tiny bit. I see him taking some baby steps forward out of his shell, but then he catches himself from going any further, and retreats back in."

George straightened himself in his seat. "There's a girl who likes Jimmy? Are you sure?"

"To be perfectly honest, Mr. Rivers, Sasha confided in me that she was thinking about asking him to the Sadie Hawkins dance this Saturday – you know, where girls ask boys to a dance – and she wanted an objective opinion. I'm not sure she trusted her girlfriends on this one."

George hesitated. "What's she like?"

"She is the sweetest girl, one of the most popular girls in school, and she'd be very sensitive to the trauma that Jimmy's been through. In fact, that's one of the reasons she wanted to get my thoughts – she didn't want to put Jimmy in an awkward position that might make him uncomfortable and do more harm than good."

"Wow," George marveled. "I like her already!"

"I was hoping you'd say that. I just think this could do a world of good for Jimmy, and the potential benefits of getting him away from that pier, so to speak, far outweigh anything bad that could happen, especially with Sasha."

"I totally agree! What can I do? I don't want to betray any confidence that Sasha might have placed in you."

"You know, when girls talk to their friends about boys, they are putting feelers out, so I think we're ok. Did you tell Jimmy you were meeting with me this afternoon?"

"Yes."

"Maybe you could tell him I just wanted to let you know how well I thought he was doing in class, and that during our conversation, you noticed a poster on the wall about the Sadie Hawkins dance and asked me about it."

George stood up to leave and shook Mrs. Keeler's hand. "Thank you so much for keeping an eye out for Jimmy and for letting me know about Sasha. I can see why you're his favorite teacher!"

"Of course, Mr. Rivers. Good luck, and let me know if there's anything else I can do to help."

When he got home, George went straight to his son's room. The door was closed. Naturally, he thought. Shutting out the outside world. He knocked.

"Come in!"

George opened the door and found Jimmy lying on his bed and reading a book. "How was your day today?" he asked, cheerfully.

"Pretty good," Jimmy answered without lifting his eyes from the book.

George couldn't see the title of the book. "What are you reading?"

Jimmy held up the book for his Dad's inspection: *The Ingenious Gentleman Don Quixote of La Mancha.*

George's face brightened when he read the title. "That is absolutely my favorite play!"

"I hate the ending," Jimmy groused.

"I know, but the play is different from the book. Alonso Quijana lives as Don Quixote."

"We talked about that...but he still dies."

George didn't dare offer in Cervantes' defense that everyone eventually dies, so he changed the subject.

"Hey, I saw Mrs. Keeler today."

Jimmy put down the book. "What did she want?"

"Just to tell me how well you're doing in school."

"That's it?"

"Jimmy, you have to give yourself some credit. After your Mom died…"

"She didn't die," Jimmy interrupted, testily. "She was killed!"

"You don't have to remind me, Jimmy. I'm just saying she wanted to tell me how impressed she is with you, and with how you've turned things around. I think she really cares about you."

"Yeah," Jimmy admitted. "She's cool."

"Anyway, I saw a few posters on the wall about a Sadie Hawkins dance this weekend. Are you going to go?"

"Dad, you have to be asked by a girl to go."

"Would you go if a girl asked you?"

"No one's going to ask me, so it doesn't matter."

"But, what if a girl *did* ask you? Would you go?"

"Dad…," Jimmy whined.

"I'm just asking."

"OK, if I answer, will you please stop?"

"I promise."

"Probably not, then."

"I know you're afraid of letting anyone get close to you…"

Jimmy interrupted his father, again. "I'm not afraid!"

"But," George went on, undaunted, "when a girl asks someone to a school dance, it's not a marriage proposal, it's just to have someone to dance with and have fun. You're a seventeen-year-old boy – you should be having fun!"

"Whatever. It's not a big deal, anyway, because it's not going to happen."

"I think it's a big deal, and so would Don Quixote! It takes a lot of courage to ask someone out at your age."

"Dad, I'm done with this conversation. You promised!"

"Just hear me out. As I was saying, do you think Don Quixote, the Knight of Chivalry, would disappoint any girl who put her ego on the line and asked him to accompany her to a dance?"

"Probably not," he said. "Are we done, now?"

"Yes. And I agree. Don Quixote de la Mancha never would let any girl down. OK, I'll have dinner ready in about an hour."

George left the room, leaving the door open...in so many ways, he hoped.

The next day, Jimmy was in the front room watching TV, waiting for his Dad to get home from work. When George walked in the door, Jimmy clicked off the TV and pounced.

"OK, what's going on?"

"Nice to see you, too," George responded cynically. "My day was fine. Thanks for asking."

Jimmy didn't bite. "You know what I'm talking about. Did Mrs. Keeler put you up to it?"

"Whoa, slow down, Speed Racer! What are you talking about? Put me up to what?"

"That whole spiel about the Sadie Hawkins dance. I got asked to go today."

George felt his cheeks beginning to redden – he hoped Jimmy hadn't noticed. "You're kidding, right?"

"No, I'm not!"

"Well, it's just a coincidence." The instant those words left his mouth, George wished he could have taken them back.

"Dad!" Jimmy protested. "You don't believe in coincidences."

George knew he was busted. "Alright, maybe Mrs. Keeler mentioned something about a girl wanting to ask you to the dance. You know, she really cares about you...Mrs. Keeler, I mean. I have to tell you, when we were talking about it – and this might seem weird to you – I felt your Mom's presence. Almost like she was speaking to me through your teacher."

"Fine." Jimmy clicked the TV back on, simultaneously turning his Dad off.

George didn't take the hint. Finally, he asked, "Well?"

Without taking his eyes from the set, Jimmy replied, "I said 'yes.'"

By the time they sat down to dinner, Jimmy had time enough to realize he was way out of his league on this one – and that he had no one else to turn to.

"So, Dad," he spoke up nonchalantly, "have you heard of a TV show called *The Mod Squad* ?"

"From the Seventies? The last great decade?"

Jimmy hated it when he said that, but... "Yeah, that's the one."

"That used to be one of my favorite shows! I can even remember the cast: Michael Cole played Pete Cochrane, Clarence Williams III played Linc Hayes, and Peggy Lipton was Julie Barnes." George chuckled, adding, "I used to have such a crush on Peggy Lipton. I think every teenage boy did. Long, straight, ash blond hair, short skirts, long legs, and drop-dead California gorgeous."

"Gross, Dad! That's way too much information!" Jimmy frowned.

"You forget that..." George caught himself before he dug the hole any deeper. "Anyway, why do you ask?"

"I guess this dance has a 'Back in Time' theme, and Sasha wants us to go as Pete and Julie from *The Mod Squad*."

"And we have a name!" George said with fanfare. "Sounds exotic! What's she like?"

"Dad, please," Jimmy blushed. "She's pretty much the way you described Julie...and very nice!"

"I suppose she's smart, too," George teased.

"Yep."

"Wow, the complete package! So, this 'Back in Time' thing... you can dress up as anyone from any time in the past?"

Jimmy nodded.

"I wonder why she picked *The Mod Squad?*"

"She said she thought I might be a little nervous to do a costume thing right off the bat, and she said Pete from *The Mod Squad* would be pretty easy."

"She *is* smart! Of the three, Pete was the most conservative. At least, he dressed the most conservatively – button-down shirts, long sleeved t-shirts, and jeans, basically. Julie's going to be the one to tie you to the show."

"Sweet!" Jimmy exclaimed. "So, I can just wear what I normally wear?"

"Pretty much. We'll probably be able to find what you'll need at a record store...a t-shirt with a peace sign on it and aviator sunglass-es, and you'll be set.

"How are you getting to the dance? Is it at your school?"

"Yeah. Sasha said she'd pick me up."

"What time?"

Jimmy didn't hear the question. He was a million miles away, lost in his thoughts.

George waved his hand in front of his son's face. "Earth to Jim-my, come in!"

Jimmy snapped out of his funk – kind of. "Sorry, what did you say?"

"I asked you what time Sasha was going to pick you up."

"7:00'

George could tell something was bothering him. "OK, what's the matter?"

Jimmy hemmed and hawed, then finally blurted out, "I just don't understand it. I mean, Sasha could have any boy in the school, and she asked me. I'm nervous. I don't know what to do!"

"Well, I don't know about all the other boys in school, but I do know that you've got something none of them have."

Jimmy looked at his father quizzically.

"You've got you!" George exclaimed. "There is no one else like you. You are totally unique. You said Sasha's a smart girl. Let me tell you something about girls – they are very intuitive. Maybe she sees in you what I see in you – a wonderful human being, and a rockstar! Anyway, whatever it is, she asked *you*. She wants to be with you just the way you've always been around her. Your job is easy. You just have to be yourself!"

Jimmy felt like an 800-pound gorilla had been lifted from his shoulders.

"Thanks, Dad," he said from the bottom of his heart. "So, will you help me find what I need?"

"I'd love to!"

* * *

By the time Saturday rolled around, Jimmy was a nervous wreck. He did like Sasha, and he desperately wanted to make a good impression. He just was tucking in his t-shirt when the doorbell rang – at 7:00 on the dot.

"Jimmy, I think she's here," George called up to his son. "I'll get the door."

"No, Dad, I'll get it! Jimmy shouted, hopping down the stairs.

Too late. George opened the front door and, suddenly, he wasn't in the new millennium anymore. Far from it...like 40 years. The same long, straight, ash blond hair – secured by a thin leather headband around her forehead. The same denim miniskirt, the same white lace embroidered peasant girl top, the same angelic face...It was uncanny.

He managed to compose himself just in time, recovering with, "Julie Barnes, I presume?"

Peggy Lipton's doppelganger flashed an incandescent smile and held out her hand. "Nice, Mr. Rivers. I'm Sasha. It's a pleasure to meet you."

George shook hands with the reincarnation of his high school crush, but before he could invite her inside, Jimmy cut in.

"Sorry," he said to Sasha, slightly out of breath. "I wanted to answer the door."

"Wow," she grinned, taking stock of Jimmy's off-white, peace-sign emblazoned, long-sleeved Henley t-shirt with the aviator glasses hanging from the three-button placket. "Look at you, Pete Cochrane!"

Jimmy felt his face flush, but there was nothing he could do about it. "Thanks! And you look great!"

"I was just about to invite her in," George said.

"We really don't have time right now, do we Sasha?"

Sasha picked up on Jimmy's cue. "Maybe later, Mr. Rivers?" she suggested.

"OK, but let me get one picture of Pete and Julie before you go," George insisted.

When Sasha stood beside him and put her arm around his waist, Jimmy felt a surge of electricity course through his body. His pulse quickened even more as he sheepishly put his arm around her shoulders and subconsciously drew her closer for the picture. Her arm was so lithe and her skin so warm! He wished he could have frozen that moment and kept it forever.

Jimmy was in such a state of so many new emotions, the next thing he remembered was driving in Sasha's black convertible Mustang – and it registering that she had missed the turn for school.

"Hey, I think we should have turned back there," he warned over the music.

Sasha looked at Jimmy. "If we were going to school," she purred slyly, a sparkle in her eye.

"But what about the dance?"

"That was just an excuse to ask you out without you going all deer-in-the-headlights on me."

"And these clothes?"

"They're fun, aren't they?" she said, flashing that 1,000-megawatt smile. "We at least had to act like we were going to the dance!"

Actually, Jimmy wouldn't have changed anything about what

was unfolding.

"So, where *are* we going?"

"To the carnival!" she replied with a flourish. "I love carnivals. We used to go every year. Tonight's the last night, and I thought it would be much more fun than the dance!"

She paused. "You're not upset, are you? If you really wanted to go to the dance, I can turn around."

"Not at all. You just surprised me, that's all. To be honest, I'm just happy to be with you. It wouldn't matter where we were."

"Awww, that's sweet!" she grinned. "I didn't think you'd mind...I kind of had you pegged for a rule-breaker."

Jimmy turned to his pretty chauffeur. "Why do you say that? You hardly know me."

Sasha was quick with her response. "Do you remember the first day of school when Mrs. Keeler asked everyone to tell the class which person in history you'd most like to meet and why? You said Captain Kirk."

"Yes," Jimmy recalled, "and everyone laughed."

"Everyone except me," Sasha corrected. "I was intrigued. Then when you explained how he became captain of the Enterprise by changing the rules of the captain's test that was created to be unsolvable, I knew I had to find out what makes Jimmy Rivers tick."

"Geez, if I had known that..."

Sasha interrupted him by looking him in the eye, putting her hand on his knee and giving it a little squeeze. "Well, now you know," she smiled.

Again, her touch sent shockwaves through his system, and he probably *would* have gone deer-in-the-headlights had he not been jolted from his impending stupor by Sasha turning quickly into the carnival parking lot.

"Here we are," she announced merrily. She parked the car in the first space she came to, about a hundred yards from the entrance. "Race you to the ticket booth!"

With that challenge, she jumped out of the car and started running towards the carnival's main entrance. Jimmy took off after her and managed to get to the booth at the same time.

"Tie goes to the girl," she squealed with delight. "Now you have to kiss me!"

Jimmy froze.

"Oh, come on, you big baby. Just on the cheek," she claimed, indicating the spot with her index finger. "Not on the lips! Ewww..."

Jimmy leaned in for her cheek, but just as he was about to plant his kiss, she quickly swiveled her head so his smooch landed full-on on her lips.

"Oops!" she grinned.

Then, she turned to the woman in the booth and bought two tickets.

Jimmy still was savoring the hint of Sasha's strawberry lip gloss around his mouth when the deep voice of the burly ticket-taker gregariously bellowed, "Do my eyes deceive me? Julie Barnes and Pete Cochrane! Two-thirds of the *Mod Squad*...step right up!"

Sasha handed him the tickets, but he wouldn't let them pass. He demanded to know where Linc was.

Jimmy *did* step right up. "He's attending a Zen Buddhist conference at the Great Vow Zen Monastery in Oregon."

"Yeah," the ticket-taker said, letting them in, "that sounds like him."

Sasha beamed at Jimmy. "There you are! Now, let's go have some real fun!"

And fun they had. The next two hours were filled with bearded ladies and sword swallowers, knife throwers and fire eaters, the Tilt-a-Whirl and the Ferris Wheel, and enough funnel cakes, cotton candy, and Pepsi to fuel a sugar rush to the moon.

Speaking of the moon, when Sasha grabbed Jimmy's hand to hurry him along from the distortion mirrors to see the Globe of Death daredevil motorcycle riders, she sent him over it – the moon, that is - and they held hands the rest of the night.

After their second ride on the Ferris Wheel – a ride much cozier than the first – they dialed down the activities to a food court where they shared a hot dog and a star-lit conversation that had Jimmy shedding some of his deepest inhibitions. For the first time since his mother had been killed, he felt like talking about her to someone other than his therapist.

"There's more to it, you know," he said, randomly.

"More to what?" Sasha asked gently, sensing what was about to come.

"Captain Kirk." And, after almost six years, Jimmy finally shared his story.

Sasha listened silently as Jimmy related in painstaking detail going to the mall with his mom to get a Tony Hawk skateboard for his eleventh birthday – how they had just entered the mall in the middle of the day and how he had heard what he thought were firecrackers going off. But there were people running and screaming, and he saw bodies on the ground...and lots of blood. They started to run too, but one of the gunman's bullets pierced his mother's back. She staggered forward as far as she could – just a few more steps – before collapsing and, in her final moments, using her body to shield him from harm.

Tears were streaming down Jimmy's cheeks. "Her last words to me were, 'Don't be sad, Jimmy. I love you and I'll always be with you. "This is not the end."' And then I felt her body go limp on top of me."

Wiping the tears from his face, Jimmy apologized, "I'm so sorry! I didn't mean to be such a downer," he sniffed.

"Stop it!" Sasha said firmly. "I have had the most wonderful night with you! I'm honored that you trusted me enough to tell me. Your mom is an incredible woman."

Sasha lifted Jimmy's chin, and for the second time that night, he felt her lips on his. This time was different. "And I think you're an amazing boy!"

Her kiss brought him back from that horrible day to the beautiful girl hugging him in the carnival food court.

"Wait a minute," he realized aloud. "You said 'is.' My mom '*is* an incredible woman.'"

"I guess I did, didn't I," Sasha agreed.

"That's just it," Jimmy explained. "I've never been able to wrap my mind around talking about her in the past tense."

"Well, I'm sure she's still with you – you just can't see her."

"My therapist basically says the same thing – nothing is what it seems."

He paused for a moment. "What do you think she meant when she said, "This is not the end?""

"I don't know. Maybe that you'll see her again in heaven?"

"Maybe. But, when I said there's more to it, I was talking about Captain Kirk."

"I'm not sure I'm following you."

"He changed the rules!"

"Right..."

"I want to change the rules, too. I want to change how our shopping trip to the mall ended," Jimmy blurted out.

Sasha caressed his tear-stained face. "Oh, sweetie, you might be reaching for the stars on this one."

"Maybe so, but I just can't accept life the way it is and not as it should be."

Sasha's face brightened. "OK, look, there's a fortune teller over there," she chirped, trying to lighten Jimmy's mood and pointing to a booth across from the food court. "Let's see what his or her crystal ball says."

"A fortune teller? Really, Sasha?"

"Come on, it'll be fun," she said, pulling on his hand. But Jimmy wouldn't budge.

"These guys are quacks!" he declared. "We'd be wasting our money."

"Said the boy who wants to travel through time with a fictional captain named Kirk." She nudged him in the ribs. "Come on, where's the open mind?"

"OK, OK," Jimmy conceded. "I see your point." He stood up and put his arm around Sasha's shoulders, and she put hers around his waist. Anyone who saw the young couple walking towards the Fortune Teller booth never would have guessed that they'd only been 'together' for a few hours.

Sasha stepped through the fortune teller booth's purple velour curtain first with Jimmy right behind her. Their eyes had not yet adjusted to the darkness when a soothing voice greeted them.

"Welcome. You will find a couch to your right. Please sit down and make yourselves comfortable."

A pale light gradually filled the room, just enough for the teenagers to make out the owner of the gentle voice sitting across from them in an oversized chair that could have been a throne in another setting. He was not quite old and dressed conservatively – not at all what Jimmy thought a fortune teller should look like. Truth be told, he looked more like an accountant.

The seer noticed the confusion on the young couple's faces. "I don't look like what you think a fortune teller should look like, do I?"

"Not really," Sasha answered, sheepishly.

"As you may come to find out," the fortune teller explained, "nothing is as it seems." He reached behind his chair and pulled out a rectangular piece of wood and handed it to Sasha.

"What do you know about this piece of wood?" he asked.

She stared at it, weighed it, and looked at it from every angle. "It's brown," she concluded, "and heavy." Then, she handed it to Jimmy.

After a perfunctory examination, he added, "It's about two feet long, a foot wide, maybe six inches thick, and it seems really solid."

Jimmy handed it back to the fortune teller. "Very good. In fact," he confirmed, "it is Australian buloke, the hardest wood in the world. But, knowledge is so limiting and deceiving. It is why Einstein said, 'Imagination is more important than knowledge.' Now, pay close attention."

The fortune teller's caveat in mind, Jimmy and Sasha watched intently as he ceremoniously held up the slab of wood with his left hand and, in front of their astonished eyes, promptly put his right hand through the center of the hardest wood in the world as if it had the consistency of a cloud. Then he withdrew it.

"How did you do that?" Jimmy asked in awe.

The fortune teller's response sent shivers through the teenagers' bodies. "I see the world not as it is, but as it should be. In my world, nothing is impossible."

Sasha elbowed Jimmy in his side – he had spoken those same words at the food court.

"Do it again," Jimmy demanded. "Except this time, let me hold the wood."

The fortune teller smiled. "You are the doubting Thomas. Let me tell you something, though – Thomas never doubted. But it's a good parable."

Neither Jimmy nor Sasha understood what the fortune teller was talking about, but Jimmy gladly accepted the hardwood – and the fortune teller repeated the exercise of putting his hand through the Australian buloke and removing it without damaging either the wood or his hand.

This time, Jimmy sat in stunned silence. Sasha still didn't know what to say.

"Did I blow your minds...open?" the fortune teller asked.

They both nodded their heads.

"Well, then, now you are ready," he said. "I want you to close your eyes, but leave your minds open and focus only on my words."

Jimmy and Sasha did as they were instructed...and they became aware of an intoxicating aroma, almost like incense, filling the air. It wasn't hallucinatory, but they began to feel swept up in a wave of elevated consciousness.

"You are familiar with the Spanish explorer, Juan Ponce de Leon, I trust," the fortune teller began.

The teenagers nodded in unison.

"He was searching for the Fountain of Youth in what is now called Florida. Of course, he never found it – not because it didn't exist, but because he was looking in the wrong place. He was looking outside, when he should have been looking inside..."

Jimmy was completely dialed in. Sasha wasn't far behind, as the fortune teller continued.

"In a few moments, you will see a large wall reaching higher into the sky than your eyes can follow."

The fortune teller waited. But, not long.

"I see it!" Jimmy exclaimed.

In the next moment, Sasha chimed in. "Me, too!"

"Look very closely," the fortune teller said evenly. "On your side of the wall, you will see Lucifer, Death, and Impossibility. On the other side, you'll see the exact opposite. You will see God. And Life. And Possibility."

Again, the fortune teller waited patiently.

"Oh, my God," Jimmy muttered under his breath.

"How do you do that?" Sasha wanted to know.

"I'm not doing anything other than opening your minds so that you can see what no one wants you to see. If you look more closely, still, you'll find yourselves."

Sure enough, as Sasha looked deeper inside her mind, she did find herself – but not on the side of the wall she would have preferred. "I'm on the wrong side," she groaned.

Jimmy discovered the same thing about himself. "Why am I on this side?" he objected. "I believe in God."

"Yes, you do. You both do," the fortune teller replied calmly. "But, do you believe what He says? He sent His Son not only to save us from ourselves, but also to remind us of our divine inheritance.

"Jesus assured us that if we had faith and did not doubt, nothing would be impossible for us. But, no one believes Him...and that's what puts you on the wrong side of the wall, as you call it. You cannot be on both sides at the same time. By that, I mean that you either believe that all things are possible, or you don't."

Sasha opened her eyes. "Who are you? You're not really a fortune teller."

"No, I'm not," he answered. "You are in charge of your own fortunes by the choices you make. So, in effect, you are the tellers. I'm more of a fortune listener."

She looked at Jimmy. But, he was so entranced that he was oblivious to everything else, as if he was in another universe. "What about

Jimmy?" she asked. "Where is he right now?"

"He's about to tell us. He may be on the wrong side of the wall for now, but he refuses to accept things that are not as he wants them to be."

Sasha was incredulous. "How could you possibly know that?"

"Never mind how I know, just listen. He's about to find a gate."

Jimmy was so far inside the moment, nothing else existed except the wall – and the fact that he wanted to get to the other side. The fortune teller was right, he thought to himself, staring at the wall, and trying to keep up with the stream of consciousness that was flooding his mind. Nothing is at it seems. What about that Australian buloke? What was that all about? But there are rules and laws... whose are they, though? They're not God's rules, they're man's rules. If they're man's rules, then they can be changed. Just like Captain Kirk changed the test! This is my test. Who says things are impossible? Not God! Man does. What does man know, anyway? Edison says only about one-millionth of one percent of all there is to know. So, man doesn't know anything! I have to get to the other side!

"I see a gate!" Jimmy announced, suddenly.

Sasha stared at the fortune teller in amazement. Who was this man? she wondered.

"It's narrow," Jimmy continued, "and about twenty feet off the ground."

He fell quiet as he tried to figure out a way to get to the narrow gate. The wall was completely sheer. The landscape was devoid of anything that might give him a boost. Lucifer was taunting him, telling him it was God's way of tormenting him by putting the gate so close and yet so far away.

Jimmy chose to ignore the serpent's temptation to doubt God and, instead, turned to the fortune teller. "I can't get there," he fretted from deep within his trance. "Help me."

"I already have," the fortune teller acknowledged. "You have to make a choice. You have to choose which you want more – to stay focused on 'can't' or to enter the narrow gate. I will tell you the choices are mutually exclusive. If you choose 'can't," you won't. If, however, you choose 'can,' you will free yourself from the prison of can't and from all its limits, and you *will* enter the gate. As always, the choice is yours."

"What's happening?" Sasha asked desperately.

"Be patient, my child. He's about to tell you his story and reveal his choice."

Sasha watched over Jimmy as a mother watches her new-born baby sleep, excited and frightened at the same time. She finally admitted to herself what she had been trying to talk herself out of the whole night. She was falling in love with him. He was her new-born love, and she prayed to God to help him choose wisely. What was going on inside his mind?

She didn't have to wait much longer for an answer.

"He's moving!" she shrieked.

"Yes, he is," smiled the fortune teller. "He's about to reveal his choice to you. There's no stopping him now."

Sasha could no longer contain the tears that had welled up in her eyes. They spilled down her cheeks in a torrent as Jimmy's body slowly rose to the ceiling...and then through it! She raced back through the purple velour curtain to see Jimmy hovering in the air, ten feet above the top of the fortune teller's booth.

A crowd had begun to gather, with people pointing at Jimmy floating, thinking they were witnessing a great magic trick.

"I'm at the gate!" Jimmy called out. "I'm going through it!"

He reached for the handle, pulled the gate open, and took the first step of his journey into a world where time did not exist.

The moment he stepped past the narrow gate, his body vanished, seemingly into thin air, right before the appreciative crowd's eyes. They erupted into spontaneous applause, thrilled by the fortune teller's magic.

"How did he do that?" a voice mused.

"Smoke and mirrors," another answered.

"Like Tupac at Coachella. Probably a hologram, or something like that," a third voice offered.

Apparently satisfied with one of the explanations, the crowd dispersed as quickly as it had formed.

Sasha, was not satisfied, however.

"What just happened?" she begged of the fortune teller, her body quivering uncontrollably. "Where is Jimmy?"

"Jimmy has freed his mind. He is no longer bound by earthly constraints or by the rules of Man. Go home, Sasha. You'll see him in the morning. I promise."

When the fortune teller put his arm around her quaking shoulders to steady her nerves, Sasha at once stopped shaking. She was bathed in a calmness and warmth she had never felt before. She looked into the fortune teller's eyes and knew she could trust him.

"I believe you," she whispered. She kissed the fortune teller's cheek and started towards the parking lot.

2

Jimmy, on the other hand, was far from content. He was overwhelmed by his newly found freedom. He actually had *flown* up to the narrow gate, but once he stepped through it, the ground had risen up to greet him and he had something solid on which to stand. He was grounded in a sense, but not, on the other side of the wall.

"Now what?" he wondered.

He peered in every direction, trying to get his bearings – and in the far-off distance, he spied what he thought to be a windmill.

"Why not?" he shrugged. And he started off in the direction of the structure. It didn't register that he didn't feel his feet on the ground.

As he got closer and realized that it truly was a windmill, he was distracted from his meanderings by a commotion to his left, and though Jimmy had witnessed so many incongruous sights that day – including the one in front of him – he still couldn't believe his eyes. A knight arrayed in armor had tilted his lance at the windmill. He dug his heels into his horse's sides, shouting at his companion, "Thou hast seen nothing, yet, Sancho!"

"No way!" Jimmy uttered. But, his eyes had not deceived him. The horse and rider charged the windmill at full gallop, and Jimmy winced at the moment before impact.

But the fear that had occasioned the wince turned to confoundment as the rider's lance pierced the side of the windmill, revealing it to be the most hideous giant snake that Jimmy ever could have imagined. The mortally-wounded serpent let out a wail that shook the sky like thunder, and the ground shuddered when its lifeless body finally fell.

The squire raced to the victorious knight and threw his arms around his master gushing, "I will never doubt you again!"

"Of course, you won't, Sancho, for I have just vanquished Doubt!" the knight boasted.

Sancho held on to the knight, much as a young child clings to a parent's leg on the first day of school...and schooled he had been. But, when the knight noticed Jimmy slowly making his way towards them, he cautioned, "Sancho, we are not alone." The squire released his grip and wheeled around to face the intruder.

Jimmy stopped a few feet from the knight's horse and the squire's donkey.

"You are..." Jimmy began in awe, but he couldn't pronounce the next words.

So the rider filled in the blanks for him: "Don Quixote de la Mancha, at your service!" he said proudly. "And this is my friend, Sancho Panza."

The squire nodded as Jimmy tried to wrap his mind around the surreal scene unfolding before him. Without success. Don Quixote and Sancho Panza shared a laugh. Then, the elderly knight tried to put Jimmy's mind at ease. "Nothing is as it seems, my friend."

Jimmy wasted no time on the familiarity of what the knight had said. "You're not insane! Those windmills really are giants!" he gushed.

"Sanity and madness are in the eye of the accuser," Don Quixote waxed, benevolently. "Too much sanity may be madness, and the maddest of all, to see life as it is and not as it should be."

This time, Don Quixote's words slapped him out of his stupor. "Those are my words!" Jimmy exclaimed. "And the fortune teller's!"

"Then we share a kindred spirit," Don Quixote trumpeted. "But, you know the fortune teller?"

Sancho could sense Jimmy's confusion. "Youngish guy – heavy on the 'ish' – dresses conservatively, looks like an accountant."

"Yes!" he practically shouted. "That's him!" Nothing could surprise him now, he thought. He was wrong.

"Wait," he gathered himself. "How can that be?"

Don Quixote replied, "You have to understand, my friend, that time does not exist on this side of the wall. The same fortune teller who has freed your mind has freed ours, too."

"But that's impossible," Jimmy countered. "You are fictional characters!"

"Have you learned nothing from the fortune teller? Look over there," he said, pointing to the fallen serpent. "I have slain Doubt!"

"You have, indeed, master!" Sancho cheered.

"OK," Jimmy persisted, "but Cervantes killed you off in the book. How do you explain that?"

"He did...but, obviously, I wasn't satisfied with that ending, so I changed it!"

Jimmy swallowed hard. "Captain Kirk!" he uttered just loud enough to be heard.

"No, I am Alonso Quijana, Don Quixote de la Mancha, champion of chivalry, defender of the oppressed, keeper of justice and vanquisher of impossible dreams.

"I fight the unbeatable foe. I run where the brave dare not go. I fight for the right, without question or pause. I am willing to march into Hell for a heavenly cause. And I will strive with my last ounce of courage to reach the unreachable star.

"This is my quest, my friend, to follow that star, no matter how hopeless, no matter how far. And make no mistake, I *will* reach that star!"

"Here, here!" toasted Sancho Panza.

Every nerve in Jimmy's body was on fire. Sasha had told him moments ago that *he* was reaching for the stars, and now he was in the company of someone just mad enough to make it happen!

"I believe, Don Quixote!" Jimmy effused. "But, tell me, where did you change the ending?"

"It was when Dulcinea del Toboso visited me on my deathbed," he recalled fondly. "And she said, 'Sancho, a man died. He seemed a good man, but I did not know him. This is not the end. Don Quixote is not dead. Believe, Sancho, believe.' And then, she kissed me."

Dulcinea's words, "This is not the end," almost floored him. They were his mother's last words!

Jimmy did not remember the kiss...but that didn't stop Don Quixote! "It was the kiss of eternal life," he explained. "'Love conquers all,' wrote the poet, Virgil. Even Death, I presumed, and so I chose to live and sprang to life, reborn, re-energized, and rejuvenated. That, my friend, is how I got on this side of the wall."

Jimmy couldn't contain his excitement. "I, too, have a quest, Don Quixote. Dulcinea's words were my mother's. In her dying breath, she told me she loved me, and then, incredibly, she added, "This is not the end." I never accepted her death. I must find out what she meant!"

"Please tell me the circumstances of your mother's journey," the knight errant insisted.

Jimmy recounted the events of his ill-fated trip to the mall with his mom, the gunman's murderous rampage, and his mother's enigmatic last words.

"When I got a little older," he went on, "my Dad told me that he had forgiven the killer, and that he blamed the news media for the carnage. He explained how the media had given a voice to the voiceless, a way for those who feel they have been wronged by society – whether real or imagined, and have no hope, no friends, no one to hear their tales of woe – to go out in what he called a blaze of infamy. Thanks to the media, they get their fifteen minutes of fame, and a public forum – everyone knows their names, what they look like, how they have been wronged, and what they had to say. My dad believes my mother would still be alive if the media hadn't given the cowards an 'easy' way out and turned them into celebrities in the process."

Don Quixote and Sancho Panza listened intently, and without interruption. When Jimmy finished, the knight chose his own words very carefully.

"It is written in the Good Book that for anyone to enter the Kingdom of Heaven, he must enter as a child. In your youth and innocence, you have left your door – your mind – open... even though you did not know to what. Let's say possibilities. And the fortune teller walked in and led you, by your own choices, to me.

"Your father is a wise man. To change the outcome, we must change the premise."

"But that all started so long ago," Jimmy lamented.

"My young friend," Don Quixote reminded, "you forget that we are on the side of the wall where time does not exist! There are only windmills to the naked eye. Remember, though, nothing is as it seems."

Then he pointed straight ahead. "Look over there. Tell me what you see."

Jimmy peered into the distance. Looming large on the horizon was the biggest windmill he ever had seen. It was enormous. No, enormous didn't do it justice – it was bigger than any mountain he had seen. But it hadn't been there before, he thought.

"It always has been there," Don Quixote assured. "It's just that now you can see it. It is The Premise of which your father spoke! And it must be vanquished. Take away the celebrity of mass murderers and you take away the mass murderer!"

Jimmy stared at the imposing windmill. "How big do you think it is?"

"To appear so large at this distance, I would say the arms are nearly two leagues long."

"Leagues?" Jimmy asked.

"In your frame of reference, about three miles long!"

"But that's…"

Don Quixote stopped him mid-sentence. "Remember where you are and that nothing is as it seems. Now, hop on Rocinante," he said, patting a spot immediately behind him on his horse's extra-long saddle.

Sancho helped Jimmy onto his master's horse, and when he was securely in place, Don Quixote removed a medallion from around his neck and handed it to Jimmy. The medallion depicted a knight sitting high atop his steed, his lance at the ready.

"It was my father's," Don Quixote explained. "I want you to

have it."

Jimmy was taken aback. "I can't take this! It was a gift from your father to you."

"Now it is a gift from me to you. Put it around your neck. I insist. It will bring you good luck!"

Gratefully, if reluctantly, Jimmy placed the medallion's thin gold chain around his neck. "Thank you so much, Don Quixote!"

The knight turned to face the road ahead. "And now we ride!" he called out with reckless abandon, urging Rocinante into a full gallop. "Sancho, our next adventure beckons!"

When the giant windmill was well within reach, Don Quixote shouted over his shoulder, "Your father's Premise is defended by the Knight of the White Moon. He is my sworn enemy, and a formidable opponent. He is a wily one and will stop at nothing to defeat me. Do not be tempted by his distraction. Hold on tight to what you want to happen!"

"I'm on it!" Jimmy yelled above the din.

Don Quixote leaned forward and whispered something in Rocinante's ear and the horse charged at the windmill as if shot from a cannon. The chivalrous knight lowered his lance and steeled himself for combat. Jimmy hung on for dear life.

Squinting through his watery eyes, Jimmy was gobsmacked at the size of The Premise. It had to have been taller than Everest, he thought; and it was, by more than one thousand feet.

"It's too big!" he hollered into the wind.

"Nonsense!" shouted Don Quixote. "Stay focused! The bigger they are, the harder they fall! Once it falls, so, too, will its outcome. It is as vulnerable as Achilles. Its heel is just to the right of the door!"

Jimmy peered ahead at the door – in time to see it fly open and the Knight of the White Moon emerging from within, spurring his horse onto a collision course. His lance was firmly set on Don Quixote's heart.

"There you are!" Don Quixote proclaimed over the wind. Then, he shouted behind him, "Jimmy, your time has come!"

The sound of his name startled him. "How did you know..."

Don Quixote cut him off. "When I tell you, you need to take the reins and my lance, and aim for The Premise's nerve center, an area about seven feet to the right of the door, at a level even with the handle. The Knight of the White Moon is mine!"

"Are you good?" Don Quixote checked one last time.

"I got this!" Jimmy shouted.

"Now!" the Man of La Mancha yelled, springing into action.

Trailing behind on his donkey, Sancho was astounded by the sight unfolding before him. In one deft move, Don Quixote handed Rocinante's reins and his lance to Jimmy, and, with an agility belying his years, hopped on top of his saddle, steadying himself with the saddle-horn. Neither knight was backing down.

At the instant before the Knight of the White Moon's lance could do any damage, Sancho heard his master's voice rebound off the giant windmill: "Lay on, Carrasco!" and he saw his master leap from Rocinante, flying through the air faster than Carrasco could react, and tackling the Knight of the White Moon off his horse. The two knights tumbled to the ground, but only one stood up. Don Quixote de la Mancha planted his foot squarely on his arch-nemesis' chest and raised his arm triumphantly.

The vicious sound of Rocinante's galloping hooves reminded Sancho that the day was not done. He quickly turned his attention back to Jimmy, who was coaxing the mighty horse to go even faster. Don Quixote's lance was aimed precisely at the target seven feet to the right of the door, even with the handle. Jimmy would not be denied.

"MOMMMMMMMMMMMMMMMMMMMMMMM!" he roared, as the lance found its mark. A bright flash of light blinded Jimmy, and a thunderous boom rattled his senses. His body shook. Or was it being shaken?

"Jimmy," he heard a familiar voice calling his name. "Jimmy. Jimmy...wake up!"

Whether the fog in his mind began to lift allowing the voice to register, or the voice cut through the fog and brought him back to his senses, wasn't clear. But, Jimmy opened his eyes and stared straight into his mother's loving eyes.

"Mom!" he cried out, bursting into tears. He sat bolt upright in his bed and hugged his mother so tightly to his chest that she had a difficult time breathing.

"You're alive!" he sobbed.

"Of course, I'm alive," she said soothingly. She rubbed his back, trying to calm her son down. "You just had a bad dream!"

When he finally was able to compose himself, Jimmy stammered, "No, Mom. It was an impossible dream!"

"An impossible dream?" she repeated, noticing Cervantes' book on the floor next to his bed. "You must have fallen asleep reading *Don Quixote*. Anyway, pull yourself together because Sasha's on her way over. She seemed really anxious to see you this morning, for some reason. Did everything go ok at the dance last night?"

Jimmy didn't answer. He still was trying to figure out what just had happened...and what was happening now.

"Jimmy? Are you alright?" his mom worried.

"Better than ok," he muttered, still dazed and confused.

"Alright, then, I'll let you get ready." She stood up to leave – but before she had taken a step towards the door, Jimmy choked up again.

"Mom, I really, really love you!"

"I love you, too, sweetheart!" his mom chuckled. "That must have been some dream! By the way, where did you get that medallion around your neck? It's very handsome!"

In another part of town, the fortune teller smiled and took apart his booth. It was time to move on.

Part Three

I

Jimmy cradled the medallion in his hand, staring at the knight sitting atop his steed, lance at the ready. It couldn't have been a dream. Could it? Don Quixote had given him the medallion that had been a gift from his father, just before they had set upon the giant windmill, The Premise, and the Knight of the White Moon. He had changed the ending, fulfilling his mother's prophecy as she died on top of him, shielding him from the gunman's bullets.

She was alive! How had she known? Did she? Was there really a shooter at the mall when they went to get the Tony Hawk skateboard for his birthday? Or, was it all a dream? But what about the medallion? His Mom hadn't seen it before. What the hell! Why would she have? She's been dead for the past six years! Or had she been?

"I'll ask Dad," he thought to himself. Then, "Wait! I could ask..."

The sound of the doorbell scattered the pieces of the mind-blowing puzzle he was trying to put together. "Sasha!"

"I'll get it," Jimmy heard his Mom call out.

"Oh my God," Jimmy panicked. "Sasha's going to freak when she sees Mom!" He threw on a pair of jeans and a t-shirt, splashed some water on his face, and thought about dragging a brush though his hair, but scrapped the idea when he looked in the mirror and realized it would be pointless.

He practically fell down the stairs, taking them as fast as he could while trying to figure out how to explain what was going on. His heart was pounding wildly when he burst into the living room and found his Mom and Sasha chatting casually around the coffee table.

Celeste Rivers stood up. "There you are, sleepyhead."

Noting her son's disheveled appearance and the bewilderment

that left him temporarily speechless, she smiled, "Jimmy, are you sure you're ok? You look like you've seen a ghost!"

"Mom, you have no idea!" he blurted out, breathing heavily. That's all he could muster. He was fighting a losing battle trying to gain control of his senses.

Turning to their guest, Celeste asked, "Sasha, can I get you anything to eat or drink?"

"No thank you, Mrs. Rivers, I'm fine. I've got church in a few minutes."

"Well, be sure to say 'hi' to your mom and dad for us. This must be such an exciting time for all of you!"

Sasha smiled politely. "It has its ups and downs. But, it's never dull, that's for sure!"

"Well, I'll leave you two alone. Have a beautiful day, Sasha."

"Thanks, Mrs. Rivers. You, too!"

As soon as his Mom left the room, Jimmy whispered nervously, "Can you believe it?"

Sasha was exasperated. "No, I can't, Jimmy! Where did you disappear to last night?"

"Sasha, my Mom is alive!" he proclaimed.

"Really, Jimmy, that's the best you can do?" Her tone suggested frustration, but her eyes couldn't mask the hurt.

Jimmy was baffled. "Oh my God," he gulped, "you don't remember!"

"Oh, I remember perfectly. We were having a great time at the dance, or so I thought, and then, poof! You disappear into thin air." She looked away so he wouldn't see the tears welling up in her eyes.

"Sasha," Jimmy pleaded. "Look at me...please!"

He waited until she turned back to him. Then, it was his turn to tear up. Gathering himself, he gently held Sasha's head in his hands to steady her gaze and said firmly, "I traveled through time and brought my mother back to life."

Of all the excuses Jimmy could have laid upon his girlfriend, that was the most unexpected. Sasha twisted her head out of his grasp. "Are you on drugs?" she practically shouted. "You were with

Lisa, weren't you?! That skank has been trying to sink her claws into you ever since we started dating."

"I was not with anyone named Lisa," Jimmy protested. "I was with Don Quixote!"

"Omigod, stop talking!" Sasha had heard enough. "I have to go!"

"No, Sasha, wait!" Jimmy insisted. "You have to hear me out. We never made it to the dance. We were on our way, dressed as Pete and Julie from *The Mod Squad*, but you said you wanted to go to the carnival, instead."

Sasha couldn't hold back her tears any longer. "Ok, now you're scaring me, Jimmy. I really have to go!" She pushed by her bewildered boyfriend saying she'd call him later.

"You don't even remember the fortune teller?" he called out after her, in a last-ditch effort to save himself.

To his utter surprise, Sasha paused. She turned around and stared at Jimmy. At the exact same moment, they said to each other, "Through the purple velour curtain."

Jimmy's mind raced ahead – was this proof that it hadn't been a dream? Or had they, somehow, shared the same dream?

Sasha started to shake uncontrollably. "I thought it was my mind trying to work through you disappearing."

"I did disappear alright, but not with Lisa!"

Sasha frowned. "But traveling through time is impossible! And bringing your Mother back to life?"

"That's just it," Jimmy boasted. "Those things are only impossible because we think they're impossible. We have to change the rules!"

"Captain Kirk!" Sasha remembered, her face lighting up at the realization that her boyfriend hadn't cheated on her. She leaned in to Jimmy and kissed his lips with a mythological sweetness that would have tempted the gods of Olympus.

"I really have to go," she said when their lips parted. "But I'll call you after church."

Jimmy, still savoring the deliciousness of her kiss, was speechless.

Sasha smiled, pecked him on the cheek and hurried off to join her family at church.

⋆ ⋆ ⋆

Meanwhile, from a darkness so deep that light didn't even bother trying to go there, a sinister voice sneered, "How could this happen?"

"I don't know," a wicked subordinate groused.

"You're sure of the count?"

"Yes, I triple-checked. There's definitely one missing."

"Do you have a name?"

"Not yet."

"This is bad…very, very bad!"

"I know," the junior demon fretted. "Do you think we have to tell him? Maybe we can…"

"Tell me what?" hissed another voice, dripping with venom.

The evil spirits trembled at the sudden interruption.

"Sorry, your majesty," the junior demon apologized, fear accenting his every syllable. "I didn't know you were here."

"How could you not know I was here!" bellowed the evilest one of them all, dressing down his minion. "I am Satan, the Devil, central to all dark places and all dark thoughts." Then he demanded again, more forcefully, "Tell me what?"

The junior demon was too afraid to confess, so the senior demon spoke up. "The count is off. A soul might have escaped."

"That's impossible!" Satan shouted. "Count them again!"

"But, I've counted them three times," the lesser demon answered meekly.

"What part of 'count them, again' did you not understand? We have to be sure!"

"What if it's true that someone escaped?" the senior demon asked.

"Then we'd have a real problem, and I'm not talking about the one who escaped," Satan scowled. "It would mean that there's a person on earth who has overcome Doubt. And against that person we have no defense."

"Can't you just kill him?" the junior demon offered, naively.

Satan bristled at his minion's ignorance. "No, I can't just kill him! God took away my authority, you idiot! I can't lift a finger against His children."

"But you *can* set the table," the senior demon interjected.

"Yes, in such a way that His children who have not been stripped of their authority exercise their free will and choose to turn away from Him and to use their authority against each other. Doubt is my greatest weapon! It's why Adam and Eve lost Paradise, why Peter fell into the sea while he was walking on water, why His children don't live forever, and why things appear to them to be impossible. By stupidly choosing to doubt Him, they disconnect the conduit that God provides for them, through which they gain access to His authority over all things. And I mean *all things*. There are no exceptions. So, that includes us. And time travel!"

"Time travel?" repeated the senior demon.

"Yes, it is the only possible explanation," Satan groused. "If this had been the so-called 'Second Coming'...well, we all remember what happened the first time Jesus the Christ came down here. It would have been a mass exodus. You see, people can't just do things on their own. Thinking that they could is what got them here in the first place. Their souls were already dead. So, if it's true that someone escaped, then there had to have been an accomplice. Someone from earth unfettered by Doubt...But how would that accomplice have found one lost soul from among the hundreds of millions we have here without being noticed?"

Satan answered his own rhetorical question. "He, or she, couldn't have! Which leads to one inescapable conclusion: said accomplice had to have traveled back through time and changed the circumstances that led to the possible escapee's death in the first place."

The senior demon frowned. "You're worried that, if it's true, this accomplice would tell everyone about traveling through time and bringing someone back to life."

"Not really," Satan replied, smugly. "If people didn't believe the

Son of God, why would they believe some alleged accomplice? I've done my job well. God's children have been blinded completely by Doubt. They'll simply call the accomplice crazy. Our friends at the church will call him or her a heretic or a blasphemer. What really worries me is that this accomplice eventually might figure out what it really means to have been created in God's image."

"What *does* it mean?" asked the junior demon.

"I can answer that by telling you what it means for us. Do you remember what happened when Jesus arrived in the county of the Gergesenes? He came upon two of your brother demons who had possessed two men and He ordered them out and into a herd of swine, and then the swine ran off a cliff and perished in the sea. We have no choice but to comply to the will of those who are connected to God!"

"Like *Ella Enchanted*!" the junior demon chirped.

"Yes, like *Ella Enchanted*," Satan grumbled, "but this is not a fairy tale, and there is no happy ending for us!

"Clearly, the accomplice hasn't figured it out, yet – if, indeed, such a person exists – but we can't take the chance that he, or she, eventually discovers what they've had all along. Even if no one else believes them, and everyone thinks they're crazy, the power of one would destroy us. Jesus assured God's children that He had given them the authority to trample on serpents and scorpions, and over all the power of the enemy, and nothing by any means would hurt them.

"Well guess what? We are the serpents and the scorpions and the enemy He was talking about, but I've pulled the wool of Doubt over their eyes, and they don't believe the Son of God, incredible as that seems! As I said, it has been my tour de force, my greatest accomplishment, to set the table in such a way that His beloved children choose not to believe the One who never would lie to them and, instead, choose to believe the one who always will lie to them!"

"Bravo!" the two demons cheered.

Satan's mood soured. "But, again, if this accomplice does exist, he, or she, could ruin everything! We can't take the chance that whoever it might be will figure out that they have authority over us. Verify the count one more time, and if it is confirmed that someone has escaped, find out who it was and identify the accomplice. Keep me informed every step of the way.

"Now, go!" Satan ordered. "I have a call to make."

The demons quickly set about their task and in the next minute, the phone began to ring in the office of the church where Sasha and her family were attending Mass.

* * *

Jimmy lay on his bed, staring at the ceiling, trying to sort out the last six years of his life. He checked his phone every three minutes, hoping to see that time had sped up so he could talk to Sasha – to no avail. He desperately needed to talk to her...she was the only one he could confide in. But confide what? That he had traveled through time, changed The Premise, and brought his Mom back to life? Or that he simply had had an incredible dream. Every time he came close to writing it off as a dream, he was stopped by the coincidence of Sasha having dreamt about the fortune teller, as well, and about the purple velour curtain, not to mention Captain Kirk! And what about the medallion he was cradling in his left hand? Where had that come from? His Mom hadn't seen it before, but how could she have? She'd been dead for over six years. And, try as he might, he couldn't remember it before the dream. Or was it a dream?

He looked at his phone, again. Another three minutes had gone by. This was torture! He hated time! It was the worst invention ever concocted by the human race. If only Adam and Eve hadn't chosen to doubt God! But, maybe I'm not bound by time, he considered, so why couldn't I speed it up?

The sound of his phone ringing at that precise instant shook him out of his discontent. He checked the caller ID.

"Sasha!" he answered, practically shouting into the phone.

"Jimmy, are you ok?" she asked, caught off-guard by his ardor.

The sound of her voice calmed him down, but only a little. "I'm sorry. I just feel like I've been lying on a bed of hot coals waiting for you to call. I really, really need to talk to you!"

"Me, too!" she said, her voice becoming more animated. "I called as soon as I could. I couldn't wait to tell you. Guess what! The priest's sermon today was on Matthew 17:20, the verse about Jesus telling his disciples that if they had the faith of a mustard seed, nothing would be impossible for them...I suddenly remembered in my dream that the fortune teller put his hand through a solid block of wood like it wasn't even there!"

"The Australian buloke!" Jimmy exclaimed. "I remember that, too!"

"But the priest said Jesus didn't really mean that nothing was impossible. He said it was just hyperbole."

She had pushed one of Jimmy's hot buttons. "I know, that always has bothered me! Adam and Eve didn't believe what God told them and look what happened to them. Now, priests are telling us what the serpent said to Adam and Eve – not to believe God, or the Son of God.

"That's why the fortune teller said "nothing is as it seems" – we have to question everything, including the possibility that I did travel through time, changed The Premise, and brought my Mom back to life."

"Wait, what's this about a Premise?"

Jimmy explained his dad's theory, and that Don Quixote told him that to change the outcome of his mother's death, he had to destroy the Premise of the news media's connection to mass murderers.

Sasha's tone changed. "Jimmy, I'm scared. Why is this happening to us?"

"I don't know. But we need to follow it and see where it takes us. Something is definitely up."

She hesitated. "I'm not sure I want to know."

"Come on," Jimmy encouraged her, "where's the girl who likes to break the rules, kidnap her boyfriend and take him to the carnival instead of to the school dance?"

"I still don't know what you're talking about," she said. "That must have been before the purple velour curtain, but I like the thought!"

Jimmy could sense a smile turning up the corners of her mouth. "Good. I'll pick you up in about twenty minutes."

"Ok, but I can't be gone all day. There's a news magazine coming to our house at 7:30 tonight to interview my Dad, and we all have to be there."

"A news magazine? Why?"

"Jimmy, my Dad's running for President!"

"What? Are you kidding me?"

"We really do have a lot to talk about!"

2

Sasha was waiting for Jimmy when his blue Camaro pulled up in front of her house. It was noon, and the day was bright and sunny. She was wearing skinny blue jeans, a white tank top, and brown ankle boots, and as she walked to the car, a slight breeze teased her blonde hair as if it was a wind machine and she was in the middle of a model shoot.

Jimmy hurried out of the car to get the door for her, and when he opened it, she flashed him an incandescent smile that would have melted butter on the spot. It had the same effect on his heart.

"Thank you, kind sir!" she cooed, gently sitting down and swinging her legs into the car.

As soon as Jimmy took his place behind the wheel, she urged, "Let's get out of here!"

"Is anything wrong?" Jimmy asked as he pulled away from the curb.

"Not really, I guess. It's just that my Dad has all his advisers at the house helping him to get ready for this interview – Ralph from the Liberation Party, Al from Believe in Family, Father Simon, and a couple of others I didn't know – and I heard them saying they'd be willing to use the force of government to restrict personal freedoms basically to shove their agendas down everyone's throat."

"Kind of an end justifies the means sort of thing," Jimmy offered.

"Exactly! It sucks!"

"I'll bet they didn't want you to leave this afternoon."

"You see? This thing about restricting personal freedom is starting already. Just drive!"

"I don't want your Dad to be mad at me," Jimmy fretted.

"He's not mad at you, he's upset with me. But, we *do* have to talk. And it can't wait."

"I know, right? This thing is freaking me out!"

Sasha placed her hand on his knee, sending those familiar shock waves through his entire body.

"Of course, I'm right," she purred. "I'm always right, aren't I?"

Jimmy could barely think. "Ok, where shall we go?" he stammered.

"That's better," Sasha smiled, giving his knee a playful squeeze before taking her hand away. "How about Dairy Queen. A blizzard sounds really good right now!"

"As you wish," Jimmy replied, channeling Westley's gallantry from *The Princess Bride*. He drove to the DQ near Colorado Boulevard and Exposition. That wasn't the closest store, but he chose it because it sat back off the intersection, partially hidden in a smallish outdoor shopping center, which made it much less crowded than the more visible outlets. Unless a girls' soccer team, whose coach also knew of its relatively secluded location, was celebrating a win with the girls' favorite ice cream treat.

This time, there were no soccer teams in the store when Jimmy and Sasha walked in – in fact, there were no other customers at all. The girls' soccer team either hadn't had a game or they had lost. Sasha ordered a small cookies and cream blizzard, and Jimmy chose a medium-sized Orange Julius. He wished aloud that he still had the option of having an egg added to the drink. The manager said something about salmonella, and Jimmy reminded himself again how much he hated that the world had become so obsessed with the illusion of safety.

They sat at a table in the back of the store for added privacy, just in case, and Jimmy dispensed with the lid and the straw of his Julius, drinking straight from the cup to enjoy the full effect of the egg-less, chopped ice and foam concoction.

"So, where were we?" he began.

"Let's start with your disappearance last night," Sasha suggested.

"Right. But do you remember anything leading up to that? I'm talking about your dream."

"Well, you said we were going to the Sadie Hawkins dance at school dressed as Pete and Julie from a show called *The Mod Squad...*"

"But you wanted to go to the carnival, instead."

"Honestly, I can't remember," she admitted dejectedly, staring straight into her boyfriend's beseeching eyes. The remnants of Orange Julius foam on Jimmy's upper lip momentarily distracted her.

"You have a little...," she started to say, then she crooked her index finger and beckoned him to come closer to her. They both leaned over the table, and she gently kissed the foam from his lip. The touch of their lips triggered her memory.

"We kissed!" she beamed. "Yes, I remember the kiss!"

Jimmy was so relieved...and this time, he took the initiative and they shared another delicious smooch.

"You're really good at that," Sasha smiled.

"You started it," Jimmy reminded her. "In the food court."

"What food court? We still don't know for sure..."

Jimmy cut her off, "Ok, let's keep going. What do you remember next?"

"The purple velour curtain, the fortune teller...and when he put his hand through the block of wood, saying he saw the world not as it is, but as it should be."

"Exactly!

"This is where I lose you, though, or lost you...whatever," she frowned. You said you saw a gate. That's when you disappeared."

"Right!" Jimmy exclaimed. "I went through the gate to the other side of the wall."

"A wall?"

"Yes, there was a huge wall. God was on one side and we were on the other side. And I levitated to a gate high up on the wall that led me to God's side of the wall where Time did not exist."

"Was Lisa on that side of the wall?"

"No! Only Don Quixote and Sancho Panza. I swear!"

"Well," Sasha hesitated, "we still don't know for sure if we were both trying to work through a very awkward situation, and this is what our minds came up with."

Sasha's words rang true. Neither of them was convinced that what they had experienced was anything more than a shared dream, or a weird coping mechanism.

"But my mind is open," she assured Jimmy, "and I'm going to give you the benefit of the doubt because you're so darned cute sitting there with more foam on your lip."

Jimmy took his cue, and leaned over the table so Sasha could clean him up again. They both knew he purposely had taken the next gulp of his drink in such a way as to deposit more foam on his upper lip.

Sasha made sure she was very thorough, then leaned back, asking, "So, what happened next, after you went through that gate?"

Jimmy took over from there. He told her all about Don Quixote, changing the rules, the giant windmills, the Premise, and the Knight of the White Moon. And about ramming Don Quixote's lance squarely into The Premise's vulnerability. He spoke of the bright flash and the thunderous boom – and then his Mom waking him up that morning to tell him his girlfriend was on her way over to see him.

They both sat there in a daze, weighed down by the inconceivability of what Jimmy just had described.

"I don't know, Jimmy," Sasha shook her head. "It just seems like such an impossible dream."

"Did someone say, 'Impossible dream?'" a voice from above startled them. "That is my calling card! Have you forgotten about the medallion?"

Jimmy and Sasha looked up to see an older man in a Dairy Queen uniform smiling down at them. Jimmy recognized him immediately. His name tag read, "Don Q."

"It's you!" he practically shouted. "Don Quixote!"

Sasha could not believe her ears. She just sat there, stunned, unable to speak.

"Hello, Jimmy!" the Man of La Mancha said with a sparkle in his eye.

Jimmy started to stand, but the knight errant stopped him. "Stay seated, Jimmy. We don't want to cause a stir."

"How...What...?" Jimmy couldn't finish a sentence. Sasha still was speechless, her face flushed with the sudden realization that Jimmy's fantastic story – and what they supposedly had experienced together – might not have been a dream at all.

Don Quixote deflected the conversation towards Sasha. "Aren't you going to introduce me to your beautiful friend?"

Barely lassoing the runaway thoughts galloping through his mind, Jimmy apologized, "Forgive me, Señor Quixote. This is Sasha."

The Man of La Mancha took her hand in his, bowed gracefully, and gentlemanly kissed it. "At your service," he said elegantly; and to Jimmy, "She's a keeper, young man. Your Dulcinea!"

Jimmy's cheeks reddened to the color of Sasha's. "What are you doing here?" Before the knight could answer, he added, "And how did you get here?"

"Breaking the rules, my dear boy. Man-made rules aren't rules at all, except to the extent that we choose to accept them. I don't choose to accept them! Neither did your Captain Kirk, as you explained to me. Neither did you. You have a medallion to prove it!"

Jimmy had forgotten about the medallion hanging around his neck underneath his shirt – the gift from Don Quixote's father to his son that had been passed on to him. Instinctively, he reached inside his shirt and produced the ancient trinket.

Finally able to escape her temporary paralysis, Sasha reached over and held it in her hand, examining the image of the knight sitting high atop his steed, his lance at the ready.

She was finally convinced. "So, it wasn't a dream after all," she marveled, sotto voce. "It really happened!"

Jimmy silently chastised himself for forgetting to mention the medallion. He still wasn't used to the idea, either of the medallion or of anything that had happened in the past twenty-four hours.

"Yes, it did," Don Quixote assured them both. "By the way, do you get the Dairy Queen thing? DQ...Dairy Queen...Don Quixote!"

"You're amazing!" Sasha admired.

"No, the two of you are," the Man of La Mancha replied. "You've taken your first steps into the freedom that has been provided for you from the very beginning, a liberation that you otherwise never would have known existed."

"But why us?" Jimmy inquired innocently.

"That is for you to find out. It was because of The Question you asked a very long time ago."

Sasha shot a glance at her boyfriend, whose intense stare might have burned a hole through Don Quixote in another context.

"A question I asked? What question?" he implored.

"I am only the messenger," the chivalrous knight responded, "your guide, if you will. You must keep seeking until you find your own answers."

"But, it started with his Mom getting killed at the shopping mall," Sasha cut in. "When she said, 'This is not the end,' before she died."

"Actually, it started long before that," Don Q answered.

Sasha's face lit up. She was fully invested now. "Omigod, that's it! The fortune teller said that he saw the world not as it is, but as it should be. When she said, "This is not the end," was Jimmy's Mom acknowledging that she shouldn't be dying? Did she know the fortune teller?"

The hint of a gratified smile teased Don Quixote de La Mancha's visage. "She's a clever one, Jimmy! The two of you are finding the pieces to an incredible puzzle and you're starting to put them together. You will be astonished when that happens.

"Now, listen carefully. There's no time to waste! The next piece is in Glenwood Springs. You must go there immediately. What's the saying? Don't pass 'Go', don't collect two hundred dollars."

"You mean right now?" Jimmy asked dubiously.

Now, the knight errant was all business and didn't mince words.

"I mean five minutes ago! Go to Glenwood and seek out John Doe!"

Jimmy was flabbergasted. "John Doe! You want us to drop everything, drive almost three hours to Glenwood Springs? To try to find a man with no name?"

"No, my friend," Don Q replied evenly. "As I have said, I am just the messenger. The choice, as always, is yours. You can choose to continue seeking, or you can choose not to. You can choose to believe me or not. I will ask you to consider this, however – you are in a Dairy Queen talking to Don Quixote. You traveled through time. You changed The Premise. Your mother is alive. These are the choices you have made that have gotten you this far..."

Sasha grabbed her boyfriend's hand. "Jimmy, we have to go to Glenwood!" she insisted. The man of La Mancha reminded them, "If you seek, you will find. Always remember, there are no impossible dreams."

Jimmy looked at Sasha. God, she was so beautiful! "What about your Dad's interview? You have to be back before 7:30."

Sasha checked her watch. "Ok, it's almost 1:00. Roundtrip to Glenwood is about five-and-a-half hours, right? That would give us an hour up there to find John Doe and try to figure this thing out. We have to try!"

"Do you want to call your parents?"

"No! In fact, I'm turning off my phone. What would I tell them? That we're going to Glenwood Springs right before my Dad's big interview? To look for a John Doe?"

Jimmy leaned in towards his girlfriend and they shared another kiss. Then, he looked up at his mentor, but Don Quixote had vanished as suddenly as he had appeared. The teenagers wasted no time getting out the door, and as Jimmy backed his car out of its parking space, he shouted, "Brace yourself, I'm gonna go fast!"

"Jimmy Rivers, are you one of those fast-talking men my father warned me about?" Sasha ribbed, channeling just the right amount of mock indignation to flush her boyfriend's cheeks.

"Sasha," he chafed, "that's not what I meant!"

She smiled mischievously, and whispered into his ear, "Well, I might be one of those fast women your mother warned *you* about!" Lingering over her last syllable, she gently blew into his ear, then nibbled on his earlobe.

Jimmy just about lost it. His Camaro swerved into the next lane, narrowly avoiding the car in his blind spot.

"Sasha!"

"Oops," she giggled, sliding back into her seat. "Did I do that?"

Jimmy snuck a peek at Sasha's playful eyes and said with a wry grin, "I'll take a rain check."

"I don't recall one being offered," she demurred.

"Check the fine print!"

"No one ever reads the fine print."

Their banter continued as Jimmy merged into westbound I-70 traffic from Sixth Avenue, and they started up the hogback.

"There's the Red Rocks exit," Sasha trilled. "Do you remember our first date?"

Jimmy blanched, racking his brain. After an uncomfortable minute, he admitted dejectedly, "I don't, Sasha. I'm sorry. All I can remember is the stuff leading up to the carnival. You're going to have to fill in some of the blanks from the last six years."

She quickly put his mind at ease. "That's cool," she said brightly. "Now, we get to go through the excitement of all our firsts, again! So, you have to take me on another 'first date' to a concert at Red Rocks.

"The only thing I'm going to say about it is that we saw Bruno Mars from the seventh row and it was magical. And I'm not talking about Bruno! Don't get me wrong, he was great...but the magic was all you!"

"Great!" Jimmy winced. "How am I going to live up to myself?"

"Did you hear what you just said?" Sasha laughed. "Well, I, for one, cannot wait! How lucky can a girl get?"

Jimmy glanced at the long, lean, perfectly-proportioned body of the girl leaning back in the passenger's seat. "I'd say I'm the lucky one!"

"Hey, Mister, eyes on the road!" she grinned, catching him in mid-ogle.

Totally busted, Jimmy tried to change the subject. "Anyway, speaking of filling in some blanks, how did *we* get so lucky?"

"You honestly don't remember?"

"Unfortunately, no. The only thing I remember about the last six years of my life was the deep void of my Mom being gone. I didn't hang with anyone. I didn't have a girlfriend. Basically, I only talked to my therapist and to my Dad."

"OK. You might say we ran into each other at my soccer game last spring," Sasha recalled with a smirk. "Well, truth be told, I ran into you. Literally. You were standing near the sideline, and I was chasing after the ball before it went out of bounds, and a girl from the other team kind of ran into me and pushed me right into you. Full on! And you just stood there, like a rock, and caught me. I don't think you budged an inch."

"I must have been inspired," he said offhandedly, trying to imagine her gorgeous body pressed into his.

"So, there I was, in your arms," Sasha continued, "and you were holding me tightly. And I didn't really want it to end, but I had to get back in the game."

"Hmmm, I wonder what I was doing at the game? I don't even like soccer."

"I think you were crushing on one of the girls on the team," Sasha chuckled. "Anyway, we had a moment when I was in your arms and gazed into your eyes. All I could do was say, 'thanks,' and run back onto the field. After the game, you started walking away, but I caught up to you and thanked you properly for catching me. I offered to buy you lunch the next day at school. You said it wasn't necessary – I still don't understand how you could have misread my signs – but I insisted. And the rest is what you'd call history!"

"I swept you off your feet!" Jimmy crowed.

"Oh my God, no!" Sasha countered. "Unless you're counting you catching me on the sideline. Otherwise, it was like I had to hold your hand the whole way through the haunted house called 'girls.' But, you were so adorable!"

Jimmy cringed at the realization that her account of their courtship probably was spot-on, but he bravely tried to save face.

"Ok, I'll take that!" he said.

"Take what?" his bemused girlfriend asked.

"That I'm adorable!"

Sasha promptly turned up the volume on the radio. "Do you know the name of this song?"

He knew it was one of Rihanna's earlier hits, but he couldn't come up with the name.

"It's called *Shut Up and Drive*!" Sasha teased. Then, she leaned over and kissed him on his cheek. ""'Adorable' definitely is your middle name!"

In another ten minutes, they passed the sign for the Buffalo Herd Overlook at Exit 254, where Interstate 70 crests at Genesee, and they could see the different ranges of the Rockies framed between the road and the overpass, and their spirited conversation abruptly stopped so they could savor the wonder of nature's perfect postcard.

"It's so beautiful!" Sasha rhapsodized.

"Yes, you are!" Jimmy flirted, sneaking another peak at her lithe body straining in all the right places against the fabric of her tight jeans and tank top.

"So, this is how it's going to be," she chastened him with delight. "If I've told you once, I've told you twice, now, keep your eyes on the road!"

"Yes, ma'am!"

Finally focused on the road ahead, Jimmy shared Sasha's sense of wonder at the majestic Rockies, resplendent in their yellow-gold-and-orange autumn finery – and the young travelers drank it all in as they drove by Evergreen, down Floyd Hill, past Idaho Springs and Georgetown, and through the Eisenhower Tunnel to the other side of the Continental Divide.

The fall colors were amplified in Silverthorne, Frisco, and Copper Mountain, but it was when they dropped into the Vail valley that their breath truly was taken away. Nothing could have prepared them for what they saw as they came around the bend from East

Vail into Vail. It was as if they had discovered Cortez' El Dorado, the legendary "Lost City of Gold." The entire valley was glowing in the powerful sunlight of a cloudless day. Talk about national treasure!

As did Tulio and Miguel, the adventurers continued on that road through El Dorado, and Sasha kept filling in whatever blanks she could from the "lost' six years of Jimmy's life – the ones that included his Mother after he had destroyed The Premise. It was all so fantastic and implausible at the same time that he had to fight the urge to dismiss the whole thing as a wild dream, one which had been scary real. But, the medallion…and Señor Quixote.

Still, the details she shared were strangely familiar. Kind of like going to a foreign country for the first time and having the unmistakable feeling of déjà vu, of having been there before…maybe in a previous life. Everything she related to seemed to strike an intimate chord, even though he couldn't quite remember or put his finger on it.

When they passed Avon, Jimmy needed a break. He couldn't wrap his mind around anything that Sasha was saying, and the effort was beginning to take its toll.

"Hey, can we change the subject for a few?" he pleaded. "My head is spinning! Tell me about your Dad."

"You mean Senator Fenimore?" Sasha shot back with more than a hint of sarcasm in her voice. "He hasn't been much of a father for the past few years. I mean, I know he has a lot on his plate, but he might as well be married to Ralph and Al and Father Simon. Don't get me wrong. I love my Dad – I just miss him."

* * *

Senator William 'Bill' Fenimore was a rising star in the rank and file of the Republican Party. A second-term United States Senator from Colorado, he had distinguished himself as a passionate, charismatic, and able politician steeped in the conservatism of his party and in the dogma of the religious right.

At 47 years old, he was as squeaky clean as any politician came

– or any non-politician, for that matter. He had a political science degree from Georgetown University, where he had met the woman who would become his wife, Alice, three years his junior, in a Greek mythology class. He had abstained from sex until his wedding night, he didn't smoke, or drink, or do drugs, and he went to church every Sunday. He wasn't a God-fearing man as much as he was a Catholic Church fearing man, but he looked good on paper. He knew he had wanted to be President of the United States since Richard Nixon had tousled his hair in 1974.

He and Alice had two children: Cooper, 21, a senior at the University of Colorado in Boulder; and Sasha, 16, a junior at Benjamin Franklin High School in southeast Denver. He didn't have the hubris of the hare, but he did have the tortoise's steadfastness – and the good sense to know that the religious right and its deep-pocketed backers would be the ones to butter his toast. So it was, that early in his political career, he had maneuvered himself to become the darling of Faith in US leader, Ralph Petiole, of Al Dobson, head of the Faithful Horizon, and of the ultra-conservative, billionaire Joak brothers, Henry and Jasper. Bill Fenimore wasn't a leader, but he was a pragmatist and a good soldier, and he jumped through every hoop his handlers put before him.

In Senator Fenimore, the Joaks, Petiole, Dobson, and Cardinal Phelps of the Catholic Church knew they had political gold. If heat can be described as the absence of cold, then the senator's political capital derived from the lack of suitable candidates to run against him. To put it bluntly, America was being deprived of her best and brightest by the vetting process from which no skeleton in any closet could hide. Alice played her role as 'the good wife' perfectly, but Cooper and Sasha could see through their father's façade and gamesmanship – and while they loved him dearly, his superficiality and the long hours he had chosen to spend away from his family in favor of his advisers had alienated them a bit. More than a bit, actually. But their mother had taught them well, and when the cameras were rolling, they were the dutiful children expected of candidates running for this country's highest office, and, for the most part, they made good choices outside of the klieg light glare, as well.

If the political pollsters were to be believed, America was less than a year away from leaving behind the democracy provided for her by her founding fathers and embracing the "new democracy," a misnomer describing the Partnership of the Right: an unholy alliance between the ultra-right conservatives calling themselves True Believers, the ultra-right aristocracy and the fundamentalist religious right. According to the pollsters, the country couldn't have cared less about this unseemly marriage between money and the church, and forget about the Constitutional provision for the separation of church and state.

Cardinal Phelps should have known better. If his priorities had been properly aligned, he would have heeded Paul's warning in his first letter to Timothy: "For the love of money is a root of all kinds of evil; and some people, craving money, have wandered from the true faith and pierced themselves with many sorrows." But, he had a different agenda, as did his predecessors Caiaphas and the high priests who persecuted Jesus. He, too, had chosen the wrong master to serve.

Suffice to say that politics and other things of man make strange bedfellows, but none stranger than Cardinal Phelps in bed with the Joak brothers. And Bill Fenimore was their puppet.

3

By the time Jimmy and Sasha reached the magnificent towering cliffs of Glenwood Canyon, their conversation had turned to the mystery at hand. Where would they find Don Quixote's enigmatic John Doe? They were debating how best to use their time, when they came upon several bouquets of flowers along the side of the interstate, presumably placed there by the grieving family of a loved one who had succumbed to injuries sustained in a car wreck at that spot. That spot was about 50 yards from Exit 119, just east of Glenwood Springs – the off-ramp for No Name, Colorado.

"That's it!" exclaimed Sasha.

"That's what?"

"No Name! When men without identification are processed through police headquarters or through hospitals, their names are listed as "John Doe.""

"Keep going…"

There was no stopping Sasha. "I don't believe in coincidence, Jimmy. Those flowers at the side of the road in that precise spot means there was an accident there...and where are people in accidents taken? To the hospital!"

"You don't think those flowers were for our John Doe, do you?"

"I don't know, but I do know the first place we should look for him is at a local hospital."

Sasha powered up her phone and looked up hospitals in Glenwood Springs. Valley View Hospital was the first entry, and they decided it would be a good starting point. She read the directions to the hospital to Jimmy and they got off the highway at Exit 116 and headed south on Grand Avenue towards Aspen. They turned left on 19th Street, and straight ahead at Blake Street, when they saw the huge hospital complex. Comprised of the Valley View Hospital and the impressive Calaway Young Cancer Center, its enormity and architecture belied its mountain town locale.

They followed the signs to the sprawling hospital's upper east parking lot and jogged through the Main Entrance to the Registration desk. Jimmy breathlessly asked if there had been any John Doe's admitted recently. The woman at the desk dutifully checked the roster and, after a few moments, looked up at the teenagers and told them a John Doe had been admitted early that morning, and that he was in intensive care on the fourth floor in Room 407.

Jimmy squeezed Sasha's hand. They were directed to Elevator C, and when the elevator doors opened on the fourth floor, they discovered a warm waiting area with a large fireplace in the middle that looked like it belonged in a ski lodge. Walking past the fireplace towards the nurses' station, they saw a sign indicating Room 407 to the left.

"Can I help you?" a nurse asked, as they approached.

"Yes," Jimmy answered. "We're here to see John Doe in Room 407."

The nurse was puzzled. "How did you hear about him?"

"Don…," Jimmy began, but before "Quixote' left his mouth, Sasha interrupted him.

"We were supposed to meet Jimmy's uncle for breakfast this morning at the Hotel Colorado, and he didn't show up, which is totally not like him. If something had come up, he would have called us. He does have a history of medical issues, so we decided to check here before going to the police."

"What's your uncle's name?" the nurse asked Jimmy.

"John Battista," he replied, not missing a beat and winking at Sasha.

The nurse wrote down the name, then looked up at the teenagers. "And what are your names?"

"I'm Jimmy Rivers and this is Sasha Fenimore."

The mention of Sasha's name caught the nurse by surprise. "Are you Senator Fenimore's daughter?"

"Yes, I am," Sasha smiled warmly, putting the woman more at ease. She was her father's daughter, after all.

"Well, you can tell your father that he has my vote!" she said cheerfully. Then, she stood up and walked out from behind the nurses' station to show them to Room 407.

"It's not a medical issue," she told Jimmy solemnly on the way. "The man was found unconscious by a jogger very early this morning near Glenwood Springs Middle School. He was beaten up very badly and his throat had been slit. He lost a lot of blood. It's really touch and go right now."

They stopped outside the door marked 407. "He's been in and out of consciousness, but he did mention your name," the nurse whispered to Jimmy.

Sasha's heart skipped a beat. Who was this John Doe, and how could he have known Jimmy's name? she wondered. "Has he said anything else?"

"No. He's very weak. I shouldn't even let you in there, but we need to establish his identity, if he really is your uncle. You can have five minutes. I'll be right outside the door if you need anything."

Jimmy and Sasha slipped into the room quietly. In front of them, a thirty-something man, his face badly bruised and his neck heavily bandaged, laid in bed hooked up to a phalanx of medical apparatuses, intravenous solutions, and oxygen.

For a few seconds, they just stood by the door, unsure what to do next. Needless to say, they never had seen the man before.

Sasha finally uttered under breath, "John Battista? That was quick."

"It's really my uncle's name. My mom's brother," Jimmy whispered back.

At the sound of Jimmy's voice, John Doe opened his eyes, spied the two teens by the door, and beckoned them closer. When they reached his bedside, he opened his hand and Sasha instinctively latched on to it.

"Can I get anything for you?" she asked softly.

In a surprisingly strong voice, considering the damage to his throat, he answered, "Don't worry about me. Nothing is as it seems. There are larger issues at play."

Jimmy's eyes widened. Everyone was telling him that. It couldn't be a coincidence. "Who are you?"

"I am a friend of the fortune teller."

Chills swept through the teenagers' bodies at the mention of the fortune teller. Could this really be happening? It was all so surreal!

The stunned teenagers just stood there in disbelief, trying to process the unimaginable. Finally, Sasha broke the awkward silence. "What happened to you?" was all she could come up with.

"Don't be alarmed," John Doe sought to assure them. "I was attacked by three men I encountered last night at the Southeast Denver Christian Bible Church."

Sasha gasped. "That's my Dad's church!" and she turned to Jimmy, adding, "My parents were there while we went to the dance."

Appalled, Jimmy asked, "Why would these guys from a church do this to you?"

"Because I was telling the parishioners they were being led the wrong way," came the short response.

"What do you mean?" Sasha inquired.

"The church was sponsoring a financial planning seminar, specifically about providing for loved ones – and for the church, of course – after passing. So, they had lawyers and insurance agents who belonged to the church making sure that everyone had life insurance policies and had their wills in order."

"I'm not following you," Sasha confessed. "How is making financial arrangements for after you die being led the wrong way?"

"Listen carefully," John Doe explained. "First of all, because the only infidelity is for live men and women to vote themselves dead. And, secondly, because the church was, in effect, leading them to the slaughter."

Jimmy was confused. "I don't understand."

"You will," he assured him, "but you must keep searching. Again, nothing is as it seems."

Those words finally hit home! They were a confirmation that what Jimmy had been taught to believe, and that most of what he had chosen to accept as the way things were, were all wrong. The fortune teller had taken it a step further, echoing his own words about seeing the world not as it is, but as it should be...before putting his hand through that block of Australian buloke wood. The implication was coming over loudly and clearly – that they had the authority to control the world around them, but the wool had been pulled over their eyes without them knowing it – and, blindly, they had accepted it. They had locked themselves up in prison without knowing the keys to their jail cells were in their back pockets. It wasn't a dream at all! It was a nightmare. Reality, that is.

The sound of Sasha's voice interrupted the stream of consciousness racing through his mind. "How did you end up in Glenwood?" she asked the man.

"I came to see a doctor, ironically. So, I caught the Greyhound bus out of Denver just after midnight. As soon as I got here and started walking into town, these three men I recognized from the church jumped me. They must have followed me on the bus."

"Which doctor did you come to see? Is he here in the hospital?"

John Doe managed a weak smile. "Doctor John Henry Holliday is his name. But, listen my time here is short. You must go. They're looking for you!"

The teenagers were stunned to hear that people were looking for them, and from the urgency in the dying man's voice, it sounded like they meant to do them harm.

"What do you mean?" Jimmy asked anxiously. "Who's looking for us?"

"And why?" Sasha implored.

"Follow the trail," the man said with growing difficulty. "Go past...," he started to say, but he coughed violently before finishing his thought. After an uncomfortable couple of moments, he squeezed out, "Tombstone. This is not the end." And John Doe closed his eyes.

Jimmy's and Sasha's knees started to shake at the mention of his mother's last words. They almost jumped out of their skin when the nurse knocked on the door and entered the room.

"I'm sorry," she apologized, "but I'm going to have to ask you to leave for now. He needs his rest."

The teenagers followed the nurse out of the room, allowing themselves one more look at the fortune teller's friend. The moment they turned their heads, he opened his eyes, suddenly, just long enough to meet their gaze with a subtle wink. Then he closed them again.

Outside of the room, the nurse asked Jimmy, "So, is he your uncle?"

Jimmy hesitated. "I'm afraid not."

The nurse pressed for anything they could tell her. "How did he know your name? Did he say *anything*?"

"I'm not sure, and not really," Jimmy stonewalled.

"He did ask for a doctor, though," Sasha said purposefully. "Doctor John Henry Holliday."

The nurse's brow furrowed. "Doc Holliday?" she repeated, skeptically.

"Yes," Sasha answered. "Is he a doctor here?"

"Doctor John Henry Holliday?" she repeated.

Sasha was starting to get impatient. "Yes!"

"Doc Holliday was a dentist and a gunfighter in the Old West. He died here in Glenwood in 1887. Where the Hotel Colorado now stands, and where you said you were going to meet your uncle for breakfast." She paused for a moment, then continued, "That's funny. What a coincidence! Anyway, you can hike to his grave, if you'd like."

The thought hit Jimmy and Sasha at the same time – where there were graves, there were tombstones!

Trying to mask his excitement, Jimmy asked casually, "Is his grave nearby?"

"The trailhead is just a few blocks north of here, at 12th and Palmer. Just go to 12th Street, turn right to Palmer, and you'll see a historical marker at the start of the trail. It's a short hike up to the cemetery."

Jimmy and Sasha thanked the nurse for her time and hurried as fast as they could out of the hospital without attracting attention. The thought that they possibly were being followed was in the back of Jimmy's mind, but he didn't let on.

"Do we have time?" he asked Sasha when they reached the car.

She checked her watch. "We'll be cutting it close, but nothing ventured, nothing gained."

Five minutes later, they were relieved to find out that the nurse hadn't exaggerated – Jimmy parked the car on Palmer Street near the marker that read "Linwood Pioneer Cemetery at Potter's Field," and wasted no time starting up the dirt trail to find Doc Holliday's resting place.

Twenty yards up the trail, he noticed that Sasha was not behind him. He turned around to see her reading a sign off to the side of the trail.

"Come on, Sasha!" he urged. "We don't have time to read historical markers."

"Jimmy, wait!" she called out. "You have to see this!"

Quickly retracing his steps, he was about to ask his girlfriend what was so important about the sign, when he noticed the picture, and every nerve in his body began to tingle.

"My God, it's him!" he nearly choked, staring in disbelief at the picture of Doc Holliday that accompanied the brief history of the dentist-cum-gunfighter. John Doe was Doc Holliday!

"Do you really think so?" Sasha asked, uneasily.

"I don't know, but the one message that's crystal clear is that nothing is as it seems. Whoever it was in the hospital mentioned 'tombstone,' though. We need to check it out. It was important enough for him to say it. Hopefully, it will help us to figure out whatever it is that's going on!"

The adrenaline that surges through teenage bodies at the drop of a hat powered them up the steep, half-mile trail in no time, and an arrow on a sign labeled "Doc Holliday's Grave' pointed out the direction to the gravesite. The graves in the cemetery were scattered about the hillside haphazardly, so they split up to cover more ground. After only a few minutes, it was Sasha who spied a fenced off area and called out, "I think I found it!"

By the time Jimmy joined her, she was standing next to a gray monolith-type tombstone that read simply, "Doc Holliday, Age 36 years, 2 months, 25 days." A gray stone marker several feet in front of the tombstone was inscribed, "This memorial dedicated to Doc Holliday who is buried somewhere in this cemetery." The fenced off area was littered with randomly strewn playing cards from admirers as a testament to Doc's passion for gambling, and a small sign alongside the fenced off site, similar to the one at the trailhead, reminded of the dentist's celebrity – and, for Jimmy and Sasha, of his uncanny resemblance to John Doe. Or vice versa.

"It's got to be him!" Sasha claimed, on reflection. "Think of all the incredible things that have happened since yesterday." She paused. "But I don't get it."

"I don't, either' Jimmy admitted. "I want to go back to Valley View and talk to Doc."

There was no question in Jimmy's mind that John Doe was, in fact, the reincarnation of Doc Holliday.

"Jimmy," Sasha hesitated. "The time." It was almost 3:45.

"We'll make it, I promise," he assured her, not a doubt in his mind. Sasha had plenty for both of them. She didn't say anything, though, as they scampered down the hill. They made it back to the hospital in less than fifteen minutes.

It helped to know where they were going this time, and when they arrived at the nurse's station on the fourth floor, they found their nurse talking to two orderlies and a hospital security guard.

"There they are," the nurse pointed her finger at Jimmy and Sasha when she saw them.

Ignoring the others, Jimmy asked urgently, "Ma'am, can we talk to Doc, er, John Doe," he caught himself, "one more time? I think I know who he is."

In a tone more animated than somber, the nurse replied, "He's gone."

Jimmy was crestfallen. "He died?"

"No! I mean, I don't know. He's not in the room. I was sitting at my desk about ten minutes ago, and I noticed his monitors had stopped working. So, I went into his room to check on them, and he was gone. Disappeared."

That was the security officer's cue. "I need to ask the two of you some questions, if you don't mind."

Sasha nudged Jimmy with her foot. "I really need to go to the restroom, first," she told the guard.

"Me, too," Jimmy chimed in.

The security officer directed them to the restrooms in the waiting area, and the teens made good their escape. They sped out of the parking lot and were snaking their way through Glenwood Canyon in no time.

Sasha calculated the time they needed to get her back to her house in time for her Dad's interview.

"My Dad's going to kill me!" she stated matter-of-factly.

"We'll make it!" Jimmy insisted.

No sooner had Jimmy's assurance left his mouth than a traffic report came over the radio of a jackknifed semi in the eastbound lanes of I-70 near Georgetown, and that traffic was backed up past the Eisenhower Tunnel. The announcer said motorists could expect delays of an hour or more in getting back to Denver.

Sasha looked at Jimmy. "That's it, it's official. I'm dead."

"Turn the radio off!" Jimmy ordered. "Please. We don't need any negativity creeping into our minds. You're not going to be late!"

"That's the only way back to Denver!" she frowned, switching off the radio.

Jimmy looked over at Sasha intently. "You never should underestimate my determination. I don't know how, but we'll find a way to get you back in time."

Suddenly, Sasha's mood changed. "That's a good look on you," she observed. Then, from out of the blue, she added, "I love you, Jimmy."

His heart nearly stopped at the mention of those three words. The L-bomb. He gazed into her eyes. She wasn't kidding.

"I love you, too," his voice quavered. Once he said it, though, it felt so right. Regaining the reins to his senses, he chirped, "There it is. Love always finds a way!"

"Maybe so," she smiled, "but how many times do I have to tell you? Eyes on the road!"

The moment he turned his head, she took the opportunity to sneak in a kiss on his cheek, giving his thigh another loving squeeze, which still sent shivers through his body. He hoped he never got used to her touch.

"Now what?" she asked, realizing they had negotiated the L-bomb rather effortlessly.

Jimmy already had moved on, though. He collected himself – sort of – and offered, "Let's try and figure out this Doc Holliday thing. I mean, it was important enough for Don Quixote to reveal himself to us and to send us on this wild goose chase. There has to be something that we're missing!"

When they exited the canyon, Sasha typed Doc Holliday's name into the search engine of her phone. "Ok, here we go. Let's see...he was born on August 14th, 1851, in Griffin, Georgia, and he was an award-winning dentist..."

She read the next few lines to herself.

"Whoa!" she squealed.

"What is it?"

"It says here that he participated in the most famous gunfight in the Old West...the "Gunfight at the OK Corral." But here's the thing – it took place in Tombstone, Arizona!"

Jimmy's face flushed with the thrill of recognition, as when someone meets "the one," and they "just know."

"That's gotta be it!" he exclaimed. "Type in "Tombstone' and "Doc Holliday' and see what comes up." As an afterthought, he added, "Please."

Plenty came up, and the teens lost track of time devouring the facts about the legendary gun battle that pitted the Earp brothers

– Wyatt, Virgil, and Morgan – and Doc Holliday against the outlaw Cowboys Ike and Billy Clanton, Frank and Tom McLaury, and Billy Claiborne.

After reading aloud the lengthy Wikipedia account of the gunfight that took place on October 26, 1881, and resulted in the deaths of the McLaurys and Billy Clanton. Sasha followed several of the redirects for more clues to John Doe's – or Doc Holliday's – cryptic 'Tombstone' message. Which, ultimately, proved to be of no help, as they essentially repeated the same information from different perspectives or sources.

Jimmy sighed in obvious frustration. "I don't know, Sasha. I'm just not feeling it."

"I know. But, we've got to be on the right track. Maybe we're just looking in the wrong place."

"Maybe," Jimmy weighed. "Try "Gunfight at the OK Corral," and see what that brings up."

She typed the five words and pressed "enter," read through the newest entries, and noted wistfully, "More of the same."

Jimmy was not about to be denied, however. "Well, check the footnotes at the bottom of the Wiki page. See if anything different comes up."

Sasha scrolled down the page towards the footnotes, and she paused at a subheading that caught her eye. "This is different," she remarked. "It says, "Popular culture/fiction and television.""

"Ok, let's try that," he said, hopefully.

"It lists a bunch of titles having to do with that whole era." She started at the top and read the titles to Jimmy. Most of them had to do with Wyatt Earp, Tombstone, or related incidents and accounts. Nothing out of the ordinary.

"Wait!" Jimmy called out, after hearing one that captured his fancy. "Read that one again!"

Sasha repeated, """Sceptre of the Gun," an original *StarTrek* episode.""

"Captain Kirk! That *has* to be it! Follow that link!" His heart was pounding.

"Aye aye, sir!" Sasha responded, as if to a military officer's command. She found the page and began reading: "'On stardate 4385.3, the Federation starship USS Enterprise, under the command of Captain James T. Kirk, is instructed to make peaceful contact with the Melkotians, the mysterious alien inhabitants of Theta Kiokis II, but is warned away by a strange space buoy that orders it not to proceed to the Melkotians' planet.

"'Ignoring the warning, Kirk takes the Enterprise to the planet anyway. Captain Kirk assembles a landing party consisting of himself, First Officer Spock, Chief Engineer Montgomery Scott, Chief Medical Officer Dr. Leonard McCoy, and Navigator Ensign Pavel Chekov and beams down to the surface of the planet to make contact. The Melkotians are angered by this and imprison the team in a psychic illusion that takes the form of the town of Tombstone, Arizona, on Earth on the historic date October 26, 1881.

"'Kirk and his companions quickly realize they are now impromptu characters in a bizarre reenactment of the legendary 'Gunfight at the O.K. Corral.' Kirk and his team are playing the role of the infamous Cowboys: Kirk as Ike Clanton, Scotty as Billy Clanton, Bones as Tom McLaury, Spock as Frank McLaury, and Chekov as Billy Claiborne. They are forced into a confrontation with the Earp brothers, lawmen Virgil, Wyatt, and Morgan Earp, and Doc Holliday. This is the team's punishment for trespassing and violating the Melkotians' strict privacy, a duel to the death, played out as one of the most famous historical events in the Wild West with the crew on the losing side.

"'They encounter various inhabitants who treat the Enterprise crew members as if they are the people whose roles they are playing. That is especially true for the Earps, who are belligerently determined to kill them at the appointed hour, or sooner if they have an excuse. The crew try every means available to them to prevent the fight, but nothing works. They are physically prevented from leaving the town, the Earps cannot be pacified, and the Sheriff refuses to interfere apart from suggesting the tactic, unacceptable to the Enterprise crew, of ambushing the Earps. The stakes rise further when

Chekov is romanced by a local girl named Sylvia. She is harassed by Morgan Earp, who kills Chekov when he interferes. As a result of this tragedy, Spock realizes that this suggests that events in the Melkotian creation can be altered from what happened in reality, as the real Billy Claiborne survived the gunfight (as did Ike Clanton).'"

Jimmy gulped. "Sasha, I don't think my Mom was supposed to die at the mall. Like Chekov. That's what she meant by, "This is not the end!'"

Sasha continued: "'That glimmer of hope is dashed when an improvised gas grenade they plan to use on their enemy totally fails on testing, thereby erasing their one possible advantage. Spock remarks that it should have worked, but the hour of the fight comes before he can explain his reasoning. When the crew refuses to go to the corral, they find themselves immediately teleported there and cannot escape.

"'The team fear for their lives, but Mr. Spock explains his realization. He notes that the gas bomb should have worked according to physical laws; its failure implies that what they are experiencing is not real, despite appearances, but is an elaborate illusion occurring in the minds of the crew that is only as real as their minds accept it to be.'"

"Nothing is real!" Jimmy interrupted. "What happened next?"

Sasha picked up where she left off: "'Spock's will is strong enough for him to believe this logical conclusion that nothing in this situation can harm him, but he has to convince the others of the same, as any lingering doubt will prove deadly. Kirk orders Spock to mind meld with each member of the team, in an attempt to wipe away any and all doubt from their minds and convince them that the bullets from the Earps' guns are mere phantoms and will pass through their bodies without injury.

"'The shootout replays as history dictates, but when the Earps fire their revolvers, their bullets have no effect as Spock predicted. Kirk tackles Wyatt Earp but does not kill him and tosses his gun to the ground. After the fight is over, the Melkotians return Kirk and the rest of the landing party to the Enterprise – including Chekov, whose attraction to Sylvia clouded his perception of the false reality enough for him to survive.'"

When Sasha finished reading, she looked over at Jimmy, who was deep in thought. She reread the part about removing all doubt from their minds and the bullets passing through their bodies without injury. She was astounded. "Do you think it's possible?"

"Yes," Jimmy answered evenly. "That's how we got here in the first place. Remember you were telling me about the sermon your priest gave this morning? And how it bothered you that the priest was telling you Jesus didn't really mean what He said? This is just taking it to the nth degree. I told you, I've never believed that anything was impossible – just that some things haven't been done *yet*! Or figured out *yet*!

"Which is why it's bugging me so much. We are so close to figuring this out. It's a test, just like for Captain Kirk. Except ours is a test of faith. He changed the rules. That's what we have to do.

"It's like they're all taunting us, daring us to go further. Go back to the part about the gas bomb and Spock. Read it again."

Jimmy turned his head towards Sasha and smiled. "Please."

"You're learning," she smiled back.

"I'll say!"

Sasha scrolled up to the passage. "Ok, here we go... "The team fear for their lives, but Mr. Spock explains his realization. He notes that the gas bomb should have worked according to physical laws; its failure implies that what they are experiencing is not real, despite appearances, but is an elaborate illusion occurring in the minds of the crew that is only as real as their minds accept it to be..."

Jimmy stopped her there. "So, Spock recognizes that the whole scenario was not real, but actually an elaborate illusion occurring in the minds of the crew. It was only as real as their minds accepted it to be. Any doubt that the bullets would not harm them would have killed them.

"Oh my God, hold on!" he exclaimed, trying desperately to keep up with the thoughts flooding his mind.

There followed several minutes of intense silence as Jimmy began to put together the pieces of the puzzle. Finally, he announced, "When we choose not to believe in the physical laws of man, this perceived reality around us does not exist. It's all an illusion. To keep us from the freedom that was intended for us! It's the blue pill of *The Matrix!*

"That's what everyone has been trying to tell us! The fortune teller, Don Quixote, Doc Holliday…," his voice trailed off.

Sasha sat there in a state of bewilderment. "Are you saying reality is not real?"

"It's only as real as we believe it to be. I told you that ever since my mother was killed, I took the red pill. I just couldn't accept the way things were instead of the way they should have been."

Sasha's face brightened. "The fortune teller said the same thing!"

"Exactly! And Don Quixote. We've been lied to, and since we have chosen very poorly to believe the lies – that what we are told are rules or laws are impossible to change – we are stuck in this horrible reality of man that we have been tricked into choosing to accept that some things are impossible. It's our fault, though. We brought it on ourselves by our terrible choice to accept man's rules and, in doing so, to reject God's Word that nothing is impossible! And as Jesus said, if we're not with Him, we're against Him. We're on the wrong side of the wall!"

"That's where Captain Kirk comes in!" Sasha carried on Jimmy's thought. "We can change the rules, too! And get on God's side of the wall!"

"We have to…if we can change our thoughts! Read the next part, again…please!"

"Spock's will is strong enough for him to believe this logical conclusion that nothing in this situation can harm him, but he has to convince the others of the same, as any lingering doubt will prove deadly…"

"Stop!" Jimmy begged. "I've heard those words before!"

"Which words?"

"“Nothing in this situation can harm him." Something like that." He racked his memory, then enthused, "Nothing by any means can harm you. It's from a Bible verse!"

Sasha entered the words into her smartphone. "Here it is. Luke 10:19. "Behold, I have given you authority to trample over serpents and scorpions and over all the power of the enemy, and nothing by any means shall hurt you.""

Jimmy's mind was in overdrive. "Sasha, this is incredible! A counselor read me that verse after my Mom was killed. Now that I think about it, he looked a lot like the fortune teller."

"No way!"

"Way!" Jimmy maintained. "Youngish, dressed conservatively, looked like an accountant. And Doubt is what killed Adam and Eve! Eliminate Doubt and you eliminate death. That's why Kirk ordered Spock to mind-meld with the other crew members. They doubted, Spock did not. When there's no doubt that bullets cannot harm you, they'll pass right through you like the fortune teller's hand through the Australian buloke. Nothing by any means shall hurt you!"

Sasha shook her head, playing the devil's advocate. "That would mean everyone's lying to us...or that they don't know any better."

"Except God and Jesus!" Jimmy interjected. "But no one believes them. Isn't that ironic? We've chosen to doubt the two who never would lie to us!"

"And Doubt brings death!"

"That's what Doc Holliday meant!" Jimmy cried out. "Eliminate Doubt and you eliminate Death!"

The sudden shift in the conversation caught Sasha by surprise. "Where did that come from?"

"Remember, he said, "The only infidelity is for live men and women to vote themselves dead?" I haven't been able to figure that one out until now.

"The financial planning seminar at the church! Doc said he thought he got in trouble because he tried to warn the parishioners that the church was leading them the wrong way by encouraging them to sign up for life insurance policies and wills.

"Well, by signing on the dotted line for those policies, they were signing up to die and voting themselves dead! And it's all about money!"

"The root of all evil," Sasha reflected. "I never thought about it like that."

"No one has because we've all been taught that we don't have a choice. And we've chosen very poorly to accept that we don't have a choice – and that Death is inevitable. But they are our own choices that are killing us!

Jimmy was in a state of super-consciousness. He was starting to connect the dots of the unholy alliance between church and money. Aristocracy and religion, and personal agendas leading everyone astray. He saw everything and he saw nothing.

"Jimmy!" Sasha shrieked, startling him back to earth. She couldn't believe her eyes. "Isn't that Denver?"

Jimmy saw the Queen City of the Plains glistening before him as they drove over the hill at Genesee Park. His eyes darted to the Camaro's clock. 5.49.

"It is...but it can't be!" he said in disbelief. "We haven't even gone through the tunnel, yet!" Then, he questioned himself. "Did we? And where's all the traffic?"

He quickly switched on the radio in time to hear the latest traffic report: "Plan on an extra two hours to get back to Denver from the mountains as a jackknifed semi in the eastbound lanes near Georgetown has turned Interstate 70 into a parking lot."

Jimmy and Sasha looked at each other in amazement. Neither of them could process what was happening.

At last, Sasha volunteered, "I honestly don't remember going through the tunnel. We couldn't have missed it!"

"We didn't!" Jimmy insisted. "I've had my eyes on the road the whole time. Well, most of the time," he admitted wryly. "And I never saw the jackknifed semi, either!"

Sasha checked her watch to make sure of the time, and shook her head. "It's right. We got here in less than two hours, and the radio just said it was going to take us an extra two hours to get back to Denver.

"Could we accidentally have gone another way around the tunnel?"

"There's no other way that would have gotten us here faster than I-70."

"Well, I still don't remember going through the tunnel or being stuck in traffic."

"Neither do I!"

"How could we have missed it? Do you think we're dead? Maybe we died in the wreck with the jackknifed semi, and this is an out-of-body experience?"

Jimmy flashed his lights at the car in front of them – and the driver ahead signaled to get out of the fast lane to let them pass.

"I don't think so, unless that guy in front of us is Haley Joel Osment and can see dead people."

Sasha was incredulous. "This is all too weird. What happened to the tunnel and the traffic?"

"I don't know! But, I *do* know this is something else we have to keep just between the two of us until we figure it out. People will think we've lost our minds. Maybe it was just luck."

Sasha's consternation lifted at the mention of "luck."

"Hey, do you remember studying about James Russell Lowell?

Her question caught Jimmy by surprise. "Wow, that was random." He thought about it for a moment. "Wasn't he one of America's Fireside Poets in the nineteenth century?"

"Very good!" Sasha grinned. "Mr. Randall would be very proud that you were paying attention in his class. Anyway, he wrote something that I'll never forget: "Luck is the prerogative of valiant souls. The fealty life pays its rightful kings.""

Then, she added, "You're just like him, you know."

"James Russell Lowell?"

"No, goofball. Don Quixote de la Mancha! You are a valiant soul, my knight in shining armor, and one of life's rightful kings. And luck is your prerogative."

She rested her arm on Jimmy's leg for the rest of the trip. Very little was said as they both savored the contentment and the conundrum of the moment.

It was 6:15 when they pulled up in front of Sasha's house. They shared an extended kiss before Sasha broke it off, saying she had to go. She opened the door, then leaned back over to Jimmy and kissed him tenderly one more time. He watched his Dulcinea fluidly and gracefully make her way to the front door. It was sheer poetry in motion.

She had dropped the L-bomb on him, he mused, and as she turned and waved to him before disappearing into the flurry of activity he noticed through the living room window, he knew that he had meant it when he returned the favor.

Coming down a bit from Cloud 9, Jimmy noticed the yellow "low fuel' light had illuminated on the fuel gauge, so he stopped at a gas station to fill up on the way home. His mind was a thousand miles away as he topped up the tank when a voice from the other side of the pump said, "You're not paying attention."

It was as if a hypnotist had snapped his fingers and brought his subject out of a trance. Jimmy's heartbeat quickened. He recognized the voice, and peered around the pump to see a youngish, conservatively dressed man who looked like an accountant. The fortune teller!

"It's you!"

"Hello, Jimmy," he smiled. "I understand you've met some of my friends."

Jimmy stumbled over the words all fighting for attention at the same time. "What is happening?" was all that came out.

"I can't tell you," the fortune teller replied calmly. "You have to find out for yourself, or it will be meaningless. But, you are on a journey and Truth is on the other end. You must not stop until you find it. When you do, you will be disturbed. Then, you will be amazed."

"I'm already amazed!" Jimmy gushed.

"Yes. You are on the right track. But, you have not arrived...yet! As I said, you must pay attention."

"What have I missed?" Jimmy asked, uncertainly.

"Think. What did Sasha tell you when she called you after

church?"

Jimmy thought back through all of the incredible events that had taken place that day, and recalled, "She talked about the verse in the Bible about Jesus telling his disciples if they had faith as a mustard seed, nothing would be impossible for them."

"Matthew 17:20," the fortune teller said. "The disciples had asked Jesus why they couldn't cast the demons out of a young boy and cure him of his epilepsy. Jesus' entire response was, "Because of your little faith. For truly, I tell you, if you have faith the size of a mustard seed, you will say to this mountain, "move from here to there," and it will move; and nothing will be impossible for you." Now, you are wondering about how you missed the tunnel and the traffic?"

Jimmy was dumbfounded. Absolutely stunned. Was the fortune teller telling him that he had moved a mountain? No way! That was impossible! Or was it? He had been determined to get Sasha back home in time for her father's interview, and he had tuned out all distracting, negative stimuli…

His mind was swimming in a sea of seemingly impossible occurrences that had taken place over the past 24 hours. But he had been awake for the drive! He couldn't have been dreaming. Or was he? Was this a grand illusion, another Land of Oz? Instinctively, he clutched the medallion around his neck and gathered his senses as best he could.

He started to ask the fortune teller another question. Doc Holliday had said that "they' were looking for him. He wanted to know who "they' were. But the fortune teller had vanished as quickly as he had appeared.

* * *

At about the same time, in that deepest, darkest corner of the underworld, two demons hissed, "That's her!" and they rushed to tell their prince. They found him in earnest conversation on the phone.

"Hold on," Satan told the person on the other end of the line as he looked impatiently at his evil minions.

"Sir, we have the name of the soul who escaped!" the senior demon announced.

"Well?" Satan demanded.

"Her name is Celeste Rivers," the junior demon divulged.

"What do you want us to do?" asked the senior demon, his voice oozing menace.

"Find out who changed The Premise. It had to have been someone close to her."

"Do you want us to arrange to have whoever it was killed?"

"No!" Satan bellowed. "We can't afford another martyr. Just find out who it was and follow him. We have other ways. Remember, even if he says anything, no one will believe him. Keep me posted."

Satan returned to his phone call. "We have the name of the soul who escaped."

"Good!" whispered the hushed voice on the other end of the line. "But I have to go. The interview with Senator Fenimore is about to start."

"OK, but I don't have to tell you what will happen if you disappoint me!" he hissed.

⋆ ⋆ ⋆

"I'm home," Jimmy called out as he walked through the front door.

"You're just in time," Celeste Rivers answered, patting a space on the couch next to her. "The interview with the Fenimores is about to start."

Jimmy plopped down next to his mother, physically and emotionally exhausted from the race to Glenwood Springs and back.

"Did you get together with Sasha?" George Rivers asked.

"Yeah."

"What did you do?"

"We took a drive to the mountains to see the colors," Jimmy replied, giving no hint of the extraordinary events that led them to Glenwood…and back.

"Look, there she is!" Celeste proclaimed, pointing to Sasha on the television screen. "She's such a beautiful girl!"

Jimmy perked up when he saw his girlfriend, whose lips he had savored not even an hour before.

"It's so exciting!" his mom added.

"What do you mean?" Jimmy asked, uncertainly. Could his mother know? After all, she had been dead for six years before her son, with the help of the fortune teller, had traveled through time, met up with Don Quixote de la Mancha, and changed "The Premise," which had brought her back to life, apparently without skipping a beat since the day she had been killed.

"That you might be dating the daughter of the next President of the United States, silly. What did you think I meant?"

She didn't know.

"It's probably his election to lose," his Dad piped in. "There are too many skeletons in everyone else's closets. He's got the backing of the Joak brothers, the Catholic Church, the Faith in US, and the Faithful Horizon. They have the resources and the wherewithal to destroy anyone who gets in their way."

"Oh, come on, George," Celeste downplayed. "It can't be as bad as you make it sound. We know the Fenimores. They're good people. They have good values. And, frankly, I don't see what's wrong with this country moving back towards its religious roots..."

George was incredulous. "So, I guess you have no problem with the Inquisition."

"Of course, you go to the extreme."

"It's not an extreme. It's called learning the lesson of history so as not to make the same mistakes. The marriage of politics, religion, and money is the most unholy of all alliances. You're assuming that religious leaders will lead us closer to God. What if they have their own agendas that are not part of God's agenda? They were the religious leaders of the day that convinced Pilate to crucify Jesus. And we saw, again, how money and power corrupted during the Inquisition. Why would you want to go there, again? You know the expression: fool me once, shame on you; fool me twice, shame on me…All I know is that if you really pay attention to the rhetoric of the Joaks and of those ultra-conservative Christian groups, they are preaching a message that is the exact opposite of what Jesus stood for…and died for."

"George, you know you're preaching to the choir. I'm just saying…"

"Hey, you guys," Jimmy interrupted. "You're missing the interview."

Truth be told, so was Jimmy. He didn't hear a word of what the Senator was saying, not because of his parents' debate, but because of his fixation on his girlfriend. And on the fantastic occurrences that had played out before them in the last forty-eight hours. He needed time to sort out his thoughts, and his parents' discussion was too distracting. He would have left the room, but he didn't want to take the chance of missing the pre-arranged signal he and Sasha had come up with for her to let him know she was thinking of him – using her right index finger to gently scratch her right temple twice.

About seven minutes into the interview, the camera zoomed in on Sasha when she was asked what she thought of her father running for President, and before she answered, she scratched at her right temple twice with her index finger.

Jimmy was in heaven. His girlfriend was on national television, using their secret language to tell him she loved him!

Was that a reach, he wondered? Was he reading too much into the temple scratch? But she had told him she loved him when he dropped her off at home a little over an hour ago. He had known he loved her ever since their first kiss in the carnival's food court, dressed as Pete and Julie of *The Mod Squad.* She had been the only one he trusted enough to talk to about his mother's death, besides his therapist. Still, he hadn't told the therapist some of the most intimate details he had shared with Sasha, even after six years!

Sasha was the one who had insisted on going to the fortune teller's booth. Who was she, really? he wondered. Was she an angel sent from heaven to get him to open up? She was *his* angel, that much was certain.

Jimmy checked out, replaying in his mind the incredible events of the past 24 hours. Stepping through that purple velour curtain into the fortune teller's domain had led him to the other side of an enormous wall, a side on which seemingly everything was possible – including meeting up with Don Quixote de la Mancha and his faithful manservant, Sancho Panza, who weren't fictional at all. Don Quixote had given him a medallion of a knight sitting high atop his steed, his lance at the ready – and together, they had engaged Don Quixote's sworn enemy, the Knight of the White Moon.

The Man of La Mancha dispatched the Knight of the White Moon, and Jimmy destroyed "The Premise' – refusing access to the avalanche of free publicity accorded to mass murderers – which had the effect of changing the circumstances that had led to his Mom's death. Thus, the voiceless never made the connection between killing innocent people and fifteen minutes of "fame," so there wasn't a shooter at the mall when he and his Mom went shopping for that skateboard for his eleventh birthday. It was as if she never had been killed. Only Jimmy knew the truth. And Sasha. She believed him, and believed *in* him…and she loved him!

She had seen the medallion – and Don Quixote, in the guise of a Dairy Queen employee, offered additional proof that it wasn't just a fantastic dream. He had sent them on an urgent, mysterious quest to Glenwood Springs in search of John Doe, who turned out to be Doc Holliday, the legendary gunfighter from the gunfight at the OK Corral. Though he died 127 years ago, they had found him in a hospital bed in Room 407 of the Valley View Hospital on his deathbed after a savage beating at the hands of three men who belonged to the Southeast Denver Christian Bible Church – coincidentally, the same one the Fenimore family attended. And he said that he was a friend of the fortune teller!

He and Sasha had discovered a connection between Doc Holliday and Captain Kirk, Jimmy's hero for having been the one to figure out that the only way to pass the test to become Captain of the Enterprise was to change the rules. Jimmy had wanted desperately to change the rules to bring his mother back to life. In the *Star Trek* episode, "The Sceptre of the Gun," Spock determined that when physical laws are disregarded, the reality based on those physical laws does not exist – that what seems to be real is, in truth, an elaborate illusion that was only as real as the crew accepted it to be.

Jimmy finally had caught on. "Sasha," he'd said, "If a lie is repeated often enough, it becomes accepted as the truth. If we choose not to believe in the physical laws of man, then this reality around us does not exist. It's all an elaborate deception to keep us from the freedom that was intended for us – and is waiting for us once we change our choices!

"That's what everyone has been leading us to – the fortune teller, Don Quixote, Doc Holliday...the "reality' around us is only as real as we believe it to be. I told you that ever since my mom was killed, I just couldn't accept the way reality was instead of the way it should have been!

"That was the message from the fortune teller. We've been lied to, and since we've chosen very poorly to believe the lies – that the rules and laws that have been accepted are impossible to change – we are stuck in this horrible pseudo-reality that we've been tricked into accepting as gospel truth. We have brought it on ourselves by the choices we have made. Captain Kirk showed us that we can change the rules if we choose to change what we believe!"

Had he and Sasha changed the rules? Somehow, they had made it back to Denver from Glenwood Springs in only ninety minutes, a trip that normally would have taken an hour longer *without* traffic – and there had been a traffic delay of over two hours on top of the normal driving time. Had they moved a mountain? Jesus said that if a man had the faith of mustard seed and didn't doubt, nothing would be impossible for him and he could move a mountain, but no one believed that's what the Son of God really meant. How could you *not* believe the One who never would lie to us, the One who has authority over all things? Jimmy wondered. He never had doubted that he could get Sasha back to Denver in time for her Dad's interview on TV that same night...and she hadn't been late.

Doc Holliday also had said something troubling to him – that people were looking for them, and it didn't sound like they were hoping to exchange recipes. Who was looking for us? And why? The same thugs who tried to kill Doc? But they were from a church, the same one that Sasha's family belonged to.

Hours before his attack, Doc had been warning parishioners not to sign up for the life insurance policies and wills at the financial "wellness' night the church had been sponsoring because they would be signing their death warrants. And what was "The Question' he had asked so long ago that the fortune teller and Don Quixote said had triggered this inconceivable sequence of events? How did they know?

Right then, Jimmy's stream of consciousness was abruptly interrupted and he sprang to his feet. "Get out of here!" he shouted, loudly.

Celeste scrambled to console her son, hugging him close to her. "Jimmy, no one is here! You fell asleep watching the interview. You must have had a bad dream."

Jimmy's eyes darted anxiously around the room. His Mom was right – no one was there. But the demon he thought he'd seen looked so real!

He sighed and sat back down on the couch. He was not convinced, but it would have been pointless to pursue it.

He noticed another program on the television. "Is the interview over?"

"Yes," his father replied. "I'm sure you can catch it online in a few minutes, if you're interested."

"How'd you think it went?"

"Typical True Believers politics. Pro-life. Anti-HERO. Pro-business. Anti-global warming. Cut taxes. Here's an interesting one, though – legalize marijuana."

"What?" Jimmy asked incredulously.

Celeste was indignant. "I can't believe Bill supports the legalization of pot," she rued. "It's a gateway drug!"

"It's just about the money," George observed.

"Well, the Bible says money is the root of all evil. The only thing that money will be good for is paying for the social costs of a stoned society."

"Honey, you don't have to vote for him."

"Who else is there to vote for? There are so many skeletons in everyone else's closet, it's like a house of horrors on Halloween. Except it's every day of the year."

"Dad, I think you hit a nerve," Jimmy chuckled.

"That's right, laugh," his Mom groused. "But, I'm telling you, nothing is what it seems."

Jimmy gasped. Those five words slapped him in the face. The fortune teller, Don Quixote, Doc Holliday...and, now, his own mother?!

His mind was swirling as Celeste excused herself to go upstairs. Was it all a coincidence? Did she know she had been murdered by a gunman at the mall six years ago and that her son had traveled back through time to change The Premise and bring her back to life? In her dying breath, after all, she had told him, "This is not the end." Now, he was beginning to believe it had been the catalyst that had set him on this mind-bending journey. But to where? And to what end? The fortune teller had told him his journey had begun even sooner, when he had asked The Question. What question???

"Dad," he blurted out. "Do you believe in time travel?"

George was floored by the randomness of his son's question. They had been discussing the politics of Senator Fenimore. "My gosh, Jimmy, where did that come from?"

"Well," Jimmy persisted, "do you?"

George thought for a few moments. "I seem to recall Einstein talking about wormholes and bending universes. But I think it's pretty far-fetched."

"But, do you think it's possible?"

George hesitated. "Not really, I guess."

"But, Dad," Jimmy insisted. "You *have* to think it's possible!"

"Why, son?"

"Because if you don't, it puts you on the wrong side of the wall."

"What wall are you talking about?"

"Look, suppose there's a fence..." Or, a giant wall, he thought to himself. "On one side of the fence, there is God. On the other side of the fence is the opposite of God – say, the Devil. On God's side, everything is possible. On the other side, things are impossible. You can't be on both sides of the fence at the same time. The second you choose to accept something as impossible, it puts you on the wrong side of the fence!

"When Peter was on God's side of the fence, he was walking on water. When he doubted, just for an instant, it put him on the other side of the fence, and he sank. So, you see, you *have* to believe it's possible so you're on the right side of the fence!"

George could sense the urgency in his son's argument. "OK, Jimmy, that's a very interesting point of view. I never thought about it that way..."

"That's because Father Simon never told us!" Jimmy practically shouted. "No one has, except for Jesus. The only thing our religious leaders tell us is that that's not what Jesus meant. They're leading us to the wrong side of the fence!"

"Jimmy, where is all this coming from?"

Jimmy hesitated. "Do you really want to know?"

"Yes."

"OK, here goes. I'm glad you're sitting down. Six years ago, when Mom took me to buy that skateboard for my birthday, she was killed by a gunman at the mall. With the help of a fortune teller, I traveled back through time and changed The Premise that led to her death and brought her back to life."

Jimmy stopped immediately. He saw the look of consternation on his father's face. "I know it sounds incredible, but you have to believe me!"

George chose his words very carefully. "Jimmy, Mom told me you had a nightmare last night and you thought she was dead, and I believe it was such a vivid dream that it has had a profound effect on you. Listen to me, your mom hasn't been dead for the past six years. She did not die and come back to life last night."

Jimmy was not to be denied. "But, Dad, do you think it's possible?"

"No, Jimmy," George said firmly. "*That* is not possible."

Jimmy was crestfallen. His Dad was on the wrong side of the fence.

* * *

"Wow, that was close," the junior demon winced.

"What were you thinking?" his mentor reprimanded. "The kid saw you!"

"But, Satan told us to find out who changed The Premise – that it had to be someone close to Celeste Rivers. So, I just…"

"So, you just got caught!" the senior demon finished his sentence. "I told you to follow at a distance. The only success we have is when no one sees us coming!"

"I didn't think anyone could see us."

"Well, you thought wrong. Don't you think if someone could change The Premise, he probably is not like all the others? And he might be able to see us?

"We have to sneak up on people, or they'll know to fight back and they might figure out that they can control us. Now, we've lost our element of surprise. He'll be on the lookout for us."

The junior demon tried to calm his mentor. "Well, the only one who saw us was the son, and no one believed him."

"Isn't that ironic," the senior demon mused.

"What?"

"That no one believes the son. They didn't believe the Son of God, either. Anyway, it's a good thing you got out of there quickly."

"Can I tell you something?" the younger demon asked sheepishly.

His mentor's exasperation was palpable. "What?"

"I didn't exactly leave by choice," he admitted.

"What do you mean?"

"I mean, the kid yelled at me to "get out," and I felt like I didn't have a choice. It felt like I had been expelled by some mysterious power or force."

The senior demon's eyes narrowed. "You know what else? In your clumsiness, I think you've stumbled onto the one who changed The Premise. We have to tell the Prince!"

Part Four

I

"Jimmy!" Sasha called out.

Amid the frenzy of hundreds of teenagers excitedly gossiping about the Sadie Hawkins dance over the weekend and hurrying to get to their first period classes, the sound of his girlfriend's voice cut through the din as a soft kiss in the morning gently rescues a loved one from the hurly-burly of a nightmare.

Jimmy stopped, his heart a-flutter, turned around, and easily picked out the most beautiful girl in the world from the throng of high-schoolers surging around him.

"Well?" she asked, expectantly, when she caught up to him.

"You look fantastic!" he smiled, drinking up her loveliness. He still wasn't quite used to the boyfriend-girlfriend thing – for him, it had only been a little over forty-eight hours.

Sasha rolled her eyes. "Not that, goofball, but thanks." And she scratched her right temple twice with her index finger.

"Oh, that!" he said, feigning ignorance. "I fell asleep on the couch."

Sasha's shoulders drooped, as if all the air had been taken out of her sails.

Jimmy's face lit up. "I'm just teasing. Of course, I saw it! I wouldn't have missed it for the world!"

Sasha elbowed her boyfriend in his ribs. "You're such a brat!" she huffed in mock anger. "I have to get to class." She started to walk away.

"Wait! I do, too." They shared the same first-period civics class. "I'm sorry. Let me make it up to you."

Without looking at him, Sasha tapped her cheek. When Jimmy

leaned in for the kiss, she quickly turned her head and planted a full-on smooch on his lips.

"There. All better," she cooed.

⋆ ⋆ ⋆

"Mr. Rivers, Miss Fenimore, good morning," their civics teacher, Ben Hamilton, loudly greeted them as they strolled into his classroom. "Glad you could join us!" Jimmy quickly surveyed the room. It was full, except for two seats in front. His eyes darted to the clock on the wall – sure enough, they were late. But how? Maybe another wrinkle in time, he thought...

"Good morning, Mr. Hamilton," Sasha replied with a bright smile and a barely perceptible nod. A smile and nod from Sasha Fenimore could defuse any potentially awkward moment. And it worked again. It always did.

"We were just talking about your father's interview last night," their teacher continued.

"Great," she muttered unconvincingly, the wattage of her smile turned down significantly.

Noticing his prized student's discomfort, Ben Hamilton sought to reassure her. "Sasha, like it or not, your father is the face of the True Believers ideology that may well occupy the White House next year. He is a decent man and I'm sure he's a wonderful father. That said, he also belongs to the public, representing a political party whose platform must be debated so that it will be an informed citizenry that exercises its right to vote responsibly in next year's election. The right to vote is the pillar of democracy – government of the people, by the people, and for the people. It carries with it the burden of great responsibility. We have a duty to be informed in order that we do not exercise our right ignorantly or recklessly. This discussion is nothing personal – it's about the very public policies of the party he represents."

"Thanks, Mr. Hamilton. Still, I think I'd rather be at the dentist's office getting a root canal."

That tickled the class's collective funny bone.

"And Ronald Reagan wanted to be in Philadelphia on March 30th, 1981," her teacher spoke over the laughter. "But, Sasha, he didn't get assassinated, and you won't, either. So, let's get started... This is a civics class. By the time you leave my class, I want you to be able to fight through all the blather and BS of an election, to have the mindset of studying both sides of the issues, and the confidence to form your own opinions.

"The True Believers have said that they support the courts having the option to impose the death penalty in capital murder cases. In the same breath, it is decidedly pro-life when it comes to abortion. How can it be pro-life and pro-death at the same time?

"The apparent contradiction has been made manifest several times in recent years when pro-life extremists have killed doctors who perform abortions."

The teacher might as well have lit the fuse to a Roman candle for the fireworks that ensued.

Then something remarkable happened: Jimmy Rivers raised his hand. Jimmy rarely – OK, never – opened up in class and Mr. Hamilton was quick to call his name before he changed his mind.

Emboldened by the events of the past forty-eight hours, Jimmy spoke confidently. "I know this is supposed to be a legal issue – determining legally, and scientifically, when life truly begins – but from this discussion, and from the discussion outside of this classroom, it seems to me that it eventually boils down to a religious issue.

"The True Believers are all about bringing God back into public schools despite the constitutional provision for the separation of church and state. But that's beside the point. The point is, according to the True Believers, God is fair game in this election."

Jimmy was on a roll. "So, here's the thing: God is definitely pro-choice! He created us with free will. Even though He knows we are going to make bad choices, He never has, and never would, take away our ability to choose. If He did, He would turn us into puppets, and where's the glory in that?

"Now, God wants us to exercise our free will responsibly, just like you do, Mr. Hamilton. He gave His Ten Commandments to Moses to pass along to us, and one of them is "Thou shalt not kill." All this talk about capital punishment, killing abortion doctors, abortions… God told us not to kill, but He's not going to take away our ability to choose freely, even if we choose poorly to disobey. Instead, He sent His Son to re-teach us the lessons we either did not learn or ignored, so that we could exercise our 'right to vote' in accordance with His will and reclaim our divine inheritance."

Ben Hamilton was stunned. Jimmy's classmates were stunned. Sasha was amazed. No one knew what to say. But, as the bell saves a boxer dazed by a powerful right cross at the end of a round, the sound of the buzzer signaling the time had come to move on to the next class saved Mr. Hamilton and his class, and the students filed out into the chaos of the hallways.

"Jimmy!" Sasha gushed, grabbing his hand before they parted. "Where did *that* come from?"

"I honestly don't know," he replied in a state of semi-bewilderment. "I've never even thought about it before."

Sasha was beaming. "I know what it is. You freed your mind this weekend, and you opened yourself up to all possibilities. And you know who the Source of all possibilities is! I want to get there, too!" She kissed him on the cheek. "See you at lunch!"

She gently patted him on his backside to scoot him to his next class.

* * *

Meanwhile, at the Southeast Denver Christian Bible Church, the phones were ringing off the hook. The day that had started off so well for Father Simon in the aftermath of Senator Fenimore's interview was about to take a decided turn south.

"What do you mean, 'he's gone?'" the priest agonized plaintively.

"We have turned this hospital upside down. We've checked all the security footage," explained the chaplain at the Valley View Hospital. "The patient in Room 407 just disappeared into thin air!"

The voice of Joyce Odell, Father Simon's secretary, cut in over the intercom. "Sir, I have Jasper Joak on Line 2."

The knot in Father Simon's stomach grew to the size of a beach ball. "I have to go," he told the chaplain. "Be sure to let me know the minute you find anything out." He pressed Line 2's flashing button. "Good morning, Jasper. What can I do for you?"

"Don't 'good morning' me!" the elder Joak brother's voice thundered. He and his brother, Henry, ran Joak Industries, a multi-level conglomerate that had netted the brothers a combined net worth of over $100 billion and afforded them ample resources to further their own ultra-conservative political agenda. "You said you were going to take care of that bastard who was warning everyone not to sign up for our life insurance policies and wills. So, imagine my surprise when Sheriff Gisbourne called to say that he escaped!"

"Jasper, that's probably overstating it a bit," he tried to console one half of the True Believers' greatest benefactors. "I just got off the phone with the chaplain up there, and he said he'd been summoned to administer last rights."

"Then, where's the body?" came Joak's booming retort.

The shakiness in Father Simon's voice mimicked his trembling hand. "Well, that's just it. It seems..."

"Nothing is as it seems," Joak bellowed. "And what about Sasha Fenimore?"

"What about her?" the harried priest stammered.

"Sheriff Gisbourne says she and a friend of hers paid a visit to the guy just before he vanished. Her friend told the nurse he thought he might be his uncle."

"But that can't be!" Father Simon protested. "Sasha was home for her dad's interview last night. She couldn't have been in Glenwood Springs yesterday. She was in church with her family until noon. Did the nurse say what time she supposedly was there?"

"Right before he disappeared. Around 4:00, she said."

"That's impossible," the priest insisted. "I was just reading in the paper how a jackknifed semi on I-70 added an extra two to three hours to the drive back from the mountains yesterday afternoon. Is the nurse sure it was Sasha?"

Joyce Odell' voice came across the intercom, again. "Sir, I have Ralph Petiole on Line 3."

"Jasper, Ralph's on the other line. Can I call you back?"

"Make sure you do! There are a lot of loose ends and I want to hear that they've all been tied up."

Father Simon switched lines. "Hello, Ralph."

Ralph Petiole, head of Faith in US and Senator Fenimore's head campaign manager, didn't have time for pleasantries, either.

"Have you seen the YouTube video? It's going viral!"

"What are you talking about?"

"Some kid at Benjamin Franklin High School going on in civics class about how God is pro-choice!"

Father Simon's world was crashing down around him.

"Obviously, as part of the religious right," Petiole screamed, "we can't be seen as opposed to God! So, how can we be pro-life when this kid very convincingly portrays God as pro-choice? You have to do something!"

This can't be happening, the beleaguered priest thought to himself, but before he had a chance to gather the rest of his scattered thoughts, his secretary interrupted his conversation, again.

"Father, Cardinal Phelps is on Line 1."

"Ralph, I have to go. I'll call you back."

Joyce Odell cut in, again, her voice beginning to sound as frazzled as his own nerves. "Sir, the red line!"

"Joyce, please tell the Cardinal I'll get right back to him," and the weary priest picked up the dedicated line.

"Simon, we've got a situation!" Satan snarled.

"I know, Sir, I've just heard."

"Well, what you don't know is that this young man's name is Jimmy Rivers, and whoever he is, it was his mother who escaped. Too much of a coincidence, Simon. He has to be the one who changed The Premise."

"Oh my God," Father Simon marveled into the receiver.

Satan howled, "How many times have I told you never to say

that name in my presence! There's more, Simon...do you know who this kid's girlfriend is? Sasha Fenimore! And guess where they were yesterday afternoon!"

"Jasper said she was seen in Glenwood," the embattled priest flinched.

"Yes! Talking to the same John Doe who was outside your church Saturday night telling everyone not to sign up for the life insurance policies and wills!"

"Sir, that just can't be. She couldn't have been there and made it back to Denver in time for the interview. That's just impossible!"

"You're forgetting who you're dealing with here! This kid seems to be connected. I shouldn't have to tell you, of all people, that nothing is impossible for those who are connected! That's beside the point, though. What was John Doe doing in Glenwood Springs? You said you were going to take care of him!"

"I thought I did. I got a text at 3:30 yesterday morning from one of the men I sent after him saying the threat had been eliminated. But, I told you killing people was a little out of our league and that it would have been better if you had done it."

"Well, you see, here's the thing," Satan said, his voice dripping in sarcasm. "I have been stripped of all my authority, I can't lift a finger against His children. So, I'm stuck with having to try and trick them into choosing to use the authority they still have against each other. That's where you come in. In setting the table so that they choose to turn away from Him, your predecessors and I have turned them into very fallible entities. Those cleaners you hired didn't take care of anything – in fact, they made things worse! That's what I have to work with – screw-ups, including you!"

"What did I do?" Simon complained.

"It's what you haven't done. It's your job to perpetuate the lies that God's children have accepted as Truth. If there are people in your sphere of influence who still believe what Jesus told them, then you haven't done your job. You have to create Doubt in everyone's mind, damn it! That's how I tricked Adam and Eve out of Paradise. That's how I got to Peter while he was walking on water. You remember that, don't you? He was as close as anyone ever was to reconnecting with Him and reclaiming his divine inheritance.

"But no one believes it," the Devil snickered evilly. "They think it's just a fantastic story. Doubt is the key, Simon! You have to do a better job of instilling Doubt in everyone's mind, especially in Jimmy Rivers' mind, or we will lose everything. You'll have the opportunity. He is Sasha Fenimore's boyfriend, after all. Have the Fenimores invite the Rivers family to dinner and make sure you're there. Then, do what you have to do to plant that seed of Doubt and make sure to water it as often as you can.

"Impossibility is your best watering can. His children are so far removed from the Light, they can't see through the darkness to the Truth that nothing is impossible when they are connected to Him. Doubt severs the connection, and that's why they're vulnerable. Bring scientists into the picture to stress that some things simply are not scientifically possible."

"They tried that with Roger Bannister," Father Simon replied feebly, "but he still ran the mile in under four minutes."

"Yes," Satan countered, "but he still died, didn't he! It's immortality that they have the hardest time with. Even if they believe that it was the faith of the blind man that allowed him to see, or the faith of the paralytic that enabled him to pick up his bed and go home, they still don't believe that a human being can live forever!

"It is my crowning accomplishment! All it takes is one seed of Doubt, one gust of wind to make the water-walker blink, and they separate from Him, and they drown in the Sea of Doubt, losing everything He has provided for them."

Properly chastised, Father Simon promised to do better.

"See that you do, Simon. Make no mistake – this Jimmy Rivers is the biggest threat to us since Peter. He definitely is connected...for now. He sees things that no one else does. He destroyed The Premise and helped his mom escape, although he's not 100% convinced it was not all just an incredible dream – and he cast out one of my demons from his parents' house last night. Thankfully, his parents did my work for me and convinced him that *that* was a dream...but it wasn't."

"What are we going to do?" Father Simon asked unsteadily.

"There's no need for panic. Just keep doing what you and your colleagues have been doing since He was here. But do it better! Plant those seeds of Doubt, and I'll do the rest. Now that I know who he is, I can set a proper table for Jimmy Rivers."

Satan paused for effect. "And, Simon, you won't want to let me down *this* time!"

★ ★ ★

Ralph Petiole slammed the phone down in the war room of the Believe in Family building in Colorado Springs, which was serving as the de facto headquarters for Senator Fenimore's "Partnership of the Right' campaign team. He was frustrated.

"He said he'd call back," he announced to the hastily gathered meeting of the ultra-right's best and brightest minds. Besides Petiole, the emergency meeting included Al Dobson from Faithful Horizon, Amon Smith from the Community of Light, the Sacred Path's Pat Bateman, and Annabelle Garton from the Blessed Unity, as Henry Joak was being video-conferenced in.

"This may be above Simon's pay grade," Pat Bateman offered. "Do you think we can get Cardinal Phelps on the line?"

"It's worth a try," seconded Amon Smith.

No sooner had the last syllable left Amon's mouth than the phone began to ring. The caller ID identified the caller…it was Cardinal Phelps.

Petiole picked up the receiver. "Your Eminence, we were just going to call you. Al's here, and Amon, Pat, and Annabelle. Henry's with us, too, via video conference."

"Good morning, everyone, I'm glad you're all there. It saves me some phone calls. Listen, we've got a real problem here. I'm sure you've seen the video."

"Yes, we have."

"Well, first off, take it down."

"We've already tried. We haven't been able to decode it."

The prelate's voice rose in exasperation. "Just find the person who posted it and convince him or her that it goes against church teaching."

Amon Smith joined the conversation. "What teaching is that, Your Eminence?"

"I don't know, Amon! Make something up. You can always fall back on the writings of the church fathers. Tell them God didn't mean to give everyone carte blanche when it comes to the exercise of free will. There are limits!"

"Your Eminence, this is Pat Bateman. We don't know who posted it. That was our first thought, too. However, when we called the teacher – a Mr. Hamilton – he said he collects his students' cell phones and iPads before every class to avoid distractions, and he returns them after the classes are over."

"Well, someone had to have recorded that kid's testimony!"

"We asked Mr. Hamilton if anyone either inside or outside the class could have made the recording without him noticing. He said there was no way it could have come from outside the class due to the perspective from which it was shot, and there was no way anyone inside the class could have made the video without him noticing. The kid was sitting in the front row, right in front of him."

"So, it's another grassy knoll is what you're telling me," came the cardinal's annoyed response.

There was an uncomfortable silence. Then, the cardinal continued, "OK, here's what you have to do. Call a press conference for the Senator as soon as possible. This has to be contained immediately. Tell him to start out with some politically correct mumbo-jumbo about how free speech is one of the basic tenets of democracy, and about how everyone is entitled to their own opinion.

"At the same time, people who hear the messages must be careful not to take them at face value. Doubt is the key. He must create doubt. I'm told the young man is the Senator's daughter's boyfriend. He should go on record as saying what a fine, respectful person he is, but that as well-meaning as the message is, it's out of context, and that religious issues never are so simple.

"Then, he needs to distract them. Have him bring up the Houston Equal Rights Ordinance as an example. Equal rights is a no-brainer, right? But, it's not so simple – if HERO is passed, it could allow men dressed as women, or who identify as female, to go into women's bathrooms. He should say that, as a husband and a father with a daughter, he doesn't want the possibility of any man legally invading the privacy women have a right to expect in their bathrooms."

"Bravo, Your Eminence!" applauded Annabelle Garton. "A masterful stroke!"

"Your Excellence," chimed in Al Dobson, "that's all well and good, but don't you think that by making such a big deal about a random student's opinion in a civics class that we are fanning the flames of a small brush fire and possibly turning it into a raging inferno?"

"Al, your concern is appreciated, but your thought process is naïve. First of all, this is no random student, and we will talk more about that later. Secondly, this video has gone viral, and it's going more and more viral by the second. It's *already* a raging inferno, as you put it. With so many disenfranchised Christians in this country – disenfranchised *voting* Christians, I might add – we can't give them any more excuses to turn away from us, and away from the Senator. We have our marching orders!"

"Understood," said the leader of Faithful Horizon.

"Very well, then, I think we're all on the same page. I'll release my own statement this afternoon. Gentlemen – and lady! – I cannot emphasize enough how important this issue is. This is not just about the White House. It's much bigger than that. This is end-of-times stuff!"

* * *

"There he is!" Sasha grinned widely when Jimmy arrived at her locker. She was waiting for him with Hannah McAuliffe, her cousin and teammate on the soccer team. "We thought you might be too big to have lunch with the little people."

"Hi girls! Sorry, I'm late. I had to talk to Mrs. Rodgers after class about the homework assignment." It took a moment for Sasha's comment to register. "Wait, what?"

Sasha raised her eyebrow. "You don't answer your cell phone anymore? I've called and texted you like ten times."

Instinctively, Jimmy felt his front pockets. The phone wasn't there.

"Oh crap, I forgot to get it at the end of Hamilton's class. Can we stop by and pick it up on our way out?"

"So, you *still* are going to eat with us?" Hannah needled.

"OK, what's up?"

"You mean you haven't heard?" Sasha asked as they made their way through the throng of students racing to lunch.

"Heard what?"

"That you're an Internet sensation. You've gone viral!"

"What are you talking about?"

"That's right," Hannah joined in. "For that little pro-choice speech you gave in Hamilton's class."

"Someone was recording that?" he asked, turning the corner to their civics class.

"Did you forget something, Mr. Rivers?" Ben Hamilton was standing just outside the door to his classroom, brandishing Jimmy's cell phone in his right hand.

"Yes, thank you, Mr. Hamilton," Jimmy replied as his teacher handed him his phone.

"I should warn you...people are looking for you," his teacher added.

The sound of those words struck a nerve. "Why does everyone keep telling me that?" Jimmy fretted aloud.

"I don't know about everyone, but I've heard from Senator Fenimore's campaign and from ABC News, for starters..."

"My dad called you?" Sasha asked, incredulously.

"Not your dad, but his campaign manager, Ralph Petiole."

"Ugh," Sasha rued. "I really don't like that man."

Jimmy was shocked. "Why? And who posted the video?"

"That's what Mr. Petiole wanted to know. ABC News just wanted to talk to you. But, in answer to your question, I don't know how that video came to be in the first place. I had everyone's cell phones and iPads, and even if I hadn't, I would have noticed someone recording you because it looked like whoever did it was in front of you – and you were sitting in the front row. That's the *really* strange part.

"Anyway, enjoy your lunch. I have some papers to grade." And with that, Ben Hamilton stepped back into his classroom.

"Come on," Hannah urged. "We're not going to have enough time to get to Duffeyroll."

The three friends debated the issue of the mysterious post during the ten-minute ride to the Duffeyroll Café, but when they sat down to lunch, Hannah changed the subject.

"OK, enough about Jimmy. I have some other news," she enthused.

Sasha's face lit up. "What is it? A boy?"

"No. Well, kind of," Hannah blushed, "but not really. I got a job at Joak Exploration!"

"And?" Sasha pressed, with a sparkle in her eye.

"OK," she confessed. "And, the HR guy who hired me is totally hot!"

"There it is!" Jimmy joined in, welcoming the distraction from his Internet mystery.

"So, what's his name?" Sasha demanded, desperate for details.

"And which came first?" Jimmy needled. "The job or the hottie?"

"His name is Tom Farrell, and, Jimmy, the job came first!"

"Wait a minute," Sasha suddenly remembered, "I thought you hated Joak Industries."

"I do! But, I'm going to expose the Joaks for the creeps they are, and what better way to get the dope on them than from the inside?"

"I'm not sure you want to be messing around with the Joak brothers," Jimmy cautioned.

"Jimmy, I want to be an investigative reporter. And I want to go to Northwestern. This would be my ticket!"

Sasha checked her watch. "Hey, guys, we have to get back."

⋆ ⋆ ⋆

By the time they returned to campus, the rest of the school had had a chance to get caught up with Jimmy's new-found celebrity, and if he was uncomfortable with it before lunch, the glare of attention in the hallways when he got back from lunch made it worse. Much worse. For a lot of reasons, not the least of which was that it put him at loggerheads with his girlfriend's father, which, in turn, would put her in a very awkward position.

"Attaboy, Jimmy!"

"Give "em hell, Jimmy!"

"Stick it to the man!"

"Ooooh, what's Sasha's dad gonna say?

"Sasha's sleeping with the enemy!"

It seemed like everyone had something to say. He turned to his girlfriend and apologized.

"Sasha, I'm so sorry. I never wanted this to happen. I had no idea this even *could* happen. That's what I get for raising my hand in class. You know how much I respect your father."

"Jimmy, I know," and she kissed him before they went their separate ways to class. "This doesn't change a thing," she assured him. "I know you didn't mean anything by it. It's not a big deal."

But it was a big deal!

When Jimmy got home from school, his Mom was waiting for him on the front porch. "I guess you got your fifteen minutes of fame," she said with a smile when she saw him. "Who knew it was going to be like this!"

"I know, right?" Jimmy replied. "That's what I get for raising my hand!"

"How did it get online?"

"That's just it, Mom. No one knows. Mr. Hamilton collects everyone's phones and iPads before class, and he said he didn't see anyone recording it from inside or outside the classroom. He would have because I was sitting in the front row."

Celeste thought for a moment. "Do they have surveillance cameras in the classrooms?"

"No, just in the hallways."

She let the mystery pass. "Anyway, the phone hasn't stopped ringing. Everyone's seen it."

"I know. It's gone viral," Jimmy frowned.

"Reporters, too. The *Denver Post, USA Today*, CNN, ABC News..."

"Mom, I don't want to talk to anybody. I didn't ask for this. I just answered a question in class!"

"A question," she repeated under her breath. That gave Celeste Rivers reason to pause. "Something about a question," she murmured, alone in her thoughts.

Jimmy's heart skipped a beat. Was she starting to remember? Don Quixote said this whole thing with the fortune teller had begun with a question. And Doc Holliday had confirmed it. The Question he had asked a long time ago. "Mom, what question?" he asked, cautiously.

"That's it!" she perked up, as if waking from a trance. "With all this commotion, I almost forgot. Alice Fenimore called and asked us to dinner on Friday night. She wants to show us some of the pictures she took of you and Sasha before the Sadie Hawkins dance.

Jimmy came crashing down to earth. What pictures? he wondered. Sasha picked him up and they went straight to the fair. Then, it dawned on him – the pictures were a part of the missing six years of his life. "Well, that's going to be incredibly weird," he muttered.

"Jimmy, Bill Fenimore is a big boy and he can take care of himself. He's been in the kitchen for a very long time, so I'm sure he can handle the heat. Especially the unintended heat from a teenage boy. Besides, I'm sure this is all going to blow over in a few days. Much ado about nothing. It probably won't even come up."

"I hope you're right, Mom." But, Jimmy knew better.

"Why don't you help yourself out, then, by talking to one of these reporters? They're not going to let up until they get something out of you. You can tell them what you just told me. That should pull the rug right out from under whatever story, or angle, they think they have."

Elevating his profile was the last thing in the world that Jimmy wanted. People – presumably, nefarious – were looking for him and Sasha. It wasn't as if they were hiding, though. Hiding in plain sight was more like it...especially, Sasha, with her dad campaigning to be the next President of the United States.

He knew from his journalism class that his Mom probably was right – the reporters would not back off until they got what they wanted. So, he reasoned, the quickest way to get out of the spotlight, ironically, would be to jump into it so everyone could see for themselves that there was *nothing* to see. And they would move along.

"OK, I'll do one interview," he said, finally. "Which one do you think I should do?"

Celeste thought carefully for a moment, then suggested Madison Munro from ABC News.

"I've followed her career since she got started about thirteen years ago, I think, and you can trust her. She's very capable, she seems very empathetic, and she can deliver a punch if one is needed. Always with a velvet glove, though. There's just something about her. I can't quite put my finger on it, but it goes beyond her reporting. It sets her apart...in my mind, anyway. She'll treat you well. Oh, and one more thing. She's looking into a possible tie-in to a story she did in 2003."

"Mom, I was four years old back then!" Nevertheless, Jimmy's curiosity had been piqued.

* * *

In a place so dark and completely devoid of light, Satan had just finished briefing his progeny on the menace of the past forty-eight hours.

"So, do you think this intruder, this Jimmy Rivers, is the vanguard of the Second Coming?" the antichrist prodded.

"Well, you're here, aren't you? That means the possibility cannot be dismissed."

"Is he The One?"

"I don't think so. But, I keep hearing about a fortune teller…"

"A fortune teller?"

"Yes. Someone who is gradually peeling away all the layers of Doubt I've worked so hard to pile on to keep their minds closed so they can't see the Truth that's right in front of their eyes. I'm sure it had something to do with that damned gospel!"

"You're talking about Thomas, aren't you?"

"Yes," the Prince grumbled. "That damned gospel of his! I did everything I could to discredit him. Hell, I even tricked them into attaching 'Doubting' to his name. But, I didn't get to his gospel before his followers hid it in that clay pot and buried it in Nag Hammadi.

"And, then seventy years ago, there it is, unearthed for all the world to see. My ultimate trump card exposed – Death is not inevitable! His words are burned into my memory: 'These are the secret sayings which the living Jesus spoke and which Didymos Judas Thomas wrote down: And He said, 'Whoever finds the interpretation of these sayings will not experience death.' Jesus said, 'Let him who seeks continue seeking until he finds. When he finds, he will become troubled. When he becomes troubled, he will be astonished, and he will rule over the All.'"

"The 'All' includes us, doesn't it?" the antichrist moaned, wistfully.

"Yes," his father answered, his voice tinged with anxiety. "The Truth is right in front of them and they still can't see it."

"Kudos to you, father!"

"Yes," he perked up, his mood a little less sullen at the thought. "With a little help from my friends…Cardinal Phelps, Father Simon, and those idiots of the ultra-right brigade telling everyone that Jesus didn't really mean what He said when He said nothing was impossible…"

"Just like what you told Adam and Eve in the Garden of Eden

– that God didn't really mean what He said when He warned them they would die if they ate the forbidden fruit!"

"Exactly!" Satan was feeling it now. "And let's not forget the scientists, and the teachers, and everyone else who have chosen to believe that death is inevitable, even though Jesus, the one who never would lie to them, told them that whoever discovered the real Truth would not experience Death."

The antichrist shook his devilish head. "Isn't it absurd that it's the free will that God provided to His children that has gotten them into the mess they're in? They are choosing to believe that they don't have a choice!"

The two devils shared a sinister, conspiratorial laugh before the antichrist's mood darkened, again. "What can I do to help?"

"You are my Trojan Horse," Satan replied. "People see you as a gift. They don't see you coming. That's the greatest advantage we have – no one sees us coming, so they don't know they have to fight. Always keep your enemies close to you – that way, you know what they're thinking and what they're doing. You can help best by continuing to trumpet the financial benefits of insurance policies and wills...Leave Jimmy Rivers to me," he finished, relishing the thought.

2

"Hello, Madison? This is Jimmy Rivers."

"Jimmy!" the reporter from ABC News said excitedly into her phone. "I'm so glad you called!"

The teenager was flustered. "You're welcome," was all he could come up with.

"Listen, I really want to talk to you about what happened in school today, but I've got a special report that's going to air at 7:00 tonight. You should watch it. Can I call you in the morning?"

"Sure," he replied. "I have a break tomorrow at 10:00. Would that work?"

"Perfectly. I'll call you at 10." She looked at the caller ID on her phone and repeated the number to Jimmy. "Is this a good number for you?"

"Yes, that's my cell phone."

"Ok, talk to you tomorrow. And Jimmy, thanks, again, for calling me back!"

No sooner had he hung up the phone than his father shouted up the stairs, "Does the Internet superstar need an engraved invitation to dinner?"

"Coming!" he replied, bounding down the stairs to be greeted by the sumptuous aroma of beef stroganoff, his favorite meal.

Celeste said grace, and Jimmy dug in. Between bites, he recalled the details of his civics class experience.

"And these are thoughts you've never had before?" his mother asked after he finished describing his controversial classroom testimony.

"No, not that I can remember. They just mysteriously popped

into my head."

"Speaking of mysteries, how about that video?" George reminded.

"It's so odd – maybe 'odd' is not the right word – coincidental, let's say, that Madison Munro, of all people would be calling to speak to Jimmy," Celeste offered. "George, do you remember that incredible story about that man and the minivan she was involved with back in 2003?"

"My gosh, that's right!" her husband recalled. "I forgot about that. Something about a man driving his car off a cliff to rescue a girl."

Jimmy noticed the clock on the wall and put his fork down. "Time out!" he interjected, forming the letter "T' with his hands. "I have to hear more about this, but it's almost 7:00."

"And that's important because?" his father asked.

"When I spoke with Madison, she said to watch her special tonight at 7:00. Maybe it's about what happened back then."

George hurried into the living room and turned on the television just in time.

"Is that her?" Jimmy gasped, staring at the the brown-haired, brown-eyed reporter.

"Yes," his mom confirmed

"She's kinda cute!" he admired. "For an old person, I mean."

George shook his head. Madison Munro was thirty-two years old. As an on-air personality, she took her appearance as seriously as she did her reporting. She hated the stereotype that people tended to open up more, initially, to attractive women, but she played the game. And she played it well. She kept herself fit, dressed impeccably, and while she would never would be mistaken for a model, she was the girl-next-door who immediately put everyone at ease with an infectious personality made up of equal parts effervescence, intelligence, and charm that drew people in, yet masked a steely determination to get to the bottom of a story. Yes, she was the ultimate gamer – and when she locked on to a story, it was game over.

"Good evening, this is Madison Munro, and I'm standing on the spot near the top of Berthoud Pass where, during my internship with ABC News, I witnessed the most extraordinary event in my reporting career – in my whole life, actually – and a mystery that endures to this day.

"Four young, extreme skiers – World Champion Dirk Daemon, Sarah Hughes, Jake Johnson, and Rachel Espair – were making their way through a terrible snowstorm to the X Games in Winter Park, Colorado. Rachel was in the lead car with all the gear, and the others were about a quarter of a mile behind in a second car, when an avalanche came crashing down this very mountain and swept Rachel's car off the road and over this cliff.

"Moments later, a minivan arrived on the scene, and I saw a man, probably in his forties or fifties – ancient, by a teenager's standard – jump out and engage in an animated conversation with the other young skiers but Rachel's frightened friends wanted no part of what he was saying.

"So, he ran back to his minivan, backed it up as far as he could, and yelled out the window, "Get out of the way!"

"He floored the accelerator and drove his minivan right over this same cliff where the avalanche had swept Rachel's car down the mountain!

"Unthinkable, right? We're just getting started. The conditions were so bad that search and rescue operations could not be initiated...but, as it turned out, it didn't matter. Rachel showed up on the doorstep of her parents' house about thirty minutes later with a blanket around her shoulders, an improbable story, and a huge debt of gratitude to this mysterious man in a minivan who has not been seen or heard from since."

With the hook properly set, the special report broke for commercial.

Jimmy was stupefied. "Are you kidding me?" he finally managed.

"It's such a fantastic story," his father allowed. "I can't believe it's been thirteen years and they still haven't found the guy. Or his minivan. It's like D.B. Cooper all over again."

"D.B. Cooper?" Jimmy asked.

George explained, "He hijacked a plane between Portland and Seattle back in the early Seventies, let the passengers off in Seattle, got paid a $200,000 ransom – which was a lot of money back then – then parachuted out of the plane on its way to Mexico City. There was a massive manhunt for him, but they never found him or the money. Heck, they never even identified him."

"Honey," Celeste interjected, "D.B. Cooper was a criminal who hijacked planes and extorted money. This man is an angel who miraculously saved a young girl's life. There's a big difference."

Having been a party to his own unexplained and miraculous occurrences over the past three days, Jimmy was completely invested in his parents' discussion. "Yes, but is there a difference between miracles and mysteries? Neither of them can be explained."

"That's a good observation," said George. "I would say that all miracles are mysteries, but I'm not sure all mysteries are miracles."

"Either way," Celeste agreed, "we can't take things at face value. We have to pay closer attention. Nothing is what it seems."

Jimmy's pulse quickened at his mother's mention of those five words. They were the fortune teller's. And Don Quixote's. And Doc Holliday's. He asked himself again, did his mother know? She didn't act like it, and actions speak louder than words. The sound of Madison's voice interrupted his troubled train of thought.

"Here on Berthoud Pass in Colorado's Rocky Mountains, nothing is what it seems..."

It was all too much for Jimmy. How many times was he going to be slapped in the face with those words? It couldn't have been a coincidence. The universe was trying to get through to him! But, which universe? His phone vibrated. Sasha's urgent text read, "Turn on Channel 7 now!"

"I'm watching it!" he texted back.

"...Joining me at the spot where her car was swept off the road and down this steep embankment by an avalanche thirteen years ago is Rachel Espair. Also with us is Sarah Hughes, who was traveling with Rachel in a car right behind hers."

Turning to Rachel, Madison continued, "Rachel, what can you tell us about that night, December 24th, 2003?"

"Well, the weather was terrible that night," Rachel began. She looked much younger than her thirty-two years with her mermaid-colored hair and her "shag' cut. Her hazel eyes pierced Jimmy's soul as she recalled her Christmas Eve ordeal.

"Dirk, Jake, Sarah, and I were on our way to compete in the X Games in Winter Park. The three of them were riding in Dirk's SUV, and I had all the gear in my car. We wanted to get there early to enjoy all that fresh powder and to kind of chill before the craziness of the Games.

"Anyway, it was coming down real good, and there was no visibility because of the wind, so we stopped at Jenny's Diner in Empire. That's when we first saw him."

"Him, being the man who would rescue you later that night?" Madison confirmed to eliminate any confusion.

"Yes."

"What can you tell us about this man?"

"He was just this old man who was driving a minivan we passed a few miles down the road."

"Rachel, you were 19 at the time, and to teenagers, anyone in their thirties is old. So, how old was old?"

"Probably about the same age as my Dad, which would have put him in his forties. My Dad is an accountant, and he had that same kind of look."

A shiver went down Jimmy's back. "No, no, no, no, no, no, no," he gulped. "It can't be!" His phone vibrated again.

"OMG!" Sasha texted.

"What can't be?" George asked.

Jimmy hadn't realized he had been speaking aloud.

"Sorry, I was just thinking to myself."

"What is it, sweetie?" his mother wanted to know.

"It's nothing, really." But he knew he had to come up with something quickly to pacify his parents. "I was just thinking, wouldn't it be weird if this old man turned out to be D.B. Cooper?"

It worked. "If he survived jumping out of that airplane, D.B. Cooper would be in his seventies or eighties," George explained. "It couldn't have been him."

They turned their attention back to the interview. Jimmy's stomach was doing somersaults.

So was Sasha's, five miles away. "Can you believe it?" came her next text. "The fortune teller???"

"I know, right?" he texted back.

Jimmy looked up at the television. "The guys were giving him a hard time about driving so slowly," Rachel was saying, "but the weather was so bad! Dirk was driving the way he skied – like a bat out of hell. I remember Sarah telling Dirk to ease up on the old man, that he would be old one day, too."

Sarah jumped in. "Dirk repeated that line from The Who - "Hope I die before I get old." It's so crazy. He died a few months later in a car accident in Honduras."

"That's right," Madison recalled "So tragic... But, getting back to the so-called old man, did he ever mention his name?"

The girls looked at each other and shook their heads. "It never came up," Rachel admitted. "When I think of him, though, this always stuck in my mind – he randomly told the guys that Disney really goofed with *The Lion King.* That they had a great opportunity to give Mustafa and Simba a problem that required wisdom and brawn, and that they could have worked together using youth and age to solve it. That way, younger generations would learn to appreciate their elders for what they had to offer rather than just telling them to get out of the way.

"Instead, he said Disney copped out and chose to show children the ugliest part of life – the lion king's own brother plotting and carrying out his brother's murder."

"Then he said something about Adam," Sarah recalled.

"Adam?" Madison inquired.

"Yeah, the dude from the Garden of Eden...and how he lived to be over 900 years old. As if that ever could happen!"

Madison thought back to her Christian upbringing. "Well, it

says in the Bible that God created us to live forever."

"That's what the old man said!" Sarah added. "And you believe those stories?"

"We're getting a little sidetracked here," Madison quickly got back en pointe. "Keep going, Rachel. What happened next?"

"Well, Dirk wanted to leave, and whatever Dirk wanted, Dirk got. I apologized to the old man for Dirk's and Jake's behavior, and we wished each other a Merry Christmas. The next time I saw him..."

"Wait," Madison interrupted. "Let's not get ahead of ourselves. So, you started driving again. Had the storm let up at all?

"No, If anything, it had gotten worse. I needed Dirk to slow down, so I led the way up the pass. And this," she indicated with her right hand, "is where the avalanche swept me off the road."

The reporter turned to Sarah. "What were your thoughts when you saw Rachel's car go over the edge?"

"I was so scared!" Sarah replied. "I thought she was dead. We got out of the car. My knees were shaking so bad, I could barely stand. We were all in shock. Dirk said something stupid like, "Wow, that could have been us," but no one knew what to do.

"A snow plow guy came up behind us and called the police. They were there in, like, fifteen minutes, and then people from search and rescue started showing up."

"And the old man, as you call him?" Madison asked.

"Yes, he was there first, like right away. He drove up in that minivan, jumped out and asked for a volunteer."

"For what?"

"He told us he was going to drive his minivan off the cliff and save Rachel!"

"Obviously, he didn't have any takers, but weren't you a little curious? I mean, that was a pretty bold, pretty bizarre, statement."

"Now, I am, for sure! But at the time, no. Just really upset and scared. Dirk told him he was crazy. I'll never forget what the old man said. He said, "If it's crazy to see things not as they are, but as they should be, then, yes, I'm crazy!"

"He didn't have crazy eyes, though. They were so calm...like he knew something that no one else did. To tell you the truth, when I looked into his eyes, I almost volunteered, but I couldn't get the words out of my mouth.

"He turned to Dirk, specifically, for help, but the world champion at taking risks and going to extremes wanted no part of him. He didn't see what I saw…"

"The look in his eyes," Madison guessed.

"Yes."

Jimmy's phone vibrated again. "It has to be him!" Sasha had typed.

"Or another "friend' of his," he sent back.

The sound of Sarah's voice caught his ear, again. "Then he backed up his minivan as far as he could, punched the accelerator, and drove off the cliff in the exact same spot as Rachel's car."

"What did you do?"

"We ran to the edge and tried to see if we could see his lights, but the visibility was too bad. We couldn't see a thing. It just looked like the snowstorm had opened its mouth and swallowed him and his minivan up whole...like the whale that swallowed Jonah."

Madison swiveled back to Rachel. "What do you remember when you went over the edge?"

"It was *so* surreal! I didn't have one of those "Oh, shit!" moments, didn't even scream. It was all so quiet…"

"Even though the car was rolling over and over?" Madison queried, trying to stay even-faced.

"Yeah, I just stayed focused on a positive outcome and prayed. But, I must have blacked out because the next thing I remember was two strong arms pulling me out of the car."

"The old man's?" Madison presumed.

"Yes. He carried me to his minivan which was just kind of floating in the air."

"Floating?"

"That's the only way to describe it."

"And it flew you home?" the reporter led her witness. "Was there anyone else in the minivan?"

"I really don't know anything else. It was all too much. I passed out. The next thing I knew, I was standing at my front door with a blanket around my shoulders. And my mom bursting into tears when she opened the door."

"And no sign of the old man or his minivan?"

"No sign of the old man or the minivan."

Madison faced the camera. "Stay with us," she told her viewing audience. "We'll be right back."

Jimmy stood up from the couch.

"You're leaving?" his father asked dubiously. "Aren't you the least bit curious about this man?"

"I am," Jimmy deadpanned, trying his best to fake nonchalance. "But teachers don't care about old men and minivans when it comes to getting homework turned in on time. I'm going to the library to finish up. I'll stream the rest of it later. Ciao!"

As soon as the front door shut behind him, Jimmy called Sasha, trying not to hyperventilate.

"Sasha, this is too much...I have to see you!"

"I know, me, too! But my parents," she hesitated. "It's a school night."

"Tell them we're going to the library to study. I'll be there in ten minutes."

⋆ ⋆ ⋆

Jimmy hopped out of his car the moment he saw Sasha emerge from her house. He hurried to the passenger side and opened the door for his girlfriend.

He was rewarded with that luminous smile of hers that could light up any black hole. "Such a gentleman!" she purred, sitting down and swinging her legs into the blue Camaro.

Jimmy ran back around the car and took his place behind the wheel. He was about to turn the ignition when Sasha exclaimed, "Wait! I forgot something."

He looked at his girlfriend, who leaned in to him and kissed him sweetly on the lips. "There," she grinned, "now, we can go."

She paused. "Oh, and where are we going, again? I'm guessing it's not the library, and the carnival's not in town."

"Very funny!" Jimmy replied, as he pulled away from the curb. "The next best thing. Dairy Queen. I have to talk to Don Quixote!"

"Jimmy, you really know how to show a girl a good time!" Sasha rhapsodized. "In the last 72 hours, you traveled through time, changed The Premise and brought your Mom back to life, introduced me to Don Quixote, took me on a wild goose chase to Glenwood Springs where we met Doc Holliday, you somehow moved a mountain, you're a viral sensation, and now we're going to see the Man of La Mancha, again.

"How are you going to top all that?"

He shook his head. "I'm not sure. The only thing I'm pretty sure of is that we're just getting started. Somehow, we've gotten involved in something that is so much bigger than anything we could have imagined."

Sasha laid her hand on Jimmy's knee, sending him over the moon. "Like I said, you really know how to show a girl a good time!"

The Dairy Queen was completely empty when they walked in – no customers, no one behind the counter.

"Hello?" Jimmy called out uncertainly.

"Sorry," an unfamiliar voice answered back. "Have a seat and I'll be right with you."

They started to sit at one of the tables nearest the counter when the voice said, "Take the same table you had yesterday afternoon. That one's too visible. They're looking for you."

Jimmy froze. It wasn't the voice from out of nowhere that startled him, or that the voice knew where they had sat the day before. It was the reminder that something presumably sinister was in the cards for them.

Sasha squeezed his hand. "Come on," she encouraged gently. "Let's go to the back."

Jimmy peered cautiously around the corner. Their booth was empty. They sat down next to each other and waited, his mind a thousand miles away.

Finally, he blurted out, "How did whoever it was know who we were and where we sat?"

"Maybe he was working yesterday and saw us when we came in," Sasha guessed. "Maybe he's in the back and he can see us on a security cam."

"Yeah, maybe, but he also said people were looking for us. That's really got me creeped out. Doc Holliday said the same thing!"

"Omigosh, you're right," Sasha recalled. "I almost forgot."

"I don't think Don Quixote is here," Jimmy mumbled, impatiently. "Hello?" he called out, again.

This time, a familiar voice responded. But it wasn't that of Señor Quixote.

"The fortune teller!" Sasha whispered excitedly in Jimmy's ear.

But, they still didn't see anyone.

"Where are you?" Jimmy asked uncertainly.

"You're still not paying attention. You can't see what's right in front of you."

"I'm not following you," Sasha said, seemingly talking to a ghost.

"People spend their whole lives missing the magic every moment has to offer because they are outside of the moment, thinking about everything but the moment. Their thoughts are framed in the context of what they've chosen very poorly to believe. In other words, everyone is so distracted, they can't see what's real, the Truth that's right in front of their eyes...And the Truth is that I'm sitting right across the table from you!"

The teenagers gawked at each other. They didn't see anyone sitting across from them.

"Clear your minds and focus on the present," the fortune teller's voice advised them. "Climb inside the moment!"

Jimmy and Sasha did their best to redirect their thoughts, to no avail.

"I still can't see you," Jimmy fretted.

"Focus, Jimmy. You can do it. Just like when you came into my booth at the carnival. Open your mind and clear away your doubt."

"I see you!" Sasha cried out, all of a sudden, staring at the conservatively-dressed man sitting across from them.

Jimmy was right behind her. "There you are!"

"Bravo!" the fortune teller cheered. "An encore performance!"

"Encore?" Jimmy asked quizzically. "Did you see the video from Mr. Hamilton's class?"

"No, Jimmy," Sasha joined in, staring directly at the fortune teller. "He was the one who shot the video!"

"And to you, young lady," he addressed Sasha, "welcome to life outside the prison!"

There was no stopping her now. "And that was you who drove the minivan over the edge of the road on Berthoud Pass and saved that girl's life thirteen years ago, wasn't it!"

"It was," the fortune teller replied calmly.

"But they said you were an old man," Jimmy protested.

"Teenagers," the fortune teller smiled. "Everyone is old to you!"

Jimmy felt his cheeks beginning to flush. "I never thought you were old," he stammered. "Well, maybe I did – but I did say on the 'youngish' side."

"Heavy on the "ish," though, right?" the fortune teller winked.

"The girl said your car was floating," Sasha continued.

A light went on in Jimmy's head. "You're changing the rules just like Captain Kirk! And Spock! The whole Tombstone thing...you're changing the physical laws."

"Your journey has been fruitful," the fortune teller smiled. "But, not so much changing as choosing to disregard. These so-called laws you're talking about...whose laws are they? Are they God's laws?"

"Well," Jimmy considered, "they're natural laws, scientific laws, like the law of gravity in this case."

"But, whose science is it? Did God say, "What goes up must come down?""

"No, man did."

"So what you're saying is that these are man's laws."

"When you put it that way, I guess they are."

"I *am* putting it that way," the fortune teller said firmly. "And, I am telling you that all of this, this reality, as you call it," he continued, spreading his arms out wide, "is an illusion. A grand illusion. The only legitimacy it has is your belief in it.

"You have chosen to believe that you have no choice, thereby imprisoning yourselves in this mirage created by Satan to keep you from the freedom that was intended for you. But, he has no authority over you. He is not your jailer. You are! And since you are your own jailers, you have the key to unlock your prisons and to reclaim Freedom. By your choices, though, you have used that key to lock yourselves up instead of to free yourselves."

The fortune teller's words hit like a phantom punch. Jimmy and Sasha were floored, unable to wrap their minds around what the fortune teller was telling them.

Noting the confusion on their faces, the fortune teller insisted, "Stay with me. This is "end-game' stuff. Jimmy, when you traveled through Time, that was not a dream or a one-time thing. You were so determined to change The Premise and bring your mom back to life that you were able to suspend your belief in this "reality," and you entered a universe parallel to this one where Time does not exist.

"Can either of you think of such a universe where Time doesn't exist?"

"Heaven," Sasha volunteered.

"Yes," the fortune teller answered, "but here on earth."

Jimmy's eyes widened in astonishment. "Oh my God," he marveled, "you're talking about Eden, aren't you!"

"Bingo!" exulted the fortune teller. "God created the Garden of Eden right here on earth...what do you think happened to it after Adam and Eve chose so poorly? Do you think it just disappeared?

"Well, Eden didn't go away – Adam and Eve did, if you'll recall. They stepped into a parallel universe, east of Eden – a parallel universe based on the deceit created by the Father of Lies, Lucifer, who you also know as Satan, or the Devil, or the Prince of Darkness.

"You see, when God, who has ultimate authority over all things, and through Whom all authority exists, stripped Lucifer of any access to His authority and banished him to the underworld, the former angel of light could not lift a finger against God's children. The only way he had to get back at God was to lie and deceive, and trick His children into using their free will to choose to accept this grand illusion, lock themselves into it, and throw away the key. Lucifer has no authority, no power over you. Truly, the only 'power' he has over you is your belief in it – your very *poor choice* to believe in it, I might add.

"Remember when I put my hand through that block of buloke, the hardest, densest wood in the world? Who said it was the hardest, densest wood in the world? Did God say it? No! It's a thing of Man, and things of God always trump the things of Man. God's law, if you need to put it in those terms, is that everything is possible when you are connected to Him through belief and you do not doubt."

The teenagers sat dumbfounded, trying desperately to process the fortune teller's words.

"Look," the fortune teller persisted, grabbing the candle on the table. "In this universe, we have chosen to believe Lucifer's lie that we have no choice, right?"

He then promptly stuck his finger in the flame...and left it there. For three whole minutes, as Jimmy and Sasha watched in amazement. When he removed his finger from the flame, it was completely unscathed. Not a hair was singed, not a molecule tainted. Incredibly, it was the same color of pink fleshiness as before he put it in the fire.

"In Eden, God's children have authority over all things, including fire," the fortune teller explained.

"But, we're in this universe," Sasha protested meekly.

"Are you?" the fortune teller asked with a gleam in his eye. "Or have you stepped back into Eden? Have you considered that the universes might overlap?"

"The floating car!" Jimmy erupted. "Gravity is a thing of Man! That's how Peter was able to walk on water. When he stepped out of the boat, he stepped out of this universe and into Eden's overlapping universe where all things are possible because he didn't doubt Jesus!"

Sasha gasped. "Peter! It can't be a coincidence! Another Peter's creator – Peter Pan's, I mean – said, 'The moment you doubt whether you can fly, you cease forever to be able to do it.'"

"Yes, but not forever," the gratified fortune teller corrected. "Mr. Barrie was speaking to the difficulty of changing beliefs once we've chosen to accept them. But difficulty does not imply impossibility. There always is choice, and if we choose to change our beliefs, we can change our world by stepping out of this universe and stepping back into the universe that was created for us originally, where everything is possible.

"Make no mistake. Eden *did not* disappear. When they chose not to believe God and instead to sit at the table of deceit Lucifer prepared for them, Adam and Eve stepped out of Paradise and into the parallel universe east of Eden where your authority is limited and all things are finite.

"Sadly, we still are choosing to accept Lucifer's invitation to sit at his table and digest his lies. The time has come to step away from that, from the illusion that God cannot be trusted and from the illusion that we don't have a choice. When we finally choose to step away from the table, we will step out of this false reality and back into Paradise."

The fortune teller paused for a moment to allow his words to sink in. Then, he continued, "I know this is a lot to wrap your minds around, but you have to stay with me. Let's get back to gravity. Again, when the Son of God told Peter he could walk on water, and Peter did not doubt, he stepped out of this illusory universe and back into Eden's parallel universe where everything is possible.

"But, he blinked when that gust of wind came up and had a moment's doubt. That was a choice he made, a choice to doubt Jesus, and, in choosing to doubt Jesus, he was thrust back into the universe where things are finite and not possible; and he fell into the sea.

"What did Jesus say to him when He rescued him? 'Peter, why did you doubt me.'"

The fortune teller addressed Jimmy directly. "You asked a question a long time ago, when you were very, very young, that challenged the core of this illusion and started you on this journey. That is why it is said that the only way to enter the kingdom of heaven is as a child. You are on the cusp of discovery. It is The Question that matters. You must not blink!"

Jimmy and Sasha were reflecting on what the fortune teller was telling them when a voice from behind startled them.

"Hey kids, we're getting ready to close. I'm gonna have to ask you to finish up."

They both looked over their shoulders. It was the Dairy Queen manager who was speaking to them.

They turned back to the fortune teller. He was gone. Vanished into thin air. Or back into a parallel or overlapping universe? Sitting on the table in front of them were the remnants of an Orange Julius and a cookies and cream blizzard.

Jimmy and Sasha stared at each other. When had they ordered those drinks?

⋆ ⋆ ⋆

Less than a mile away, in the Polo Club, just off East Exposition Avenue, the antichrist shouted into the phone, "But, what about the intruder? He's getting closer."

"Don't you worry about Jimmy Rivers," his father snapped. "I said I'd take care of him. He might have found the way out, but he has an Achilles Heel, and it's called Sasha Fenimore. He *will* blink, my son, and he *will* fall!"

3

Jimmy's phone vibrated next to his bed. Instinctively, he looked at the clock on his dresser, even though he just had checked it five minutes ago: 1.07.

It was a snapchat from a pouty-faced Sasha, lying awake in her bed, wearing a black Victoria's Secret tank top that said "Angel' across the chest. Then, came the text, "I can't sleep!"

"My God, you're beautiful! I wish I was in a bed with you right now."

He stared at the message he just had typed. It was as if his fingers had a mind of their own. He did agree, though. But, he couldn't send it. She might get the wrong idea. Or be offended. Or think he was a perv. It was too soon. Or was it? He had only known they were boyfriend and girlfriend for a few days, but, clearly, it had been much longer than that. How far had they gone? he wondered.

"Are you awake?" came Sasha's next text.

Oops. The distraction of her photo and the ensuing debate with his fingers over the appropriate response had delayed the acknowledgement of her text. He recovered from his consternation, and decided to push the button to erase what he had typed – but his fingers had the last laugh. Instead of the "erase" button, his index finger "accidentally" pushed the "send" button!

"Oh no!" he panicked. His heart was racing as he furiously typed out an apology, ruing the fact that no one had invented a way to retrieve inadvertent texts.

His fingers still weren't cooperating, however, and auto-correct was slowing him down. He couldn't get his apology out fast enough!

His phone vibrated, again. Sasha had beaten him to the punch:

"Awww, thanks! Play your cards right and you might get lucky' – and she finished it off with a winking, smiley-face emoji.

That threw him for a loop – and somewhat answered his question about how familiar they had been before he had traveled through time and reset his reality. This time, his fingers, having been vindicated, chose to cooperate and he got the "erase' button right. Instead of apologizing, he flirted, "You better be careful, I play a pretty mean game of 'Go Fish!'"

"Bring it on, Rivers! Luck is a lady," she flirted right back.

Jimmy didn't know where she was going with that. He typed in a question mark.

"Silly boy! Guys always wonder if they're going to get lucky with a girl, but the girl already knows." And another smiley face.

"So, what do you know?" His fingers were getting ahead of himself, again.

Satisfied that she had her boyfriend hooked – and that she had set the hook firmly with a proper tug – Sasha worked her feminine mystique by deftly changing tack.

"I know that we have to figure out what question you asked so long ago that started you out on this journey. Well, us, really."

Jimmy shook his head and chuckled. He knew she had him outnumbered. Hopelessly outnumbered! How do girls get so good at "winning" so quickly? They must be born with it, he sighed.

"Wow!" was all that he could come up with.

"Seriously," came her next text. "I've been thinking about this since you dropped me off. Everyone keeps telling you that everything that's happening is because of a question you asked when you were very young. If you can remember what the question was, maybe we can figure this out."

Jimmy was suddenly overcome with emotion. Tears welled up in his eyes. The events of the past three days had been incredible. From the fortune teller to Don Quixote, to traveling through time to changing The Premise and bringing his Mom back to life, to Doc Holliday and moving mountains, to the viral video and parallel universes, all wrapped up in being with the most extraordinary girl he ever could have imagined, was almost too much. And, it would have been if no one had believed him.

"Sasha, thank you for believing me! No one else would. If you didn't, I'm not sure I would myself. It's almost as fantastic as Alice following the white rabbit through the looking glass or Dorothy going to Oz. Am I dreaming?"

His phone rang. "Hi…Listen to me, Jimmy Rivers!" she cut in before he could get another word out. "Don't you go getting second thoughts on me now that you've brought me this far! You're the one who told everyone in class about Captain Kirk changing the rules. Whose rules were they? Man's rules, not God's rules! Human beings make mistakes, bad choices. God doesn't. So, really, it's more likely than not that what we've blindly chosen to accept as the Truth on earth is not the real Truth at all, and everyone else is crazy, living in a dream world – nightmare, actually – not you!

"You've opened my eyes and my mind and shown me that nothing is what it seems. Don't even think about trying to close them, now. I'm not going back and neither are you. *We* took the red pill. We're going to follow this together and see where it takes us!"

Jimmy winced. He knew she was right, yet he had to unload. "But, parallel universes and the Garden of Eden where everything is possible? That's so far beyond viral! It's not funny anymore, or provocative. That's hallucination territory. Everyone would think I'm on drugs, or worse. They'd send people in white uniforms to wrap me up in a straight-jacket and take me to rehab or to the psych ward. And the church would accuse me of heresy."

"Stop right there!" Sasha demanded. "Are you not hearing my words? People would have thought Kirk was on drugs, too, if he had told them about choosing to change the rules before he did it. Everyone's minds are so closed, they can't see what you're seeing. What we're seeing. You have to show them before it's too late!

"Oh, and speaking of choice, do you know where the word "heresy' comes from? I learned this in religion class – it comes from the Greek word for "to choose." Isn't that ironic? The church uses a word to describe the ultimate sin that has its root in the free will that

God provided for us!"

"Who are you?" Jimmy marveled.

"I'm just a girl who believes you. Probably the only one," she laughed. "But, here's the thing, Jimmy. You opened my mind. When you told me about the Sadie Hawkins Dance, and the carnival, and the fortune teller, and changing The Premise with Don Quixote to bring your mother back to life, I became a heretic. I had to choose to open my mind to consider the possibility that what you were telling me was the truth, instead of simply rejecting it as an unbelievably ridiculous excuse you came up with to be with Lisa when you disappeared at the dance. That's just it – if it hadn't been so unbelievable, I probably wouldn't have given you the time of day.

"So, I unlocked my mind a bit – to consider that you might be telling the truth, or maybe just out of curiosity – and when you told me about the fortune teller and the purple velour curtain, that's when Truth kicked the door wide open and I came face to face with what I had been keeping locked out. To be perfectly honest, at first, I was shocked. But that turned to amazement very quickly because what came pouring in seemed so right. I just knew that you had to be connected. To the real Truth, maybe. Who knows?

"But, I do know that George Bernard Shaw said, "All great truths start out as blasphemies' – and that you might be chasing down the greatest blasphemy, the greatest Truth of all."

"Oh my God, that's it!" Jimmy practically shouted into the phone.

Sasha was startled by his sudden outburst. "What's "it"?"

"Blasphemy! I think I just figured out what "The Question' was!"

Sasha's eyes widened, waiting for the "Great Reveal." But, instead, she got only silence.

Finally, she could stand the suspense no longer. "Sweetie, are you going to share?"

"Sorry," Jimmy replied, his mind still in a fog. "I was just trying to remember the details. It happened when I was five or six years old, and we were learning about Noah and the ark in Sunday School. I think we were doing some kind of art project, coloring in the animals or something, and one of the kids asked why God killed all the rest of the people and animals.

"The teacher answered something like, "Because those were bad people who sinned against God."

"And then I raised my hand and asked, 'Do you mean God is going to kill us if we make a mistake? That doesn't make sense. I thought God loved everyone. Why didn't He just send Jesus to help everyone like He did at Easter?'"

"Jimmy!" Sasha exclaimed. "That's amazing! You came up with that when you were five or six years old? You didn't hear that from your parents?"

"No, it just popped into my head like the "God is pro-choice" thing did at school. Anyway, the teacher didn't have an answer, so she told me she'd ask the priest and get back to me the next Sunday. I remember the priest coming over to our house that night and having a long conversation with my parents. He asked them the same thing. He didn't believe that I thought of that myself and wanted to make sure my parents weren't questioning the teaching of the Church and passing along their uncertainty to me.

"My Dad didn't appreciate the insinuation that he was lying, and he got a little upset. He assured the priest that they never had had any such conversation about Noah with me, that the question was totally my own, and that it was a legitimate question.

"Then he really got going. He said that as long as they were on the subject of church teaching, he wasn't comfortable with the practice of the clergy, supposedly men of God, denying Communion to those who were not part of the Roman Catholic club, as he called it. Or the practice of withholding Communion from those who didn't vote the way the Church thought they should vote."

Jimmy gasped.

"What is it?"

"I just remembered who the priest was. It was Cardinal Phelps from New York! He was Father Sam back then'

"What a small world!" Sasha exclaimed. "You know Cardinal Phelps is very involved in my Dad's political campaign, right?"

"Yeah. Well, I don't know what he's telling your Dad, but he told my Dad that he didn't understand the ways of the Church, and he recommended several writings from what he called 'the church fathers' for my Dad to read and enlighten himself.

"That was the wrong thing to say to my Dad," Jimmy chuckled. He said, 'Enlighten me? You're the one with your head in the sand. Are you telling me there's been no inspired thought in over two thousand years? The church fathers were human beings and, as all human beings, they were just as fallible as every other human being. What if they had a personal agenda like Caiaphas did? A personal agenda that was so far apart from God's will, yet it would have been preserved and handed down through the ages by the blind acceptance of tradition.'

"Then, my Mom joined in. She reminded Father Sam that when Jesus offered His body and blood at the Last Supper, it was for the salvation of all mankind, and that Jesus always was reaching out to the outcasts in society. She said Jesus was all about inclusion, while it seemed that the Church was all about exclusion.

"That's when we stopped going to church. Mom and Dad think our church leaders are leading us further away from God instead of closer to Him."

Sasha chewed on Jimmy's words. "I never thought about it like that, but I can see where your parents are coming from. Jesus didn't hang out with the churchgoers. It seems like He always was with those who needed to hear His message the most – the tax collectors, the lepers, the prostitutes, the criminals… all the outcasts outside of the church.

"But let's get back to 'The Question.' You asked it and you were chosen. Or, maybe not so much chosen as you proved yourself. No, not proved yourself. That doesn't sound right, either. Maybe it's because you're on the right path. You're just like Captain Kirk. You chose not to blindly accept things the way they were – you chose to focus on the way things should be."

Sasha heard it just as soon as the words left her mouth.

"The fortune teller!" they enunciated at the same time, chills running down both their spines.

"Jimmy, this is incredible! You know how Jesus said that in order to enter the kingdom of heaven, you have to enter as a child? That's because children's minds are completely open to receive the Truth.

"But, what's one of the first things parents teach their kids? That there's no such thing as Santa Claus, that it's impossible for anyone to do what Santa Claus does. And that puts them on the side of the fence away from God! Let me guess, you honestly believe in Santa Claus, am I right?"

"I always have," Jimmy admitted. "Or, let's just say that I've always left my mind open to the possibility of Santa Claus. I've never believed that anything was impossible. I've always thought that whatever was said to be impossible just hadn't been done, yet...or discovered. Like parallel universes. I'll bet that's where Santa Claus is!"

"So, that puts you on God's side of the fence, in His universe! You're probably the only one, and that was revealed when you asked that question about Noah."

"I see where you're going. We all have free will, but God knows the choices we're going to make. I don't think I'm the chosen one, or anything like that. I'm just the one who chose differently."

"Like Robert Frost said, the path less traveled has made all the difference! God knew you would choose not to accept your Mom's death."

Sasha hesitated. "Oh no, Jimmy, I just had a terrible thought..."

"Wait, I think I know what it is," Jimmy interrupted. "No, I don't think God killed my Mom because He knew the choices I would make. I don't know why everyone thinks God is a killer. Everyone's afraid God will strike them down and kill them if they step out of line. Nothing could be further from the Truth. I mean one of the Ten Commandments He gave to Moses is 'Thou shalt not kill.' He's not going to do what He tells us not to do! He created us in His image. If He tells us not to kill, then that's because He doesn't kill.

"The Lord's Prayer says, 'Thy will be done on earth as it is in heaven...' His will is very clear. Besides the Commandment, Jesus said if someone hits you on the cheek, you should give him the other cheek to hit. There is no "an eye for an eye, a tooth for a tooth' crap!

"And God revealed Himself to Moses," Jimmy continued, as if, yes, he was in another universe. "Why Moses? Because He knew the choices Moses would make and because He knew the Israelites would be open to receive Him through Moses. Why? Because through Moses, He would offer them freedom from hundreds of years of slavery, oppression, and torture. They were ignorant and uneducated, but they understood what freedom meant – the opposite of the only thing they knew – and, really, they had nothing to lose. So, they chose to open themselves up to the hope that Moses offered through God.

"Then they were freed. With freedom comes responsibility, but Moses knew they still were ignorant and uneducated. All they understood was fear. That's all they had known for generations. There was no way for them to wrap their minds around God's unconditional love and what it meant. So, in order to get them to toe God's line, Moses wrote the first five books of the Old Testament from a glass half-empty perspective based on fear, rather from a glass half-full perspective, based on love. The Israelites were to fear God as they had feared Pharaoh and the Egyptians because that's what they knew. They had no concept of God's all-encompassing and unconditional Love. So, Moses used fear to convince them to adhere to God's Word.

"That's how the story of the Great Flood came to be told. If you screwed up, God would wipe you out. I'm not saying there wasn't a Great Flood - I'm just saying that God knew that Noah was the only one who would listen to Him. And the choice of who got saved was man's, not God's. Only Noah was dialed in to God and heard His message. Just like it was in the Garden of Eden. God didn't kill Adam and Eve. They brought death upon themselves by the poor choices they made. God simply doesn't interfere with free will."

Sasha was stunned. Speechless. Blown away.

"That's it!" Jimmy realized at that moment. Jimmy was on the other side of the wall and the floodgates were wide open.

"God didn't choose me. I did! By the choices I made. I just refused to accept that my Mom's death was the way life was supposed to be. When someone is pronounced "dead," our minds shut down in acceptance. But, in bringing Lazarus back to life, and in His own resurrection, Jesus showed us that Death was not absolute. And I refused to accept the absolute, according to Man."

"And your Mom told you that it wasn't the end, too," Sasha added. "That was a huge hint. Do you think she knows?"

"I'll admit I have thought about it…I can't say for sure. But, I do think that's why God doesn't intervene when bad things happen to good people! You know that's one of the arguments that nonbelievers make: if there is a God, why does He let bad things happen to good people?"

Jimmy answered his own question. "Two reasons. First, He doesn't want to interfere with our free will, and turn us all into puppets. Second, because how else would we learn? We learn from our mistakes, but if we don't think we're making a mistake, we don't learn.

"Omigosh!" Jimmy shuddered at the sudden realization. "Death is a mistake! It wasn't meant to be. It came from a mistake Adam and Eve made, but here's the thing. They didn't choose for us! That would negate the free will that God gives to everyone, and choosing to think that we don't have a choice puts us on the side of the wall away from God, and that's where Death is. It's a huge mistake to choose the wrong side of the wall. That puts us in the wrong universe. Everything over there is a terrible mistake, including Death.

"Someone has to stand up and say this is wrong, that we're going the wrong way! Jesus already tried to tell us that, but no one believed Him. He told us we were created in God's image. And what is that image? To live forever as masters of our universe. And that's what Thomas said Jesus told him, too – that whoever finds the Truth never would taste Death. Jesus said nothing is impossible for us if we have faith. He also told us that we have been given the authority to trample on serpents and scorpions and over all the power of the enemy so nothing by any means would harm us.

"Was He lying to us? No! He was challenging us to recognize our mistakes, to learn from them, to choose to turn around and to seek the Truth, to choose to seek to rediscover our divine inheritance and find our way out of the Darkness by rediscovering our partnership with God. He has granted us full access to His authority over all things – our part of the deal is to not doubt, to have faith and to believe Him. Not just believe in Him, but also *believe* Him!

"God didn't kill my mom. The gunman did. But I refused to accept that her death was part of God's master plan, the way things were supposed to be. After all, He created Adam and Eve to live forever as masters of their universe in Eden, and He still is creating us in His image to live forever. Death is definitely a mistake, but we are choosing not to see it that way, choosing blindly to accept it, choosing the wrong universe where Death does exist. Since we don't see it that way, though, we aren't choosing to change our minds. Could I be the only one? I don't know, but that's when we met the fortune teller and this incredible journey began."

Neither of them spoke for the next few minutes, allowing what Jimmy had said to sink in.

Then, Sasha said quietly, "Jimmy, I don't know what to say. If they didn't believe Jesus, why would they believe you? Where are these thoughts coming from?"

"I honestly don't know," he whispered, completely spent. "It's like a revelation or something. Since I never shut myself off to the possibility of Santa Claus, maybe subconsciously I left the door open to all possibilities, and God was teaching me, getting me ready, even though I wasn't aware of it. Maybe, I was open to the lessons and they became part of my DNA, and then, when everything was perfectly organized, assimilated, and processed in my subconscious, to the point that I would not doubt, fear, or disbelieve when I became consciously aware of it, and that's when 'the dream' happened. And the journey began."

"Jimmy, I'll admit, I'm a little scared. Where do you think it's taking us?"

"I have no idea, Sasha. But, right now, I'm exhausted, and I've got that interview tomorrow."

The abrupt change of subject caught Sasha by surprise. "What interview?"

Jimmy perked up. "Shoot, in all the excitement, I forgot to tell you. Madison Munro wants to talk to me about the video."

"Madison Munro called you?"

"Hey, don't act all surprised. I got a lot of calls about that video."

"Sorry, I didn't mean it that way," she apologized. "I just meant it's so crazy that your diatribe made the national news!"

Jimmy laughed. "Wow, diatribe. There's a word!"

"Come on, Jimmy," Sasha complained.

"I'm just pulling your chain. I really can't believe it, either. I do want to talk to her about the alleged old man, though. If it was the fortune teller, the age thing doesn't add up. He should be close to sixty by now, but you've seen him – he doesn't look a day over thirty-five."

"Exactly! You know, I've met Madison before, when she interviewed my Dad. She's a sweet lady, but she's like a pit bull on crack when she latches on to a story. She's definitely onto something, Jimmy, and I'm guessing she knows it has something to do with the fortune teller, even though she probably doesn't know what, or who, it might be right now. You can trust her."

"Thanks, Sasha!"

"Time for bed?" she asked, gently.

"Time for bed," he agreed. Then, he smiled. "I still wish I was in bed with you."

"Well, I have to admit you're playing "Go Fish" very well.... so far! But, I don't want you to get overconfident or anything," she cooed.

"Never!" Jimmy protested. "Goodnight, Sasha. I love you."

"I love you, too, Jimmy. Sweet dreams. See you in a few hours."

Part Five

I

Jimmy came down the stairs to breakfast about twenty minutes earlier than usual and surprised Celeste in the kitchen. "Good morning, Mom!"

She looked up at the clock, then at her son, dressed and ready for school. "Good morning! You're up early."

"Yeah, it's a big day and I wanted to get an early start. I've got that phone interview with Madison this morning at 10:00, and I still have a little homework to get done before then," he explained, sitting down at the table. "I still can't believe all the uproar that video caused."

"Well, the 'pro-life-pro-choice' issue is a pretty sensitive topic, especially with the election coming up," his mother replied, pouring him a glass of orange juice. "And I know you didn't mean it, but you put Senator Fenimore and the pro-lifers in a kind of tricky spot. A reporter asked Cardinal Phelps to comment, and you should have heard him trying to dissect your comments. He said they were well-meaning, but very naïve.

"Then, he went totally off-topic, trying to distract everyone with his Biblical scholarship, as if to ridicule any lesser mortal's temerity to question his interpretation of Scripture, and defaulted back to his smarmy rebuttal that you needed to read the church fathers. Now, does any of that sound familiar?"

"About that," Jimmy voiced, getting to the real reason for his early rise. "Do you and Dad ever regret not going to church anymore?"

"OK, where did that come from?"

"It just seems that I was part of that problem, too," Jimmy fretted.

"You're talking about the question you asked in Sunday School about Noah..."

"Yes."

Celeste picked her words carefully. "You were not the problem, Jimmy. You were only five years old, for heaven's sake. But, when Father Sam – now, Cardinal Phelps – came into our house and basically accused your father and me of lying, that was a problem. A huge problem.

"And your father turned the tables on him, challenging him on the exclusivity of the Church in denying Communion to those who weren't part of the Roman Catholic club, as he called it, even if they believed in Jesus and the Holy Trinity. He asked Father Sam how, in good conscience, he could defend a 'rule' that clearly was not what Jesus would have done. Or did, for that matter. Jesus was all about inclusion! In sacrificing His body and blood, He didn't exclude anyone from His salvation.

"Father Sam said it was blasphemous to question the traditions of the Church and told us in no uncertain terms that we needed to strengthen our faith by refamiliarizing ourselves with the teachings of the church fathers."

"All great truths start out as blasphemies," Jimmy repeated what Sasha had told him.

His Mom smiled. "You know how, looking back, you always can think of the perfect thing you wish you would have said? That would have been it. But, in the heat of the moment, your heart races ahead and your brain can't keep up.

"I said something about the church fathers being human and just as fallible as the rest of us. What if they made a mistake, or had an agenda like the religious leaders who condemned Jesus, the Son of God? If no one questioned the errant tradition, then that mistake would be passed on to all future generations, and we never would find our way back to God.

"Your father and I feel that our church leaders are leading us the wrong way, and that if we just turn a blind eye to it and accept it, then we have become part of the problem, instead of part of the solution. So, when we chose to stop going to church, it wasn't the end…"

Jimmy's heart skipped a beat. She said it, again – "this is not the end' – and, again, he was tormented by the possibility that his Mom knew she had been killed and that he had brought her back to life. Maybe once could be written off to coincidence, but twice? Especially since she practically had reiterated his conversation with Sasha from just a few hours ago.

Celeste hadn't stopped talking and he had temporarily zoned out. When Jimmy realized this, he asked, "Wait, what did you say?"

"When?"

"Just now. About this not being the end."

"I was saying that just because we stopped going to church, it was not the end of our relationship with God. In fact, it was the beginning, our first step in our journey back Home, like the prodigal son.

"Jimmy, we all are prodigal children, squandering our inheritance – our divine inheritance – by choosing foolishly to follow the wrong leader. But the instant we choose to repent, to turn back to God, and to ask for forgiveness, He's not holding our feet to the fire for the poor choices we made that led us away from Him and waiting for us to crawl all the way back to Him. No, He's rushing to where we are, to greet us and to welcome us back on the spot, without condemnation or condition – and to celebrate our return with a great feast.

"That's why your father and I believe that taking a bite of the forbidden fruit was not Adam's and Eve's poorest choice. Their worst choice was to choose not to turn back to God and ask for forgiveness after they had disobeyed. Because, as Jesus told us, they would have been forgiven immediately, and they would have re-inherited Paradise."

Celeste paused to let her words sink in. She could see her son was deep in thought, trying to work through them.

"I know it's a lot to think about, but while you're at it, here's something else. God sent His Son to save us after we had become hopelessly lost. Well, not hopelessly, obviously, but let's just say we couldn't find our way back to Him and we kept wandering further and further away.

"Think about Jesus' time on earth. He wasn't sent here just to save us, He also came to set the record straight and to shine His light on the way back Home, on the path back to God. Because we had gotten the message, the Word, wrong, and we were going the wrong way.

"But, guess what...in the Revelation, John tells us that Jesus is going to come again. Now, why do you suppose that is?"

Celeste answered her own question. "Because we still haven't gotten the message right! And we're still headed in the wrong direction! And, who's leading us the wrong way? Our religious leaders! That's why He has to come again.

"So, our blind allegiance is just as sinful because we, too, are missing the mark. You forced your father and me to open our eyes and to make a choice when you asked that question about Noah. We knew we made the right choice because, in making it, we both felt the celebration of God welcoming His prodigal children back to His kingdom."

She added, "Jimmy, our minds were closed. Our lamps were out of oil, and we couldn't see the bridegroom. But, you opened our minds and refilled our lamps, and we could see Jesus among us, and we have followed Him to where we are now.

"This probably was a lot more than you bargained for, but the short answer to your question is, 'No, we do not regret for a second not going to church, as it is, anymore.'"

Jimmy could not hold back any longer. "Mom," he blurted out, "do you know the fortune teller?"

Celeste's heart skipped a beat, and she quickly changed the subject.

"What I know is that you will be late for school if you don't hurry up and get going!"

"But, Mom!"

"Don't 'but Mom' me," she admonished, and she shooed him out the door with a kiss on the cheek and a toasted whole-wheat bagel with cream cheese wrapped in a napkin in his hand.

★ ★ ★

"Seven hundred million dollars!" Henry Joak exclaimed gleefully.

"And that's with two months to go," grinned Dagmar Dawson, Director of Corporate Communications for Joak Industries.

Jasper Joak did not share their joy. He had called the early morning meeting when he heard the number of states pushing for the legalization of marijuana had reached double digits.

"And what about the taxes?" he groused.

"Well, sir," Dagmar fidgeted, "it looks like they'll come in at around $70 million for the year."

Jasper pounded his fist on the conference table. "Goddamn it!" he thundered. "How is it that we can spend all the money we have on rolling over our political opposition with such success, but we can't figure out a way to avoid these taxes? I think it was better before this march to legalization! I still don't understand why we have to support it!"

"There are too many fronts, sir. We would lose, in more ways than one. The number of political races is finite, identifiable, manageable. The legalization of pot campaign is more of a grass-roots movement, so to speak, kind of like standing in front of the stampede to abolish Prohibition."

"Right. And look what happened to Al Capone," Jasper countered. He had it all until the IRS got involved. The goddamn IRS... they have to have their fingers in everyone's pie!"

"Come on, Jasper," his younger brother intervened. "We have to roll with times. We're still making a helluva lot of money."

Jasper was inconsolable when it came to losing money. "We have the money that says we don't have to roll with anything! I hate paying taxes! That's our seventy million dollars and the government is stealing it from us. We never had to pay it before!"

Henry changed course. "Look at our friends on Wall Street. They're having to pay billions of dollars in fines for cheating Main Street during the Great Recession, but if you make $200 billion by cheating and only have to pay a fine of $15 billion, then that's still an extremely profitable enterprise. Plus, we get the politicians off our backs."

"It's a great business model," Dagmar chimed in. "Profits from bending the rules – alright, let's call it what is: profits from breaking the rules are extraordinary, and our Wall Street brethren view the fines they have to pay *if* they get caught simply as a cost of doing business. Maybe that's the way you should look at the decriminalization issue."

"And," Henry added, "it will be good to get out of the shadows. It was a huge risk we took when we got into bed with the drug lords – our farms and their distribution network – and the money was worth the risk. The model still works. But, as you know, there's been someone snooping around our operation in Westcliffe."

"I've already talked to The Cobra about that. The problem has been eliminated with extreme prejudice. I'll tell you what, though, he's not happy about our legalization platform, and when he's not happy, things start to happen. Bad things."

* * *

The moment the 10:00 buzzer sounded over the intercom, Jimmy bolted out of Mrs. Keeler's class. He passed Sasha in the hallway, gave her a quick kiss, and called out over his shoulder, "See you at lunch!"

"Good luck!"

He made his way to the baseball field just in time. At 10:05, his phone rang and "Madison Munro' popped up on the caller ID.

"Hello, this is Jimmy," he answered his phone.

"Hi Jimmy, it's Madison. Is this a good time?"

"It is."

He was nervous, not knowing what to expect – almost like asking a girl out on a date for the first time. But Madison knew her way around nervous suitors and uncomfortable witnesses, and she had done her homework. She asked him about last weekend's Sadie Hawkins dance, which only increased his level of anxiety, and when he answered with a perfunctory, "It was fine," she talked at length about what a nightmare hers had been. Her plan worked. By the time she had finished, Jimmy was completely at ease, and that's when she went to work.

"So, do you have any idea how many 'hits' you've had in the past forty-eight hours?" she asked.

"Not really," Jimmy replied sheepishly. "I haven't been following it. My friends keep talking about it, though."

"Try twenty-three million, and still counting!"

Jimmy truly was shocked. "That's amazing! I can't believe it."

"Well, believe it, Jimmy. It's a sensitive subject, and you definitely hit a nerve. Apart from the obvious political significance, there are a lot of disenfranchised, or disaffected, churchgoers out there and I think your comments really resonated with them."

"I don't know what to say."

Madison laughed. "Well, you sure knew what to say, yesterday. Where did that come from?"

"Honestly, I don't know. I mean, I never raise my hand in class, but there I was, saying these things that, looking back, seem so well thought out, but were totally spur-of-the-moment."

"Kind of like speaking in tongues, it sounds like. Do you think it was the Holy Spirit talking through you?"

Jimmy hesitated. "I don't know about that."

The determined reporter wouldn't back off. "I'm guessing you have a pretty open mind."

Wow, she's as good as advertised, Jimmy thought to himself. "I've been told that," he replied.

Madison knew she was on to something, but she could hear herself leading the witness, so she took her foot off the gas pedal.

"Listen, I know you're in school right now, and don't have too much time. I'm hoping we can set up a time to meet and do a formal interview on camera."

"Sure, I guess." He hesitated. "When were you thinking?"

"Will you have time tonight? I could be at your house at 6:30."

"Tonight!" Jimmy gulped. That caught him off-guard. This was going too fast – way too fast – and he was starting to have second thoughts about all the publicity.

Sensing his reluctance, Madison put on the full-court press. "Look, Jimmy, I've been around stories for a long time, and I've developed a kind of sixth sense about them. I don't know what it is, but all six of them are screaming that there's something big here, and they've never let me down before. I have a feeling that this is your moment, and we – you – have to seize it!"

Jimmy was astonished. Of course, she was right, but she couldn't have known just how right she really was. Truth be told, he didn't know, either. His hand started to shake from all the adrenaline coursing through his veins. Also, he was desperate to ask about the fortune teller...

"Jimmy, are you still there? Stay with me...did you see my special on the old man and the minivan last night?"

It was like she was inside his head. He instantly gobbled her bait – hook, line, and sinker. There was no holding back. "Yes, I did! I'm really curious about that old man. And his age."

Bingo! He just validated her instinct. She had gotten the same feeling when she first saw Jimmy's video as she had when she interviewed Rachel Espair about the man who rescued her – and she wondered if, somehow, the stories might be connected. "Old man" had been Rachel's description, and that of the other kids, but age is so relative, especially to teenagers and twentysomethings. Everyone is old to them.

And, now, Jimmy asks a very personal question, not about any of the fantastic things that happened that night on Berthoud Pass, but about the man's age – as if he had an idea as to who he might be! So, she gave her hook another gentle tug.

"Jimmy, I'd much rather have this conversation in person. Phone calls are so one-dimensional. You can ask me whatever you want to know about the man after we do the interview."

Jimmy's curiosity trumped his trepidation. "OK," he agreed.

"Do you want to check with your parents to see if tonight at 6:30 works?"

"No, it's fine. My Dad plays volleyball on Tuesday nights, and my Mom has Bible study. Do you need my address?"

"2318 White Rabbit Road?" she asked

"That's it."

"Thank you, Jimmy. I'm very much looking forward to meeting you tonight."

"Me too."

* * *

Two thousand miles away, a meeting already was underway in the Cardinal's Office of the Archdiocese of New York at 1011 First Avenue.

The antichrist had not been able to sleep last night, so troubled was he over what he perceived to be Cardinal Phelps' weak public response to the viral video controversy, and he had summoned the company jet at 1:30 in the morning to whisk him to New York City and a personal audience with the cleric.

"What else could I say?" the cardinal protested. "The kid didn't leave me a lot of room, ecumenically. I have to be very careful not to overstep the bounds of the Church, or I will be called to Rome and probably be replaced."

The antichrist got a chuckle out of that. "Replaced and reassigned, not removed. You still would be of service to us. We've already seen to that. Did you think it was just by accident, or by the grace of God – ugh, I hate that phrase – that the pedophiles among your fellow clergy are still working for the Church?

"My father's influence extends to the highest corridors in Rome. He can have you replaced and reassigned to a small parish in South America if it suits him, and you'll still be working for us – and, so, too, will the priest who takes your place in these posh surroundings.

"So, now, you have a choice: a parish among the Mapuches in southern Chile, or New York City. But, I digress..."

"What would you have me say?" the defeated Cardinal mumbled.

The antichrist beamed. "Father will be pleased with your choice. We've come a long way together. The separation of church and state is about to come down like the Berlin Wall, and then we will have free reign to impose our will on the governance of the United States and the rest of the world. I mean, who would ever question the Church's motives?"

The antichrist paused for effect. Then, he answered his own question. "Jimmy Rivers!" he pounded his fist on the prelate's desk. "You only slapped his hand, yesterday. He needs to be squashed!"

"I understand," came the Cardinal's meek response.

"Good!" the antichrist bellowed. "Now, here's what Father and I want you to do. Distract them! God's children are so easily distracted – it worked in the Garden of Eden and it continues to work to this day. Make them blink. They always blink. Get them to sit at the anti-contraception table and serve them up a pro-life menu!

"If parents don't want condoms passed out in schools, then they have to be pro-life and it validates the Church's pro-life position. Talk up abstinence! The capital punishment issue will be reduced to white noise in the beautiful music of their daughters not being encouraged to have sex in elementary school, or middle school, or high school.

"It's win-win. We get the distraction of all the social and emotional dysfunction of unprotected sex outside of marriage that keeps them from getting back on the path to rediscovering who they really are, and they don't recognize the power they have over us."

"Even better, no one will hear Jimmy Rivers' voice above the uproar. It literally will be drowned out, and so will he, figuratively!"

The Cardinal's mood brightened. "Yes, yes...that will work!" Then, somberly, he added, "But, he still will be a pretty big loose end."

"The last thing we want to do is turn Jimmy Rivers into a martyr. If anything happens to him, everyone would blame the pro-life extremists and we'll be back to Square One. Rest assured that we've got other plans for him. He will get distracted, he will blink, and he will fall!"

The antichrist stood up to leave. "Now, if you'll excuse me, I have a meeting with Jasper Joak. He is just as confused as you were, and he needs to see the big picture. I can help him."

He shook the Cardinal's hand and left the building. The Cardinal was beginning to realize that when you sell your soul to the Devil, there truly is hell to pay.

⋆ ⋆ ⋆

Jimmy saw them too late. The hallways at Benjamin Franklin High School seemed unusually crowded as he fought his way through the hordes of giddy, hormone-sotted teenagers all headed to lunch at the same time. Then, abruptly, the crowd miraculously parted, as the Red Sea had in Moses' day. Except it wasn't Moses doing the parting – it was Lisa Gallagher, Torri Bridger, and Hayley Summers looking like they just had stepped out of an *American Eagle* catalogue, making their way through the hallway.

Sasha had warned him about Lisa, but there still were significant blanks from the past six years that needed to be filled in. He had succeeded in avoiding her for almost two days...until now.

"Jimmy Rivers!" she exclaimed with delight, stopping right in front of her prey, while Torri and Hayley dutifully positioned themselves on either side of him. He was trapped.

"Look at you, all famous and everything!" Lisa said with a sparkle in her eye. "And now you don't have time for the little people," she sighed with a pouty-face that must have been rehearsed a thousand times in front of a mirror.

She was in his personal space, and it was unnerving. "I wouldn't say I'm famous," Jimmy stammered.

"Oh, look, girls, he's blushing!" she laughed, gently running the palm of her hand down the side of one of his reddened cheeks.

"That's so cute!"

His face burned even brighter at the feel of her touch. He was completely helpless and Lisa knew it.

"I was just wondering," she continued her flirtatious advance, "if you could…"

"If he could what?" Sasha suddenly cut in, stepping in front of Torri to link arms with her flustered boyfriend.

Jimmy breathed a huge sigh of relief at the sound of Sasha's voice and her cavalry coming to his rescue. Only the most trained eye would have caught Lisa's momentary annoyance, so quick was she to regain her composure from her rival's inconvenient appearance. Sasha saw it, though, and reveled in it.

"Oh, hi, Sasha!" Lisa recovered with feigned nonchalance. "Where did you come from?"

"It's nice to see you, too, Lisa," came Sasha's even response, sprinkled with the tiniest hint of sarcasm. "It looks like I got here just in time."

"Don't be silly," Lisa smiled mischievously, taking a step back out of Jimmy's personal space. "I was just going to ask Jimmy if he could help me with my math homework after school. Right girls?"

Torri and Hayley obediently backed up their leader, after which Lisa insincerely remarked, "Hey, you two should come over Thursday night. My parents are out of town and I'm having a few friends over to celebrate teachers' planning day on Friday."

"Thanks, Lisa, we'll think about it," Sasha lied.

Turning back to Jimmy, Lisa brazenly inquired, "So, Jimmy, will you be able to help me this afternoon?"

"I can't today. I have plans right after school."

Lisa was not about to take "no' for an answer. "Well, maybe another time," she winked. "Come on girls!"

After only a few steps, Lisa called out over her shoulder, "Don't forget about Thursday night!" and the Queen Bee and her drones disappeared around the corner.

"Omigod, thank you!" Jimmy exhaled. "*That* was uncomfortable!"

"At your service,!" Sasha replied brightly, affecting a quick curtsey. Then her playfulness morphed into seriousness. "Lisa Gallagher is not one to be trifled with. Be careful around her, Jimmy."

"Uh, hello! Did you not see how I totally had that whole situation under control?"

"Oh, I saw alright!"

"No, really."

"OK, let's hear it," Sasha grinned, crossing her arms. "This oughtta be good!"

Jimmy hesitated, trying to find the right spin.

"I'm waiting!"

"I got this. It was all part of my master plan."

Sasha was unconvinced. "Master plan, huh?"

"Yeah, I was stalling Lisa and those other two to give you a chance to step in and stake your claim!"

"Stake my claim? So you're assuming that there is something of value here that I would want to be mine?" she asked with mock cynicism.

Jimmy shifted his feet. "Of course!"

"Well, don't just stand there...enlighten me."

Jimmy didn't have to be told twice. In one motion, he leaned in to Sasha, placed his arm around her back, and dipped her until her head was inches from the ground.

"I was so buzzed from last night, and excited about today, that I forgot my wallet, so I'm going to let you take me out to lunch!"

"Wow!" Sasha quipped, "you really know how to sweep a girl off her feet!" Secretly, though, it felt so good to be the girl in Jimmy's strong arms.

"So, you are agreeing that there is something of value here."

"And if I said "no?" she teased.

"Let's just say that, if I were in your current position, I'd consider my answer very carefully!" he grinned.

Sasha had had her fun. "Ok...now, don't get all big-headed on me, but, yes, there is something of value here."

Jimmy pulled his girlfriend back to her feet, and she gave him a playful shove.

"Where do you want to go?" she asked, straightening her clothes.

"Is Hannah coming?"

"No, she's at Joak, doing all the paperwork for her internship."

"Ok, then Ellyngton's," he replied tongue-in-cheek. It was one of the premier – and most expensive – restaurants located in the historic Brown Palace Hotel in downtown Denver.

"Subway it is!" Sasha said matter-of-factly, not missing a beat.

The Subway shop located in Cherry Hills Marketplace was only two miles from school, and, therefore, one of the most popular lunchtime destinations for Ben Franklin students. It was almost impossible to get a table – except for today. Between bites of his meatball sub, Jimmy asked, "So what is it between you and Lisa?"

Sasha looked up from her double-chicken chopped salad and reminisced, "We used to be really good friends. We hung out, played sports together, had sleepovers. Then, it all changed in eighth grade."

"What happened?"

"Hugh Taylor is what happened. She was totally crushing on him. I mean big-time. You know how girls can get, especially with their first loves."

"Not really," Jimmy said.

"Ok, well, it's everything. 24/7. It pretty much defines your whole existence. Anyway, she was ready to take it to the next level – which in middle school means announcing you're boyfriend and girlfriend – so she was kind of stalking him, waiting for the right moment.

"The moment came when Hugh stayed after school for some extra credit, and he was alone in a classroom, and Lisa made her move. She walked into the room and locked the door behind her. She told him how much she loved him and that she wanted to be his girlfriend."

"Let me guess...that didn't go over so well."

"Right?! I mean, what boy wants to have all that laid in his lap? Especially in middle school! But, it gets worse..."

"I'm guessing this is where you come in."

"Hugh tried to let her down gently, saying he liked her a lot, but he liked other girls, too."

"And your name came up."

"Yes, even though I never did anything to encourage him, especially since I knew how Lisa felt about him. And we've been rivals ever since. In her mind, anyway. I've tried everything to make things right between us, but she just won't let it go.

"Anyway, enough about Lisa Gallagher. I want to hear about Madison Munro! How did the phone call go?"

"It was amazing. She was amazing," Jimmy enthused. Then, he paused. "Scary, really."

"Scary? In what way?"

"She said she had a sixth sense about a bigger story than just the video."

"I warned you. What did you tell her?"

"That's just it. Nothing! She just said her instincts were screaming and they've never let her down. Something about how this is our moment, hers and mine, and we have to seize it."

"Wow, Jimmy," Sasha observed. "Those are some pretty serious instincts. But how could she know anything about all this?"

"I don't know. Unless she's another one of the fortune teller's "friends." But she was talking about the Holy Spirit and open minds..."

"I told you she was good! How do you feel, though? Do you feel like you can open up to her?"

"I do. It was almost like a relief to talk to her. I mean, she was getting so close, it would have been cool to be able to talk to someone else about what's been going on – someone who is not connected to all this, but receptive. Someone who would not call me crazy or accuse me of being on drugs. Someone who would hear me out with an open mind...someone like you, actually, but detached.

"What do you think?"

"I told you I thought you could trust her."

"Yeah, I think so, too. I'm still a little nervous that it's going too fast. I mean, I can barely keep up with everything that's been happening myself! Just think where I was just 72 hours ago...and she wants to do the interview tonight!"

"Tonight?" Sasha gasped. "Where?"

"At my house at 7:00. That's what I mean. There's no time to process all this before then, and even if there were, I wouldn't know where to begin."

"Do you mind if I tag along?"

"Mind?" He reached across the table and took her hands in his. "I was hoping you'd ask me that!"

Their eyes locked.

"Jimmy...," she breathed his name so sweetly.

His heart fluttered.

"We have to get to class!" she giggled.

"Wow! So, that's how it's going to be," he said wryly, reeling from her flirty cold shower. "It's on, girl!"

The two teenagers finished their last bites and hurried back to school. They had been so engrossed in their conversation – and with each other – that neither of them had noticed the man in the dark suit sitting two tables away from them. Watching them, listening to them. And he had heard every word!

2

Tom Farrell helped Hannah with her chair at Ellyngton's. The celebrated restaurant still was crowded with power-lunchers, and the teenager was more than a little self-conscious about what she was wearing.

"Mr. Farrell, it really wasn't necessary to bring me here. I'm not exactly dressed for this. I would have been perfectly happy at McDonald's."

"McDonald's!" the Human Resources head of Joak Exploration harrumphed. "All those papers you signed at the office mean you're part of the Joak Industries family, now, and this is how we welcome new employees – and interns – into the family.

"You may think you're just an intern, but the Joaks have invited you into their family, and you will be treated as part of it. The Joak family does not do McDonald's. Not even for the fries," he smiled.

"What the Joak family does do," he added, "is put its best foot forward at all times. These are the types of places you'll frequent while you're here at Joak. And, as you mentioned, you'll be expected to dress accordingly.

"Business professional. The Joaks are kind of old-fashioned in the sense…"

"Good afternoon, Mr. Farrell!" a server interrupted. "Can I start you off with your dirty martini, three olives?"

"Yes, thank you, Marla."

"And for you, Miss?"

"I'm good with water," Hannah answered, "but can you bring me some lemon slices, please?"

"Of course, right away."

"Thank you."

"As I was saying," Tom continued after Marla excused herself to do their bidding, "the Joaks are old-fashioned in the sense that they have their own ideas as to what constitutes a professional appearance for women.

"No slacks. Skirts or dresses only, over the knee. Nylons are a must, closed-toe pumps no higher than three inches, hair pulled back, very light make-up, stud earrings only, clear fingernail polish."

Marla returned with the dirty martini and lemon slices, and asked if they needed more time with the menu.

Hannah hesitated, still trying to digest the Joak Industries dress code.

"Do you like Cobb salads?" Tom asked her.

"I do, yes," she said timidly.

Tom ordered for the two of them. "The young lady will have the Cobb salad, and I'll have the Angus burger, medium rare, with cheddar cheese, and fresh fruit on the side."

"Right away, Mr. Farrell," and the dutiful server wasted no time getting their order to the kitchen.

The HR chief redirected to Hannah. "Any questions about the dress code?"

"No, sir, Mr. Farrell," she replied respectfully.

"Oh, and one more thing...please call me Tom."

* * *

"Abraham Isaac Carter, where have you been? Do you have any idea what time it is? And why weren't you answering your phone?" Leticia Carter's voice boomed from the kitchen the second her 11-year old son walked through the front door.

Whenever his mother used all three of his names, Isaac knew he was in trouble.

"I'm sorry, Mama, my phone died. I couldn't call you."

"And whose fault is that? Lord almighty, I hate these teacher planning days. Now, get yourself cleaned up. Supper's almost ready."

As a single parent working two jobs, Leticia Carter knew how important it was to provide a semblance of stability and structure for her only child. Supper was promptly at 6:00, leaving plenty of time for homework and play before lights-out at 9:00 on school nights.

Isaac came back into the kitchen and sat down to a plateful of macaroni and cheese, a mixed green salad, and a cup of tomato soup. Leticia said grace, thanking the Lord for watching over her wayward son, this day, in particular. It was 6:00 on the dot.

"I wasn't wayward," Isaac objected, and before picking up his fork, he reached into his pocket, pulled out a $100 bill, and put it on the table.

His mother nearly choked on her food at the sight of the big bill at a time they needed money so badly.

"Where did you get that?" she demanded to know. "I better not hear anything about you 'finding' it!"

"I didn't 'find' it, Mama," he replied, savoring his first bite of his favorite dish. "I earned it. I did a favor for a man and he paid me $100. And it was almost $200!"

"What man, Isaac? And what favor?" Leticia asked, trying to remain calm. "Do you remember our talk about 'stranger danger?'"

"Yes, but I was only taking the letters to the mailbox by the park this morning like you asked me to, and he was there, standing by the mailbox with a big envelope in his hand. And he asked me if I'd do him a favor.

"I told him I wasn't supposed to talk to strangers, and he pulled out the $100 bill and said all he needed me to do was hold on to the envelope for him and come back to the mailbox at 5:30. If he was there, I'd give him back the envelope and he'd give me another $100 bill. If he wasn't there, he told me to put the envelope in the mailbox and keep the $100.

"And, Mama, I knew we could use the money!"

"That was it?" Leticia asked.

"That was it. I put the envelope in my backpack and went over to Lincoln's house. On my way home, I stopped back at the mailbox a little before 5:30 and waited for him for a while. I was hoping to get that other $100 bill, but he never showed up and the mailman came, so I put the letter in the mailbox and ran home."

"Honey, I appreciate where your heart was – and don't get me wrong, we do need the money – but you could get in a lot of trouble. You don't know what was in that letter."

Isaac frowned and put down his fork. "I'm sorry, Mama. Maybe we should call the *Denver Post.*"

"Why should we call the newspaper? What can they do?"

"Well, the envelope was addressed to them."

Isaac's attention to detail always had impressed his mother and his teachers, but Leticia still was agitated.

"Child, I'm sure the newspaper gets hundreds of letters a day..."

"But this one was one of those big, manila ones like you bring home from work sometimes," he interjected, "and the name in the return address space said 'Roland Thomas.'"

* * *

Ralph Petiole just had pulled into the parking lot of the world headquarters of Believe in Family, when his dedicated burner phone vibrated.

"Yes, Sir," he answered crisply.

"Ralph, we have a problem," Satan began. "It's like a wildfire in Southern California being whipped up by the Santa Ana winds. It's starting to jump all boundaries – almost out of control, I'd say."

"You're talking about Jimmy Rivers."

"I'm talking about everything – Jimmy Rivers, the escape, John Doe, the video, some mysterious fortune teller, Roland Thomas..."

"Wait," Senator Fenimore's frazzled campaign manager cut in. "Who is Roland Thomas?"

"He's nobody right now, but he could be somebody very soon. We'll cross that bridge if we get to it. Anyway, the kid is about to be interviewed tonight on ABC News."

"What?" Petiole practically screamed into his phone. "Can't

you do anything?"

Ralph was mortified the moment he heard the words come out of his mouth "I'm sorry, Sir," he apologized profusely, not wanting to be on the business end of the Evil One's wrath.

It was too late. "You know I have no authority!" Satan wailed.

If Satan hadn't needed the flag-bearer of the Partnership of the Right so urgently, he would have seen to his co-conspirator's immediate termination with extreme prejudice. Unfortunately, no one had Senator Fenimore's ear like his campaign chief, and for what he was about to run by him, he managed to overlook the indiscretion.

"As I was trying to say," the Evilest One continued, regaining his composure somewhat, "I don't know what the ABC News thing is about, but it can't be good for us. Cardinal Phelps has a press conference scheduled for tomorrow morning at 10:00 in New York, but I'm afraid it might be too late.

"We have to strike, and strike quickly to contain this wildfire!"

"Are you saying what I think you're saying? Take out Jimmy Rivers?"

"Absolutely not!" Satan howled. "Look what happened when Pilate washed his hands of Jesus! The damn news media would be all over it, asking questions, digging into his past, trying to put all the pieces together, and what if they did? What if they solved the puzzle!

"No, we're not going to kill Jimmy Rivers. I've got other plans for him. Remember, we didn't kill Peter either when he was walking on water. All it took was a gust of wind for him to fall. We have that gust of wind for Jimmy Rivers...and her name is Sasha Fenimore."

Ralph Petiole's face blanched. "You're not saying what I think you're saying," he pleaded incredulously.

"Yes, Ralph. Killing Sasha Fenimore is our only option at this point."

"Why are you telling me?" his voice trembled.

"Because I want *you* to run it by her father."

Ralph's body convulsed as the enormity of what the Devil was telling him to do sunk in. He broke out into a cold sweat.

"But, why?" he stammered. "What possibly could be gained by asking the Senator to sanction his own daughter's murder?"

"He has to be prepared. He can't fall apart. It would be an opportunity for him to act presidential. He must be ready!"

Ralph's head was spinning. How had it come to this? Seventy-two hours ago, they were on autopilot to the White House. Now, in the parking lot of Believe in Family, he was being told to tell Senator Fenimore that the White House depended on him signing off on the sacrifice of his own daughter for the greater good. How had it all gone so wrong?

"Look at it this way, Ralph," Satan explained. "The Senator will get an avalanche of sympathy votes. And, he'll have the opportunity to forgive her killer and get the same props John Paul II did when he forgave Mehmet Ali Agca. There will be no stopping him.

"It will be the final nail in Jimmy Rivers' coffin. He will be destroyed, rendered irrelevant, not even a footnote. Nothing he says will matter, again...if he says anything, that is. I could see him crawling into a hole and never coming out."

The devious genius of Satan's plan began to register, and Ralph finally caught his breath. It *would* be a public relations bonanza, but the words still stuck in his throat as he wrestled with broaching the subject with the Senator.

The Evilest One added, "There is a Biblical precedent, after all. Abraham was ready to kill his own son for God. I'm not asking anything different."

"But, it was just a test of faith. Even though he was ready to do it, God called it off."

"Yes, but the point is, he would have done it. It's the same test of allegiance. Except I'm not going to call it off."

"I think I'm going to be sick." And Ralph Petiole opened the car door and threw up onto the Believe in Family parking lot.

3

The doorbell rang at 2318 White Rabbit Road a little after 6:00. Jimmy opened the door to a reporter with a hidden agenda and her cameraman. The cat had a firm grip on Jimmy's tongue, so Madison broke the ice.

"Hello!" she said brightly. "I recognize you!"

"I recognize you, too," he stammered.

"This is my cameraman, André," she introduced.

Jimmy snapped out of his momentary stupor, shook hands, and invited them in.

"I know we're a little early, but I wanted a chance to talk a bit before we started the interview."

"Yeah, me, too," Jimmy agreed. "I was curious about that man in the minivan."

"Hi, Madison!" Sasha called out as she came down the stairs into the front room.

"Sasha!" Madison exclaimed. "What an unexpected pleasure! What are you doing here?"

"I'm kinda with Jimmy," she smiled, as they hugged.

"Kinda?" Jimmy huffed. "She's my girlfriend!" he insisted.

Madison grinned. "Well, aren't you the lucky one. This just gets more and more compelling by the minute."

"I love your dress!" Sasha admired, noting Madison's gray, above-the-knee, cap sleeve sheath with bow detail around the neck. "Is it a Tahari?"

"Wow, you do have an eye, don't you! Yes, I got it on sale at Nordstrom's." Madison was ready to get down to brass tacks. "So, how long have the two of you been together?"

Jimmy hesitated. He had no idea.

"About seven months," his girlfriend answered.

Looking at Sasha, Madison inquired, "Has your father said anything to you about the video? I mean it really shoots down his pro-life agenda."

"No, we actually haven't had a chance to talk about it. This is all happening so fast, and he's tied up with the campaign."

"Well, Dick Cheney's daughter is gay and it didn't seem to hurt his political career." Turning to Jimmy, she asked, "Are you ready for all of this?"

"I'm not sure I like all this publicity," he groaned.

"As we talked about on the phone, whether you're ready or not, the spotlight has found you. Trust me, it's not going to let go, especially when it finds out about your pretty girlfriend, here. And, don't kid yourself, it always finds out!

"As I also told you, I have this strange feeling that this is just the tip of the iceberg."

Jimmy seized his opportunity. "You're right, it has found me. I got so many calls from so many reporters. But that's one of the reasons I called you back. I'm curious about that 'old' man in your story about what happened on Berthoud Pass. The girl said the guy looked like an accountant."

"Yes, Rachel's dad is an accountant, and she said he had that look about him. Football players have a look, basketball players have a look, models have a look...I guess accountants have a look, too."

"Right. I have no problem with that. It's the age thing. She thought he was about her dad's age, in his forties, which would put him in his late fifties by now."

"OK, I'm not sure where you're going with this," she demurred, subtly leading him in the direction she wanted him to go.

"I think I know who this old man could be," he admitted, not playing his cards all at once, "but the age doesn't match."

"We think we know who he might be," Sasha chimed in. "He could be a fortune teller we know."

"I knew it!" Madison beamed, her instincts confirmed.

"You know the fortune teller?" Jimmy wondered aloud.

"No, but I knew there was more here than met the eye! I mean, how could there not be? Flying cars, miraculous rescues, mysterious men, incongruous videos...So, tell me about this fortune teller. You've both met him, obviously."

"Yes," the two teenagers answered in unison.

"And here's the really strange part," Jimmy continued, his comfort level elevated. "The first time was in a dream that we both had."

"Oh my," Madison gasped, under her breath. "Parallel universes!"

"That's what the fortune teller said!" Sasha marveled at her prescience.

"For the past thirteen years," Madison explained, "I've been trying to wrap my mind around what happened that night on Berthoud Pass – doing a lot of research, talking to professors and scientists about quantum physics and mechanics, interviewing spiritualists and theologians, and, as strange as it sounds, that's the only explanation that is somewhat consistent with everything that happened.

"I'd like to meet this fortune teller!"

"I get the feeling he only reveals himself to those who are open to receiving him," Jimmy backed off, hoping to remove himself from an intermediary role. "I think he'll want to meet you, too, though. When you least expect it."

"There are others, too," Sasha joined in. "Don Quixote, Doc Holliday, Captain Kirk..."

"It's getting late, Madison," André interrupted.

Madison looked at her watch and frowned. "Time flies when you're having fun, doesn't it? Well, clearly, we have a lot more to talk about, but André's right. We have the interview to do."

"Please," Jimmy begged, "nothing about the fortune teller or any of this other stuff."

"Of course, not," Madison assured him. "We're nowhere near ready for any of that, and it's not part of the public record. Let's go over how I envision tonight's interview and stop me if you have any questions or if I'm going in a direction that makes you uncomfortable."

Jimmy nodded his head. "Ok, thanks."

* * *

At the sprawling world headquarters campus of Joak Industries in Wichita, Kansas, Jasper Joak was engaged in a spirited discussion with the antichrist.

"Explain to me, again, why we are supporting the legalization of marijuana," Jasper whined. "It is putting a big dent in our profits!"

"Think of it as long-term greed," the antichrist clarified. "It's an investment in our future."

The elder Joak brother looked perplexed.

"What have we learned from the very beginning? That God's children have the tendency to exercise their free will very badly. We need to insure that the tendency is reinforced so that they continue to choose poorly...unless you want one of them – and all it takes is one – to figure out that by exercising their free will wisely, as God advised them, they actually have authority over us, and there's nothing we can do by any means to change that.

"If they discover the true meaning of what Jesus tried to tell them, and choose to believe it, then they will have authority over the 'All,' as Thomas put it...and that means us! So, we have to do everything we can to impair their ability to make good choices. Our friends in the clergy have helped immeasurably by telling their parishioners that Jesus didn't really mean what He said when He told them that nothing would be impossible for anyone who had the faith of a mustard seed.

"And parents, teachers, scientists, and adults, in general, have done us a big favor by shoving impossibilities down young people's throats, first by telling them there is no such thing as Santa Claus. Then, when they are open to accepting impossibility as an explanation for things that have not been done yet, or things that cannot be explained yet, they have the tendency to choose very poorly to accept the impossibility explanation uncritically, and they separate themselves from God and from access to their divine authority through Him.

"And it takes them out of Eden, where everything is possible, and puts them into our parallel universe where bad things happen to them, where there are limits, including the Ultimate Limit, and where you make lots and lots of money!"

Jasper listened intently as the antichrist continued.

"We can't take it for granted that no one will figure it out. This Jimmy Rivers kid is a big problem, but, not to worry, he will be dealt with. However, he is a reminder that we have to do everything we can to continue to bombard God's children with distractions, 24/7 – lie, cheat, deceive, whatever – to impair their ability to make wise choices and to trick them into choosing to sit at our table. That's where pot comes in.

"We want people to believe it's no worse than alcohol. Think of all the poor choices His children make when they are drunk! Now, introduce 'stoned' into the mainstream, and you add layers upon layers of impairment gaining general acceptance in society. And," the antichrist chortled, "they actually have chosen to believe our lies that it is not a gateway drug!

"Jasper, we're only one step away from the White House and from being able to impose our will, unopposed, over the entire world. That's long-term greed!"

Jasper was convinced. "Well, when you put it that way!"

"And another thing, the legalization of pot will legitimize your operation in Westcliffe, and you won't have to be looking over your shoulder all the time."

"Speaking of that, The Cobra has neutralized the threat down there."

"Are you sure? Because he really botched the John Doe job in Glenwood!"

"Yes, it has been confirmed. The body has been disposed of."

"Well, that's one loose end tied up. But, as you are well aware, there are too many more. Let me ask you a question – since we're planning a long-term coup, in effect, what's the first priority in any coup?"

"Getting control of the military?" Jasper guessed.

"We'll have that when we get the White House. But the first order of business for any successful coup is gaining control of the media outlets. I understand that ABC News is about to interview Jimmy Rivers on national TV tonight. We are not in a position to stop it, unfortunately, but it would be nice to get to a place where we could.

"My father and I would like you and your brother to see about gaining a foothold in the industry. If Carlos Slim can become the largest single stockholder of the *New York Times*, you and Henry should be able to buy into that game, as well."

"We've already turned over that stone in some or our biggest markets, and we're looking to expand our sphere of influence. Tom Farrell is our point man."

"Good," the antichrist said. "See that he gets the job done."

"But what about the interview tonight?"

"Senator Fenimore has a press conference scheduled for tomorrow morning to control the damage. And steps already have been taken to, as you so delicately put it, 'neutralize' Jimmy Rivers."

4

Jimmy sat across the coffee table from Madison in the living room of his parents' house in exactly the same spot where, only two days earlier, he had found his newly-resurrected (or not) mother chatting amicably with his beautiful girlfriend he hadn't known he had.

This time, he and a reporter from ABC News were awaiting the signal from her cameraman that they would be "live," while his girlfriend of seventy-two-hours-cum-seven-months stood to the side, beyond the camera lens' reach, giving him the thumbs-up sign and blowing him good-luck kisses. It all was so surreal!

"Are you nervous?" Madison asked, never taking her eyes from the three fingers André held over his head.

Truth be told, Jimmy's heart was pounding. "It's just so hard to process everything that's happened since Saturday night."

"I'm sure it is. But, just think of it as you and I having a casual conversation like you would with one of your friends from school."

André lowered his ring finger and Madison whispered, "Here we go!"

Then, the middle finger came down, followed by the index finger, the red light on the top of his camera illuminated, and he pointed at Madison.

"Good evening, I'm Madison Munro, and I'm sitting with Jimmy Rivers, Denver's Internet sensation, whose video about pro-choice went viral yesterday, and shows no sign of letting up."

Turning to Jimmy, she began, "Thank you for visiting with us, tonight, Jimmy. "

Jimmy nodded his head. "It's a pleasure, Madison."

"First of all, I have to ask you, did you have any idea you'd get this kind of response when you made this video?"

"Actually, I had no idea that anyone was recording what I was saying. Mr. Hamilton, our teacher, collects all of our cell phones and iPads before class. And I didn't see anyone else with any kind of recording device. I just was responding to a question he asked in class."

"Well, the video is out there, but just in case there is anyone watching who has not seen it or heard about it, can you go over the question, again, for us?"

"Sure. Mr. Hamilton asked how the True Believers can be pro-life and pro-death at the same time. He was referring to how it supports capital punishment and a pro-life agenda, in terms of abortion, at the same time."

"Your answer was quite something!" Madison enthused, while maintaining her reporter's detachment. "Was it something you had been thinking about for a long time, or discussed with your parents, or a teacher, or a religious leader, or anyone, before?"

"That's just it, Madison. I never had thought about it, at least consciously, until Mr. Hamilton brought it up in class. And I never raise my hand. I just..."

Jimmy hesitated for a moment. He looked at Sasha and scratched at his temple twice with his right finger. It was their secret signal to let the other person know he or she was being thought of.

"Anyway," he rejoined Madison, "the thought just popped into my head from out of nowhere and I felt like I was being nudged somehow to add to the class discussion.

"I knew it was against the rules to talk about God in public schools, but since the True Believers want to put God back in schools, I thought it would be fair game. And I remembered from Sunday School that God created us in His image with free will. So, He's definitely pro-choice."

Jimmy was on a roll. "One of the Ten Commandments is, "Thou shalt not kill," and all this talk about capital punishment, and abortion, and killing abortion doctors to prevent abortions, goes against

His commandment, but He's not taking away our ability to choose freely, even when we choose to exercise it against His will.

"Instead, He sent His son, Jesus, to remind us to exercise our right to vote, so to speak, in accordance with His will."

Madison started to ask Jimmy another question, but there was no stopping him. "I'm sorry, There's another thing...can I keep going?"

"Of course," she responded, with just a hint of hesitation that Jimmy noticed, but disregarded. She hated to be surprised in an interview, especially on camera, and knew she was taking a big risk handing the reins over to her interviewee.

Jimmy again scratched his right temple twice, staring at Sasha, and he repeated the conversation he had with her in the wee hours of the morning.

"God is not a killer. Why would He tell us not to kill, and then turn around and kill people, Himself? That would be hypocritical. It's so Old Testament, you know, an eye for an eye, and a tooth for a tooth. Jesus came into the world not only to save us, but also to set the record straight because we still hadn't gotten the Word right. He wanted to remind us of our divine inheritance and show us the way Home.

"Instead of an eye for an eye and a tooth for a tooth, Jesus taught us that if someone hits us on the cheek, then we should give our attacker our other cheek to hit.

"He gave us the Lord's Prayer that says, "Thy will be done, on earth as it is in heaven." Which means that we should strive to live our lives the way God does. If He tells us not to kill on earth, then He's not a killer in heaven, either. After all, He didn't kill Lucifer when His trusted angel of light betrayed Him.

"In the Old Testament, Moses wrote the first five books in such a way as to scare his followers into living according to God's Ten Commandments because his followers understood fear, not love: "If you step out of line, God will strike you down." They were ignorant, uneducated slaves with absolutely no concept of God's unconditional love.

"But, along comes Jesus when we're able to understand, and He tells us that God is all about unconditional, everlasting love – a love that is so great as to be incomprehensible even though we're ready to receive the message. God is Love. Period. End of story. The two most important Commandments, according to Jesus, are centered on Love. When we stepped out of line, God didn't condemn his prodigal children, He sent His Son to save us! And to show us the way back Home. God is the landowner in the story of the prodigal son! And when we turn back to Him, He rushes to greet us and to celebrate our choice to repent with a great feast."

Madison was just as dazed as Sasha had been when she first heard Jimmy's astonishing testimony, and that's precisely why she hated to be surprised on camera.

"But what about Noah and the flood?" was all she could manage.

"That's the question that got us kicked out of church. I asked it when I was five years old. We were doing an art project in Sunday School about Noah's ark, and another kid asked the teacher why God had killed all those people and the animals. The teacher said it was because the people had sinned against God.

"I raised my hand and asked, "If God loves us so much, then why would He kill us for making a mistake? Why didn't He send Jesus to help us like He did at Easter?""

"You and your family got kicked out of church because you asked a question?" Madison inquired, dubiously. "Maybe that's why you don't like to raise your hand in class."

"I never thought of that," Jimmy mused. "But, let me tell you this. We weren't actually kicked out of church. The priest came over to our house and accused my parents of putting false thoughts in my head because he didn't believe a five-year-old could come up with them on his own."

"Did they?" Madison asked. "You have to admit, that's a pretty advanced thought."

"I know it is. But, my parents and I never had that conversation. Again, I have no idea where it came from, and that was the truth."

"Did the priest accept that?"

"No. So, basically, he was accusing my parents of lying, and that didn't go over too well with them. They took turns pointing out some other inconsistencies in the ways of the church, in the hands of priests like Father Sam, and decided right then and there that they no longer wanted any part of it."

Madison quickly interjected, "Wait, did you say "Father Sam? Father Sam Phelps, as in Cardinal Phelps, the leader of the Catholic Church in North America?"

"Yes, that's the one. He told my parents they didn't understand, and that they should re-read the teachings of the church fathers. But, my Dad stood his ground, saying the church fathers were human beings, prone to the same fallibility as the rest of us, and there are so many times in history when men of God either misunderstood the Word of God, were led astray, or had their own agendas that were apart from God. Or, like Moses, maybe, who got the message across in a way that Israelites could understand thousands of years ago, which obviously has evolved.

"And then my mom added that Jesus was all about inclusion, and the Church was about exclusion. Jesus didn't exclude anyone when He sacrificed His body and blood for our salvation, but the Catholic church and others say you have to be a member of their 'club' to receive communion. Nothing could be further from the Truth. She reminded Father Sam what Jesus told Thomas: "Split a piece of wood and I am there, lift a stone, and you have found me," alluding to the fact that the magnificent edifices erected in the name of God should be torn down because they distract from the true meaning of the Word. Which told her that the leaders of the Church were leading us away from God, instead of closer to Him, and we chose to stop going to church."

"So, you weren't really kicked out of church, per se, your parents just had a problem with the inconsistencies, in your words, of what the church's leaders were preaching to you."

"Right. I mean, God is the Ultimate Truth. The Truth is constant and consistent under all circumstances. And do you want to know how we know we're being led the wrong way? It's because Jesus has to come again. The Second Coming. We still need to be saved from ourselves and shown the way Home because we still haven't gotten the message right!"

André was signaling "cut' by drawing a finger across his throat, and Madison was quick to pick up his cue.

"Jimmy, unfortunately, I'm afraid our time is up..."

"Do you want to know about Time?" he cut her off. "There's so much more!"

"I'm sure there is, but it will have to keep for now. Thank you for allowing us into your home."

"Thank you, Madison!" Jimmy never had felt more alive.

When the red light on André's camera went off, Madison let out a deep breath. "Oh my God, Jimmy, why didn't you tell me about the whole "God is not a killer' thesis and about Cardinal Phelps?"

"You didn't ask. Besides, I never know anymore what's going to come out of my mouth, or when it's going to come out."

"I think you were absolutely brilliant!" Sasha exulted, rushing over to give her boyfriend a big hug...and kiss. "You're my hero!"

"He's my hero, too, Sasha," Madison said, taking off her microphone. "That was very brave of him."

Turning to Jimmy, she confided, "We have so much more to talk about, and I'd like to meet that fortune teller. But I have to go – deadlines are deadlines. I'll call you tomorrow and see when we can get together. You have my number, too, in case you ever need to get in touch.

"Jimmy, as I said, what you talked about on camera tonight was very brave, but you better keep your head down. They're going to come after you big-time!"

No sooner had the words left Madison's mouth, than the house phone started to ring.

Jimmy grabbed Sasha's hand. "Let's get outta here!"

⋆ ⋆ ⋆

"Hey, don't you go to school with that boy?" a woman nudged her 24-Hour Fitness workout buddy.

Lisa Gallagher looked over from her stationary bike and took out her ear buds.

"What?"

"Don't you go to school with that boy?" her friend repeated, indicating the TV monitor above her.

Lisa gazed up. "Omigod, yes," she exclaimed. "That's Jimmy Rivers! What's he doing on TV? Is it about that video?"

"Yes, but he's saying some even crazier shit." She paused and looked over at Lisa. "You know, he's cute. I'd totally do him."

"Ewww, that's disgusting! You're, like old."

"I'm only 26," she said with a gleam in her eye, "and look what hooking up with Ray J did for Kim K! I'm just sayin', this Jimmy of yours is going to be way more famous than Kim K!"

"That's still gross," Lisa replied, putting her ear buds back in her ears. But, she never took her eyes off the TV monitor. And, subconsciously, she started pedaling faster.

⋆ ⋆ ⋆

"Yes, I saw the interview!" Cardinal Phelps practically shouted into his smartphone.

"Has he called you, yet?" Father Simon asked, patiently.

"No, but I'm sure…" The sound of the Cardinal's burner phone interrupted him. "There he is now. I'll have to call you back."

He swiped his finger across the face of the dedicated phone to accept the call. "If you're calling about the interview, yes, I saw it."

"Actually, I was calling just to chat and see how your day was," Satan sneered sarcastically. "Of course, I'm calling about the damned interview! This is turning out to be the biggest threat we've had since Peter!"

The cardinal tried to placate the Evilest One. "I'm sure you have some gusts of wind up your sleeve..."

"Of course, I do," he snarled. "But it's not just Jimmy Rivers.

You've had parishioners running for the exits in droves, and this will make it a hundred times worse! We have to have God's children in church so you can continue to sow and cultivate the seeds of Doubt in their minds.

"I mean, I don't have to tell you how bad it will be if they start believing Him."

"Who, Jimmy?"

"No!" Satan screamed. "Jesus! We can't have them start believing what He told them, that they have power over us! I've got a hurricane up my sleeve, as you put it, for Jimmy. But, it's the idea that threatens. It's like Victor Hugo said, "Nothing else in the world is so powerful…as an idea whose time has come."

"So, leave Jimmy Rivers to me. You have to attack the idea! I want you at Fenimore's press conference in Denver tomorrow morning. I've already spoken with Ralph, and my son is flying back to New York, as we speak, to pick you up.

"The Senator is going to talk about the dangers of pro-choice, and, lucky for us, God's children are so easily distracted. They'll forget all about Jimmy's mumbo-jumbo when he talks about condoms being passed out in schools and their daughters having sex in middle school.

"Then, it will be your turn. Do what you do best – create Doubt! Drive home the hyperbole angle. And be very cardinal-like. Tell the world you are praying for Jimmy's soul because he's on the path of heresy and blasphemy that will put him in Hell for eternity. Remind them of that ridiculous wordplay that the only way to heaven is through death to this world. That reinforces the mistake in their minds – not only that Death is inevitable, but also that it must be embraced.

"They'll believe you, instead of Jimmy, instead of Jesus, instead of Thomas, and instead of God. I've already got them so lost in the dark, there's no way they can find their way back to Him by themselves. We have to make sure that they choose to follow you deeper into the darkness. And, then, you have to keep them there, in the prison of Can't, by continuing to emphasize that they have no choice! And I will see to it that Jimmy's 'there's-always-choice, get-out-of-jail-free' card 'light' is extinguished permanently.

"It's time to get my public relations man, Leon Tusk, involved. He'll bombard his social media platform with our lies. People, even supposed Christians, won't admit it, but they worship thirty pieces of silver more than they do God, and Tusk has so much money, they'll blindly follow him, no questions asked.

"So, give them a reasonable doubt, Cardinal, or even an unreasonable one. That's all it takes. Leon will do the rest. They will blink!"

5

"I'm so proud of you, Jimmy!" Sasha said admiring her boyfriend from the passenger seat of his car. "Where shall we go?"

Jimmy's cell phone started to ring, and he powered it down without checking the caller ID. "Thanks, Sasha." Then, he frowned. "You know, for the past six years, I've pretty much gotten used to people leaving me alone…"

Sasha stopped him right there. "That was a different reality. Or universe maybe, remember? Jimmy, you got your mom back!"

"Right. That's right. I couldn't be happier about that. It's all the other stuff. I thought I'd be ready for it…maybe, I should have waited to do the interview."

Sasha rubbed his shoulder. "I think it's all related. I mean, you can't have one without the other. You have to shine your light! Did you ever stop to think about who might be coming after us? I have. I would imagine the Devil would not be too happy about you undoing Death. He shrinks in the Light!"

His girlfriend's comments went right over his head. It was her touch. It always did the trick. He snapped out of his brief uncertainty and angst, but still didn't want to go anywhere he might be recognized.

"I just don't feel like talking to anyone right now."

Sasha shifted gears quickly. "I know, let's go to a movie!" she said cheerily, noticing the marquee for the Chez Artiste movie theater ahead on the left."

There were no TV monitors in movie theaters, Jimmy reasoned, so he pulled into the parking lot and they walked inside.

"Hi there!" the ticket taker greeted them as they checked the movies and times.

"Hi," they both smiled back. Jimmy was relieved she didn't recognize him.

"*Poseidon*?" he wondered aloud. "Didn't that come out a while ago?"

"Yes, it's part of our signature classic movie series on Tuesday nights. It's been pretty popular."

"What do you think?" Jimmy whispered to his girlfriend. "It starts in five minutes. We'd have to wait at least an hour for the other two."

"It sounds perfect!"

As Jimmy bought the tickets, Sasha's phone vibrated. It was her father calling. She powered her phone down and walked hand-in-hand with her boyfriend into the lobby, where she bought them a large popcorn and root beer to share.

Jimmy was surprised at just how popular the classic series was when they entered the theater. They found two seats a few rows from the back and settled in as the lights began to dim.

Sasha was starved and started in on the popcorn, so mesmerized by the image of Zac Efron – her not-so-secret celebrity crush – in the first trailer that she didn't notice the small note dropped in her boyfriend's lap by a person sitting behind them.

Jimmy looked over his shoulder. There was no one there. He looked at the note and made out the words, "Meet me in the men's room. FT."

The fortune teller! Sasha was in her own world, completely oblivious to what was going on. He leaned over to her and excused himself to go to the bathroom.

The fortune teller was the only one in the men's room when Jimmy walked in.

"Boy, do I have some questions for you!" Jimmy said when he saw the familiar accountant-like man. "The first one is, why all this cloak and dagger stuff?"

"I have my reasons." He paused, considering whether to elaborate...and decided against it. "I saw the interview. You were very good. Very good! I just wanted to tell you that you're on the right path and to not stop until you find the Truth."

"What Truth?"

"You'll know it when you find it. Just stay focused, no matter what, and don't ever lose that focus."

"On whatever it is I'm looking for?"

"Yes. And on what you want to happen. They'll do everything they can – and I mean everything – to distract you, but remember, they have no power over you. The choice of what to focus on is yours. There always is choice. Always! You must choose wisely!"

"Who is "they?""

"Let's just say there are those out there who are not as excited as we are that you're on this path and that you're getting warmer by the day."

Jimmy was confused by the fortune teller's cryptic message, and he tried to recall something he vaguely remembered Sasha mentioning to him earlier in the car, but wild horses could not have kept him from his next question.

"You told us that you were the old man in the minivan who saved that girl on Berthoud Pass. How could it have been? The age thing doesn't work?

"I mean, you seem to be in your thirties, but the man in the minivan probably would be in his fifties or sixties by now."

The faintest hint of a smile turned up the corners of the fortune teller's mouth. "How long do I have to be with you? Haven't you learned by now that nothing is what it seems?"

"Yes, but..."

The fortune teller looked Jimmy squarely in the eyes. "Do you remember me telling you that I see the world not as it is, but as it should be?"

"Yes, that is coming through loudly and clearly from you and from your friends."

"Good. Well, the world as it should be is that we should be living forever. That's how we were created. But, our parents chose poorly and brought Death into the world by mistake. More precisely, they stepped out of Eden and into Lucifer's reality in the universe east of Eden where Death exists. This is key, though. Death is not inevitable. It's a mistake, the result of a poor choice. And you can change your universe by choosing to change your thought that you don't have a choice.

"My thought was that if I was going to live forever, I didn't want it to be in the body of what we subconsciously have chosen to associate with that of a 900-year-old man.

"So, if you pay attention, you'll discover that, while scientists can describe the aging process, they don't know what triggers it. Without getting too technical, the process is governed by telomeres, which are essential parts of our DNA. They protect our chromosomes from degradation as they replicate, similar to the plastic tips at the end of shoelaces. And there's an enzyme called telomerase that shields the plastic tips from decay.

"As our cells regenerate over time, there is not enough of the telomerase to go around, and our telomeres begin to shorten until there is no more protection for our DNA. Our chromosomes are compromised, they begin to degrade, and that's when the aging process begins.

"That, basically, is what happens. Can you guess what triggers the shortage of telomerase?"

Jimmy just stared at the fortune teller, imploringly.

"It's the choice to accept the inevitability of Death! That's our 'goal,' in effect. We are programming ourselves to die, and our mind-body synergy works to achieve that goal by not producing enough telomerase to keep our telomeres from shortening and that's how our chromosomes are compromised over time.

"I chose to change the rules...and, in making that choice, I moved west, back into Eden's universe where everything is possible. From there, I chose to focus on increasing the telomerase in my DNA strands to protect my telomeres from disintegrating, and voila! Thirty is the new sixty."

Jimmy was lost, even though the proof was right in front of his eyes.

"Look, Jimmy, I know this is a lot, but think of where you are, where you've been, and what's happened over the past seventy-two hours. Remember your Captain Kirk, and, above all, Jesus reminded us that we have been created in God's image, and that hasn't changed since He created Adam and Eve. When we follow through on our part of our partnership with God by choosing to believe in Him, and, just as importantly, by choosing to believe in what He says and not to doubt, we are transported back into the universe where nothing is impossible.

"Absolutely nothing...including increasing the telomerase in our bodies to protect our telomeres and our DNA!"

Jimmy frantically tried to connect the fortune teller's dots...to no avail.

"Jimmy," the fortune teller's voice cut in, "the movie's about to start. You better get back to Sasha."

The sound of his girlfriend's name brought him back from the parallel universe into which he had been nudged to explore.

"Right!"

"Oh, and one more thing," the fortune teller added. "Pay close attention to the movie. It was not by chance that this particular movie was playing at this theater at this particular time. Someone is watching over you, knowing what choices you will make, but allowing you to make them."

The fortune teller's words barely registered as Jimmy scrambled, mentally and physically, to get back to Sasha. He sat down next to her just as the opening credits had begun.

Outside the Chez Artiste movie theater on Colorado Boulevard, a man in a dark suit waited patiently in his car.

* * *

Ralph Petiole left the Believe in Family world headquarters right after Jimmy's interview on TV. The teenager's words reverberated in his mind over and over: "God is not a killer. God is not a killer. God is not a killer." Who the hell does this kid think he is? But, really, who is this kid? What 5-year old child asks why God killed all the sinners during Noah's time, but later changed His mind and decided to send His Son to save sinners? If God has perfect knowledge, then He wouldn't ever have to change His mind. A change of mind and a change of heart implies imperfect thoughts or reasoning.

Ralph was not a religious man. He was cut of the cloth of pragmatism, of forging alliances to shove agendas – his agenda – down people's throats. He could see the writing on the wall: America was turning right, extreme right, and the ultra-conservative religious right was only too happy to accommodate. The Partnership of the Right had the presidential timber the country wanted – Bill Fenimore was political gold. And his blind ambition – or willingness to turn a blind eye – easily could be manipulated by the Partnership in its secret quest for global domination.

In fact, Fenimore and Petiole were birds of a feather – political chameleons changing colors to embrace any ideology that would get them the power they both craved. Ralph wondered how no one in the Partnership had seen this coming. After all, "the kid," as he called Jimmy, made sense, he admitted to himself, and he could see the Senator's electorate slipping away.

"What the hell!" he screamed, as his preoccupation with Jimmy nearly got him steamrolled by a speeding 18-wheeler when he mindlessly tried to merge into the northbound lanes of Interstate 25.

Chastened but not contrite, he quickly obsessed again over Jimmy Rivers. "Holy Crap!" he pounded his fist onto the steering wheel – except this time, his invective was not directed at a reckless truck driver. If it wasn't for this kid, he would not be driving to Denver on this mission from hell (literally and figuratively) to tell Senator Fenimore that he had to sign off on having his only daughter killed. Killed for the greater good, though. Damn it, the kid was right! He could see it – clearly, since his mind wasn't in the total lockdown promulgated by the church. He wasn't of them, he was just with them. He hadn't drunk their Kool-Aid. Why would God tell His children not to kill, and then turn around and do what He told them not to do? And the whole pro-life, pro-choice debate – of course, God is pro-choice! He gave His children free will and He never takes it away, even when they make choices that go against His will.

What was it that he'd heard in church so long ago? Love the sinner, but hate the sin? How had Cardinal Phelps gotten mixed up with Satan, anyway? It probably went back to those religious leaders who condemned Jesus because He called them out on their personal agendas that were not consistent with the Word of His Father. Clearly, that is the dark side of tradition: what if the tradition is wrong? What if it misses the mark? Then, that sin will be perpetuated throughout eternity unless someone has the temerity to stand up to the church, to the church fathers, and to the tradition – and to call them out on it.

Galileo did it, and the church killed him – and Galileo had been right! Déjà vu. Jimmy Rivers is a modern-day Galileo, and they're going to kill him, too, by killing Sasha! Why?

Because this unholy alliance has been going on for so long. God doesn't kill, but those under Lucifer's influence can be tricked into doing so – proof positive that an unholy alliance exists. This is so messed up! And it's all predicated on the poppycock premise that there is a God. But, how could there not be a God when Satan was doing everything in his power to lead people away from Him?

Ralph's burner phone started to ring and interrupted the downward spiral of his stream of consciousness.

"Hello, sir," he sang out to his master.

"I just spoke with the Senator," Satan replied. He's expecting you. How far along are you?"

"The traffic's not so bad. Probably about 45 minutes to go. Did you tell him why I'm coming?"

"No, just that you needed to speak with him in person and that it was urgent."

"Could it be that maybe…" Ralph stopped in mid-sentence. "Whoa!" he exclaimed. "What just happened?"

"What is it?" Satan demanded. "You sound like you just saw a ghost."

"It wasn't a ghost, but it was like I suddenly snapped out of a different reality...a reality in which everything was possible and Jimmy Rivers was right."

He could feel Satan's cold blood starting to boil, and he quickly assured, "Don't worry, it was just some sort of bad dream. I'm as dialed in as ever. Right or wrong, I know what I have to do and why I have to do it. I can see the big picture, and I'm not going to let this kid get in our way!"

"OK, Ralph," Satan relaxed. "You had me worried for a moment, though."

* * *

"Sir," Madison Munro pleaded into her cell phone. "We have to pursue this Jimmy Rivers angle further."

Her producer at ABC News was not convinced. "I think we'd be getting off track. The real story is Senator Fenimore's campaign – following up and trying to gauge the impact of Jimmy's video and your interview. I mean, the Partnership of the Right was sailing along to the White House in smooth waters, and now this. Is it a ripple in the water or a tidal wave that will sink their ship?"

"Sir, you're absolutely right. But, with all due respect, I think you'd be better off assigning someone like Gus to that angle.

"You want to talk tidal waves? Jimmy Rivers is just a drop of water in this tsunami, and I need to dig much deeper. You know my instincts never have let you down before."

Cal Everett couldn't deny that Madison Munro was a throwback to a bygone era. She reminded him so much of himself at her age. She had that intangible sixth sense that enabled her to sniff out stories overlooked by her peers, and she had the passion and the tenacity to find all the pieces to a puzzling narrative and to put them together.

He sighed. "OK, give me one reason I should let you stay on Jimmy Rivers."

Madison had been waiting for just the right time to spring her case on her producer. She had spent nearly a year researching quantum physics and mechanics – all on her own time, sacrificing any semblance of a personal life. This was her moment of truth.

"Cal, are you sitting down?"

"'Cal?' Oh no," he groaned, knowing full well that she only used his first name when she needed something...usually to go beyond the limits of mainstream journalism. "Lay it on me."

"Parallel universes!" she blurted into her phone.

"Omigod, Madison, you've got to be kidding!"

"Hear me out, Cal, I've done my homework. On my own time, mind you."

"No wonder you don't have a boyfriend!" her producer stammered, shaking his head. "Madison, you need to unplug once in a while. You have to have balance in your life or you'll burn out."

She ignored his well-meaning caveat and forged ahead. "It started about a year ago, when I went to visit my uncle in California. He's a 95-year old retired nuclear physicist, living by himself after my aunt died a few years ago, so I try to visit him whenever I can."

"Hold on right there. You have an uncle who is more than 60 years older than you?"

"OK, Cal, back off. He's my Dad's uncle, so I guess that makes him my great uncle, or something, but I've always called him "Uncle John.'"

"Go on," he allowed, a hint of exasperation in his voice.

"Thank you. As I was saying, I paid a visit to Uncle John about a year ago. He walks two miles every day, attends lectures, frequents the opera, and uses a telescope and trigonometry to triangulate how fast and how high planes are flying past his living room window in their approach to San Francisco International Airport."

"I get it. He's engaged."

"Right. Anyway, I asked him if he ever got lonely, and he said his family pops in from time to time, and, of course, there are the five o'clock Friday afternoon get-togethers with some of his friends at the Alpine Inn...formerly Rossotti's."

"And?" Cal asked, his voice dripping in impatience.

"And...," Madison draws out for effect, "I asked him "which friends'?"

She paused, toying with her Type A producer.

"And? Come on, Madison, I don't have time for games!" he groused.

"Cal, you're no fun anymore," she grunted. "So, I ask him who his friends are, and they are like a Who's Who in physics, mostly retired like my uncle, but who love nothing more than getting together at the end of the week at the Alpine Inn. You're probably wondering how many friends he meets with every Friday afternoon."

"Not really."

"Well, aren't you going to ask me, anyway?"

"OK, Madison," he humored his star reporter." "How many friends does your uncle meet with at the Alpine Inn, formerly Rossotti's – you see, I have been paying attention – every Friday afternoon at 5:00?"

"Up to 50!" she emphasized gleefully. "Meeting every week for five hours, from 5:00 to 10:00, and sitting at these long picnic tables in the courtyard in the back of the restaurant. And here's the best part – it's a biker bar! Don't you love the incongruity?!"

"I'm still listening."

"Anyway, I asked him what they talk about for so long? He answered, "Well, Madison, we talk about contemporary physics, of course." And I thought to myself, that's 50 of the best and brightest minds in physics exploring cutting edge theories and debating where the science is headed."

"And?" This time, the tone in Cal's voice had changed from intensely disinterested to marginally curious.

"So, then I asked him if there was any consensus among them in terms of what they thought would be the next frontier in physics. And, without missing a beat, Uncle John said, very evenly, "Parallel universes.""

Cal abruptly leapt from marginally curious to genuinely interested. "OK, you got me. I know how you feel about coincidences...

but what does this have to do with Jimmy Rivers?"

"I'm not sure, yet, but guess who Jimmy's dating."

"I don't know."

"Sasha Fenimore!"

There was no one better at putting two and two together than Cal Everett. Except, maybe, Madison. "So, by your refusal to accept coincidences, you think that, somehow, Jimmy Rivers and the Fenimores are connected by parallel universes."

"And Rachel Espair and the man and the minivan on Berthoud Pass thirteen years ago!"

"You've got to be kidding!" her wary producer erupted. "How do you propose to make that leap?"

"I'm not sure, but that's why you have to let me stay on Jimmy Rivers."

Cal relented – it was pointless to argue. "Fine, but you let me know just as soon as you find that missing link. Hell, you probably know it already."

"Come on, Cal," Madison grinned mischievously, "would I ever hold out on you?"

They both knew the answer to that, and Madison ended the phone call determined to find the fortune teller…who she had "forgotten' to mention to her beleaguered producer.

6

"I have given you the authority to trample on serpents and scorpions and over all the power of the enemy. Nothing by any means ever shall hurt you." That's from Luke 10:19."

Isaac loved their nightly Bible readings before bed, but the 11-year old boy looked at his mother quizzically after she read the verse from Luke.

"But, Mama, why do bad things happen, then?"

"Faithlessness," came Leticia Carter's quick reply. "People just don't believe. Do you remember the story of Peter walking on water we read about a couple of weeks ago?"

"Yes. Jesus told Peter he could walk on water, so he stepped out of the boat and he was doing it."

"Then what happened?"

"There was a big gust of wind and Peter got nervous and he fell in."

"Why do you think people get nervous?"

"They think something bad might happen?"

"That's right. So, when the wind whipped up the waves, Peter switched his thinking from believing what Jesus told him and doing something that everyone thought was impossible to expecting something bad would happen because he couldn't swim. He doubted Jesus just for a second, and that's all it took for him to fall in the water.

"So you see, it's not Jesus' fault that we get hurt, it's ours. And, it's even harder for us, because Peter only doubted for a second, but we've been taught to doubt for over two thousand years. That's a 2,000-year blink, which means that we've had our eyes closed to the Truth for a very long time, so we just started to believe the Devil's lies because we couldn't see anything else, and that's why bad things happen.

"Then everyone – scientists, religious leaders, teachers – tell us that Jesus didn't really mean what He said, and we choose to believe them because our eyes and our minds are closed, and we accept that bad things are a normal part of life. And so they are. End of story."

"That's really sad, Mama."

"Yes, it is, baby." Then, Leticia continued, "And I'll tell you something else. You know the man who started the company I work for, Henry Ford, once said, "Whether you think you can or you can't, you're right." Do you understand what he meant?"

Isaac thought for a moment. "Whatever you think about will happen?"

"Right," his mother beamed. "So, as much as you can, you want to think about what you want to happen and not blink. We have to learn from Peter's mistake, or we will keep repeating it."

"Were you worried when I was a little late getting home tonight?" her son asked.

"Guilty as charged,"' Leticia admitted.

"Well, stop it!" Isaac demanded with a sparkle in his eye. "You don't want anything bad to happen to me, do you?"

"Of course, not, baby. It's just easier said than done because there's so much evil out there, and you're just a child."

Isaac's eyes narrowed. "OK, think about this. I was named after Abraham and Isaac, right? And you told me that Abraham totally trusted God when God told him to sacrifice Isaac who he loved so much. And Abraham was about to do it, but just before he stabbed Isaac, God sent one of his angels to tell him not to. You told me it was a test of faith. Abraham never blinked, and it worked out."

Leticia Carter shook her head in wonderment. "That's why Jesus also told us that to enter the kingdom of heaven, it must be as a child." She reflected, "The thing is, as you get older, you lose that youthful innocence and your mind starts to shut down in the graveyard of acceptance. You start to accept things the way they are instead of the way they should be because everyone tells you that you have no choice. We've all been battered down by the Devil's nonstop barrage of Doubt. It's 24/7.

"And, in the end, the wool has been pulled so completely over our eyes, we just choose to give up. We simply accept that the world is evil and there's nothing we can do about it. Especially when bad things keep happening. It's a vicious circle: Bad things happen, so we worry about them happening, which invites more bad things to happen, which makes us worry more, and so on and so on."

Isaac's mother was on a roll. "I never made this connection before, but you know who Thomas Edison was, right?"

"Yes, the man who invented the light bulb."

"That's right. Well, did you also know that it took him 2,000 tries to figure it out? And when someone asked him how it felt to have failed 2,000 times before he got it right, Edison said he didn't look at it as having failed 2,000 times. He thought of it as a 2,000-step process of discovery.

"So, maybe I'm in the 1,000th step of getting to where I need to be. Maybe it will take 10,000 steps. A Chinese philosopher said that the journey of a thousand miles starts with a single step. The key is to keep putting one foot in front of the other and to never give up until you get there.

"The sad thing is that a lot of people take those first steps, but somewhere along the way, they choose to give up. We have to remember that things that happen to us along the way are facts, not the Truth. When we make mistakes, they are guides to learn from that will lead us to the Truth. The Truth that Jesus told us about in Luke 10:19."

"Wow, Mama," Isaac marveled, as her words sunk in. "I like that!"

"Not bad for an old dog," Leticia hugged her son. "But, you were the one who opened my mind for those new tricks to come in. And I promise to try to stop worrying about you. It doesn't mean I don't care, it only means I trust God like Abraham did."

Just then, Leticia's phone rang. She looked at her watch – it was after 9:00. She checked the caller ID: it read, "Denver Post."

"Baby, it's the newspaper!" She took the call. "Hello?"

"Hello, is this Leticia Carter?"

"It is."

"Ms. Carter, this is Don Stottlemeyer. I'm the editor of the *Denver Post*. I hope I'm not calling too late."

"It's ok, I was just reading a bedtime story to my son."

"Is your son Abraham Isaac Carter?"

"Yes."

"You called earlier and left a message about a suspicious package your son sent to us in the mail today?"

"Yes, sir. He told me a man paid him $100 to put a large manila envelope in the mailbox this afternoon if he didn't come back by a certain time. My son noticed it was addressed to your newspaper."

"Ma'am, would it be possible to put your phone on "speaker' so I can talk to both of you?"

Leticia turned to Isaac. "Baby, the man from the newspaper wants to talk to you about the guy who paid you to mail the envelope this afternoon. Is that okay with you?"

"I guess so," Isaac replied, uncertainly. "He seemed like a very nice person, though."

Leticia switched her phone to speaker mode. "I'm sorry, what's your name, again?"

"Don Stottlemeyer from the *Denver Post*."

"Yes, Mr. Stottlemeyer, I got the part about the newspaper. Isaac and I both are on the phone."

"Hello, Isaac. I wanted to ask you a couple of questions about the man who paid you to send us that envelope today."

"OK."

"Were there a lot of stamps on the envelope?"

"Yes. Seven of them. I counted."

"Was it bulky, like there was something in it besides paper?"

"Well, it was heavier than most letters, but it didn't feel like there was anything else in there besides a lot of paper."

"And the name on the return address was Roland Thomas?"

"Yes, sir."

"Do you remember what he looked like?"

"He was tall and thin and wearing a New York Yankees baseball cap. Oh, and he had a dark brown backpack. That's what he was carrying the envelope in."

"Your Mom called earlier and said that he paid you $100 at about 9:00 in the morning to bring the envelope back to him at the mailbox at 5:30 this afternoon, and that he'd give you another $100. Is that right?"

"Yes, but he never came back. And he said if he didn't come back to put the envelope in the mailbox and keep the $100."

"Did he seem nervous to you?"

"Maybe a little, but it was more like he was in a hurry. He was very nice."

Don Stottlemeyer had to make another phone call right away. "Ms. Carter, Isaac, thank you very much for your time, and for letting us know about the envelope. Again, I'm sorry for calling so late, but I wanted to follow up as quickly as possible. It's probably nothing, but we have to take these things very seriously. Have a good rest of your night."

"Goodnight," they responded in unison, and Leticia hung up the phone.

"And goodnight to you, too," she said, kissing her son's forehead. "Now, we are going to undo all of Thomas Edison's hard work," and she turned off the light and closed Isaac's door.

Meanwhile, back at the *Denver Post*, Don Stottlemeyer quickly dialed thc phone number to Joak Industries.

* * *

"Oh my God," Sasha remarked as she and Jimmy left the movie theater hand-in-hand.

"I know, right?" Jimmy exclaimed. "The fortune teller was spot-on about the movie!"

"Not the movie, goofball. I'm starving. You know we completely missed dinner."

Jimmy's words suddenly registered. "Wait, what? When did you see the fortune teller?" Then it dawned on her. "It was when you went to the restroom, wasn't it?"

"Yes, but,..."

Sasha didn't let him finish. "First, Lisa Gallagher, and now the fortune teller. I can't leave you alone for a second," she said tongue-in-cheek. "Why didn't you tell me?"

"I couldn't – the movie was just starting. I'm telling you now, though."

They kept walking. Jimmy didn't say a word. They were almost to the car when Sasha stopped.

"Well?" she demanded petulantly.

"Well, what?"

"What did he say?"

"Oh, so you do want to know," he teased. And she jabbed her elbow into her boyfriend's ribs.

"Ow! Ok, I'll tell you! He said not to tell you anything until you gave me a kiss. On the lips!"

"Well, Mr. On The Lips, guess what? Now, I don't want to know," she said, feigning indifference. "You guys with your puny plans."

God, she's beautiful Jimmy thought to himself as he opened her door and she slid into his car.

He ran around to the other side and hopped into the driver's seat, but before he could turn on the ignition, Sasha leaned over to him, stopping at the last possible moment before their lips touched.

"That was so corny, Jimmy Rivers, but you're lucky – I'm a sucker for corn." And she planted a kiss on his mouth that was sweeter than any buttered corn he ever had tasted.

She pulled away. "So, what did the fortune teller have to say?"

Her kiss had short-circuited all of Jimmy's nerve impulses. He couldn't focus. "I can't remember," he said weakly, still marooned in the throes of passion.

"Jimmy!" Sasha practically shrieked.

Talk about a cold shower! But, it cleared the cobwebs and reconnected the circuitry.

"He said it was no accident that *Poseidon* was playing at this theater at this particular time, and that we should pay close attention.

"Oh my God!" she exclaimed, again, this time with a hint of sarcasm at the underwhelming reveal.

"What?"

"I'm even hungrier than I was a few minutes ago!"

"Right!" Jimmy didn't need any more reminders. He fired up his Camaro and turned left out of the parking lot. Even though they both had been warned that they were being followed, neither of them noticed the headlights that illuminated behind them as Jimmy made a right turn from East Amherst onto South Colorado Boulevard. The headlight menace remained at a discreet distance, just beyond notice, duplicating the blue Camaro's every move. Which is not to say that Jimmy made all the right moves.

"So, where shall we go?" he asked.

"Come on, Jimmy. You're the boy with a cute girl in your muscle car. And you're in the driver's seat!" Sasha wasn't going to let her boyfriend up for air, and she loved every minute of his discomfort.

Jimmy was so outnumbered, and he knew it. He looked at her fake pout, completely baffled at how gorgeous she was as she looked out the passenger window – to keep from laughing! – and at how well she played the game. It's just not fair, he thought to himself.

But he played along, as best he could, by turning on the radio, determined not to say another word until Sasha did. One would have thought that, freed of the Sasha distraction, he might have noticed the same headlights from the movie theater behind him. He didn't.

Ten minutes later, Sasha gasped, when she realized their culinary destination. "Denny's? That's your plan to get laid?"

Jimmy's cheeks reddened instantly. Not even the cover of darkness could save him from the embarrassment of having his innermost thoughts thrust into the open for all the world to see – meaning, of course, his girlfriend, because in the few short days that he could remember, she had become his whole world. And he was at a distinct disadvantage – not only because of his gender, but also because he had traveled through time, changed The Premise, and had no recollection of the ensuing six years. Had they done it? he wondered, his mind racing so fast that he forgot to respond to her question.

Her eyes twinkling, Sasha continued her assault. "You know, I got a text from Hannah this afternoon. The HR guy from Joak took her to Ellyngton's for lunch today. That's how you impress a girl!"

Jimmy stammered, "This is the only place I could think of that would be open this late, besides Burger King!"

Sasha recognized it was time to let up before she crossed that fine line between teasing and hurtful. "Silly boy," she giggled playfully. "It's so fun to pull your chain! You always take things so seriously. Believe me, there is no place I'd rather be than sitting with you late at night in your car in a Denny's parking lot."

Jimmy let out a huge sigh of relief. "That's not fair! You've known about our relationship since Day One, whenever that was. I only have the last four days to go by."

"You're right. I'm sorry," the words came out, dripping in insincerity. "And I suppose I haven't been entirely truthful. There is somewhere else I'd rather be right now."

"I knew it!" he chirped, triumphantly, proud for having salvaged one meaningless score at the end of the game.

"I'd rather be inside Denny's getting something to eat and hearing your thoughts about *Poseidon*," she insisted with a gleam in her eye.

Take away Jimmy's score. "Wow! You do have an evil streak in you," he declared.

The man in the dark suit watched the flirting teenagers traipse into the restaurant.

* * *

Ralph Petiole pulled up to Senator Fenimore's neatly trimmed, two-story brick house at 37 Skylark Lane at precisely 9:00 pm. There was a warm glow emanating from the windows of the Mediterranean style architecture wholly inconsistent with his appointed mission. His head ached from rehearsing over and over myriad explanations as to why the Senator had to agree to have his daughter killed, and each rehearsal made him more sick to his stomach.

His heart was pounding as he walked up the steps towards the arched, oversized front doors. He felt faint. It was real. No more practice. He almost turned around...but the consequences of not delivering Satan's directive meant an inevitable meet-and-be-killed introduction to The Cobra.

When Ralph had enlisted the financial support of the billionaire Joak brothers, without whose seemingly bottomless pockets they never would have been on the verge of taking over the White House, he knew there would be a price to pay, but he never could have imagined that the price would be The Cobra, the notorious, fugitive former leader of the ruthless Los Hermanos drug cartel! How could he have known that a significant part of the conservative industrialists' empire included an illicit marijuana plantation (for lack of a better word) in the Wet Mountains just east of Westcliffe, Colorado? Nobody had known! The Joaks had recognized they knew nothing about the distribution of an illegal drug, so they had paid an enormous bribe to the warden of the Mexican prison where The Cobra was incarcerated and, just like that, the former drug-lord-cum-assassin was a fugitive from justice and a part of the team.

Still, he berated himself for the choices he'd made that had gotten him into this almost untenable predicament, and it's likely he would have done so for several more minutes if the front door hadn't opened.

"Hello, Ralph!" greeted Alice Fenimore's cheery voice. "Bill said you'd be stopping by, and I happened to look out the window and saw your car." She was used to seeing her husband's campaign manager stressed out, but she couldn't remember ever seeing him as anxious as he was on her doorstep. "Is everything ok?"

Ralph tried unsuccessfully to regain his composure and he gave Alice a perfunctory hug. It was all so surreal. He was about to ask her husband's permission to have their daughter killed. "Yeah, it's fine. Just normal campaign stuff."

A hug from Ralph Petiole? Ralph Petiole never hugged anyone, Alice thought in his awkward embrace. Something was not right. "Well, come on in," she said, extricating herself from his arms. "Bill's in the study. Can I get you anything?"

"No, thank you, Alice. Wait, on second thought, I could use a glass of water."

"Are you sure you're alright? We saw the interview."

She hit a nerve. "That kid!" he practically exploded. "Nothing good is going to come of this, mark my words!"

"For heaven's sake, Ralph, you worry too much. He's just a boy getting his fifteen minutes of fame. You're the man with the plan."

"It's my job to worry," he sighed, "and, yes, for better or worse, I'm the man with the plan."

"Well, from the look of things, you might be taking your job a little too far. Come on, Bill's waiting."

Ralph followed Alice to the study. She knocked on the door before opening it, announcing, "Honey, Ralph's here."

"Come in."

As she opened the door, she whispered, "Take a few deep breaths and I'll be right back with your water."

The Senator didn't make it any easier. Standing up from his desk, he demanded, "Ralph, what is so urgent that couldn't be discussed over the phone? As you know, I've got a pretty important press conference to prepare for in the morning."

The two men sat down in the leather, high-backed chairs near the fireplace. Alice returned with the water, then dutifully shut the door behind her on the way out.

Ralph took a sip of water, wiped the sweat off his brow, then leaned forward conspiratorially. "Bill, this Jimmy Rivers thing is getting out of hand. It has to stop!"

"We have the press conference tomorrow morning with Cardinal Phelps." He paused. "What else can we do?" he asked meekly.

The Senator had given him the perfect segue. "That's why I'm here."

He took a deep breath and another sip of water. "First of all, let me say that this is coming straight from the top."

"I figured that...and I'm not liking the sound of it," he frowned.

"Well, he's not really liking the sound of Jimmy Rivers, either, to put it mildly."

Bill Fenimore's face blanched at the sudden realization of his campaign manager's late-night visit. He lowered his voice, but it still seethed through his clenched teeth: "Ralph, we're not going to kill Jimmy Rivers! Beside the fact that he's a good kid and my daughter's boyfriend, we can't be in the business of killing people, let alone a teenage boy! No way! No f - - king way!"

"Bill, calm down, you have to hear me out. We're not going to kill Jimmy. It would turn him into a martyr of sorts, and we'd never be free of his shadow. His death would be burned into the nation's consciousness going into Election Day...and for years to come."

"Well, that's a relief," the senator breathed easier, momentarily placated. "So, what does Satan have in mind?"

OK, here goes, Ralph thought. "It all boils down to the greater good. For instance, over 200,000 innocent people were killed in Hiroshima and Nagasaki when we dropped the atomic bombs on those cities, but that brought an almost immediate end to World War II – and the greater good was served."

He had the Senator's rapt attention. It was like writing a term paper in college – starting out with a general, global principle or parallel and narrowing it down to a powerful thesis: serving the greater good on a very personal basis.

"Now, let's factor down the global greater good into a local common denominator. We both agree that killing is wrong. But, what if the greater good is served? And, by that, I mean the protection of unborn babies. Someone has to stand up for their rights, and if it takes killing abortion doctors to do so, then so be it. I mean, the United States set the precedent for it in World War II, right?

"I see where you're going."

"No, you don't, Senator," Ralph sighed. "Not yet, anyway.

"Do you remember the story of Abraham and Isaac in the Old Testament? How God told Abraham to offer his beloved son, Isaac, as a sacrifice to Him?"

"Of course, I do."

"And how Abraham took Isaac to the altar and was about to plunge the sharp knife into his son's body when an angel of the Lord told him at the last minute that God didn't want him to do it, after all?"

"Yes, but where are you going with this? It's so random."

"Not really, Bill. You see, God was testing Abraham's faith. He told us always to keep God first in our lives – that in order to access His authority over all things, there never could be a higher priority."

"Understood," the Senator replied hesitantly.

Ralph had arrived at his moment of truth, and it totally unnerved him. He gulped down the rest of the water, loosened his tie, shifted his weight in his chair, looked the senator squarely in the eyes, then stared directly at the floor. He couldn't bear to see the pain and anger in his protégée's eyes as he spelled out Satan's diabolical plan.

"Well, as you know," he continued, "our leader demands the same loyalty from us as God did of Abraham and Isaac. He insists that the only way to silence Jimmy Rivers is to take Sasha out of the picture the same way Abraham had been instructed to take out Isaac."

Bill Fenimore exploded. "You want me to kill my own daughter?" he hissed, trying to keep his voice from being heard outside of his study.

Ralph put his index finger to his lips signaling to the Senator to lower his voice. "This conversation cannot leave this room. Alice must not know anything about it. She'd probably have to die, too, if she found out."

"This is outrageous, Ralph," the Senator fumed. "I'm not going to kill Sasha!"

"You don't have to, sir," Ralph was quick to interject. "Satan has arranged for The Cobra to do it. You simply have to be prepared so you can act humanly and presidentially when she is killed. How you react will make a lasting impression on voters when they go to the polls.

"And remember, it's for the greater good. Sometimes sacrifices have to be made to serve the greater good."

"Quit saying that!" the Senator protested. "The greater good. Always the greater good. What in the hell do I get out of it?"

"The White House," his campaign manager replied, evenly. "We...I mean you...get the White House, and a..."

Ralph never got to finish his sentence. "Get out!" Bill Fenimore bellowed. "Get out of my house. And stay away from me!"

The embattled campaign manager gave the Senator a few moments to cool down, then added in a very somber tone, "Sir, Satan is not going to take 'no' for an answer, I'm afraid."

"Ralph, please," the Senator pleaded in a defeated, hushed tone. "I do need you to leave. I need to be alone to figure this out. Just how did you expect me to react when you came into my house to tell me that I had to sign off on my daughter's murder?"

Ralph Petiole lowered his head. Was the greater good really worth it, in this case, he wondered? "I'm so sorry, Bill. I'll show myself out."

Making his way to his car, Ralph wanted nothing more than to dig a hole, climb in and pull it in after him. But, a sudden thought interrupted his self-loathing: the Senator hadn't said "no."

★ ★ ★

"You know what your problem is?" Henry Joak asked his older brother. "You've got to quit thinking of yourself as a modern-day Al Capone."

The billionaire brother industrialists were at Joak Industries' worldwide headquarters in Wichita awaiting Ralph Petiole's signal to go forward with the plot to kill Sasha Fenimore.

"Henry," Jasper protested, "he had it all until Prohibition ended."

"That's my point!"

"That can't be your point – it's my point!"

"Look," Henry explained for the umpteenth time. "Think of it like a game of chess. We're sacrificing some profit now, like Bobby Fischer might sacrifice a knight to gain superior position to win the game. It doesn't matter how many pieces we have on the board when the game ends – just that it is our king that still is standing at the end."

"You're talking about Satan."

"I'm talking about all of us! The legalization of pot will give us another tool with which to impair the ability of the electorate to make good choices. We do not survive in a world of good choices. Our domain is the realm of poor choices.

"That's why Jimmy Rivers has to be stopped. His ability to make good choices has not been compromised, and that's what has Satan worried. His Achilles heel always has been the Truth, which he says is hiding in plain sight right in front of God's children. The Truth is that God is pro-choice, that He is not a killer, that Moses' version of the flood was meant to convince the illiterate and uneducated Israelites to toe God's line because fear was the only thing they understood – not Love. The Truth is that Death is a mistake, the result of poor choices by Adam and Eve, and by the rest of us to choose to believe that we don't have a choice in the matter.

"We've made our choice – to throw in with Satan and to rule this world. Who even knows if there's an afterlife? A bird in the hand is worth two in the bush, right? But, we'll lose it all if we can't get him to blink!

"For heaven's sake, not even his mother's death caused him to blink. The demons say he has an accomplice – some sort of fortune teller – but it doesn't matter. He still has free will, and we have to set the table of Doubt in such a way that he chooses to sit down at it and blink. This fortune teller, or whoever he is, cannot choose for him. God wouldn't allow it. Not even God will choose for him. And that's our opening.

"The legalization of pot will impair the ability of the people around Jimmy – even those closest to him – to choose wisely, and they will be our pawns. And our pawns are waiting for the green light to kill Sasha Fenimore. Satan is convinced Jimmy will blink when she is killed, and legal pot will keep the rest of God's children under our thumb."

Jasper calmed down. "Alright, I get it. I guess I just needed someone to take the time to explain it to me, instead of just telling me what to do."

Henry threw up his hands. "Hallelujah, older brother! And when pot is legal, we won't have to rely on the drug lords' distribution network. Those guys scare me, especially The Cobra. If word ever got out that we were in bed with them before legalization, Jimmy Rivers would be the least of our worries."

The phone rang in Jasper's office. "There's our boy, Ralph, right on time."

But, it wasn't Ralph Petiole's voice Jasper heard when he picked up the phone.

"Jasper, this is Don Stottlemeyer at the *Denver Post*. We've got a problem...a huge problem!"

7

"Welcome to Denny's!" their server greeted Jimmy and Sasha cheerily. The name tag on her shirt said her name was Kelsey. "What can I get for you?"

"I'll have the cranberry apple chicken salad," Sasha ordered, "with the dressing on the side, please."

"And I'll have the All-American Slam with whole wheat toast," Jimmy added.

"How would you like your eggs?"

"Basted."

They handed their menus back to Kelsey, who lingered for an extra few seconds, staring at Jimmy. Her face lit up when she made the connection. "Hey, you're that kid from the video...Jimmy, isn't it?"

"Yeah," Jimmy smiled, sheepishly.

"I just want to tell you that what you said made so much sense," Kelsey gushed. "It felt totally right, like you took a splinter out of my soul!"

Uh-oh, here goes, Jimmy thought to himself.

"You know, I was raised Orthodox Christian and went to church and to Sunday School every Sunday with my parents. But, when I got older, I started to think about some of the things that were taught to me that didn't make sense. You know, when you're a kid, you just accept what adults tell you. Then they're in your mind and you don't even think about them when you get older...but I did. And that's when I stopped going to church."

Sasha squeezed Jimmy's hand under the table and gave him a playful wink.

Kelsey continued her testimony, unabashedly. "Now, don't get me wrong. I still believe in God and Jesus and everything, but I don't trust the priests. It felt like they were leading me the wrong way. I guess you could say I became…," she hesitated. "What's the word?"

"Disaffected?" Sasha offered.

"Yes, that's it, darlin'. Anyway, as I said," she carried on, looking at Jimmy, "it felt so good to get that splinter out...like my soul was healed!"

Jimmy didn't know what to say and just nodded.

"Thanks for sharing, Kelsey," Sasha chimed in. "It really means a lot!"

"Yes, it does," Jimmy agreed, having extricated his tongue from the cat's clutches.

"That's sweet of you both, but I'm sure you didn't come in here to listen to me blab away. I'll get your order in right away."

"It's ok," Jimmy reassured their suddenly flustered server, oblivious to the man in the dark suit who took a seat at the table across from theirs. "It's refreshing to hear your story."

Emboldened, Kelsey forgot about their order. "You know, it started when I got back home from college," she plowed ahead, "and I went to church with my parents, and when the priest invited the parishioners to come up for communion, he said only those who were baptized as Orthodox could receive the sacrament.

"I couldn't believe my ears. I'm like, I can't believe this educated, man of the cloth just said that! In church, especially! I'm sure he knew that Jesus offered His body and blood for the salvation of all people, not just those who belonged to the Orthodox 'club!'"

"I mean you know who Jesus hung out with – all the outcasts. And who cast them out? Certainly not God, because they still were His children. They were their fellow human beings who judged them. What gave them the right to judge, anyway. There was only one perfect human who was without sin, and He wanted everyone to receive His salvation."

Kelsey shook her long, auburn hair as if coming out of a trance.

"Omigosh, I did it again. I'm so sorry! I'll get this order in and have your food out to you as quick as I can!"

"Really, it's ok," Jimmy reassured her for a second time. "I really appreciate you sharing your thoughts. We're totally on the same page. Jesus said, "Do not judge, or you too will be judged. For in the same way you judge others, you will be judged, and with the measure you use, it will be measured to you.""

"That's it. That's it, exactly!" Kelsey beamed. "But you're here with your girlfriend or your sister..."

"Girlfriend!" Jimmy cut in, proudly, kissing Sasha on the cheek.

"Good for you! Good for both of you!" Kelsey exclaimed before scurrying to the next table to ask the man in the dark suit if he wanted some coffee before turning in their order.

"Wow, Jimmy," Sasha enthused. "Look how complete strangers open up to you. The Truth really did set her free. You're amazing!"

"Um, excuse me," Jimmy deferred. "If you look up 'amazing' in the dictionary, your picture is going to be next to it."

"That's not fair. I told you what a sucker I am for corny lines." This time, the kiss was on the lips, and there was nothing sisterly about it.

"Now, you were saying?" Sasha asked when their lips parted.

Jimmy was confused. "I was saying?"

"About the movie, silly. I swear, if your head wasn't attached to..."

"I got you," Jimmy stopped his girlfriend's good-natured ribbing. "*Poseidon*! OK, here's the thing. You know how God created Adam and Eve to live forever, right?"

"Right."

"Well, do you think He stopped doing that? That He changed His mind and decided to stop creating His children in His image?"

"I hadn't really thought about it, to be honest. Until a few days ago, I just accepted that Death was inevitable, that we were born to die."

"That just doesn't make sense, does it? What Parent who could do anything, and who loves His children so much, would create His children to die? Especially a Parent who knows everything – changing His mind would be an admission that He had made a mistake."

"You're right. It doesn't make sense, now that I think about it," Sasha agreed.

"Of course it doesn't!" Jimmy emphasized.

Sasha noticed that look in Jimmy's eyes that she'd seen before when he was about to go off – it was one of an almost otherworldly focus and passion.

"God still is creating us in His image," he continued, "and what's that image? To live forever as masters of our universe. On His authority.

"God is the Truth and God is Love, both of which are consistent and constant under all circumstances. That includes His children making the bad choice to turn away from Him. God knows the choices we're going to make, good and bad, and He allows us to make them without direct interference. And He still loves us no matter what.

"That's why Jesus told us the story of the prodigal son. The moment we turn away from our bad choices and turn back to God, He'll be rushing out to meet us and welcome us back into His kingdom with a great feast. Death is not inevitable, it's a mistake – the result of poor choices that Adam and Eve made, and poor choices that everyone has repeated since then to accept its inevitability even though it never was part of God's Master Plan."

"Master Plan?" Sasha questioned as Kelsey delivered the food to their table.

"Yes! The Master Plan is God creating His children to live forever as masters of their universe. And that universe was Eden. The Master Plan never changed. We did. We've always had to do our part, too, but we're dropping the ball. The Master Plan was a partnership – God's part is creating us in His image. Our part is to put God first in our lives and to have the faith of a mustard seed. Faith is the conduit through which we gain access to God's authority over all things, including Death."

Sasha digested Jimmy's every word – and every morsel of her

salad – as he spoke.

Her boyfriend was just getting started. It was like he was possessed. "But, we messed up the Master Plan big-time. So, God sent Jesus to save us. The thing that everyone overlooks is the fact that He tried to save us by teaching us the error of our ways and showing us the way back Home. Unfortunately, we didn't pay attention. When there was a storm in the sea that His disciples feared would capsize their boat, Jesus wondered aloud, "How long do I have to be with you," leaving unsaid, "before you grasp the Truth." He calmed the storm, which the disciples could have done themselves if they had remained faithful and had access to God's authority, instead of putting their fear first and losing their access.

"Jesus told his disciple Thomas that whoever discovered the true meaning of His words never would taste Death. And guess what? The sad thing is that Adam's and Eve's worst mistake was their second one – choosing not to turn back to God to say they were sorry and ask for forgiveness. They would have re-inherited Eden just as the prodigal son immediately was welcomed back into his father's fold when he repented. But we keep repeating Adam's and Eve's mistakes – we believe in God and Jesus, but we don't believe them. And we're not choosing to turn back to Them to ask for forgiveness. We just keep repeating our mistakes because we have chosen to accept that we have no choice.

"Nothing changes when nothing changes, so God came up with Plan B..."

"Jimmy!" Sasha cut in suddenly, loud enough to get his attention, but not so loud as to alert the other patrons.

"What is it?"

"You're scaring me! Look at yourself...you're floating!"

"What???" Then he noticed his weightlessness, only the table keeping him from rising to the ceiling like an untethered helium balloon.

Before he could say, "What's happening?" he plopped back down on his seat.

"OK, that was totally freaky," Sasha's voice shook.

"Whoa! You think you were freaked! What if you were the one floating?" came Jimmy's bewildered response.

Then Sasha remembered how their journey began. "It was just like in the dream," she whispered, "when you were with the fortune teller."

He thought back. "I don't remember the floating part. I must have been in some kind of trance. I just remember getting on the other side of that huge wall and meeting up with Don Quixote."

"Maybe that's when you crossed over into the parallel universe for the first time," Sasha suggested. "Maybe what just happened means there's an overlap. I just remember you being completely focused and freed of doubt. It's like Doubt was an anchor, holding you down. I just saw that look in your eyes again, tonight, as you started to talk about the Master Plan."

Jimmy was amazed. "Sasha, everything is so clear to me right now, but I have no idea where these thoughts are coming from. I mean, I heard myself talking about Thomas, but I'm not sure how I knew what he said. In fact, I can tell you exactly what he said, like I was reading his words from a sheet of paper. He said Jesus told him, "Whoever discovers the true interpretation of these sayings will never taste death. Those who seek should not stop seeking until they find. When they find, they will be disturbed, they will marvel, and they will reign over the all.'"

Jimmy looked sheepishly around the restaurant. "Do you think anyone else saw me floating?"

"I don't think so. There would have been quite a reaction."

Sasha was almost right. The man in the dark suit had seen everything, but he showed nothing.

"Anyway, you were saying?" Sasha reminded.

"OK, Plan B is what actually happened because we've been so blinded by the Devil's deceit. Jesus saved us by choosing to die, descending into Lucifer's lair, and destroying the gates of hell. So, we get back Home to God's kingdom by waiting around to die.

"As we talked about, that's wholly incongruous with a God who loves us so much to see us go through so much pain."

"I get it!" Sasha blurted out. "I see the connection! When the Poseidon capsized, the captain told the survivors that they should stay in the airtight ballroom and wait until the rescuers got there. He was like the priests telling us to wait for Jesus to save us. We've stopped seeking. We haven't found the Truth. And that's why we taste Death. Waiting means dying, and that's what happened to the people who believed the captain instead of Josh Lucas.

"Josh didn't believe the captain, like you don't believe the priests. He didn't want to wait. He knew there had to be a better way. He and the others sought, and they found. That's the Master Plan, as you call it. And they didn't taste death. They survived."

"That's it, exactly!" Jimmy raved. "I've never been more sure of anything!" This time he felt himself starting to levitate and caught himself, grabbing hold of the table.

"I'm going to have to get you a weighted belt like the astronauts wear," Sasha grinned. "You've definitely got the right stuff!"

"The right stuff," Jimmy repeated. "I see what you did there! That's what the fortune teller meant when he said it was not by accident that this particular movie was playing in this particular theater at this particular time. It was a clue, reinforcing that we're headed in the right direction."

"But why doesn't he come right out and tell you?"

"Because I have to seek it and find it myself. Just as Jesus told Thomas. It has to be an active discovery, I'm guessing, not a passive one. You have to experience it to believe it. Like Thomas putting his finger in Jesus' wounds."

Sasha barely heard what Jimmy was saying. A nagging thought had been tugging at her consciousness since Sunday, and it was back. This time, though, there was a spark that enabled her to put her finger on it.

"Jimmy," she announced abruptly in a low whisper. "You're the peaceful warrior!"

"What do you mean?"

"Have you heard of the book, "*The Way of the Peaceful Warrior*?""

"I haven't."

"I can't believe I didn't make the connection right away. It's about this gymnast who's headed for the Olympics and he has a terrible accident that almost kills him, and ruins his Olympic dreams. He's lost and confused, and he's having these nightmares about death.

"One night, he can't sleep, so he goes out for a walk, or a run, I can't remember. But, he stops at a gas station and meets this old man he recognizes from his dreams.

"Does this sound familiar? Your Mom's death, your dream, the man – the fortune teller – from the dream…"

Jimmy was intrigued. "Go on," he insisted, still holding himself down.

"He calls this man Socrates, and he watches in disbelief as Socrates seemingly flies to the roof of the gas station. He asks the old man how he did it, and if he could teach him how to do it.

"Socrates tells him that he is trapped in the illusions of his mind – the fortune teller's Grand Illusion! – and he sets about rearranging the gymnast's mind so that he lives entirely in the moment, freed of all distractions. He tells him that he must focus only on the present, and he will see the universe that has been hidden in plain sight for so long."

"The peaceful warrior," Jimmy mused. "I like that."

Sasha leaned over to her boyfriend, who still was savoring the thought of the peaceful warrior and still holding himself down. He was hoping for another kiss; instead, she said quietly, "I finally thought of it because I started paying attention to the present, your present," she effused. Then, her tone took a decided turn. "Don't look now, but I saw that man in the dark suit sitting across from us at lunch today at Subway. I think he might be following us."

Jimmy waited a few moments, then casually looked over his shoulder at the man. A chill went through his body and he immediately fell back into his seat – as Peter had fallen into the sea.

⋆ ⋆ ⋆

"Hi, Uncle John, it's Madison. I hope I'm not calling at a bad time." Which reminded her to check her watch, kind of a shoot-first-ask-questions-later mentality that defined Madison Munro when she was pursuing leads for a story. There was no bad time.

"No, no," her uncle replied, "it's always good to hear from you, no matter what time it is. I was just watching the planes in their landing patterns for SFO. Is everything OK?"

Madison chuckled. "I thought you might be. Yes, everything is fine – I wanted to follow up on our discussion about parallel universes. Did you see my special report on TV tonight?"

"Yes, I did. Jimmy's a remarkable young man."

"And do you remember that report I did thirteen years ago about that girl whose car was swept off Berthoud Pass in Colorado by an avalanche, and was rescued by an old man in a flying minivan?"

"How could I forget it?"

"Well, I believe Jimmy and Rachel – that was the girl's name who got swept off the Pass – are connected by some mysterious fortune teller who exists in a parallel universe.

"The last time we spoke, you were telling me about how you and your physics friends are starting to embrace the possibility, at least, that parallel universes exist."

"That's right."

Madison hesitated. "This might sound silly, but I need them to overlap. Is there such a thing?"

"Not in string theory, or in the many worlds theory," her uncle explained. "But, the many interacting worlds theory, as the name implies, suggests that parallel universes can interact and affect our own universe."

"Bingo!" Madison exclaimed. "That's the one I'm interested in! How does it work?"

"Well, it goes something like this. In the simplest terms, quantum theory allows for multiple versions of our universe to exist. In the many worlds interpretation, every choice will influence the creation of new universes. However, all the universes that are created stop interacting with the universe from which they initially branched off.

"That wasn't good enough for Howard Wiseman. He led a team of researchers at Griffith University in Australia that took the many worlds theory a step further, hypothesizing that the many worlds can and do interact from time to time on the quantum level.

"Are you familiar with *Star Trek*? That may have been a bit before your time."

"It was, but I love the reruns. Live long and prosper!" she grinned.

"Right. It is so often the case that science fiction takes what little is known and forges ahead into the unknown and waits for science to catch up with it. In this case, Wiseman and his team are saying the larger scale interactions you see in *Star Trek* could be possible under their theory, which means it theoretically could be possible accidentally to find yourself in another dimension at random. Well, not so much at random – it would depend on choices that are made."

"I'm not sure I understand," Madison stopped her uncle. "Accidentally? You mean people wouldn't have any control over which dimension they were in?"

"No, my dear. Quite the contrary. By definition, the dimensions are unlimited. Practically, though, they are limited to the degree that one's mind is open or closed. The more open the mind, the more dimensions – or universes, as you call them – there are. If a mind opens, then the dimensions expand. Are people aware of it? Not necessarily. In fact, they probably wouldn't notice them unless they were paying attention. That's why I said "accidentally.""

"Socrates!" Madison shrieked into her phone.

"I'm afraid not," Uncle John said. "These theories are very recent."

"No, not the Greek philosopher. The wise old man from the book, "*The Way of the Peaceful Warrior*." Have you heard of it?"

"I haven't," he frowned.

"It's OK, I'll tell you about it later. Actually, I'll send you the book. You'll love it. But please keep going...this is fascinating stuff!"

"Well, an unlimited number of quantum states of a system are believed to exist simultaneously in all possible configurations until an observer forces it to adopt one state. Most of the time, the observer is not aware that the choices he or she makes, either subconsciously or consciously, force the state.

"For example, as I mentioned, Wiseman and his researchers are in Australia. Australia is home to the densest, hardest wood known to man, Australian buloke. In labeling it the hardest wood in the world, mankind has chosen – ordered, actually – that specific dimension, and to the extent that the rest of us choose to accept that state, then our collective minds have shut out any other possible realm, and the dimension is locked down. And the key is thrown away."

"I get it!" Madison chimed in. "The key to altering the state is an open mind."

"Precisely! If one's mind were open to the possibility of putting one's hand through the buloke – and I'm not talking about breaking it with a karate chop – then she would be choosing that particular dimension and subconsciously putting herself into that universe in which it would be possible to put her hand through the buloke, as if she were a ghost, while she's still in this universe. There's the overlap. And to the extent that she is not aware of the dimension she has ordered, it's accidental."

Madison's heart was racing. The fortune teller! "So, there could be flying cars in this universe if a person's mind was open enough to choose the universe in which flying cars are possible, and that universe of flying cars could overlap with the universe we're in!"

"According to the theory, yes. I should add, though, it's only a theory. Nothing has been proven…yet. For me, though it's a theory that is most consistent with the Word of God. God created us in His image to be in control of our universe, and He gave us free will. Jesus told us that if we have the faith of a mustard seed, nothing would be impossible for us, including telling a mountain to pick itself up and throw itself into the sea.

"So, we get to choose our universe, and by the choices we make, we force our universe. We are free to choose that universe in which we can order a mountain to throw itself into the sea, but we choose, instead not to believe it, and therefore order up the universe in which it is not possible. That's the ultimate problem – poor choices. We're choosing very badly a universe that is filled with limits. Even worse, we're choosing to believe that we don't have a choice. So our minds are locked down into universes in which limits exist, and we are locked out of universes in which limits do not exist."

"But if we change our choices, we can change our universes!" Madison exulted.

"That's right," her uncle affirmed.

"Thank you so much, Uncle John! You've helped me more than you could imagine. I think I've found the missing link! I have to go right now, but I promise I'll fly out for a visit very soon, and maybe without a plane," she boasted.

"Call or visit any time, Madison. I've thoroughly enjoyed our chat. Hope to see you soon. Goodbye."

Madison hung up and started to dial Cal Everett's number, but her producer beat her to the punch, and her phone began to ring.

"Cal, you're not going to believe…"

He stopped her mid-sentence. "Madison, listen to me. Why hasn't Jimmy heard from the fundamentalist Christians, the abortion doctor killers...anyone from the extreme right? I'm looking through all these comments about his video and your interview tonight, and there's nothing. It's so glaringly conspicuous. The veil of anonymity never fails to produce some of the most vile, hateful, and heinous comments, but there's nothing, not a single one. And you know how fanatical these trolls are."

Cal took the wind right out of his star reporter's sails.

"That is odd. Really odd! I never look at those comments for that exact reason."

"I know, right? Something's up. I'm starting to get a sick feeling about Jimmy. This is getting stranger by the minute, and my instincts are screaming!"

"You see what I mean? And, you have no idea how strange, Cal! Or fantastic! I just spoke with my Uncle John."

* * *

"He was going back and forth, sir, but I don't think he put his finger on it. The girl, though, said she thought Doubt was weighing him down like an anchor, and freed of Doubt, he was untethered to your reality," the man in the dark suit recalled into his cell phone as he followed Jimmy's car out of the Denny's parking lot.

"Damn, damn, damn, damn, damn!" Satan hollered. "How have things gone so far south so quickly? I mean, who is this Jimmy Rivers, really? And the Senator's daughter?"

"I don't know..." The man in the dark suit hesitated. "You don't suppose this could be Him, do you? The Second Coming?"

"No, He never gave Doubt the breath of life. He may have been close in Gethsemane, but He never blinked, and it only made Him stronger, if you can imagine that.

"You said this Jimmy Rivers is going in and out, meaning he's still vulnerable. What else did he say?"

"They talked about a dream and parallel universes. He definitely figured out the *Poseidon* clue, telling the girl that God's Master Plan did not include waiting around to die for Jesus to save them.

"Oh, yes, and he mentioned how Thomas said Jesus told him that whoever found the true meaning of His words never would taste Death."

"How did that happen? Who told him about Thomas?" Satan bellowed, his frustration boiling over. "I did everything I could to discredit Thomas. But his followers hid the gospel before I could destroy it...and they hid it very well, not only from me, but also from everyone else. It would have been OK if nobody had found those clay pots, but those damn Egyptian peasants looking for that nitrate rock for their fertilizer just happen to stumble on them after sixteen hundred years! I mean, it doesn't get more random than that. And the parchment was preserved perfectly! How does that happen, especially in my universe?"

"It was like they were meant to find those pots with the gospel in it. Again, maybe the time is coming, and God knew the choices they would make."

"Maybe, but I planned for that, too. The church was supposed to suppress the gospel, and to create Doubt as to its authenticity and to its veracity. It failed miserably."

"Sir, Jimmy said he couldn't remember being told about Thomas, and when you stop to think about a five-year old boy questioning church dogma, it makes you wonder if he's not like the apostles speaking in tongues they never had known. Could it possibly be the Holy Spirit talking through Him?"

"I don't know," Satan groaned. "What I do know is that he's got most of the pieces to the puzzle, but he hasn't put them together... yet!"

"And you still don't want me to take him out? I could have done it so many times already."

"Absolutely not!" the Devil shouted. "As I've said from the beginning, I will not turn him into a martyr!"

"We can make it look like an accident."

Satan was adamant. "You don't understand these vultures in the press. There are no coincidences, only conspiracies, and they'll always turn over every stone in their determination to prove them. That's the last thing in the world we want to happen. We can't give any more publicity than we have now encouraging His children to examine the beliefs we've tricked them into choosing blindly to accept.

"I've gotten the word out to all the priests, especially the fundamentalists in the Bible belt, in no uncertain terms. Jimmy Rivers is off limits. No death threats. No social media. No tweets. No responses to his video or to his interview or to anything else! No comments at all. He is untouchable. I don't want what is about to happen to be connected back to me or to any of us in any way. Understood?"

"Loudly and clearly. They're pulling up in front of the Senator's house right now. What do you want me to do?"

"Drive on by. He's just going home. But continue your surveillance. I want you to make sure that no one goes rogue on me. I don't want a single hair on his head to be ruffled before we take out the Senator's daughter!"

"And when will that be?" the man in the dark suit inquired.

"Just as soon as the Senator gives us the green light. He has to be on board, or this never will work."

8

Cooper Fenimore checked his cell phone for the tenth time in the last thirty minutes. 10:57. The 21-year old son of Senator and Alice Fenimore and senior at the University of Colorado at Boulder was trying to work on his senior thesis, but he couldn't focus. He hadn't heard from his roommate and partner since 7:00 that morning when they'd said goodbye to each other.

That was strange enough since they typically talked or texted six or seven times a day, but what made it even more worrisome was that his partner had told him if he hadn't heard from him by 10:00 that night to call the police.

He recalled their morning conversation verbatim.

"The police?" Cooper had repeated, taken aback. "Are you serious? Why can't you just tell me what you're working on?"

"I'm as serious as a heart attack, Cooper. And I can't tell you because then I'd have to kill you," he'd joked, trying to ease the tension in the room.

"Do you see me laughing? No, because you're not funny. What could be so important and dangerous?"

"An idea whose time has come?" his partner queried, trying to keep a straight face.

"Oh my God," Cooper complained, "Can you try to be serious for just a few seconds and acknowledge that your partner is worried about you?"

"I'm sorry, Cooper," his roommate replied, properly chastened. Truth be told, though, his attempt at humor to defuse the concern had been as much for him as it was for Cooper. He came clean. "I'm doing an investigative report on some very high profile, dangerous people. They could come after me, which means they could come after you – and the less you know, the better off you'll be."

"But, my Dad's running for President. I can get us protection. Besides, whoever you're talking about wouldn't want to open such a high profile can of worms, anyway."

"Don't be so sure. These are very desperate people joining forces with very bad people. It's a lethal mix, and they're so far under the radar that exposing them would be an incredible coup, maybe just the break I need to launch my career."

"OK, now you're really scaring me!"

"Don't worry, everything is written down and will be published if anything happens to me. And they know it."

"That's not the point. That's like saying if you get hit by a car and killed while crossing the street in a crosswalk, the driver will get a traffic ticket. You're still dead."

That's when Roland had told Cooper to call the police if he hadn't heard from him by 10:00 that night.

Cooper checked the time again. 11:07. And he dialed 911.

"Denver Police Department, the operator answered. "What's your emergency?"

"I want to report a missing person."

"What's the person's name?"

"Roland Thomas."

* * *

"I'm worried for them," the woman's voice said, as they watched the teenagers kiss in the blue Camaro.

"It's out of our hands," the male voice responded. "Our Father already has given them free will and access to His authority over all things. The challenge of Life, is the challenge of Choice – which universe to choose – and the choice is theirs alone."

"But, did Jimmy's mom have a choice? We wouldn't have gotten to this point if she hadn't been killed. Was she sacrificed to jump-start his journey?"

"The same can be said of Judas Iscariot. You have to remember that our Father is not a killer. For Jimmy's Mom and for Judas – and for all of His children, for that matter – He knows what choices they're going to make, but He doesn't interfere with them, even when they go against His will.

"In Celeste Rivers' case, He knew she would be killed by the gunman when she took Jimmy to the shopping mall.

"He sent the messenger to her years before that ill-fated trip to the mall, and he told her that there would come a time when she needed to tell her son, "This is not the end."

"She was confused. She asked how she would know when to deliver the message. The only thing he could say to her was that she would know. And then he left.

"It bothered her for weeks, but she eventually forgot about it... until she took the bullet meant for Jimmy and shielded him with her body. Our Father knew she would know when to deliver the message, which she did in her dying breath.

"And He knew the choices Jimmy would make, and that's how we got here."

"Did Satan know about Jimmy?

"That would imply the fallen angel has some authority. He doesn't. He was stripped of all his authority, all his power, when he rose up against our Father and Michael vanquished him and kicked him out of heaven into the darkness of the underworld."

"But the man in the dark suit?"

"Reactive, not proactive. And the antichrist. And Cardinal Phelps. And Father Simon. And the religious right. And the Partnership of the Right. And Faithful Horizon. And the Joak brothers. And The Cobra. And the True Believers, a name that couldn't be further from the Truth. And anyone who has been brainwashed and tricked into thinking that they have no choice but the universe away from God.

"The only thing Lucifer, or Satan, can do is slither into the Garden and sow his seeds of Doubt. Our Father's children are bombarded by that Doubt 24/7 – every second of every minute of every hour of every day of every week of every month of every year until they are worn down and finally choose to sit at the table Lucifer has set for them by accepting that they have no choice but to wait to be saved in the Poseidon's ballroom.

"Jimmy's different. Did you see his weightlessness in the restaurant when he was freed of the burden of Doubt? It was the same weightlessness Peter experienced when he was walking on water. They both chose God's universe, where there are no limits whatsoever."

"And, yet, Peter fell into the sea."

"Which matters only to the extent that Jimmy might be tricked into choosing Doubt over Belief, too. On the other hand, Peter's fall could be a lesson for Jimmy, as it should be for all of God's children, and he could choose to learn from Peter's mistake and not repeat it. Remember, Lucifer will be sending gusts of wind – blowing in the ears of God's children and trying to tempt them to choose poorly – for as long as they're in his realm.

"Again, this is the challenge of life – to choose wisely not to succumb to Lucifer's constant temptation. It is imperative for God's children not to blink – or, if they do – to choose to turn back to our Father, admitting they made a mistake. As Jesus has assured them, they will re-inherit the Paradise that His Father provided for them in His universe.

"Remember, Jesus promised them, 'I have given you the authority to trample over serpents and scorpions and over all the power of the enemy. Nothing by any means ever shall hurt you.'"

"And that's why it's so important for God's children never to choose any of Lucifer's temptations that would impair their ability to make good choices! As long as Jimmy chooses wisely the Eden that our Father provided for all His children, and avoids the poor choices of Lucifer's universe, East of Eden, nothing can harm him in any universe."

"Will he?"

"Only our Father knows. We will find out in short order, I'm sure of it."

⋆ ⋆ ⋆

"Daddy!" Sasha exclaimed, surprised to see the Senator sitting on the couch in the family room when she opened the door and turned on the hall light. "Were you waiting up for me?"

"Well, it is a school night, and it is getting late, and...oh, heck," he sighed, "is it a crime for a father to wait up for his daughter to say "hi?""

Sasha sat down on the couch next to her father and kissed his cheek. "A crime?" she mocked. "I think it's sweet!"

He put his arm around his daughter and held her close. "You know, running for President is a 48-hour a day job – and then you throw in your responsibilities as a United States Senator, and before you know it, you've become a stranger to your own family, to the people who matter most in your life.

"And then you realize that you can't remember the last time you've spoken to your daughter, and suddenly, you're aware of the huge hole in your heart, and you sit on the couch in the dark counting the seconds "til she walks through the front door."

Sasha cuddled up to her dad. "I'm not going to lie, Daddy. I've missed you," she admitted.

"I'm sorry, Sweetheart. There has to be balance. We can't get these last several months back, but we can do something about the future."

"I'm not so sure about that," Sasha smiled.

That caught the Senator off-guard. "About what? The future?" he asked, anxiously.

"No, about not being able to get time back."

"I don't understand."

His daughter giggled. "I'm just kidding, Daddy!" But, not really, she thought to herself.

"I know I'm a little late to the party, but how's your senior year going?"

"Daddy," Sasha groaned, "I'm just a junior."

"Ha! Gotcha back!" he gloated, triumphantly.

"At least I don't have food on my shirt," Sasha shot back, pointing to an area around his chest. Bill Fenimore looked down, and Sasha quickly flicked her father's nose. "Had enough?" she needled. "You might as well give up, Senator!"

He looked at his daughter's smiling face. "As Roberto Duran said to Sugar Ray Leonard in the eighth round of their second fight, 'No mas!'"

"Whoever they are," Sasha razzed, "but I get that you're throwing in the towel. You're a wise man, Bill Fenimore! The United States would be lucky to have you as their next President!"

Ever the politician, Senator Fenimore asked, "So, I can count on your vote?"

"Omigod, I'm only 16!"

Genuinely flustered, Bill Fenimore tried to save himself by changing the subject. "So, were you with Jimmy tonight?"

"Yes."

"Did you see his interview?"

"See it? I was there!"

"So you saw Madison?"

"I did. I really like her."

"I do, too. She's a driven, but fair, journalist. I miss her. ABC took her off the campaign trail, I guess so she could dig into Jimmy's story. Apparently, now I'm number two in ABC's eyes."

"You're still number one with me, Daddy!" his daughter cooed.

"I'm not so sure about that, but thanks for saying so. Anyway, what did you think about the interview?"

"I thought he was brilliant!" Sasha gushed. Then, a dark thought crossed her mind. She sat up straight. "Wait a minute, is this all about Jimmy? Because if it is..."

"Sasha, stop. Can't you at least give me credit for getting his name right?" he winked.

"I could, but his name has been in the news a lot lately, and a lot of it is tied to you."

"But not as your boyfriend, so I think I deserve some credit."

No response from his daughter.

"You're a tough one, Sasha Fenimore!"

"I learned from the best," she grinned, resuming her cuddle.

"Anyway, how is he?"

"He's wonderful. Incredible. Amazing! There's so much more to him than meets the eye."

"Clearly," her father nodded. "How's he handling all this attention?"

"He hates it as much as you love it."

Bill Fenimore chuckled. "What's not to like about it? A total lack of privacy, your every move examined under a microscope, the extreme vetting, the Internet trolls, the press...the goddamn press always nipping at your feet."

Sasha hugged her father. "It's pretty bad, isn't it?"

"You have no idea," he winced. "You are no longer the king of the chessboard, you're just a pawn. You can be sacrificed at any time."

"And, now, Jimmy."

"Yes, and, now, Jimmy."

"Daddy, have you listened to what he's saying? I know you've heard it, but have you actually listened?"

"Honey, he's trashing organized religion, the traditions that have been in place for almost 2,000 years."

"Right, but what if the traditions are wrong? What if we're being led the wrong way?"

"You're talking about some of the most devout and learned religious figures throughout time. I mean, he's even questioning Moses, for God's sake, saying the Great Flood never happened."

"And what I'm saying is that you're hearing his words but not listening to what he's saying. All he said was that God is not a killer, and that Moses was trying to reach an illiterate, uneducated group of people who understood only one thing – fear.

"Maybe Noah was chosen because God knew he would believe Him. Noah tried to warn everyone, but they chose not to believe him. It's just like Adam and Eve. God didn't kill them. He warned them about the forbidden fruit, but they chose to doubt Him, and to believe the serpent. Basically, they chose to die.

"So, maybe there was a Great Flood and God warned His children about it – all Jimmy is saying is that God is not a killer. Their choice not to believe killed them. Only Noah chose to believe Him, and only Noah and his family survived. It's very consistent with the Word of God – when you choose God's side of the fence, there is Life. If you choose the side of the fence away from God, there is Death."

Sasha was on a roll. She continued, "So, how does Moses convince the Israelites to follow him to God's side of the fence? He speaks the only language they understand, and he chooses to tell the story with God as a kind of boogeyman who will strike anyone down who steps out of His line. The Israelites bought into it because they understood fear. So, they didn't love God as He loves us, they feared Him."

The Senator shook his head and turned very serious. "Whoa, he's really gotten to you. Now, I want you to listen to me. Not just hear my words, but listen to them. Jimmy's a very dangerous young man, and I would think long and hard about your relationship with him."

Sasha sat up straight on the couch. "And if I were you, I would think very long and hard about the people you surround yourself with! Ralph Petiole, Amon Smith, Pat Bateman, Annabelle Garton. Ugh. I really can't stand Ralph. I bet he's the one who's pulling your strings, moving you like the pawn you mentioned, and telling you to tell me that Jimmy's not good for me, that he's so dangerous.

"Well, guess what...the religious leaders of the day called Jesus a very dangerous person, too!"

"You can't be comparing Jimmy to Jesus!" the Senator raised his voice.

"No, I'm not. I'm just saying that Caiaphas and all those learned religious leaders you brought up, were human, first, then supposedly men of God. As human beings, they were fallible and given to distraction by personal agendas that are very far apart from the Word of God.

"Look at Galileo! Those learned men of God forced him to recant his studies that proved the earth was not the center of the universe, that it was the earth that revolved around the sun. They imprisoned him for ten years for having the guts to challenge them, and ultimately they killed him. Why? Because he challenged what the church taught! And he was right! And what about the Inquisition?"

"Sasha, stop. I'm not looking to get into a religious debate with you, something that neither of us are qualified for. You're right. Human beings are not perfect. We make mistakes. Maybe Jimmy's making a mistake. Maybe he's not. As a father, I just don't want you to get hurt."

"So, you know about the guy following us. Is that one of Ralph's thugs?" She heard the words coming out of her mouth, but she couldn't stop them, and she knew she'd regret it.

"There's someone following you?" her father practically exploded. "OK, this has gone far enough! I want you to stop seeing Jimmy for a while until this can be sorted out."

Sasha kissed her father on the cheek. "I understand where that's coming from, but that's just not going to happen. I'm tired and I'm going to bed."

"Sasha!" the Senator called out to his daughter as she climbed the stairs to her bedroom.

"Good-night, Daddy. I love you."

* * *

On his way home from dropping Sasha off at her house, Jimmy kept checking his rear-view mirror. He almost crashed his car when a voice next to him said, "He's not following you. He knows where you're going."

The fortune teller!

Composing himself somewhat, Jimmy's voice shook, "Everyone kept telling me that 'they' were following me and I guess it didn't really register. But, when Sasha noticed the man in the dark suit at the restaurant tonight, it became real, and all of a sudden, I'm scared."

"Jimmy, the person who does not fear death is naïve and missing out on the most powerful impulse of the spirit: survival. It is the dance with Death that elevates. You've heard, 'that which doesn't kill you makes you stronger?'" That's because facing Death forces you to make a choice: to live or to die. And when you choose Life, you're choosing to elevate to God's side of the wall, God's universe where Death does not exist.

"The young man who had a car fall on his face and was facing Death, quite literally, had to make a choice. His choice to live meant he simultaneously chose to reject the belief he blindly had chosen to accept that he couldn't lift a car. At that moment, he was the prodigal son who, in choosing Life, chose God's universe where everything is possible, and he freed himself from the Doubt that prevented him from lifting cars. Had he not been faced with Death, he never would have been forced to choose to change his mind, and he would not have been able to lift that car."

The fortune teller let his words sink in for a few moments, then carried on. "Look Peter didn't know how to swim. How do you think he felt initially when Jesus told him to step out of the safety of the boat and to come to Him by walking on the water that scared him so much? It is the choice to overcome fear, or Doubt, that makes you move faster than you thought possible, to fight longer than you thought possible, and enables you to re-enter the Eden universe where everything is possible.

"The choice to overcome fear, especially when facing Death, forces you to focus all of your energy – physical, mental, emotional, and spiritual – on a single focal point that is heaven on earth, if you will. It is how Peter walked on water, how a frantic mother can lift a burning truck off her child, how you traveled through time to rescue your mother from the universe East of Eden and the underworld prison called "Hell," and how a certain fortune teller lengthens his telomeres and increases his telomerase."

Jimmy was totally transfixed by the fortune teller's words. He was in the driver's seat, and realized it was an allegory for his life.

And the fortune teller continued to expand his owner's manual.

"As I've said, the challenge of Life all of God's children face is the challenge of Choice – the choice to stay focused on Eden and to choose to reject the Devil's temptation to shift their focus to the universe East of Eden. Think of the magnifying glass. When you hold it in such a way that it focuses all the energy of the sun into a single focal point on a sheet of paper, the paper soon starts to smolder, then catches fire. That is your passionflame, your Eden – and it fires you in the direction of limitless living. However, if you shift your hand, even by a millimeter, the focus is lost. There is no fire, and you fall back into the East of Eden universe, the only one everyone knows and accepts because of poor choices and a focus that has shifted away from God almost since the beginning of Time.

"So, it's OK to fear, as long as the choice is to overcome Fear. Because it forces you to shift your focus onto Eden, and it ignites your journey back Home to the universe that God created for all His children. That, truly, is the transformative power of God's Love – transforming Fear into the passionflame that fires you back to the universe of freedom from all limits. It's only a choice away!"

"But what about Sasha?" Jimmy fretted.

"Do not worry about that girl. Her mind has been opened to receive what has been promised. She is on her own path to discovery. Until then, by choosing to overcome your fear, you will be as the Roman soldier who asked Jesus to heal his servant who was dying back at the soldier's home. The soldier believed with all of his heart, mind, and soul that his servant could be healed through Jesus. The Son was amazed at the soldier's great faith, and He told him to go home – that his faith had healed his servant. And his servant had been healed at that very instant. Jesus didn't take credit for the healing. He told the soldier that his faith had done the healing. And it is your faith that has 'healed' Sasha.

"I'm telling you that the same partnership between God and His children into which He entered from the very beginning still is intact. Our part is to choose to believe Him. I can't tell you too many times – our faith is the conduit through which He gives us access to

His authority over all things."

Checking for traffic, Jimmy looked left to turn onto White Rabbit Lane, and then looked to his right. There were no cars coming, but he also saw that the fortune teller had vanished as abruptly as he had appeared. "I wish he'd stop doing that," he thought to himself. There was so much more he wanted to say. It would have to keep for another time...he was sure he hadn't seen the last of his enigmatic guide.

His parents greeted him with thunderous applause when he walked through the door. Jimmy raised both arms in victorious acknowledgment.

"I guess you saw the interview!"

"Jimmy," his mom raved, giving her son a big hug, "we're so proud of you!"

George followed with a hearty high-five. "I wonder if Cardinal Phelps will be paying us another visit, telling us how naïve we are and how we should read the teachings of the church fathers."

"And how he'll be praying for our blasphemous souls," Celeste was quick to add.

Still trying to wrap his mind around the fortune teller's words, Jimmy gave the outward appearance of extreme fatigue.

"You must be exhausted," his mother noticed. "Why don't we all get a good night's sleep, and you can tell us all about it in the morning."

"Thanks, Mom. I love you guys!" And the three of them embraced in a warm group hug.

Celeste retreated to the kitchen to finish her tidying, and Jimmy started up the stairs to get ready for bed. He was almost at the top of the stairs when his father called out to him.

"Oh, and Jimmy?"

"Yes?" his son turned around.

"I've been doing a lot of thinking about our conversation, yesterday, about traveling back through time and bringing your mother back to life."

"And?"

"I think that it would have to be possible. I can't imagine it happening – I still think it was some sort of nightmare you had – but after hearing you tonight on TV and after what you said about Noah when you were so young, your defiance reminds me of another defiant one who challenged the authorities, and He said nothing would be impossible for anyone who believed and didn't doubt. I'll be honest, I'm not there, yet, but you've definitely opened my mind to consider all possibilities."

Jimmy ran down the stairs and gave his father a heartfelt hug. "Thanks Dad. You don't know how much that means to me! And 'yet' is a very good place to be!"

* * *

It's a funny thing about adrenaline – it will keep you going for hours and hours in the fast lane, but when it runs out, there's no gradual downshifting to slower speeds, to move over to the right lanes to get off the interstate, to find a hotel, to get a bite to eat, to take a shower, and to go to bed. No. When the adrenaline leaves your body, you hit a brick wall, and you're stranded with no place to go.

That's where Jimmy was, barely able to crawl into bed before falling asleep. It had been the longest of days and his eyes were about to close for the last time that night when his phone vibrated. He ignored it and the vibrating stopped. But, when it started again almost as soon as it had stopped, he raised his heavy eyelids just enough to see the caller ID – and he got a fresh shot of adrenaline.

"Hi Sasha!" he managed through his grogginess. "Sorry I missed your first call. I was doing my push-ups."

She wasn't in a joking mood and didn't take the bait. "Jimmy, Cooper just called. He's very upset. Roland is missing."

"Roland?"

"Cut it out, Jimmy," she chided. "This isn't funny."

Her cold slap in the face cleared away the cobwebs. "Sasha, I wasn't trying to be funny. Who is Roland?"

He could sense the frustration in his girlfriend's voice. "Jimmy!

What's the matter with you? Roland is Cooper's partner. Wake up!" she said adamantly.

"Sasha, I'm wide awake now. I don't know anyone named Roland."

"Yes, you do! Cooper and Roland and you and I hang out together when we go to Boulder. You met him just a couple of weeks after we started seeing each other. Don't you remember...?"

Sasha caught herself. "Oh, Jimmy, I'm sorry," she apologized, "that was during the missing six years."

"That's OK. I'm glad I'm not losing my mind. That missing time has to be just as frustrating for you as it is for me."

"I'm so sorry," she apologized, again. "I feel badly for my brother, and I'm worried about Roland. Cooper said he was doing some secret investigation for a story that potentially was very dangerous."

She paused. "And I'm also sad that you don't remember meeting them. You were so sweet to them. I wish you could remember."

"Why? What did I do?"

"My Dad was a total ass when Cooper came out, but what would you expect when he's surrounded by all that extreme, right-wing fundamentalism?

"Anyway, the first time we hung out together, you made a point of telling them that they wouldn't go straight to hell, as my Dad said they would, that homosexuality is not identified as a sin in the Bible no matter what anyone says, and that even if it was, there were lots of sins that every heterosexual routinely commits on a daily basis that similarly would condemn them. You said, 'So even if homosexuality was sinful behavior per the Bible, you'd have the sinner condemning the sinner.'"

Jimmy listened intently as Sasha continued.

"Then you reminded them of Jesus stepping in front of the men who were determined to stone the prostitute to death. He said, 'Let he who is without sin cast the first stone.' And, of course, the prostitute was spared.

"You asked them if they believed in Jesus, and they said, 'yes,' and you told them that Jesus said whoever believed in Him would be saved, and that He didn't list a single exception. Then, you told them about the two criminals who were crucified with Him, and how the one criminal chastised the other one when he had derided the Son of God for not saving them all. The other one stuck up for Jesus and said they deserved to be there, but Jesus, the Son of God, had done nothing wrong. And Jesus told his defender that he would be with Him in Paradise that day.

"I'll never forget that!" she beamed.

Jimmy was incredulous. "I said all that?"

Sasha chuckled, "After what's happened in the past four days, nothing should surprise you! Anyhow, that's why the four of us hung out together so much. You treated them with the same respectful humanity that you would like others to treat you. You followed the Golden Rule'

"I wish I could remember," Jimmy lamented. "So, did Cooper call the police?"

"Yes, but he couldn't tell them much. Roland said he didn't want to involve Cooper because he didn't want to put him in a dangerous spot. Think *Marathon Man*. But, he said he had an insurance policy that would keep him safe. Some insurance policy that turned out to be!"

"Hmmm," Jimmy thought. "We'll see. We don't know for sure that anything bad has happened to him. But, it probably was some incriminating information that would be made public if anything did happen to him. He would have had it sent to a media outlet, maybe the *Denver Post*."

"Omigosh, my Mom's friend, Sylvia, works in the mailroom at the *Post*. I'll talk to her first thing in the morning. Jimmy, you're magic!" Sasha admired. "I love you."

"I love you, too. Sweet dreams."

Part Six

I

Ralph Petiole's phone rang at 2:17 in the morning. He still was awake, anxiously awaiting the call.

The voice on the other end said softly, "Every way I look at it, sacrifices have to be made to serve the greater good. He justified homosexuality. He wants condoms passed out in schools. He wants to kill unborn babies. He's blaspheming the church and its leaders. He's standing between us and the White House. He has to be stopped – and without martyring him. If Satan thinks this is the only way to do that, then so be it.

"Before I sign off on it, though, I have to have his assurance that it will be quick and painless, and I have to know all the details in advance."

"Yes, sir, Senator."

★ ★ ★

Celeste Rivers gently closed Jimmy's bedroom door and went back downstairs to join her husband in the kitchen.

"I didn't have the heart to wake him up. He's been through so much these past few days and he was sleeping like a baby."

"I'm glad you didn't," George agreed, finishing his morning coffee and taking his cup to the sink. He paused. "Honey, have you had any unusual conversations with Jimmy recently?"

"You mean apart from him waking up from his dream and screaming, "Mom, you're alive!"" she remarked. "You know, now that I think about it," she recalled, "yesterday he asked me if you and I regret not going to church anymore, as if he was blaming himself for it. That was kind of out of the blue, after all these years."

George snickered wistfully, "The question about Noah he asked when he was five years old. What did you tell him?"

"I reminded him that he was not the problem, that the real problem was with the very fallible leaders of the Church, like Father Sam.

"I also asked him why he thought Jesus had to come again in the Second Coming...and he did say, "Because we still haven't gotten the message right." I told him he was spot-on. And, the fact that instead of showing us the way back Home, our leaders are leading us further and further away from the Light into a deeper and deeper darkness.

"I assured Jimmy that was the main reason we chose to stop going to church – that if you see a problem and you're not part of the solution, then you're part of the problem."

"Right. But, did he happen to mention anything about a fortune teller?" George asked, uncertainly.

Celeste's face blanched. For the second time in two days, a memory she had buried years ago, when she was a teenager, had been dug up, given an otherworldly context, and was slapping her in the face.

"A fortune teller? Why do you ask?" a barely perceptible tremor in her voice belying her shock at suddenly having connected the dots between a long-forgotten, and seemingly random, encounter a quarter of a century ago and their son.

George noticed. "What is it, Celeste?"

"I'll tell you, but first, what about this fortune teller?"

"Well, after the Fenimore interview on Monday, Jimmy told me about his dream. Actually, he wasn't sure it was a dream. He said that a gunman at the mall shot and killed you six years ago when the two of you had gone to buy that skateboard for his birthday. And that with the help of a fortune teller, he traveled through time and brought you back to life."

Ordinarily, such a fantastic tale might have elicited a shared giggle at the silliness of the prospect, but not this time. "After everything we've heard from our son, I'm not going to say it didn't happen," Celeste sighed, "but, I honestly can say I have absolutely no recollection of it. And you'd think I'd remember being shot."

"Not if somehow Jimmy changed something that led to you getting shot and, in doing that, changed the course of history," George mused. "He could have…"

"I don't know anything about that," his wife abruptly interjected, "but, yesterday, when Jimmy asked me if I knew a fortune teller, I remembered going to a psychic with my sister when we were teenagers. I didn't want to go – I told her they all were quacks – but she insisted. He could have been a fortune teller of sorts, couldn't he have?

"Anyway, this guy was clean-cut, and he didn't look the part. Actually, he looked more like an accountant, and he told me the strangest thing," she said, plumbing her memory of long ago. "You know how most of these psychics talk about relationships and jobs and spirits, and put you in touch with people who have passed? Not this guy. It felt like he looked into my soul when he told me I would have a son and that one day I should tell him, "This is not the end."

"I went along with it, and I asked him how I would know when to tell him it wasn't the end, and he said I'd just know."

George was fascinated by what he perceived to be some very disjointed pieces of a large puzzle somehow starting to fall into place. "So, have you told Jimmy that it wasn't the end, yet?"

"No. At least, not that I can recall."

"Honey, let's suppose for a minute that what Jimmy told me really happened. I mean, can this be a coincidence that you spoke to a fortune teller, or psychic, all those years ago, and Jimmy tells me that a fortune teller helped him to travel through time to bring you back to life?

"Because, if you were shot and you knew you were dying, wouldn't that be the perfect time to tell Jimmy, 'This is not the end?'"

Celeste's pulse quickened. "George, you're scaring me. What's happening here?"

Her husband shook his head. "I don't know. I didn't mean to

frighten you, but whatever it is, it's a lot bigger than you or me, or anything else in the world, it seems."

Tears welled up in Celeste's eyes. "If it's true, what a burden he's been carrying around for the past six years!"

George put his arm around his wife's shoulders. "I'm not sure he knew about it until this past weekend."

"It sounds like he's trying to reach out to us, though."

"I agree. But, let's let him sleep. We can let him know later today that we are here for him, whenever he wants to talk about whatever he wants to talk about. Non-judgmental, completely open minds. You can start out with your story of your trip to the psychic with your sister."

"Oh, George," Celeste sniffed, wiping the tears from her face, "I want to hug him right now and let him know he's not alone."

"I think he'll be more receptive when he's wide awake after a good night's sleep. Let's leave him a note and tell him we excused him from school today."

"OK, but hopefully I'll be back before he wakes up."

"Do you want a ride to yoga?" her husband asked, reaching for the car keys.

"Thanks, but it's such a beautiful morning, I'm going to run. Love you."

"Love you, too. See you tonight."

And George and Celeste Rivers kissed each other goodbye.

* * *

The serenity at the Rivers household was in stark contrast to the chaos at the Fenimore's. The Senator was in a foul mood having signed off on his daughter's murder – the guilt of a modern-day Macbeth hanging over his head – to advance his career and the agendas of the corrupt kingmakers, or what they labeled "the greater good." Jimmy had forced the Senator's hand – at least, that's what he'd been led to believe – and he took out all of his self-loathing on Sasha's boyfriend. That's how he was going to get back at him, by having her killed. He was losing her, anyway.

In the twisted logic of pro-lifers who would kill for the greater good, he would be killing two birds with one stone: inflicting the greatest harm on Jimmy Rivers, the boy who was "forcing" him to sign off on his daughter's murder, and getting himself elected to the White House. That still didn't make it any easier. He knew he was putting himself in the same category of pond scum as that of an estranged spouse killing his innocent children to get back at his wife, and it repulsed him.

Adding to his dreadful mood was the looming 10:00 a.m., press conference with Cardinal Phelps, hastily arranged by his end-justifies-the-means campaign manager on Satan's command to try to contain the damage of Jimmy's nationally televised interview last night. Ralph was set to arrive at his house at any moment – another headache occasioned by Jimmy Rivers. Being held accountable to the public was bad enough, but it was quite another to be beholden to Satan. He was stuck in the middle of a Faustian pact, and he wanted to explode.

Sasha was sitting with her mother just finishing her avocado toast when her father walked into the kitchen.

"Hi, Daddy!" she chirped, merrily.

The Senator was having none of it. "You remember what I told you last night. I don't want you seeing Jimmy anymore!"

"Bill!" Alice nearly shouted in her daughter's defense. "What's the matter with you?"

Sasha had never heard her mother raise her voice to the Senator. Tears began to stream down her cheeks.

"Did she tell you some crazy man has been following them since Jimmy's classroom stunt on Monday?"

"It wasn't a stunt, Daddy!" she protested through her tears. "He was just participating in a class discussion."

"You're telling me he knew nothing about that video?" the Senator replied, angrily. "Because it sure gave him his fifteen minutes of fame!"

"Yes! Jimmy's not like you! And that's one of the things I love about him. No one knows where that video came from!"

The Senator's heart hardened. There it was in black and white. His own daughter had rejected him in favor of the boy who had turned his life into a living hell. Never mind that it was, in fact, the Senator, himself, who had chosen his path. And he knew it.

"Could this day get any worse?" he bellowed, storming out of the kitchen and into his study, slamming the door behind him.

"Mom!" Sasha pleaded, still visibly shaken.

Alice hugged her daughter and gently stroked her long hair. "Honey, your father's under a lot of pressure. It doesn't excuse his behavior, but the kind of stress he's dealing with, especially these last few days, would cause just about anyone to react badly at times.

"This just happens to be one of those times, and I'm so sorry this thing with Jimmy seems to have been the straw that broke the camel's back.

"Running for President of the United States takes over your life, and there's no time off for good behavior – or even bad behavior. Which means it doesn't leave room for much of anything else. But, deep down, your father loves you very much.

"Tell you what – tonight we'll have a family meeting to sort all of this out."

Alice reached for the box of Kleenex on the counter and handed it to Sasha.

"Thanks, Mom," her daughter sniffed, taking three tissues to wipe her eyes and blow her nose. She felt so safe in her mother's arms. She tried to change the subject. "How's my makeup?"

"In need of a little touch-up," Alice smiled. She watched as Sasha expertly blended and buffed the streaks out of her barest foundation. Finally, her curiosity piqued, she asked, "So, is it true? Is there someone following you and Jimmy?"

Sasha tried to ignore the question by looking in the mirror and checking for blemishes. Finding none, she declared, "There we go... good as new!"

"Not quite," her mother objected. "You still haven't told me about the man who's been following you and Jimmy."

“Oh, Mom,” Sasha leaned in, as if to share a secret. “I’m not even sure he’s actually following us, but he gave me the creeps. I saw him for the first time, yesterday, when Jimmy and I went to lunch at the Subway by school, and you know how packed with students it is at lunchtime...well, I noticed this man in a dark suit because he looked so out of place among all the kids.

“Then, I saw him again late last night at Denny’s after the movie. I guess it could have been a coincidence, but neither of us had a good feeling about it.”

“Sasha,” Alice began, but her daughter cut her off at the pass.

“Mom, Jimmy needs me. I can’t stop seeing him.”

“I know, Sweetie. I wasn’t going to tell you not to see him. I just was going to say that you’re a smart girl and to keep your wits about you. Don’t put yourselves in a bad situation.”

The phone rang before Alice could finish her thought. “Hello?” she answered.

“Mrs. Fenimore, this is Jack Thompson from the *Denver Post*. Is the Senator available?”

“I’m afraid he’s in a meeting right now, Jack. Can I help you?”

“I was hoping to get a comment about your son Cooper’s roommate, Roland Thomas. He was reported missing last night.”

Alice Fenimore knew how to play the good, political wife. “Neither of us will have any comment at this time. Thank you for your concern.” And she hung up the phone.

“That was about Roland, wasn’t it?” Sasha asked.

“Yes.”

“Does Daddy know?”

“No, that would send him over the edge right now. I was hoping Roland would turn up before he found out he was missing. But, there are a lot of crazies out there, and with your father running for president...”

“Omigosh!” Sasha interrupted. “I almost forgot. Cooper told me that Roland was working on a very sensitive story about some powerful people. Roland wouldn’t tell him what it was about to keep him out of danger, but he assured Cooper he had an insurance policy that would keep him safe.

"After I got off the phone with Cooper, I called Jimmy and told him what was going on. He thought the insurance policy might have been information about the story Roland was working on that would have been sent to the news media if anything happened to him."

"Why wouldn't Cooper tell me that?"

"He probably didn't want to worry you."

"Well, that's what I meant when I told you about not putting yourselves in bad situations," Alice fretted.

"Anyway, Jimmy suggested that Roland might have arranged to have whatever information he had sent to a local news outlet, like the *Denver Post*, because they would get it quicker than any other outlet. And, Roland was so meticulous, I know he would have put his return address on it, just in case there was a delivery issue. So, I was thinking you could…"

"Call Sylvia!" Alice finished her daughter's sentence. "She knows that mail room like the back of her hand."

The sound of a car horn's two rapid beeps interrupted their covert scheming.

"That's Hannah," Sasha said, gathering her books. She looked at her mother.

"Don't worry. I'll call Sylvia right now."

"There's one more thing. Jimmy said the people who Roland was investigating probably would suspect the same thing, and if they still went ahead and tried to stop him somehow, that would mean they had the news media angle covered."

Alice thought for a moment. "He's right." Then, she shook her head. "We're really letting our imaginations run away with us, but I'll tell Sylvia to be careful and not to mention it to anyone else."

Sasha hugged her mother. "Thanks, Mom. I have to go."

Alice opened the front door and waved to her niece. She kissed her daughter goodbye, and watched her out the door, hopping down the steps to her cousin's car as a teenage girl without a care in the world. Remarkable.

* * *

At 225 Liberty Street in New York City, the editors of *Time* magazine convened an emergency meeting to reconsider its annual "Person of the Year' award in light of Jimmy Rivers having been thrust into the national – and global – consciousness just two days ago. Responding to a flurry of requests from the rank and file to throw Jimmy's name into the ring, Editor-in-Chief Misty Johnson called the meeting to order by reminding the executive editors gathered in the conference room of the magazine's long-standing criteria for its candidates: "The Person of the Year is officially the person or persons who most affected the news and our lives, for good or ill, and embodied what was most important about the year."

"And that's why I think Jimmy Rivers should be our Person of the Year," Claire Reynolds immediately cut in. "In less than 72 hours, he has singlehandedly upended the Partnership of the Right's front-running apple cart, settled in many people's minds the pro-choice-pro-life debate, ecumenically, at least, and presented the greatest challenge to the traditions of Christianity since Luther's 95 Theses."

"I don't disagree, Claire, but I think you have to take into account a body of work," David Sturn insisted. "Jimmy could turn out to be a three-day flash-in-the-pan. Andy Theus, on the other hand, has spearheaded Safety First Inc., into an international insurance juggernaut from its mom and pop roots twenty-five years ago.

"And, this year, he capped his legacy by reaching out to all the poor and otherwise uninsured with his game-changing plan to make life insurance affordable for everyone, thereby providing for generations to come.

"You can't really compare the promise of three days to the reality of twenty-five years."

"Oh, I can think of another three days that shook the world," Mario Mendoza chimed in.

The comments and opinions came in rapid-fire after that salvo.

"Are you seriously comparing Jimmy Rivers' fifteen minutes to

Jesus' third-day resurrection?"

"He's just saying you can't minimize achievement solely on the basis of time."

"Oh, yes we can! This is *Time* magazine."

"OK, but even Jesus had a body of work behind Him."

"Maybe Jimmy does, too. He asked that question about Noah and the flood when he was five years old. So, there's a gap of about twelve years there that could be worth taking the time to look into."

"Right. That could correspond to the missing 18 years between when Jesus first appeared in the temple and when his public ministry began at age 30."

"We just don't know much about him and we're running out of time."

"Again, this is *Time* magazine!"

"OK, knock it off. This is serious. Do we want to use running out of time as an excuse? We could be sitting on the story of the century!"

"And Munro at ABC News already has her fingernails dug into Jimmy's back."

"He's a 17-year-old kid!"

"Malala won the Nobel when she was 17."

"It's like the race to space. ABC was the first into orbit, but we can be first on the moon!"

⋆ ⋆ ⋆

Sylvia Brown was pleasantly surprised when she checked the caller ID of her buzzing cell phone. "Hello, Alice!"

"Hi, Sylvia, how are you?"

"Good, good, good. Busy. Everyone says print journalism is on the way out, but you wouldn't believe it from the mailroom. It's crazier than ever in here! How's the wife of the next President of the United States?"

Alice managed a weak smile. "As you can imagine, hectic doesn't even come close to describing the ups and downs."

"I saw you guys on TV the other night. Sasha and Cooper are all grown up!"

"I know it's hard to believe. It seems like it was just the other day they were running around the house in diapers." Alice paused. "That's part of the reason I called. I was hoping you could do a favor for me."

"Of course, Alice, anything. What is it?"

"Well, it's about Cooper. His roommate, actually."

"What about him?"

"I can't go into too many details because I don't know them. But, his name is Roland Thomas and he's gone missing. There's a chance it's because he was working on a story that some powerful people didn't want to come out."

Alice could sense the concern in her friend's voice. "Have you called the police?"

"No. They usually require 48 to 72 hours before they'll investigate a missing person, and we don't have the luxury of waiting that long. Especially with Bill's campaign and the national convention coming up. And besides, he could show up at any time with a perfectly logical explanation for where he's been."

"Understood. How can I help?"

"If there was foul play involved, we think there's a chance Roland would have arranged for whatever incriminating evidence he might have had to have been sent to a media outlet as a kind of insurance policy. We don't think he would have sent it to us or to one of his friends because he was worried about putting anyone he knew in danger. I was hoping you could keep an eye out for it in case he sent it to the *Post*, so it doesn't get lost in the shuffle."

"Alice, I really think you should get the police involved," Sylvia advised.

"As I said, hopefully, that won't be necessary. Because of the potential sensitivity to the Senator, we're trying to be as discrete as possible by keeping it out of the public realm, until we know for sure what's going on."

"OK."

"There's one more thing. If there is damaging information, you need to be very careful. Powerful people have powerful friends who have no problem getting their hands dirty in cleaning up their friends' messes, so to speak. I think we can be pretty sure that if we thought Roland might have sent what he knew about whoever it is to the news media, they would have thought the same thing, and they'll probably do whatever it takes to intercept that letter before anyone else gets to it.

"Have you noticed anything unusual in the mail room this morning, or anyone who doesn't really belong there?"

Sylvia thought for a moment and looked around the room. "No, just the normal staff. Well, and Don Stottlemeyer, our managing editor. He's been poking around the mail, which is kind of strange for two reasons. Once we go to print, he's never in the building this early, and he hardly ever comes down here."

Alice winced. "It could be nothing, or it could be something. I wouldn't trust him, though. Do you remember watching *Three Days of the Condor* in our journalism class?"

"Yes, and now you're scaring me," Sylvia admitted.

"I'm so sorry to ask you to do this. If you'd rather not, just tell me, and we'll think of something else."

"Oh, stop. This is the most exciting thing that's happened to me in I can't remember how long. I'm just saying...

"Anyway, tell me what I'm looking for."

Alice breathed a sigh of relief. "Thank you so much, Sylvia! So, it would be a letter or package from Roland Thomas. Sasha says he always put his name in the return address of anything he was sending. If you find it, call me and I'll come and get it."

"Oh geez, now you're asking me to tamper with the mail. I could lose my job, and much worse. That's a federal offense."

"Sylvia," Alice started to apologize...

"Alice, I'm just yanking your chain," her friend chuckled.

"Seriously, Sylvia, I know I'm asking a lot, but if the letter does exist, that would mean Roland is in grave danger and we might be the only ones who could save his life."

"I almost forgot how charming you could be," Sylvia responded, uneasily. "I'll do it, Alice. You can count on me. I'll let you know if I find anything."

"Sylvia, you're the best!"

"You say that, now. But, you're going to owe me, big time!"

* * *

"Good morning!" Hannah greeted her cousin as Sasha slid into the Toyota Camry's passenger seat.

Sasha leaned over and gave her a hug. "I hope so!"

"Why, what's going on?"

"Omigod, like everything," Sasha groaned.

Hannah looked over her shoulder as she pulled away from the curb. "Spill!"

"OK, first of all, my dad is in the worst mood ever. Did you see Jimmy's interview last night?"

"Of course, I did. I think everyone did. He was amazing! I had no idea my cousin's boyfriend had such deep thoughts. And they made so much sense. Like they say, still waters run deep."

"Yeah, well, Jimmy's 'amazing' is my dad's nightmare, and he's got this big press conference this morning to try to mitigate the damage."

"What damage? It's not like he's running against Jimmy. Except for the pro-choice pro-life debate, what Jimmy's saying is not even a political issue. Are the Democrats going to come out all of a sudden and make Jimmy's interpretation of the Bible part of their platform? This is probably all news to them, too, and they wouldn't touch it with a 10-foot pole."

"When did you get so smart?" Sasha teased. "Then, there's this whole thing about the guy in the dark suit."

"What guy?"

"I'm not sure, but I think there's this man who might be following us. Or, following Jimmy, anyway. I noticed him at Subway, yesterday, at lunch. He stuck out like a sore thumb among all the students. Then, he turned up at Denny's last night. I caught him staring at us. It was creepy.

"So, my Dad was waiting up for me when I got home, and I let it slip about this guy, and he blew up. He said I had to stop seeing Jimmy."

Hannah gave the Senator the benefit of the doubt. "I'm sure he's just worried about you. But, that's a little extreme."

"I know, right? And when he finds out about Roland…"

"Wait! What about Roland?"

"Cooper said he didn't come home last night. No phone call. Nothing. Which is really weird because those two are like peas in a pod. They talk like twenty times a day.

"Before he left yesterday morning, he told Cooper he was working on an investigative story about some powerful people. But, he didn't say anything more than that because he didn't want to put Cooper in danger, too."

"Yikes!" was Hannah's first reaction. "But," she continued, optimistically, "I'm sure he'll turn up with a great story about where he was, and you'll all have a good laugh…twenty years from now."

"I hope so," Sasha said anxiously. "Jimmy had a good idea, though. In case something did happen, he said Roland was smart enough to cover his bases and probably would have arranged to have his story sent to the news media.

"And mom is going to call her friend who works in the mailroom at the *Post* and tell her to keep an eye out for an envelope that has his name on it."

"If Roland put his name in the return address," Hannah allowed.

"Oh, he would have. You know how fastidious Roland is, and how he attends to every detail. He definitely would have written his name in the return address, just in case there was some problem with the delivery and it had to be sent back.

"And," Sasha added, "everyone's worried about the negative publicity."

"You mean besides the interview?"

"Yes. You know Ralph Petiole of Faith in US is heading Dad's campaign, right? Well, they're all so homophobic even though they claim to be Christians. They don't want Cooper coming out during the campaign. They say they can't afford the distraction. Mom hasn't even told dad about what's going on with Roland, yet. She doesn't want him worrying about the possibility that it will come out that Cooper's gay on top of everything else he's going through. Especially, if it turns out that nothing happened to Roland."

Hannah tittered nervously. "Wow, that is a rough start to the day!"

Sasha quickly changed the subject. It was too much of a downer. "Enough about me. What about you?" she asked, playfully poking at her ticklish cousin's ribs. "How was Ellyngton's?"

"Stop!" Hannah pleaded, her body convulsing, causing the car to swerve. "You're going to kill us. I'll tell you!"

Regaining her composure, Hannah rhapsodized, "It was wonderful. Tom is a dreamboat!"

"Tom?"

"Tom Farrell, the HR guy. When we walked into the restaurant, the staff snapped to attention. I told you he's gorgeous, right."

"Stats!"

"Six-foot two or three, very athletic, dark hair, blue eyes, blue suit – it had to be Armani – Italian loafers..."

"Omigod, what were you wearing?"

"Just what I wore to school. It was so awkward. But he put me right at ease. Oh, and no ring!"

"No ring? Hannah you're 17! How old is this guy?"

"Oh, come on, Sasha, let me have my crush! I'd guess he's in his mid-thirties, or so.

"Anyway, we sit down and the server brings him his usual dirty martini with three olives, and he ordered for me – a Cobb salad, which was so good!" Hannah smiled as she relived her lunch date. "I felt like such a princess!"

"OK, so you've already got a major crush on your boss. What about the job?"

"Just normal stuff around the office. Helping with the phones, the mail, filing, research, making appointments...whatever he needs help with.

"And, get this – he said the Joaks are very old-fashioned and conservative when it comes to women in the workplace. Only skirts or dresses, and they have to be over the knee. Nylons are a must, and only closed-toe pumps, no higher than three inches. My hair has to be pulled back, only stud earrings, light makeup, and clear nail polish."

"Ewww, it sounds like these guys are from the Dark Ages."

"I don't know, it kind of made me feel special, in a way. But, the best thing is, mom and I went shopping after work, and I got a whole new work wardrobe!"

"I'm glad you're excited, Hannah, but don't forget why you're there," Sasha cautioned. "All that attention from Mr. Dreamboat and your new outfits can be very distracting."

"Don't worry. I know what I'm doing. I still have my eyes on the prize. All expenses paid to Northwestern, baby!"

Hannah turned left off of East Quincy into the student parking lot at Benjamin Franklin High School. "Speaking of distractions, with all you've had going on the last couple of days, were you able to get that paper done for Mr. Hamilton's class?"

"Crap!" Sasha moaned. "Yes, I finished it...at 3:30 this morning. But I forgot to put it in my folder. It's sitting on my desk in my room."

Before Sasha could get another word out, Hannah did a quick U-turn in the parking lot and headed back to 37 Skylark Lane.

"Hannah, I don't want to make you late," Sasha objected.

"We'll make it. Besides, if we are late, I'll just have my dad write us a note saying we were kidnapped by aliens or something. Mrs. Perkins in the attendance office is cool. Trust me."

Sasha needn't have worried – the traffic gods were smiling on the teenage girls and, in no time at all, the silver Camry was turning onto Skylark Lane.

"STOP THE CAR!" Sasha shouted.

Hannah reflexively slammed on the brakes at her cousin's sudden outburst and pulled over to the curb three houses down from the Fenimore's two-story Mediterranean home.

Unnerved, she asked, "Sasha, what's the matter?"

A cold shiver went down Sasha's spine as she identified the three men walking up the sidewalk to her front door: Ralph Petiole, Father Simon from the Southeast Denver Christian Bible Church, and...the man in the dark suit.

"Turn around before anyone sees us!" Sasha demanded.

"But, what about your paper?"

"Forget about the paper...I have to call Jimmy!"

2

The phone rang several times before a voice on the other end answered, "Hello, *Denver Post.*"

"Yes, this is Leticia Carter. I'd like to speak with Mr. Don Stottlemeyer, please."

"Does he know who you are," the operator dutifully asked before disturbing the paper's busy managing editor.

"Yes, ma'am. Tell him it's Leticia Carter. He called me at my house last night and said I could call him at any time."

"Hold on, Ms. Carter, let me see if he's available."

The operator got right back on the line. "I'm sorry, Ms. Carter, he's in a meeting. Would you like his voicemail?"

"No, thank you. But, can you transfer me to the mailroom?"

"Certainly. Hold on."

"Isaac!" Leticia called out to her son while she waited for someone to pick up. "Get your things ready. We have to go as soon as I get off the phone."

"Mom," Isaac whined, "why didn't you call on your cell phone?"

"I forgot to charge it last night...the battery's dead."

"Mail room, this is Sylvia."

"Hello, Sylvia, my name is Leticia Carter. I spoke with Mr. Don Stottlemeyer last night about a suspicious envelope a man paid my son to mail if he didn't come back in the afternoon. I was worried about it, and I'm just calling to see if Mr. Stottlemeyer followed up on it. You can't be too careful these days."

That's why the managing editor was poking around the mail room, probably for the first time in the twenty-five years since he'd started there, Sylvia thought to herself. How serendipitous that she'd just gotten off the phone with Alice, who, out of the blue, also had called about a mysterious envelope that may or may not have been sent to the *Post*.

"Sylvia, are you still there?" Leticia asked impatiently, already late in getting Isaac to school.

"Yes, I'm sorry," she apologized, snapping out of her trance. Instinctively, she knew she better get as much information as she could about the peculiar coincidence. "Can I get your full name and number where you can be reached?"

Sylvia copied down the information, but she wasn't finished. "And your son's name?"

"Abraham Isaac Carter."

"How old is he?

"Eleven years old."

"Did Isaac mention anything in particular about the envelope that will help us identify it?"

"He said it was a large manila envelope that was very thick. It was addressed to the *Denver Post*. He also said there was a name on the return address." Leticia hesitated. "What was it?"

"Isaac!" Sylvia heard Leticia shout to her son. "What was the name on the return address of that big manila envelope?"

Sylvia couldn't quite make out the name that Isaac shouted back at his mom, but she heard Leticia just fine. "The name on the return address was Roland Thomas."

Sylvia's heart started to pound through her chest. Something definitely was up. She thanked Leticia for her earnestness and promised to get back to her.

As she hung up the phone, Don Stottlemeyer walked quickly past her.

"Mr. Stottlemeyer, I just got off the phone with Leticia Carter. She said she talked to you last night about a suspicious package her son mailed to the newspaper yesterday afternoon. She was wondering if it had turned up." Sylvia said nothing about her conversation with Alice Fenimore.

The harried managing editor turned around, looking as if he'd just been caught with his hand in the cookie jar. He was carrying a stack of papers under his arm that only partly concealed a large, over-stuffed manila envelope sandwiched between them.

"I'm sorry," he stammered. "What's your name?"

"Sylvia, sir."

"Well, Sylvia, you'd be surprised to know how many prank phone calls I get every week about mysterious packages, and, invariably, they turn out to be from people with overactive imaginations who watch a lot of TV and report UFO sightings.

"I'm sure nothing will come of it, but keep your eye out for anything that looks unusual, and let me know if you see anything."

How about that large manila envelope you're carrying under your arm and trying to hide? Sylvia thought to herself.

Before continuing on his way, Stottlemeyer asked, "Did Leticia, I think you said her name was, say what it looked like or who it might be from?"

"No," Sylvia lied.

"I didn't think so." And the managing editor scurried off with his prize. But not before the skeptical mail clerk spied the partially hidden name in the return address.

* * *

Jimmy felt a hand on his shoulder and turned around with a start.

"Señor Quixote!" he exclaimed. "What a surprise!"

The kindred spirits embraced. Jimmy was so mesmerized by the errant knight's appearance, he didn't hear his cell phone ringing. And ringing. And ringing.

"What are you doing here?" he asked.

"In all seriousness, I am here on a matter of great urgency," Don Quixote replied. "You must come with me at once."

"But, I have to go to school. And Sasha..."

"As I said, it is of the utmost urgency."

Jimmy didn't have to be told a third time, still oblivious to his cell phone's insistent demands. "OK, so where are we going?"

"You'll see. You drive."

They hopped into Jimmy's Camaro and the wayward knight directed him to the Dairy Queen on South Colorado Boulevard. It was the same one at which, two nights ago, he and Sasha were amazed to find the elder knight working. It was closed, of course, but Don Quixote had a key and opened the front door.

"Follow me," he instructed, and he led Jimmy to a locked door in the storeroom. The knight opened it and the two of them stepped inside. Outside, actually, into a faraway land. Jimmy's eyes were as big as silver dollars.

"Do you recognize this place?"

"Of course, I do!" the entranced teenager answered, surveying the vast landscape on the other side of the Wall, where neither Time nor limits of any kind existed. It was the place they first had met – the land of giant windmills – only four days earlier, where they simultaneously had vanquished Don Quixote's mortal enemy, the Knight of the White Moon, and changed The Premise, bringing Jimmy's mother back to life. It seemed like an eternity ago.

The wayward knight motioned to his right. "And there is Sancho Panza."

Jimmy swiveled to see the knight's faithful manservant atop his donkey, leading Rocinante towards them.

"Hello, Señor Jimmy!"

"Hola, Sancho."

After a brief exchange of pleasantries, the Man of La Mancha announced, "Come, we must go!"

In one deft move, belying his years, he took a short, running start, jumped up, placed his hands on Rocinante's hindquarters, and vaulted onto the long saddle atop his trusty steed. He extended a hand to Jimmy and helped the teenager into the saddle behind him. Jimmy marveled at the elder knight's nimbleness, but then he remembered they were in the land of no limits.

They rode for a short while – who could tell when Time doesn't exist? – up to an inn that seemed so out of place on this side of the Wall. Not of this century, if truth be told...more akin to a saloon out of an Old West that Time had forgotten.

Sure enough, when they walked inside, Jimmy found it identical to the late 19th Century watering holes he'd read about and seen on TV. In front of them, a bartender tended to three patrons sitting at the bar, saloon-girls waited on tables of what seemed to be lumberjacks and fur traders, a man at the piano was playing "Home on the Range," and in the corner to his left, Jimmy noticed a familiar face holding court at a faro table. He caught Doc Holliday's eye, and the gambling dentist-cum-gunslinger smiled ever so slightly, nodding a "Hello, kid," in return.

"It's like we're on a movie set, or something!" Jimmy gasped. "Why are we here?"

"Someone wants to see you."

No sooner had the words left the errant knight's mouth than one of the saloon girls – a very attractive dark-haired girl with red lips – accosted Jimmy.

"You're the one!" she declared above the din, noticing the knight's medallion around his neck and poking out of his shirt.

Don Quixote gathered her in his arms and quickly introduced her. "Jimmy, this is my Dulcinea!

"And, yes, my Sweet, this is Jimmy, the one I have been telling you about."

Dulcinea leaned over and gave the teenager a big kiss on his cheek, leaving a noticeable trace of red lipstick.

"I want to thank you, Señor Jimmy, for helping my chevalier defeat his nemesis, Carrasco!"

Jimmy's face flushed, almost as red as Dulcinea's lipstick. "I didn't do anything. It was all Señor Quixote! You should have seen him leap from Rocinante at full gallop and tackle the Knight of the White Moon! He was amazing!"

"You are too modest, Jimmy," Dulcinea disagreed. "Who held Rocinante's reins so steadily that Señor Quixote could time his leap so perfectly?"

"Isn't she as wonderful as she has been described?" the knight gushed, kissing her passionately in front of them.

Jimmy and Sancho looked at each other and smiled. After several moments, Dulcinea broke off the kiss in mock indignation. "Señor Quixote, I have work to do!"

Fixing her hair, she addressed the onlookers. "Jimmy, it was so nice to meet you. I hope we can have more time later. And, Sancho, keep an eye on this one," she said, motioning towards her errant knight. "I don't know how you can keep up with all his campaigns, but he would be lost without you."

"I hope so, too!" Jimmy called out after the winsome saloon girl went back to tending to her patrons.

"Do you see why she is the apple of my eye?" enthused Don Quixote.

"She is wonderful. Thank you for bringing me here to meet her. It would be fun if Sasha could meet her, too!"

"Maybe one day, my young friend. But you are mistaken. She is not the person for whom I brought you here. The person who summoned you awaits you through that curtain at the top of the stairs."

Jimmy glanced upstairs, and his pulse quickened when he saw the purple velour curtain – the same purple velour curtain that he and Sasha had walked through four days ago at the carnival that started him on this incredible journey.

Sure enough, when Jimmy walked through it, he saw the fortune teller waiting for him, sitting in a high-backed armchair. There was a Latino-looking man next to him.

Both men stood up. "Hello, Jimmy," the fortune teller greeted him. Thanks for coming on such short notice."

"I didn't really have a choice, did I?" Jimmy regretted those words as soon as he heard them.

"Remember, you always have a choice, Jimmy" the fortune teller corrected, "and there are no insignificant choices. You must choose wisely at all times; and, you have chosen wisely today.

"I'd like to introduce to you a friend of mine. This is Miki."

In his mid to late thirties and the picture of health, the man reached out his hand to shake Jimmy's. "It's very nice to meet you."

"Nice to meet you, too, Miki," Jimmy returned the greeting,

wondering if Miki had as colorful a past as Don Quixote's or Doc Holliday's, how he knew the fortune teller, and how he fit into his journey.

Noticing Jimmy's barely hidden consternation, the fortune teller interjected, "Miki has, let's say, special skills which may come in handy down the road."

Miki smiled and winked at Jimmy, immediately putting the teenager at ease.

"Now, Miki," the fortune teller continued, "Jimmy and I need a few minutes."

Taking his cue, Miki again shook hands with Jimmy and said, "I look forward to seeing you, again. The fortune teller has told me so much about you."

"All good, I hope," Jimmy looked at the fortune teller.

"All good."

Miki exited through the back hallway, and the fortune teller and Jimmy sat down across from each other.

"So, what's Miki's story?" Jimmy asked. "And what are his special skills, as you call them?"

"That will have to wait. Suffice to say that his special skills have to do with bringing drug lords to justice."

"Drug lords?" gulped Jimmy. "What do they have to do with me?"

"We will cross that bridge when we come to it. But, at this time, there is another more pressing matter that must be addressed immediately."

"So I've been told. But, why did you send for me instead of just popping up at the most random times and places like you always do?"

"For reasons that you soon shall see," the fortune teller promised. "At this particular moment, we need to be in the place where Time does not exist. If I have said it once, I've said it a thousand times, Time is the worst invention the human race ever has come up with. But, I digress.

"Now, Jimmy, you must pay very close attention to what I am

about to tell you. Without overstating it, your life will depend on it."

"Yes, sir!" Jimmy replied, resolutely.

"Good. I have given you a lot to think about, but, if we are to go any further, I need you to go beyond consideration and to make up your mind.

"Let me remind you, at our first meeting, you chose this side of the Wall, where there are no limits and everything is possible. You encountered Don Quixote and traveled though time to defeat The Premise, thereby enabling you to bring your mother back to life.

"That was not a dream, Jimmy. That was the result of all the choices you've made in your seventeen years, consciously and subconsciously, that led you to me and to this universe where Time does not exist. This universe enables you to move through the universe that you know as if Time is standing still and everything is frozen in place. Then, you chose to go back to a specific moment on the Time continuum and you changed something that happened, which, in turn, changed the course of history.

"You changed The Premise. Do you remember what it was?"

"Yes, of course, I do. The Premise was that the news media was perpetuating mass killings in the world by giving these killers their fifteen minutes of fame, giving them the opportunity to go out in a blaze of infamy. These cowards saw it as their only chance to shine a light on their unremarkable and miserable lives, on the indignations they had to endure, and to lay the blame at society's feet.

"And by committing the most horrible atrocities, the world would know they existed – everyone would know their names, see their faces, and read their manifestos. Mass killings gave them the only voice they thought they ever would have.

"So, by going back through time and changing The Premise – in effect, taking away these cowards' fifteen minutes of fame achieved at the expense of innocent lives – my Dad thought the senseless mass murders would stop, and it might give my mom another chance.

"Apparently, it worked, because when I buried Señor Quixote's lance into The Premise, and took away the fame, or infamy, my mom hadn't been killed by that gunman at the mall because he wasn't even there to wreak his havoc. He hadn't connected the dots between committing heinous acts and getting his name and face on the front page of the newspapers and the 10 o'clock news."

The fortune teller stared into Jimmy's eyes with an intensity that underscored his emergency. "Precisely."

Jimmy was completely dialed in. "That's how Sasha and I made the three-hour trip from Glenwood Springs to Denver in less than an hour."

"Yes, you were so focused on getting to Denver on time, and on not incurring her father's wrath, you didn't pay attention to the 'facts,' the gusts of wind, of why it would be impossible, including the jackknifed truck on I-70 that added another three hours to the trip. Through your belief, devoid of distraction and doubt, you subconsciously chose this overlapping universe, on this side of the Wall, that allowed you to move the mountain and make the trip on time."

"The parallel universes you told me about," Jimmy suddenly realized.

"Yes!" the fortune teller beamed. "But, there's much more. You can choose any universe just as Adam and Eve chose theirs. They did not choose for you, and you do not have to choose the one they chose."

Jimmy's brow furrowed. "I'm not sure I follow. Any universe, you said? How many universes are there?"

"Do you remember reciting those passages from the Gospel of Thomas in which Jesus told Thomas that whoever found the correct interpretation of His sayings never would taste death? That he should seek until he found, and that when he found he would become disturbed, and then he would be amazed and rule over the All?

"It's that ruling over 'the All' that counts...because there are no limits to the number of universes you can create, and it applies to all universes you create by the choices you make.

"As choices are unlimited, then so are universes. You're only limited by what you believe is possible – in other words, all limits are self-imposed. On this side of the Wall, where there are no limits, that also applies to universes. They are unlimited and you rule over them all by the choices you make.

"Forgive me for being so detailed, but it's only because this is so important. Remember Jesus telling us that nothing would be impossible for anyone who had the faith of a mustard seed? That all things are possible through God? He was speaking of this universe, on this side of the Wall. This is God's side of the Wall. It is the Eden that He created for us, and it can and does overlap with any other universe, depending on the choices we make. There are as many different universes as there are people, each of them predicated on the choices they make; and they are evolving constantly. Change your choice, change your universe.

"The most important choice is to not put anything or anyone before God. Which means that we must choose to believe what He says, not what anyone else says about anything being impossible. Doubt in the Lord is what causes people to sink. Do you remember starting to float at the Denny's restaurant last night when you were with Sasha? You were locked into the Truth, unburdened by Doubt, and you started to float. Something may be impossible in any universe chosen that is apart from God, but it's not impossible in the universe that God has chosen for His children.

"Do you see the partnership God spelled out for us?"

Jimmy hesitated. "I think so. Does it have something to do with faith?"

"It has everything to do with faith!" came the fortune teller's firm response. "God's part is giving us access to His authority over all things; our part is believing Him."

"You've said that before," Jimmy recalled. "People claim to believe in Him, but they don't believe what He says."

"Yes. This side of the Wall, this Eden, depends not only on believing in Him, but also on believing what He says. Uncompromised faith is the conduit through which His authority over all things flows to us. However, the moment we doubt, the moment we choose to believe something is impossible, the conduit is blocked, or broken, and we change our universe into one in which whatever things we chose to believe are not possible, are impossible. When Peter was walking on water, he was in God's universe which overlapped his universe – and gravity was an observation, not a "law." The things of God always will trump the things of Man on the side of the Wall apart from God.

"But, when that gust of wind came up, Peter changed his choice and he changed his universe. He chose to doubt that walking on water was possible, and at that precise instant, he entered a universe in which gravity was an inviolable "law," not an observation, and walking on water therefore was not possible...and he fell into the sea.

"As you've discovered, my young prodigal, it works both ways. You can change your choices to return to God's side of the Wall, to this Eden, where the conduit is reopened and mended, and you regain access to your divine inheritance – God's authority over all things. Nothing is impossible. It is a self-fulfilling prophecy.

"So, again, the challenge of Life and living without limits, even in this world, is the challenge of Choice – choosing Eden and bringing it with you into all overlapping universes east of Eden. That's why I have told you there are no insignificant choices and that you always must choose wisely."

Jimmy was puzzled. "I don't understand. The choice seems obvious. Why wouldn't everyone choose the universe where all things are possible?"

"Oh, I don't know. Why don't you go back and ask Adam and Eve that same question? Suffice to say that Lucifer is doing everything in his power...wait," the fortune teller caught himself, "that's a poor choice of words because Lucifer has been stripped of all access to God's authority. He has no power.

"What I meant to say, more accurately, is that we have seen the extent of what the fallen angel can do. He only can slither into our lives, as he did in the Garden, and trick us into choosing poorly to sit at his table of deceit, to partake of his Doubt and Distraction, and voila! We have put ourselves in his dark universe of limits.

"Those whispers in our minds to doubt are his gusts of wind. They come every second of every minute of every hour of every day of every week of every month of every year of our lives. He will tempt us with everything that will impair our ability to make good choices – alcohol, sex, drugs. Trust me, Lucifer is dancing in Hades over this legalization of pot initiative that is sweeping the country.

"But the important thing to remember is that he has no power over us. He's not pulling a gun on us and forcing us to choose poorly. We have only ourselves to blame, just as Adam and Eve had only themselves to blame."

"I get it!" Jimmy blurted out confidently, with absolutely no hesitation or doubt in his voice. As Jesus told Thomas, seekers first would be troubled, then amazed, when they found the true translation of His words.

"I can see it in your eyes," the fortune teller agreed. "So, getting back to the parallel universes, you've already seen how they can overlap and interact with the world on the other side of the Wall. The trick, then, is to choose the right universe.

"For example, you probably remember me sticking my finger in that candle flame at the Dairy Queen a couple of nights ago, and leaving it in the flame for three minutes."

"How could I forget?" Jimmy recalled vividly. "It was one of the most amazing things I've ever seen. You never flinched, and not a single hair was even singed."

The fortune teller explained, "That's because out of all the universes possible, I chose the one in which fire would not burn my skin, or harm me in any way. I could have left my finger in there for three hours and nothing would have happened even though I also was in the universe you had chosen in which fire destroys. That's the overlap."

"That's how you were able to put your hand through the Australian buloke! You chose the universe in which your hand could pass effortlessly through the densest wood in the world as if it was steam."

"Exactly! And getting back to the flame, if at any time I had blinked and feared the fire, my finger would have burned up in seconds...similar to Peter falling into the sea when he chose to doubt Jesus by putting his fear of the gust of wind ahead of his trust in

Him.

"Let me tell you something about Peter's experience that no one ever has spoken of before. When he fell into the sea, his total focus was on the universe in which he couldn't swim – obviously, a very poor choice. If he had kept his wits about him, though, and recognized that there always is choice, he just as easily could have chosen again the universe on this side of the Wall and stepped back up onto the water, or he could have chosen a universe in which he spontaneously would have been taught to swim.

"That is the lesson of Jesus' story of the prodigal son, as you know. If we choose poorly to accept any of the limited universes, then we can choose wisely to change that poor choice and get back to the universe on God's side of the Wall where life and living truly are without limits – as He provided for us. We would be reclaiming our divine inheritance.

"As you have said, God is not a killer, and He doesn't hold grudges. He loves us so much, that He will forgive any poor choice and, as Jesus taught, He will rush to greet us upon our choice to return to His side of the Wall. And, again, He will celebrate our return with a great feast. It is why Adam's and Eve's second poor choice – not to repent and turn back to Him – was by far their most egregious mistake."

"That's why the Carib Indians couldn't see Columbus' ships when he sailed to the New World for the first time!" Jimmy exclaimed, randomly. "I never understood the story of the Indians on the shore noticing a change in the currents hitting their island when the Niña, the Pinta, and the Santa Maria approached, but not being able to see the ships even though they had to have been within eyesight since they were close enough to affect the current. Sailing ships were not part of the universe they had chosen, so they were invisible!

"But the medicine man knew something had to be out there, and he kept staring out to sea, determined to find out what it was. He was seeking. He sought an overlapping universe in which he could see the current changers, and eventually, he found it and he saw the ships. He ran back to his village to describe what he had seen to his fellow Indians. They trusted him so much, that they chose to believe him, and they changed their universe! So, when they went back to the shore, they, too, could see Columbus' three ships.

"And that's why we can't find Eden! We have chosen the overlapping universe east of Eden where Eden doesn't exist. So, even though it's right here in front of our eyes, we can't see it! It all makes such perfect sense! Why has no one told us this before?"

"Someone has, Jimmy, but no one believed Him," the fortune teller winked. "And the others, the so-called religious leaders, have chosen so poorly to buy into Lucifer's deceit – for whatever reason, lack of faith, ignorance, agendas more aligned with Caiaphas' than with God's – that they couldn't find their way back Home to this side of the Wall if it hit them squarely in the face. Which it has.

"That's why you must never underestimate the lengths to which Lucifer will go to deceive. His survival depends on it. From this side of the Wall, we have the authority to tell him to enter a herd of pigs which then will become crazed and throw themselves off a cliff, and he will have no choice but to obey our command.

"Before I send you on your way, I must tell you that Fear is Lucifer's greatest tool of deceit. It is why God instructed Abraham to put a knife into his beloved son, Isaac. He helped Abraham to overcome his greatest fear – that of losing his son – and simultaneously stripped Lucifer of his greatest tool.

"That's why the wise man prays not for safety from the storm, but for deliverance from fear. Fear is Doubt in sheep's clothing. When one chooses fear, one is doubtful of a positive outcome.

"Remember the story of Jesus and His disciples crossing the Sea of Galilee when a furious storm arose, sending angry waves crashing over the boat so that it nearly capsized. Jesus was asleep in the stern and the frightened disciples woke Him up and begged Him to save them from drowning.

"Jesus replied, "You of little faith, how long do I have to be with you? Why are you so afraid?" He was referring to, 'I have told you I have given you the power to trample over serpents and scorpions and to overcome all the power of the enemy, and that nothing by any means ever shall hurt you,' yet, his disciples still feared and doubted. And He calmed the storm.

"The choice to fear separates you from God's side of the Wall, and you lose access to His authority over all things. What is feared then becomes reality. This authority you have been given is a double-edged sword – it will make happen whatever is focused on, good or bad. That's why we always must choose wisely. Jesus is telling His disciples that they had chosen poorly – that if they had chosen not to fear, or not to doubt, then their conduit of faith would have been unblocked, and they could have accessed His Father's authority to calm the waves...just as He did.

"Jesus is the One who never would lie to us, but no one chooses to believe Him. Even those who lived with Him. That's how nefarious Lucifer's deceit is, and everyone chooses universes on the other side of this Wall where bad things do happen. In that way, fear becomes a self-fulfilling prophecy.

"In all dangerous, life-or-death situations, then, your first choice must be Life. If you had your blue Camaro up on a jack and you were working underneath it, and it fell off the jack and onto your face, and the first thought you chose was 'I'm dead,' you would have ordered your own death. If, on the other hand, your first thought was to survive, then you would have chosen wisely – you would have 'ordered' your survival, and you would have been freed of the barrier occasioned by the poor choice that you couldn't lift a car, and you would be able to lift the car off your face, as God provided for you. Just as the disciples would have been able to calm the storm.

"Remember, nothing by any means ever shall hurt the child who chooses to believe."

Jimmy nodded his head. "I got this!" he declared, brimming with the self-assured confidence of someone knowing in advance that there will be a favorable outcome, and there wasn't a thing anyone, including Satan, could have done to get him to change his mind, and, thus, the outcome. He was in the zone....the faith zone.

"Just always focus on what I want to happen," he assured himself and the fortune teller, "and no matter how impossible it seems, I'm choosing the overlapping universe where all things are possible that God provided for us, and no harm will come to me."

"Do you believe it?"

"110%!"

"OK, then, it's time to WAKE UP!"

At that precise instant, Jimmy opened his eyes. He was in his bedroom. And it was on fire!

3

The four men gathered in Senator Fenimore's study huddled together in a last-minute huddle to make sure they were on the same page for the press conference. Everyone added their two cents' worth, except the man in the dark suit, who sat ominously quiet, monitoring everything.

Father Simon spoke for Cardinal Phelps, who already was at the Southeast Denver Christian Bible Church preparing his own remarks, along with the social media sociopath, Leon Tusk.

"His Eminence is going to create Doubt. That's all it will take. Reasonable or unreasonable, the people just need something to refocus on and to cling to that will distract them from Jimmy's fanciful and naïve version of Christian theology. And Leon will do his part, beating them over the head with it.

"It's a tried-and-true strategy. If the people don't believe the Son of God, and don't believe God, Himself – those Who never would lie to them – then there's no way they'll choose to believe Jimmy when the Cardinal and Leon get done with him."

Ralph Petiole added, "As we discussed last night, Senator, you have to drive home the point about taking care of the 'greater good.' You can leave the ecclesiastical issues to the Cardinal."

"Got it," Senator Fenimore affirmed. "But, listen, I was thinking…"

"Uh-oh, that's dangerous," Ralph quipped to nervous chuckles around the room, except from the man in the dark suit, who continued to sit in stoic observance.

"Is it too early to talk publicly about a possible running mate?" the Senator asked.

"Not necessarily," his campaign manager answered, wondering where he was going with that.

"Why? Who were you thinking of?"

"Andy Theus from SFI. All this talk about coming up with something that would distract from Jimmy. Andy would be a pretty good distraction."

"Especially coming from left field," Ralph agreed, slowly warming to the idea. "He's fresh, no political baggage, he's widely admired, and his business acumen is beyond reproach. He's always been a huge and loyal supporter of the Party. Do you think he'd consider it?"

"That's why I mentioned it...he called the other day and basically threw his hat into the ring. Said it was something he'd always had in the back of his mind, and that he was ready for new challenges. Besides, he said it would be lots of fun."

The hint of a smile turned up the corners of Ralph Petiole's mouth. "Actually, that's not a bad idea at all! Why didn't I think of it?"

⋆ ⋆ ⋆

The South Metro Fire Station 37 received the call that smoke was pouring out of a house at 2318 White Rabbit Road at 8:47 that morning, and by the time firefighters arrived on the scene ten minutes later, the home was completely engulfed in flames.

Two minutes later, Madison Munro's cell phone rang as she pulled away from The Crawford Hotel at Union Station to attend Senator Fenimore's and Cardinal Phelps' 10:00 a.m. press conference at the Southeast Denver Christian Bible Church.

She wouldn't have answered it, but it was the ringtone she had designated specifically for her producer, Cal Everett.

"What is it, Cal?" she demanded, a hint of exasperation in her voice. "I'm trying to get to the press conference."

"Forget the press conference! Jimmy's house is on fire. And he's not at school!"

Those awful words, so unexpected and menacing, would have caused anyone else as invested in a story to become unglued and their synapses to misfire, but not Madison. She spontaneously went into crisis mode.

"Crap!" she blurted into the phone. Then, "OK, Cal, I'm on my way. I need you to call André. He's probably already at the church getting set up. Tell him to meet me at the house. There's no way that press conference is going to happen."

She hung up, maneuvered her black Lexus through traffic and onto Interstate 25 South, pressed her Christian Louboutin shoe – the one perk she permitted herself – to the metal, and hit the speed dial on her phone. "Thank God I put her number in my contacts last night," she thought to herself

Sasha picked up and whispered, "Hi, Madison, I can't really talk right now. I'm in class."

"Sasha, listen to me," the reporter insisted, "this is important. Have you talked to Jimmy this morning?

A chill went down Sasha's spine when she heard the stress in Madison's voice. "No. He wasn't in first period and he's not picking up his phone. Why? What's the matter?"

Madison didn't mince words. "His house is on fire, and he could be inside."

Sasha might as well have been hit in the gut by a heavy right hand from a professional boxer. She couldn't breathe. Her eyes welled up with tears. She felt light-headed.

"Sasha! Listen to me!" Madison urged, sensing the young girl was on the verge of a panic attack. "I'll be in front of your school in five minutes. I'm driving a black Lexus. Can you meet me?"

"Y-e-e-s-s-s," the shaken girl stammered, her determination to get to Jimmy keeping her just this side of a totally incapacitating attack. Without a word, and with tears streaming down her cheeks, she excused herself and staggered out of her class.

By the time she tripped down the stairs in front of her school, the black Lexus was waiting for her. She climbed in and Madison hit the gas practically before she could shut the door. Sasha burst into tears.

With one hand on the wheel, Madison reached into her purse and retrieved a packet of tissues.

"Hear me out, Sasha," she said calmly, as the teenager dabbed at her eyes. "First of all, we don't know for sure that Jimmy's in the house. And, secondly, I've seen some truly unbelievable – call them 'miraculous' – things in my career, so you can't give up hope!"

"You're talking about that time on Berthoud Pass," Sasha sniffed, as Madison sped towards 2318 White Rabbit Road, breaking just about every traffic law in the process.

"Yes, I am," she said, and she recounted the story for Sasha's benefit, even though she knew the teary teenager already had heard it, to keep her mind occupied and hopeful...and distracted from thoughts of Jimmy's imminent peril.

"I saw a man drive his minivan over that cliff in a blinding snowstorm to rescue a young girl whose car got swept over the edge by an avalanche. I was only twenty-one, and I was horrified to see someone supposedly kill himself in front of my eyes.

"It turns out that the man didn't die, that he had some kind of flying car, and he was able to rescue Rachel and return her safely to her home. It's such an unbelievable story, you wonder if Rachel was on drugs or if she hit her head and was hallucinating, but, the fact is, I saw the guy drive that minivan off the cliff!

"Everyone else eventually wrote it off as some kind of miracle, something that couldn't be explained – kind of like those stories you hear of mothers having surges of adrenaline and lifting trucks off their children who were pinned beneath them.

"For me, though, this went way beyond that. There was something else there, something that I just couldn't put my finger on. And I wouldn't let it go. I have something of a sixth sense about these things. I'm getting the same feeling about Jimmy. There's something special about him, and I haven't quite put my finger on it...but I will!"

Madison slammed on the brakes. "We're here!" she announced.

Those two words were like a cold slap in the face for Sasha. She had become so immersed in Madison's retelling of the Berthoud Pass incident, she had lost track of the time and their whereabouts. At once, she took in the horrific scene in front of them, and, somehow, amid all the chaos, spotted George and Celeste Rivers holding each other, and watching helplessly as legions of firefighters scrambled around them, trying to save what was left of their burning house and to prevent the hungry flames from spreading to their neighbors' homes.

"There are Jimmy's parents!" she yelped, hurrying out of the car with Madison a step behind. Tears again filled her eyes as she fell into their arms and hugged them tightly, but she managed to maintain a semblance of composure.

"Have you heard from Jimmy?" she asked anxiously.

"No, I'm afraid not," Celeste answered, her voice quavering. "We let him sleep in this morning because he was up so late last night, and because of all the stress he's been under these past few days. But he's not picking up his cell phone."

Feeling herself starting to lose her grip, again, Sasha deferred to Madison. "Mr. and Mrs. Rivers, this is Madison Munro from ABC News."

"I'm so sorry we have to meet under these circumstances," the reporter empathized while shaking their hands. "You have a very special son. I have to tell you, I have a very strong feeling that this can't be the end."

For the second time in less than ten minutes, Madison's words startled her audience. George and Celeste looked at each other incredulously. "This can't be the end," couldn't have been a coincidence – could it have been?

Before they fully could wrap their minds around them, Madison had donned her reporter's hat and brought them back to earth.

"Has the fire chief told you anything?"

George spoke up. "Only that by the time they got here, the fire was too hot and the smoke was too thick to go inside to check for anyone who might be trapped. He said there had to have been some accelerant for the fire to have advanced so quickly.

"We told him we thought Jimmy might still be in the house and he said they were trying everything they could to be able to get inside. By the sound of his voice, though, I could tell he didn't hold out much hope. I mean, if he's telling us it was too hot and too dangerous for his firemen to go in with all their gear, then it's kind of easy to do the math."

Madison noticed the arrival of her cameraman, André. "If you'll excuse me, I need to set up. But, as I was telling Sasha on the way over here, you must never give up hope, no matter how impossible a situation seems. God bless."

* * *

Alice Fenimore had poured herself a cup of coffee and just settled in to watch her favorite morning show, *Good Morning America*, when the programming was interrupted by a special report. The video feed switched to a familiar reporter standing in front of a burning house.

"Good morning. I'm Madison Munro. Last night, Jimmy Rivers and I sat in the living room of his house here in southeast Denver, and we spent almost an entire hour talking about the ramifications of a mysterious video, taken anonymously, that showed him explaining to his civics class at Benjamin Franklin High School the hypocrisy of the Partnership of the Right's pro-life stance and its support for capital punishment – and why, if God were here today, He would be pro-choice rather than pro-life.

"Twelve hours after wrapping up the interview, Jimmy's house is on fire and there are unconfirmed reports that he still might be inside. It's too early to tell if this can be written off to tragic coincidence, but it's almost too much of a stretch to do so. All we can say at this point is, God, if You're here, we need a miracle."

"Oh my God!" Alice gasped, spilling her coffee. She raced to the study and banged frantically on the door. "Bill! Bill! BILL!"

The Senator finally opened the door. He was irritated. He'd made it very clear that he was not to be disturbed, and was about to chastise his wife, but she beat him to the punch.

"Bill! You have to see this! The Rivers' house is on fire!"

On hearing the news, the Senator's three associates rushed out of the study and into the family room, with the Senator close behind, and caught the middle of the news station's initial report, with the house burning in the background: "...the young man whose video and interview have gone completely viral for his challenges to the Partnership of the Right and to the traditions of the Catholic Church. Again, there are unconfirmed rumors that he still might be inside the house."

Cell phones started to ring at once. The man in the dark suit answered his and sprinted out of the house. Cardinal Phelps called Father Simon to alert him that the press conference had been canceled. The Senator picked up a call from his campaign headquarters, and Ralph was fielding requests from reporters seeking comment.

"We have no comment at this time except to say we are thankful for the firefighters' swift action and hopeful that Jimmy is not in the house."

* * *

"How could you let this happen?" Satan screamed into the phone as the man in the dark suit sped to the scene. "I told you to watch over him. We can't afford something like this happening! The Partnership will get blamed for it, the Church is under attack, and he's shining a light on the lies I have used since the Garden to keep them from realizing what it means to have been created in God's image."

He paused to assess what he'd just said. Then he continued.

"As a matter of fact," Satan fumed, "this couldn't be worse. It is exactly what I was afraid of – Jimmy getting more and more publicity, more and more eyes looking into his Truth...and we had no recourse but to cancel the press conference! I want you to find out who set that fire, and I want whoever it was dealt with in the severest way possible. I need to send a message!"

* * *

Back at the Fenimore household, the frenzy had intensified. Father Simon debated with Cardinal Phelps about the wisdom of canceling the press conference. "Your Eminence, with all due respect, think of it like this. This is 'The Show.' As far as we're concerned, there is no more important show. And the show must go on! Just as Pilate 'showed' after all the fanfare that greeted Jesus when he rode into Jerusalem on that donkey!"

"Well, that didn't turn out so well for Pilate, did it?" the Cardinal growled.

"This is not the Son of God we're talking about! He's a seventeen year-old kid who probably can't see the writing on the wall. Ours is the greatest "show' on earth, and the show must go on. We can't let him have the last word without discrediting it!"

"I appreciate your passion, Father, but your concern is misplaced. You're worried about the last word, but the greater concern is about last rites."

"I don't understand."

"The bigger picture is how insensitive we will come off as human beings running for the highest office in the land, and especially as religious leaders, if we attack a young boy who may have lost his life in a fire, or whose family just lost their house and all their possessions. You mentioned Jesus. It is not what Jesus would do."

"But why should that stop us now?" the zealous priest protested. "Nothing we're doing is what Jesus would do."

"Hear me out. Years ago, when I was in your shoes, we had a family in the church, Mark and Gale Grassley. She was Catholic, he was not, but they baptized their three children in the church, and they were among the church's highest-donating stewards.

"Mark died tragically during a family vacation to Mexico, but because he hadn't been baptized in the church, we couldn't offer funeral services for him. His grieving family was forced to go elsewhere to lay their beloved father and husband to rest. Many of our parishioners were astounded at the church's position, and as I recall, Jimmy's parents were among them. They challenged me, asking what I thought Jesus would do if He were in my position – if I thought He would refuse a funeral for Mark and his bereaved family. I couldn't answer them.

"Needless to say, we can't afford to have anyone challenge our motives with, 'What Would Jesus Do,' and not have an answer with the national spotlight on us!"

Father Simon backed off. "It's incredible how this has gone full circle...first, with Jimmy's parents, and now, with Jimmy. Who are these people?"

Ralph continued to fend off reporters' incessant clamor while, at the same time, trying to convince Alice that they shouldn't drop everything and hurry over to the Rivers' burning house to offer their support.

The harried campaign manager was adamant. "Alice, he's a Senator for the state of Colorado. He can't be seen as an ambulance chaser. It just doesn't look presidential."

"Damn your presidential priorities!" Alice yelled. "He's a father, too, and this is our daughter's boyfriend."

The sound of his wife's raised voice fetched the Senator to her side in time to hear Ralph argue, "And what would you accomplish by being there? Other than creating a monumental distraction?"

Suddenly contrite, Bill Fenimore put his arm around Alice's shoulders. "He's right, honey. We'd be like a three-ring circus in the middle of professionals trying to do their jobs and possibly trying to save a life."

Alice Fenimore sighed heavily, resigned to her proper Stepford Wife role. "I just feel so helpless."

4

In Matthew 7:7, Jesus said, "Ask and it will be given to you; seek and you will find; knock and the door will be opened to you."

Five minutes after Madison Munro begged God for a miracle, the front door of the burning house at 2318 White Rabbit Road opened, and Jimmy walked out of the flames, not a hair on his body having been singed.

For the briefest of moments, the collective emergency effort in front of the Rivers' house – that of the firefighters, the paramedics, the reporters, the police officers – hiccupped, as all eyes gaped at the incongruously surreal scene unfolding before them, their minds unable to process the sight of Jimmy calmly emerging from the fire. George, Celeste, and Sasha held each other up, paralyzed by the unfathomable.

"Jimmy!" Sasha shrieked, breaking the spell, and suddenly, the first responders swarmed around her boyfriend, and spirited him to safety – well, to a waiting ambulance, anyway.

Try as she might, she couldn't break through the police line that cordoned off the area. But Madison, hearing Sasha's struggle even though she was in the middle of her broadcast, slyly maneuvered her way through the mob to Sasha's side, with André close behind and filming her every move.

"Hey!" she yelled at one of the police officers, above the commotion. "These are Jimmy's parents, the homeowners," indicating George and Celeste who had joined Sasha at the police line. "And, this is Sasha Fenimore, Senator Fenimore's daughter and Jimmy's girlfriend. Let them through! You're on live TV, by the way."

Reluctantly, the officer let them cross the line, but it didn't get them any closer to Jimmy. Everyone wanted a piece of him, from the medical personnel trying to check his vital signs to the other emergency responders attempting to gain an understanding as to what happened and to how he got out alive with not so much as a scratch.

The paramedics were baffled when all the numbers came back "normal," except for his pulse, which posted 42, quite a bit below normal, and indicative of someone who might be sleeping. This was completely uncharted territory, and the decision was made to take Jimmy to Denver General Hospital for observation and for a more thorough examination.

As unshaken as Jimmy appeared to be, that's how agitated his parents still were. Sasha, by then, was a little more accustomed to the extraordinary events that, more and more, had become part and parcel of the "Jimmy Rivers experience," but she, too hadn't come all the way back from the edge. When Jimmy caught sight of them through the crowd, he sent a rescue worker to fetch them, and all three of them were allowed to accompany him in the ambulance. Amid a blaring siren and flashing red and blue lights, and trailed by a phalanx of paparazzi, the caravan made its way to Denver General's Level One Trauma Center.

They left the others behind to finish their jobs...the Rivers' house was a total loss, but the firefighters still needed to contain it. Paramedics stood by waiting to assist, as needed. Madison and the other reporters still on the scene scrambled to get comments from anyone they could.

Police officers kept the lookie-loos at bay, all the while scouring the rubberneckers for anyone who looked out-of-place. It was a well-known fact that arsonists and pyromaniacs often liked to stick around among the curiosity-seekers to admire their handiwork. No one caught their eye, but the man in the dark suit zeroed in on a fortysomething man wearing a Fundamental Truth Church t-shirt and a Kansas City Royals baseball cap who didn't quite blend.

In the ambulance, Sasha held Jimmy's hand tightly. This time, tears of happiness stained her cheeks. She leaned over and kissed her boyfriend's forehead, somewhat surprised to discover how cool it felt against her lips.

"I was so scared," she admitted.

Jimmy brought her hand to his lips and gently kissed it. He noticed his parents shaking from the adrenaline still coursing through their veins. There was no "fight or flight' situation to which it could be applied, so it just manifested in uncontrollable tremors.

"Hey you guys," Jimmy smiled brightly, "thanks for letting me sleep in!"

* * *

Alice stayed glued to her television set while her husband, his campaign manager, and their parish priest hightailed it to their war room at the Southeast Denver Christian Bible Church to meet up with Cardinal Phelps and Leon Tusk. The blaring sound of her cell phone shook her from her catatonia.

"Oh my God, Alice, can you believe this s - - t with the Rivers' house? Did you see your daughter on TV?" It was Sylvia calling from the mail room at the *Denver Post*.

"No, I can't!" she blurted, still shaken. "I'm so shocked with everything that's going on – the campaign, this fire, Jimmy's video, Roland...," her voice trailed off. "But, yes, I did see Sasha getting into the ambulance with Jimmy and his parents."

"Have you talked with her, yet?"

"No, she's not picking up. She'll call me when she has a chance."

"Well, speaking of Roland, that's another reason I'm calling."

Alice perked up. "Did you find the envelope?"

Sylvia hesitated. "I've got good news and less good news about that."

"Give me the good news," Alice insisted. "I could use a shot of good news right about now."

"OK, the good news is that the envelope has been found!"

"Thank the Lord!"

"But I don't have it," Sylvia added quickly.

"I don't understand. Where is it?"

"So, that's the strange thing. After I got off the phone with you, I received a call from a Leticia Carter, and she was asking about the envelope, too. She said it was her son, Isaac, who Roland asked to mail the envelope for him if he didn't meet back up with him at 5:30 yesterday afternoon. When he didn't show up, Isaac did as he was instructed. He put the envelope in the mailbox.

"Which brings us to the not so good news. It sounds like something might have happened to Roland."

Sylvia just confirmed Alice's worst fear. Cooper was going to be devastated, and she didn't even want to think about the Senator's reaction.

"You said you don't have it? Who does? Whoever does have it has to get whatever's inside to the police as soon as possible!"

"And we're back to strange. I'm pretty sure our managing editor, Don Stottlemeyer, has it. He was down here for first mail call, which is unusual in and of itself because, as I told you, he never gets to work this early and because in all my years in the mail room, I've never seen him down here.

"Then, when I mentioned to him that I had spoken with Leticia and told him that she had called to follow up on their conversation last night about the envelope, he totally denied it, saying he gets lots of crank calls and he can't remember the names of everyone calling them in.

"But, and this is a huge 'BUT'...I saw him trying to hide the envelope between a stack of papers he was carrying, and he seemed defensive when I asked him about it in the first place."

"Are you sure the envelope was from Roland?"

"100%. The envelope was bigger than the other papers he had stuck it between, and the return address was only partially hidden. I could see Roland's name."

"I'm confused," Alice admitted. "What do you think it means?"

"I'm not sure, but it could be because we've had some corporate spies here in the last several months trying to steal our exclusives and out-scoop us. Maybe he didn't want to take any chances on this one. Which could mean two things: it's potentially a very sensitive story involving some high-profile people. And, if it is, it doesn't bode well for Roland.

"If that's the case, though, you can be sure Don won't waste any time getting the story out after checking the sources. He wouldn't want to take the chance of another outlet beating us to the punch. And, you can be sure that he'll contact the proper authorities, if need be, so they can send out the cavalry for Roland! That's kind of a rule in this business, lest the paper get cited as an accessory, withholding information critical to an investigation, or some such thing."

Alice thanked Sylvia and promised they'd get together one day soon for lunch or for drinks after work. She hung up the phone and immediately dialed Cooper's number to find out if he'd heard from Roland and to tell him about the envelope. He didn't pick up, either. All this money we spend on cell phones, she groused, to speed up the communication process... She left her son a text message to call her as soon as he could.

Alice turned her attention back to the special report that had captivated the nation. Madison Munro was wrapping up:

"This is what we know so far. At approximately 8:47 this morning, Fire Station 37 received a call about a house on fire at 2318 White Rabbit Road. The house belongs to George and Celeste Rivers, the parents of Jimmy Rivers, the young man who, under mysterious circumstances, was recorded answering a question in his civics class at Benjamin Franklin High School on Monday, and identified the inherent hypocrisy of the Partnership of the Right's platform supporting both capital punishment and pro-life agendas by pointing out, quite convincingly, that God is, first and foremost, "pro-choice."

"The video went viral in record time, and then, in a subsequent interview with this reporter last night, he presented a very logical challenge to some of the traditions behind the dogma and foundation of the Catholic Church. He may not have made many friends, but he did influence a lot of people.

"Fire Chief McDaniels said that it was too early to tell for sure if the fire had been set deliberately, but the fact that it spread so quickly was a strong indicator that some sort of accelerant had been used.

"Time will tell if the Rivers house was targeted specifically because of Jimmy's thoughts and the almost instant fame they have brought him, but the coincidence was not lost upon the investigators with whom we spoke. And, there are a lot of lunatics out there.

"So, while it remains unclear at this point if this was a random arson event or if it was a message from extreme right-wing Christian fundamentalists, it is expected that an 'attempted murder' charge will be added to the laundry list of charges brought against whoever set this fire since Jimmy was inside the house.

"That being said, it's hard to say right now if this was an intentional attempt on the life of the teenager at the center of this storm. This is Wednesday morning, and ordinarily Jimmy would have been in school, but his parents felt that he needed the extra rest after all the excitement of the past few days.

"Nevertheless, leaving the question unanswered for now as to whether or not the arsonist was trying to kill Jimmy, none of us were prepared for what we were about to see when we first arrived on the scene, especially from a fire that Chief McDaniels deemed too dangerous to send his firefighters inside, and too hot for anyone inside to have survived.

"Yet, incredibly, just moments after the fire chief had spoken – as if on cue – Jimmy casually emerged from the raging inferno as if he were taking a walk in the park without a care in the world. He was completely untouched by the flames licking at his entire body, almost like he had an invisible, protective asbestos bubble around him. Not even a fiber of his clothing was burned, let alone any of the hairs on his head.

"It was nothing short of a miracle. That was the word everyone used to describe the indescribable, even those who claimed to be atheists. The term generally is associated with anything that defies explanation in this universe, but I have my own theories that tie into another miraculous event I witnessed thirteen years ago on Berthoud Pass that we coincidentally – there's that word, again – revisited in an anniversary special on this station two nights ago.

"Was it a fantastic coincidence that we chose to take another look at the Berthoud Pass miracle a mere 48 hours before the White Rabbit Road miracle unfolded before our very eyes? Or was it the universe nudging us in a direction that we otherwise would not have chosen?

"This is Madison Munro reporting in front of 2318 White Rabbit Road."

* * *

Father Simon snaked his Escalade through the back alleys of the neighborhood near the Southeast Denver Christian Bible Church. He parked the SUV behind the church and he and the Senator and Ralph Petiole entered the house of worship through the priest's entrance to avoid the reporters camped out in front of the sanctuary, jockeying among themselves for the most advantageous position from which to get a comment.

Joyce Odell, Father Simon's loyal secretary, was waiting for the men, and showed them to the meeting room where Cardinal Phelps was speaking earnestly on the phone with Leon Tusk waiting in the wings to transmit a transcript of their conspiratorial plan. As the men took their seats, around the table, the Cardinal said, "They're here now," and pushed a button to put the phone on speaker.

"Gentlemen," Satan growled, "obviously that fire was a real f - - k-up, as I anticipated, and you wouldn't want to be whoever it was who started it when I catch up to him! Do you see all the publicity the kid is getting? And the reporters in front of this church? All of them waiting to ask questions about how he walked out of that fire without getting burned!"

Father Simon tried to soothe the Devil's ruffled feathers. "Sir, I don't think any of them will make the connection with the story of Shadrach, Meshach, and Abednago. I'd go so far as to say that none of them would know the Old Testament if it fell off a shelf and hit them in the head."

"Well, someone will!" Satan screamed.

"If I may, sire," Cardinal Phelps interposed. "We've been here before, and the idiots still don't get it. Our path is clear – we must stay the course and create Doubt, however unreasonable, and discredit the source.

"The story of Shadrach, Meshach, and Abednago must be presented in the same light as Jesus saying nothing would be impossible for anyone who has the faith of a mustard seed – as hyperbole! As a fantastic exaggeration to get a point across.

"Do you think they will believe any story if they didn't believe Jesus? Nebuchadnezzar's fire was heated up seven times hotter than usual – so hot that it killed the guards who threw the three nonconformists into it. No one believed it then and no one will believe it now. They always default to disbelief'

Ralph disagreed. "But, ABC News wasn't around back then. Everybody saw Jimmy walk out of his burning house with not even a scorch mark on his clothes!"

"That's why we have to discredit the source, as well," Satan's malevolent voice came over the loudspeaker. "Our outlets will call it fake news. We'll get scientists to say it's absolutely impossible for anyone or anything to survive such a fire and, you'll see – everyone will continue to believe the scientists over the Son of God.

"'In God We Trust' means nothing to His children. All we have to do, as Cardinal Phelps noted, is give them a reasonable or unreasonable doubt and they'll follow in the footsteps of their ancestors, Adam and Eve, and choose very poorly to place their trust in Doubt.

"That moment in the Garden was my greatest triumph! And I can do it again. We just float the idea of a conspiracy theory staged by those who want to smear the Senator and your Partnership of the Right. Or, it could have been the fake ABC News staging the fire in a brazen attempt to support that reporter's agenda to link the two miracles, as she calls them.

"Either way, with Leon's invaluable help, we float the theory that whoever it was could have created a secret passageway for the kid to walk through safely, which would have been completely destroyed by the fire, and the fake news will become old news before you know it. Look, everyone had forgotten about that incident on Berthoud Pass thirteen years ago, and it would have stayed forgotten if it hadn't been for that shameless reporter bringing it up, again!"

Satan paused to let his words sink in. "So, if there aren't any questions, let's get to work! Oh, and one more thing," he added. "Senator, before you go to sleep tonight, leave your back door unlocked."

5

The second Madison went off the air, she called Jimmy. "Come on, pick up!" she pleaded into her phone.

When it went to voicemail, she hung up and pushed "redial' – then, quickly hung up, again, before it rang.

"What am I thinking?" she scolded herself, and she dialed Sasha's number.

"Hi Madison," the teenager answered the phone.

"Wow, somebody is a lot calmer than when I picked her up from school today. She must be making goo-goo eyes at her boyfriend!"

"She must be!" Sasha giggled.

"How's he doing? I tried calling him, but I realized his cell phone probably has seen better days."

"Hold on, I'll put him on. I'll let you decide. See you soon...and thank you!"

"You're welcome."

"Hey, Madison," Jimmy chirped nonchalantly when he got on the line. "What's up?"

"Oh, so that's how we're going to play it. OK, well, Mr. Not-Much-Is-Up. Same ol' same ol,' on this end," she yawned for effect. "Watched a house go up in flames, and, if that wasn't boring enough, I saw a wise guy walk out of that fire without burning a single hair on his chinny-chin-chin. You?"

"Same," he deadpanned. "Nothing out of the ordinary." There was a pregnant pause. Then, "Oh, wait, now that you mention it, I was that handsome guy who walked out of that fire. Small world."

"Did I say "handsome?" I don't think so. I'm pretty sure I said 'wise guy!'"

"Oh. Well, then, it couldn't have been me."

"Alright, Sugar Ray, you win. No más."

"Sugar Ray?"

"Good grief, you're too young. My bad. But, seriously, how are you?"

"I keep telling everybody that I'm fine, but this doctor who's checking me out says he wants to be the judge of that. Anyway, I'll spare you the suspense. I'm fine."

"I'll take your word for it. Jimmy, I have so many questions, I don't know where to start."

"I'm gonna have to call you back. The doctor has a few more tests for me."

"Of course. I'm sorry, I almost forgot you were the wise guy I saw in the fire. Be well, and I'll talk to you later. Can you pass me over to your parents?"

"You mean handsome, don't you?" Satisfied that he had gotten the last word in, Jimmy handed the phone to his father.

"Hello, Madison, this is George Rivers."

"Hello, Mr. Rivers…"

"Please call me George."

"OK, so, Mr. Rivers – George – you're going to need a place to stay for a few nights, and I wanted to let you know that I've arranged for a room for the three of you at The Crawford Hotel. Also, there will be a burner phone for Jimmy...oh gosh, I heard that as soon as it came out. Let me try that again. There will be a temporary phone for Jimmy until insurance gets him a new one.

"Is there anything else I – check that, ABC – can do for you right now?"

"That's so kind of you, Madison, but we wouldn't want to impose," he demurred politely.

"No imposition at all. It's on ABC, so impose away!"

George shrugged his shoulders. "Well, ok, then, thank you. But, really, the hotel room and phone are more than enough. Celeste and I can do some shopping this afternoon."

"Sir, I don't want to tell you what to do, but you might want to think about keeping a low profile for a few days until this gets sorted out. That fire was deliberately set. Now, whoever set it might not have known Jimmy would be in the house because it's a school day.

"But, we can't discount the possibility that someone was following your son and knew that you let him sleep in. Whoever it was will know by now that Jimmy still is alive, and they might put a tail on you to find out where he is. Let me get someone to take care of that shopping for you."

George's mood dimmed noticeably. "I never would have thought of that."

"That's what thirteen years in this business will do for you. And we'll have to sneak you out of the hospital the back way. I'll be there shortly."

* * *

Officers Mike McGregor and Houston Janney eased their squad car into the parking lot of the 7-11 near West 38th Avenue and Irving Street in the Highlands neighborhood just west of downtown Denver. They had been partners ever since Janney was a rookie on the force and was assigned to the highly-decorated 17-year veteran, and they'd been dispatched to the convenience store to investigate a report of a "man down" behind the building.

Pistols drawn, the two police officers walked around back and found a man face down on the ground, lying in a pool of blood. He had been shot in the back of the head, execution style.

"Strange," Janney remarked, holstering his gun and putting on latex gloves before turning the body over.

"Definitely not gang-related," McGregor agreed. "This looks like a professional hit. And no reports of a gunshot – could be a silencer."

"In this neighborhood?" his partner wondered aloud.

"I know. Something's not right. Houston, we've got a problem," the veteran said with a straight face.

"Really, you're going to go there, again?" It's not like Janney hadn't heard the phrase ten thousand times in his life.

McGregor smiled. "Never gets old."

The younger officer bent down and gently rolled the body over. It appeared to be that of a fortysomething man, unremarkably clothed in blue jeans, a faded yellow Fundamental Truth Church t-shirt, an unzipped blue windbreaker, and a Kansas City Royals baseball cap.

McGregor shook his head, his seventeen years of experience in the field flashing red. "Now, I really don't like where this is headed."

"What do you mean? Do you recognize this guy?"

"I recognize his t-shirt. Haven't you heard of the Fundamental Truth Church?"

"No. Should I have?"

"Maybe. They're on the news from time to time for their radical, fundamentalist beliefs. Their church is in Topeka, and they call themselves Christians, but that would be like the Devil calling himself an angel. I'd say it's one of the most odious and rabid hate groups in the U.S., if not the worst."

"How do they get away with that?"

"How does any church get away with the things they say and do that are so anti-Christ?"

Janney looked at his partner. "You've been holding out on me. You know about religion?"

"OK, no one knows this, but I graduated from the seminary before I joined the force."

"Talk about radical," Janney whistled. "That's quite a change!"

"Not really, not when you think about it. Both callings are about helping people – and even Jesus was fed up with organized religion. He said, "Split a piece of wood and I am there. Lift a stone and you will find me."

"In other words, in order to be with Him, you have to tear down these palatial, hypocritical edifices that are Christian in name only. Once you refocus on Christ by tearing down all the distractions, that's when you'll truly be with Him.

"I would have been crushed by the hierarchy and by the weight of the traditions they always default to, if I bucked the system, so to speak, so I chose the force to spread my good works.

"And, by the way, I'd appreciate it if you kept that to yourself, partner."

"Sure, Mike."

"So, let's see if this guy has any ID on him."

Janney reached under the body and found a wallet in the back pocket of the man's jeans. The driver's license belonged to Jackson Hill, 47 years old, from Topeka, Kansas.

"He's got a few credit cards in his name and about $200 in cash, so we can rule out robbery as a motive. Oh, and lookie here...his NRA card."

"Figures."

"And a concealed weapon permit."

"Damn. Giving a gun to a guy with this much hate in him is like giving heroin to an addict and telling him not to use it. Is he carrying?"

Janney felt around the dead man's waistband, patted down his legs, and checked all his pockets. He pulled out a set of car keys and some tattered newspaper clippings from the windbreaker, but no weapon.

"Nothing. Just these clippings."

"Great," McGregor lamented. "Someone either stole his gun before we got here, or it's in his car, wherever that is. Let me see those clippings."

Janney handed them over and called in their report while McGregor skimmed through the faded yellow newsprint. Forensics was on their way.

"What do they say?" Houston asked, after hanging up with dispatch.

"They're old, from 1993, 1994 and 1995...David Gunn, John Bayard Britton, George Tiller, Yitzhak Rabin. Probably a little before your time."

"Who are they? What do you think they mean?"

"Well, Yitzhak Rabin was a hero of mine," McGregor reminisced, "the only Israeli prime minister who had the Palestinians' ear. For the first time, almost since the beginning of time, there was a realistic chance for peace in the Middle East. I'll never forget his words: "We who have fought against you, the Palestinians, we say to you today, in a loud and clear voice, enough blood and tears. Enough!"

"But before a treaty could be signed, he was assassinated by an ultra-Orthodox Jew who hadn't had enough and who hated the idea of reconciliation with the Arabs. And the bastard succeeded. Taking Rabin out derailed the whole peace train. People like to speculate what the world would have been like if Kennedy hadn't been shot... same thing with Rabin. Peace in the Middle East...what a concept!"

McGregor paused to contemplate Rabin's irreplaceable loss. Then, he continued, "Anyway, Gunn, Tiller, and Britton were the first abortion doctors killed here in the U.S. by pro-lifers, as odd as that sounds.

"Five will get you ten that these clippings were this Jackson Hill's fight song and he was here to take someone out."

"Well, it looks like whoever he was going to hit, hit back harder. He definitely locked horns with the wrong person."

* * *

From the Emergency Room at Denver General Hospital, Sasha listened intently as Jimmy tried to explain the unexplainable to a police detective.

"I didn't hear anything before the fire. But then I heard a voice telling me to wake up, and that's when I saw my room was on fire."

"No, there was no one in the room with me."

"I don't know whose voice it was."

"No, it wasn't staged."

"No, we don't have an underground tunnel."

"The only way to describe it is that it was like Moses parting the Red Sea, and I walked through this kind of corridor that somehow was insulated from the fire."

"No, it wasn't hot."

"Yes, I believe in God. Really, you should know that by now."

"Yes, I believe in miracles."

"I don't know if it had anything to do with the video or the interview."

"No, I don't want to speculate."

"No, I don't believe in coincidences."

"No, I haven't gotten any death threats."

Sasha felt her phone vibrate and stepped outside the room.

"Hi, Mom."

"Honey, it's so good to hear your voice," Alice blubbered. "I was so worried."

"Mom, I'm fine. It was Jimmy who was in the fire...and, he's fine, too. I can't talk right now, but I was just about to call you. Can you come and pick me up at Denver General and take me back to school?"

"Of course, Sweetheart. I'll be there in about fifteen minutes."

"Thank you! Text me when you're here. We'll talk in the car."

Jimmy's parents were answering questions when Sasha walked back into the room.

"Yes, we locked the door on our way out."

"We never leave it unlocked."

"No, we didn't see anything or anyone suspicious."

"No, we don't keep gasoline in the garage."

"We have – or had – electric stoves."

Sasha whispered into Jimmy's ear. "We both know what this is. The parallel universes!"

Jimmy looked straight into his girlfriend's eyes. "I've got so much to tell you. You're not going to believe it!"

"Oh, my mind is about as open as it's ever been after I saw you walk – not run! – out of that fire like you didn't have a care in the world."

Sasha's phone buzzed. She looked at the text.

"It's my Mom. She's here. I have to turn my paper in. Are you going to be ok?"

"No."

Concern clouded Sasha's face. "What's the matter?"

"You're leaving me," he teased.

Sasha gently backhanded her smiling boyfriend on the arm. "Keep that up, mister, and I will be leaving you!"

"Seriously, Sasha, thank you for being here."

She kissed him sweetly on the lips. "Promise to call me when you get to The Crawford and get your phone?"

"I promise."

She reached around her boyfriend's shoulders to give him a hug. He drew her in closer...and gave her posterior a playful pinch.

Again, she affected a fake umbrage and this time slapped his hand.

"No, there's nothing wrong with you," she said wryly. "Some things never will change." Then, she bent over him and nibbled on his ear lobe, "And I hope they never will."

⋆ ⋆ ⋆

Andy Theus was watching the drama unfold at 2318 White Rabbit Road from his corner office on the 56th floor of the SFI Building in downtown Denver. Madison Munro just had signed off when his phone buzzed.

"Sir," the voice of his secretary, Emily Charles, cut in, "I have Senator Fenimore on Line 1."

The Chairman and Chief Executive Officer of Safety First International picked up immediately.

"Good morning, Bill!"

"Hi, Andy. I hope I'm not interrupting anything."

"Not at all. It's never an interruption when the next President of the United States calls. I was watching TV. Helluva thing with the Rivers house. Helluva thing."

"That's partly why I'm calling you. You of all people should know that timing is everything, but it is especially so in politics. Momentum goes back and forth, and you don't want to peak too soon.

"You've probably seen the kid's video that went viral a couple of days ago, and his interview on TV last night..."

"I have. And, I have to be honest with you – that reporter, Madison Munro, scares me. We've butted heads a few times and I can't say that I ever came out of it ahead or without a bruise or three."

"And that's the second part of the problem. Publicity. As publicity goes, so goes momentum. Right now, it's definitely switched sides."

"Bill," Andy interjected, "I don't think it's switched sides as much as it's gone away from the Partnership."

"Six of one, half dozen of the other. Anyway, I'm sitting here with Ralph, Cardinal Phelps, and Father Simon, and we've talked it over with the others, and we think it's high time to get "Mo' back on our side before this damn fire turns into a runaway train we can't stop."

"I'm with you. How can I help?"

"I'll cut right to the chase, Andy. Do you have any political aspirations?"

"You mean, beyond doing whatever I can to support the Partnership? No, not really," he lied.

"Ever since it became obvious that we were going to win the nomination, we've been vetting potential running mates, and your name kept coming up. Yours was the only one that came up without any skeletons in the closet."

Not a word from the CEO of the largest insurer in the world.

"Andy, are you still there?" the Senator asked.

"I'm sorry, Bill," Andy apologized, feigning ignorance. "You caught me by surprise. I don't know what to say."

"Well, before you say anything, I have to tell you that you'd have to step away from SFI when we get elected."

"I like the way you said, 'when we get elected,' not, 'if we get elected.'"

"Andy, there's no question in anyone's mind that we will win the White House with a landslide if you sign on. We know it might be premature to announce a running mate before the nomination, but drastic times call for drastic measures. We have to stop this Jimmy Rivers juggernaut right now! Will you think about it?"

"Senator, I don't have to. You know I've always done whatever I could to support the party. It would be a privilege and an honor to step up to the plate as your running mate, and I have no problem walking away from SFI when we get elected. It practically runs on auto-pilot, now, as it is."

Andy heard a collective enthusiastic, "Yes!" in the background from the others gathered at the Southeast Denver Christian Bible Church.

"I'm pretty sure you heard that," the Senator grinned. "That's such good news! You're doing us and your country a tremendous service! We'll be in touch shortly about how and when we'll make the announcement. You might clear your schedule for the rest of the day...and tomorrow.

"And, Andy, I can't stress this enough. Until we make the announcement, it's very important that you don't tell anyone. If it leaks out before we have a chance to announce it, it will defuse the moment."

"Not a word from me to anyone," Andy assured the Partnership. "Not until you make it official."

The two men thanked each other and hung up, each of them smugly elated that they had gotten their way.

Andy reached into his suit coat's inside pocket, pulled out his private phone, and dialed a dedicated number. When the voice on the other end answered, he said softly and with a conspiratorial smile, "It's done."

6

Alice Fenimore was so relieved to see her daughter walk out of the double doors of Denver General's Emergency entrance. She had the most brilliant rainbow aura around her. No matter what was going on in Alice's life, no matter how stressful it might be, she knew everything would work out when she was plugged into Sasha's radiant energy.

Sasha opened the door of the silver Range Rover and plopped herself down in the passenger seat. She was exhausted from all the emotion that had been coursing through her body.

"Honey, are you sure you're ok?" Alice asked, leaning over to give her daughter a big hug.

"I really am. Just laying eyes on Jimmy was such a relief!"

"I know what you mean. And Jimmy?

"He's fine, too, thank God."

"So, it's true?"

"What?"

"That he walked out of that burning house practically untouched?"

"Not practically, Mom. Completely untouched. There wasn't a single singed hair on his body!"

"It's just so unbelievable!"

"I know. If I hadn't seen him with my own two eyes, I wouldn't have believed it, either."

"What did he say?"

"He said it was like the flames parted as the Red Sea did for Moses."

"To be honest, I always thought that account of Moses parting the Red Sea just was a fanciful story."

"Probably most everyone does. Maybe it's a sign from above that Jimmy's right – that it's time we need to choose to believe God, not just believe in Him...

"Oh, and Mom?"

"Yes, dear?"

"We need to go. I have to get to school, but I need to go home so I can get my paper for Mr. Hamilton's class. I should have asked you to bring it, but there was too much going on. Besides, I need my car."

"I'm sorry," Alice apologized, putting the Range Rover in gear. "I don't know where my mind is."

Sasha winced. She suddenly remembered what happened a few hours ago when Hannah had rushed her home to retrieve her paper – the man in the dark suit walking up the steps to her house with her father, his disgusting campaign manager, and Father Simon. In all the excitement, she had forgotten to tell Jimmy.

"Mom, Daddy's not at the house, is he?"

"No. They all raced to the church when they heard the news about the Rivers' house."

Sasha breathed a sigh of relief. But her mind was in overdrive.

"How did the press conference go?"

"Postponed."

"Poor Daddy," she muttered. "I'll bet his stress level is through the roof!"

"Let's just say he's had much better days. He's got so much on his plate...with more to come!"

"Oh my gosh," Sasha exhaled. "I almost forgot about Cooper and Roland. Please tell me Roland's shown up!"

"I wish I could, Sweetheart," her mother frowned. "But," she continued with faint hope in her voice, "Jimmy's instincts were right. Sylvia said she saw the envelope from Roland!"

"Saw it?" Sasha asked anxiously. "Doesn't she have it?"

"No. She said the managing editor of the paper got to it before she could, but she was able to confirm it was from Roland. She said that if it was that important for the managing editor to come in early and poke his head into the mail room for the first time since she's been there, she was sure that it would be the paper's top priority, and that when he opens it, he'll do the right thing, depending on what Roland sent in. If he feels he needs to call the police, he will. Actually, I'm a little surprised we haven't heard from Mr. Stottlemeyer, yet, but with the fire...," her voice trailed off. "Maybe he called your father."

"I hope not! You have to tell him first so he can be prepared. You know how sensitive it is for him."

"I know, I just haven't had a chance."

"How's Cooper?"

"He's worried. He's hoping for the best, but I think he's preparing for the worst."

"He should come home. I hate to think of him all alone in his apartment."

"He wants to stay there in case Roland shows up. But some of his friends are with him, so that's good. I'm sure they're taking good care of him."

"I'll call him after school," Sasha promised.

The silver Range Rover pulled into the driveway at 37 Skylark Lane and Sasha hopped out.

"Honey, I know you're in a hurry and you've got a lot on your mind. Please be careful!"

* * *

Hannah stuffed her jeans, t-shirt, and Converses into her backpack and checked herself in the full-length mirror of the ladies room at Joak Industries' downtown Denver office.

Hair pulled back, light makeup, silver stud earrings, sleeveless black top, gray pencil skirt just below the knees, nude pantyhose, and three-inch black pumps – in fifteen minutes, she had transformed herself from hip high school senior to attractive professional woman ten years her senior.

It was one o'clock in the afternoon and she was eager to start her first day. Girls know when they look good and Hannah savored the feeling of knowing the effect she would have on those around her...namely, on the head of HR, Tom Farrell. He would be a little distracted, a little more helpful, a little more permissive, and a little more forgiving as she embarked on her clandestine, fact-gathering espionage. She smiled deviously at the woman looking back at her in the mirror. The high school intern...it was the perfect cover.

She stowed her backpack in the employees' coatroom next to the break room and reported for duty. Tom was at a meeting outside of the office, but the receptionist, Annika Anderson, greeted her warmly.

"Love your outfit, Hannah!" she said cheerfully, not a hint of jealousy in her effusiveness. "That's just what this office needs – a breath of fresh air! So, are you ready for your first day?"

"I'm excited," Hannah admitted, mildly disappointed that she would have to wait for Tom to lay eyes on her.

"Well, here's your first official task. Take this mail and put it on Tom's desk. You know where it is, don't you?"

"Yes, ma'am!" Hannah saluted smartly, a sly grin turning up the corners of her mouth. There were letters and trade periodicals of all sizes, and she used two hands to carry the unwieldy pile down the long hallway to the head of Human Resources' corner office.

The door was open and she stepped inside. She took a moment to admire the view from the cavernous office. She'd been there once before, when she'd interviewed for the position, but hadn't had the opportunity to drink it all in. She considered trying out his high-backed chair behind the huge mahogany desk but had second thoughts and went about arranging the mail according to size.

The bulkiest envelope caught her eye, and her heart skipped a beat. It was addressed to the *Denver Post*. And in big, bold letters, the name in the return address was "Roland Thomas."

It hadn't been opened.

* * *

Sasha steered her black convertible Mustang into the student parking lot at Benjamin Franklin High School with an abandon just this side of reckless. Paper in hand, she hopped out of the car, ran inside, and raced up the stairs to Room 303. She tried the handle, but the door was locked. She knocked anxiously on the door. "Come on, you have to be here," she fretted under her breath.

"Coming," a familiar voice called out from inside the classroom, and in another moment, Ben Hamilton opened the door.

"Mr. Hamilton," she blurted out, "I'm so sorry I missed your class, but here's my paper..."

"Sasha," her teacher interrupted, "come in. You have to see this," he insisted, ushering her to his computer. "How's Jimmy doing?"

"Mr. Hamilton, you wouldn't believe it. He's fine! Not a single singed hair on his body. It's a miracle!"

"That's not what they're saying," he pointed to the news conference streaming live on his laptop.

Sasha looked at the screen. Standing in front of the Southeast Denver Christian Bible Church, Cardinal Phelps, Father Simon, and Ralph Petiole were giving their version of how Jimmy had been able to walk out of his house so calmly and totally unscathed as it burned to the ground earlier that morning.

When Cardinal Phelps was questioned about the similarities to the Old Testament account of Shadrach, Meshach, and Abednago surviving having been thrown into a fiery furnace after they refused to bow down to King Nebuchadnezzar – a fire so hot that the guard who had opened the hatch to the furnace was killed from the blast of heat – he responded that it was pure hyperbole, simply a fanciful story meant to convey the victory of the people standing up for what they believed and refusing to genuflect to oppression.

"It never really happened in the literal sense," he explained.

Mr. Hamilton paused the feed. "Sasha, do you know what miracles are?" he asked rhetorically.

Then, he answered his own question. "Miracles are things that science can't explain. If you don't believe in miracles, you don't believe in a higher authority who can override the physical laws of man. What I'm saying is that this is a striking admission from one of the higher-ups in the church that He really doesn't believe in God! Do you know what he really believes in?"

Sasha was quick with an answer this time. "The Partnership of the Right!"

"Exactly."

"That rings a bell. You know, my family goes to the Southeast Denver Christian Bible Church, and last Sunday Father Simon's sermon was about Matthew 17:20, the passage in which Jesus tells us that nothing is impossible for anyone who has the faith of a mustard seed – and Father Simon said that's not what Jesus meant, that it was just hyperbole.

"That's one of the reasons Jimmy and his family got sideways with the church. He reminded me about the first time someone from this world said not to trust someone from heaven: the serpent telling Eve that God didn't really mean she and Adam would die if they ate the fruit from the Tree of Knowledge of what is good and evil. And we know how that turned out!"

"That's an interesting thesis. I never thought of that, but the Word of God really isn't my strength. Frankly, though, it doesn't seem to be theirs, either," he said pointing to the images of Cardinal Phelps and Father Simon frozen on his laptop's screen. "Let's see what else they have to say."

He hit the "play' icon and the feed continued.

Another reporter asked, "Well, how do you explain Jimmy walking out of that fire completely untouched?"

Ralph Petiole stepped up to the microphone. "I'll take this one. We believe that an investigation will show that this was a stunt orchestrated by the fake news media, in collaboration with those who oppose Senator Fenimore, to throw shade on the Partnership and to lend credence to an impossible story about something that happened on Berthoud Pass thirteen years ago. It's just a blatant, thinly-veiled attempt to boost ratings for a second-rate, fake news outlet."

Ben Hamilton exited the feed. "I've heard enough. Petiole just put it out there. You can be sure you're going to get an earful of cider!"

"Cider? What?" Sasha was confused.

"It's a quote from Damon Runyan. He was an American writer famous for his romanticized portraits of gamblers and gangsters on Broadway during the Prohibition era. He wrote, "Someday, somewhere, a guy is going to come to you and show you a nice, brand-new deck of cards on which the seal is never broken, and this guy is going to offer to bet you that the jack of spades will jump out of this deck and squirt cider in your ear. But, do not bet this man, for, as sure as you do, you are going to get an earful of cider.'"

He continued, "I think your father is a good man, Sasha, but in his desire to get to the White House, he has surrounded himself with some very dangerous people who are using him as a pawn in a secret agenda that serves only one purpose: their own! I'm not saying your life is in danger, but I'd be very careful around these men, if I were you."

"Oh my God," Sasha suddenly remembered. "The man in the dark suit. I forgot to tell Jimmy!"

Taken aback by Sasha's sudden outburst, her teacher pressed, "What man? Are you two in some kind of trouble?"

"I'm sorry, I don't have time to explain," Sasha replied, gasping for air as she rushed to the door. "I have to go. Thank you for your advice and for taking my paper!"

⋆ ⋆ ⋆

Henry Joak rang the doorbell at 4666 West Emerald Bay Street in Wichita's Delano Township suburb. He and his older brother, Jasper, didn't share a particularly close personal relationship, but in matters of their co-owned business, Joak Industries, their ultra-conservative political action committee, and the Partnership of the Right, they were on the same page and virtually inseparable. So, as he waited for his brother to open the door, Henry still was perplexed at the urgency with which Jasper had pleaded with him to come to his home.

When the door finally opened, Jasper stood, framed in the doorway, looking like he'd seen a ghost – and not a friendly one. The elder Joak held his index finger to his lips and motioned for Henry to come inside.

"How are you Henry," he offered, affecting a nonchalance that belied his obvious distress.

"I'm fine, Jasper," Henry replied as calmly as he could, picking up on his brother's cue. "Is Delilah here?"

"No, she's out tonight at a board meeting for one of her charities. I can't remember which one. It's such a nice night, I thought we could have a couple of drinks on the patio, smoke some cigars, and shoot the shit."

Anyone who knew Jasper Joak would have known he was up to something. It was not unusual for his wife of 45 years to be away at night, but the elder Joak didn't shoot the shit with anyone, much less with his younger brother. Carrying on the subterfuge of inane banter, Jasper continued, "But first, I want to show you something downstairs," and he led his brother to the soundproof panic room in the basement. And closed the door behind them.

"OK, Jasper," Henry demanded, dropping the pretense of familial amity, "what in the hell is going on?"

Jasper didn't waste another word. "I hired someone to set that fire at the Rivers house."

"You what?" Henry screamed in disbelief, his face turning blood-red. "How could you be so stupid?"

"That little punk really was getting under my skin! I mean, do you understand the damage he's inflicted on the Partnership and on the campaign?"

"Of course, I do! But, do YOU understand how much worse it's gotten since everyone around the world saw him walk out of that blazing inferno like he was going for a walk in the park?"

"I do," Jasper replied sheepishly.

"And now do you understand why Satan insisted that no one lift a finger against the boy?"

"Yes."

Exasperated, Henry asked, "Besides, how did you find someone to set the fire all by yourself?"

"I called the Corbin group in Topeka."

Henry felt his blood starting to boil anew. "The Fundamental Truth Church? Please tell me you used a burner phone, at least."

Jasper lowered his head. "I wish I could."

"Do you have some kind of death wish that I don't know about," Henry shouted. "You just put yourself in front of a firing squad. Satan is furious! He hasn't been this angry since...well, since the boy helped his mom escape."

"That's why I called you here. What are we going to do?"

"What do you mean 'we'? This is all your doing, dear brother."

"Come on, Henry, you have to help me!"

"Actually, Jasper, I don't have to do anything. Besides, what would you have me do? Tell everyone that you didn't mean to hire those thugs to set that fire? If they haven't already connected you to them through the Fundamental Truth Church, it's only a matter of time." Henry paused. "Goddamn it, Jasper, they're going to think I was in on it, too!"

"Well, if they do, I'll just tell Satan that you had nothing to do with it."

"Why didn't I think of that? I mean, Satan is such a reasonable guy," Henry replied, his voice dripping in sarcasm. Solemnly, he added, "This is bad, Jasper, really bad. Probably the worst jam you've ever gotten us into."

"I know. Nathan called just before you got here. He said the two guys he sent to do the job were both dead – randomly shot in the backs of their heads, execution style, about a mile away from each other in north Denver."

"Random, my ass!" groused Henry.

* * *

Alice Fenimore switched off the radio in her Range Rover and sat in the Safeway parking lot. She was frustrated. Anxious. Didn't know what to believe any more. She believed in her husband, and she wanted to believe in the Partnership, but their implausible denials and wild conspiracy theories to explain how Jimmy survived the fire made it more and more difficult. The problem was that the things Jimmy had said over the past several days sounded so rational – they made so much sense. But where did they come from? Until that viral video, she never had heard anything so lofty come out of his mouth. Why now? And why Jimmy?

The Partnership had gone to inconceivable lengths to distance Jimmy from comparisons to Shadrach, Meshach, and Abednego, even so far as discrediting the Old Testament account. But, what about Moses? she mused. His story was just as fantastic. He came out of nowhere to lead the Israelites out of captivity, ostensibly on God's orders, and he parted the Red Sea to make good their escape. Was Jimmy a modern-day Moses parting a fire to make good his own escape? Was he about to lead humanity out of the darkness of captivity?

If so, who were the captors? It seemed as if he was leading us away from the church, or, at least, away from the very human individuals who were in charge of the church. Were they leading us the wrong way, away from God? Did that mean that the church leaders were our captors? And that we weren't free? If this was prison, then what did freedom look like? And what…

"Omigod, Roland!" she uttered out loud, suddenly remembering the envelope Sylvia said she'd seen the managing editor of the *Denver Post* trying to hide as he hurried out of the mail room that morning. Alice had been acquainted with Don Stottlemeyer for years through the Senator's political career and, while she wouldn't have called him a close personal friend, they were chummy enough for him to have given her his direct number to contact him for whatever reason.

This certainly would qualify under the "whatever reason' umbrella. But she didn't want to betray Sylvia's confidence or put her job in jeopardy. She picked up her phone and dialed the newspaper editor's number.

"Hello, Alice," he answered noncommittally. He was swamped

trying to get all the angles of the fire to press, but this was the Senator's wife. "What can I do for you?"

"I know you're busy with everything that's going on, but the Senator and I wanted to invite you and Tina for dinner tonight. It's kind of a last-minute thing, and nothing fancy, but Ralph will be here, Father Simon, and maybe one or two others from the Partnership, and I thought you might want to be here in case they went 'on record' with anything. And," she added, "that will give me an opportunity to visit with Tina."

Don's mood brightened considerably at the invitation. "Thank you, Alice, we'd be delighted to attend," he replied, making a mental note to call his wife as soon as he hung up with the Senator's wife. "Can we bring anything?"

"No, just come over around 7:30, if that works. The boys will have to come up for air right about then.

"Oh, and Don, one more thing..."

Here it comes, the editor thought. Quid pro quo.

"Cooper's roommate might have sent a letter to the paper that could reflect badly on the Partnership. He said he had written it in the heat of the moment, and that now he was having second thoughts about sending it in. I know it's a stretch, but would you ask the mail room to keep an eye out for an envelope from Roland Thomas? He'd really like to have it back."

Alice could tell she'd hit a nerve. After an uncomfortable silence, the shaken editor tried but failed to put on a brave face. "I'm sorry, what was his name, again?"

He had been caught with his hand in the cookie jar, yet Alice couldn't call him out on it. As calmly as she could, she repeated, 'Roland Thomas.'"

"Got it," the editor said, regaining some of his composure. "I don't have to tell you, though, this will be like looking for a needle in the haystack of all the letters the *Post* receives on a daily basis, but I'll do what I can. Maybe we'll get lucky."

Why won't he tell me that he has the envelope? What's he hiding? Alice wondered. "Thank you, Don, I hope so."

The sound of another phone ringing in the car startled Alice. She turned her head towards the passenger seat and saw Sasha's cell phone on the floor. She must have dropped it in her haste to turn her paper in.

"Don, I have to go. Thanks, again, for your help. See you tonight?"

"Yes. 7:30. Looking forward to it."

Alice ended the call and reached for her daughter's phone. She saw her niece's name on the caller ID.

"Hi Hannah, it's Auntie Alice."

"Hi Auntie," her niece whispered urgently into the phone. "Is Sasha there?"

"No, honey, she's not. She forgot her phone in the car. I only picked it up because I saw it was you. Is everything ok?"

Hannah hesitated. "Auntie, Sasha told me about Roland being missing and that he was working on a kind of dangerous story. And that you all thought he'd be the one to cover his bases and send a letter to the newspaper if anything happened to him."

"Hannah, I know you and Sasha are like sisters and don't keep any secrets from each other, but we're trying to keep quiet about this and not jump to any conclusions until we have more information."

"Well, that's just it," Hannah offered. "I'm at my internship at Joak Industries, and Roland's envelope is in a pile of mail for Tom Farrell, their HR guy – and my boss!"

"What?" Alice gasped in disbelief. "Could you tell if it's been opened?"

"It hasn't been, otherwise I could have taken a peek."

"That's so odd, because a friend of mine who works in the mail room at the newspaper told me she saw it at the *Post* this morning."

"Well, it's here now. What do you want me to do?"

Alice thought a moment. "Is your boss there?"

"No, he's at a meeting. Annika said he's due back in less than an hour. She said Mr. Farrell never is late, and usually early."

"Hannah, thank you so much for letting me know. I'll call you back in a few minutes once I figure this out. There are so many moving parts."

"OK. And when you see Sasha, can you have her call me?"

"Of course. Thanks, again, Sweetie! I'll get right back to you."

The sight of the clock in the car finally registered and interrupted Alice's train of thought. Her dinner guests would be arriving in a few hours! She dashed into the store, bought the groceries – chicken cutlets, ham, Swiss cheese, asparagus, mixed greens, pasta, garlic bread, and wine – then hurried home to start cooking, all the while wrestling with what to tell Hannah.

7

By the time Madison Munro pulled alongside Denver General's Level One Trauma Center, the phalanx of paparazzi that had followed Jimmy's ambulance had tripled in size. The story that started with a simple question in a civics class three days ago had morphed into an international sensation with a life of its own. Exactly what Satan had hoped to avoid! And while the world was focused on Jimmy Rivers, the man in the dark suit was cleaning up the mess. Two members of the Fundamental Truth Church already had been eliminated, but they were only the grunts, and he was in hot pursuit of the instigators. They had been sloppy, and phone records were like breadcrumbs leading him to his prey.

At present, however, the man in the dark suit was below even Madison's vast radar screen, and as she watched the hospital's Chief Quality Officer, Dr. Flynn Athens, trying to keep the reporters at bay, she delved into a contact list the size of Vermont and found the name Cherie Slater. Cherie had hit on Madison several years before while Madison was following up on leads for an investigative piece about improper opioid prescriptions at the hospital, and Madison was not above using her sex for information. It's not that she slept around, just that she found there were a lot of lonely people, male and female, seeking an intimacy that she was willing to provide – on her terms – if she thought there would be a pot of golden information at the end of the carnal rainbow. She never initiated it, but, if needed, she let it be known she was open for business, as it were, in the most subtle ways women communicate their interest.

Madison was a single, sexual woman, and she had her needs, too, but she was married to a 'just the facts, ma'am' job that had her drop everything at a moment's notice – even if the moments had been most inopportune. So, she was forced to compartmentalize her intimacy into a type of "friends with benefits" arrangement, but always as a means to an end. Did the end justify the means, or did it make her superficial? She didn't care, as long as she got her story. To her credit, though, she never misrepresented herself or what she had to offer. Again, lonely people will take whatever they can get, and it worked for her, as long as her "friends" didn't try to possess her. To her credit, they always were excited to take her call.

Cherie was one of the head nurses at Denver General, around Madison's age, and unhappily married. Well, more bored than unhappy. She had gotten married too young. She was having plenty of sex, but the intimacy of the kiss had vanished long ago. There's a reason that when a person is paying for sex, kissing typically is not part of the transaction. Intercourse is mechanical, kissing is intimate.

And Cherie was craving intimacy. She hadn't kissed a girl since middle school when she and her best girlfriend had practiced their techniques on each other. She'd never been attracted to women as sexual partners before, but when she met Madison for the first time, she had gotten that familiar tingling she used to get when the eye contact she'd make with a man across the room was more an invitation than a casual glance. When Madison had responded to her gentle, yet purposeful, touch on the arm, they both had gotten what they wanted; and Madison received an extra bonus – the International Women's Media Foundation award for Courage in Journalism.

The nurse was thrilled to see Madison's name pop up on her caller ID.

"Well, hello, stranger!" she cooed.

Madison smiled. "I know." Not an apology, but an acknowledgment that it had been too long.

"Let me guess," Cherie divined. "Jimmy Rivers?"

Affecting innocence, Madison replied, "I'm sure I don't know what you're talking about."

"I'll see you at the back entrance in five minutes," the nurse giggled. "Oh, and by the way, in case you were interested, he's been cleared to be released."

"You know, if you weren't married…"

"Yeah, right," Cherie stopped her, "just get that cute tush to the back door!"

Twenty minutes after letting Madison in, Cherie was holding open the same back door as Jimmy, wearing Madison's New York Yankees baseball cap pulled down as far as it would go, and his parents slipped out of the hospital and into Madison's Lexus.

Madison started the car then exhorted her passengers to wait for a moment. They watched her run back into the hospital and Cherie close the door behind them. Only Celeste noticed Madison's slightly smudged lipstick and her attempts to hide a furtive grin when she returned moments later and put the car in gear.

* * *

Sasha sat in her car in the school parking lot digging furiously through her purse and backpack for her phone.

"Shit, shit, shit, shit, shit!" she murmured aloud. "Where is it?"

She had to tell Jimmy about dark suit man! Exasperated, she leaned back in the driver's seat and worked her way back to the last time she remembered having it. She hadn't had it out when she turned her paper in to Mr. Hamilton. It was in the hospital. In Jimmy's room. Her Mom had called, and she asked her to pick her up so she could turn her paper in. She'd laid it down on the floor of the passenger seat to fasten her seat belt, and…damn! Her phone still was in her mother's car.

Teenage girls without their cell phones is bad enough, but Sasha was even more distressed – she had no way of getting in touch with her Mom to find out where she was. The last thing she needed was to waste time going off on a wild goose chase looking for her phone when she had to speak with Jimmy as quickly as possible. How could she have forgotten to tell him about the man in the dark suit walking up the stairs to her house with Ralph Petiole and Father Simon?

"I guess thinking your boyfriend was dying in a house fire and then seeing him walk out of the burning house miraculously untouched by the flames is quite a distraction," she consoled herself. But still!

The conversation with herself continued. "OK, you forgot your phone in your mom's car. It's not lost. Quit beating yourself up over it. Just figure out what to do next."

She couldn't just sit there, so she turned on the ignition in time to hear Jefferson Airplane's "White Rabbit" playing on the radio and Grace Slick singing, "Just ask Alice when she's ten feet tall..."

Sasha looked at her radio in disbelief. "Ok, Grace," she spoke to it, "I can't ask Alice where she is because she's not ten feet tall and I DON'T HAVE A PHONE!"

Again, chasing after her phone clearly was not an option. The fastest way to Jimmy was a straight line, so she headed back to the hospital. It wasn't until she'd gotten to the intersection of University and Speer at the Cherry Creek Mall that it dawned on her that Jimmy probably wasn't at the hospital anymore – Madison had said she was on her way to take him and his parents to The Crawford Hotel at Union Station.

Sasha was flying completely blind, but she felt good about setting her car's GPS for 1701 Wynkoop Street. She felt even better when she found a parking space on 15th Street in front of a Patagonia store, three blocks away from the hotel. The fact that there were 45 minutes left on the meter was icing on the cake.

As she got out of her car, she couldn't help but notice a huge sign in the window of the upscale outdoor retailer advertising 50% off selected items. She hesitated. The teenage girl wanted to peek inside, if only for a moment, but the dutiful girlfriend prevailed, and she hustled to the front desk of the lavishly-appointed boutique hotel.

She was greeted with a cheery, yet obligatory, "Welcome to The Crawford Hotel," by a front desk professional – heavy on the "professional" – whose name tag said, "Olivia."

"Thank you," Sasha responded automatically. "Can you please tell me which room the Rivers family is in?"

"I'm sorry," Olivia apologized crisply, "but we cannot give out that information." And she directed Sasha to a house phone. "You can call the operator and she'll connect you to the room."

Sasha scampered to the house phone on the wall and picked up the receiver.

"This is the hotel operator. How may I help you?"

"Can you please connect me to the Rivers family's room?"

After a quick search, the operator replied, "I'm sorry, we don't have anyone by that name staying here."

Had Sasha heard Madison wrong? No. "Can you please check, again? I know they're here!"

"Miss," the operator answered curtly, "there are no rooms registered to anyone by the name of Rivers."

"How about Munro?"

"No one by that name, either."

Tears began to well up in Sasha's eyes. "OK, thank you," she said, her voice cracking. She was trying as hard as she could not to cry, but her body began to shake she was so upset with herself for having forgotten her phone in her mom's car.

Right then, just as she was about to lose it, she heard a familiar voice call out to her: "Sasha!"

Madison's keen eye had spotted Jimmy's stricken girlfriend in the lobby after parking her car in the Coohills parking garage four blocks away in an attempt to keep the Rivers family's whereabouts hidden. Ten minutes earlier, she had entrusted George, Celeste, and Jimmy to the head bellman at The Crawford, Robert, who had spirited the Rivers family to Room 331, the Crawford Suite, via the service elevator. It had been Robert's pleasure to return Madison's favors since she began staying there when the hotel opened and the pursuit of a story brought her to Denver.

Sasha fell into Madison's arms, no longer able to hold back her tears. "I'm so happy to see you!"

⋆ ⋆ ⋆

"He's so close!" a woman's voice said from another dimension. "Like Ponce de Leon searching for the Fountain of Youth. He looked all over Florida, when all he had to do was look inside. Jimmy just has to get over the last hump to break out of Lucifer's earthly prison and into the universe of freedom from all limits that was intended for him – and for all of our Father's children.

"This is where it will take the greatest leap of faith. He has to overcome the millennia of lies and deceit Lucifer-turned-Satan has tricked everyone into believing, masking them as tradition and scientific truths and convincing them there is no choice.

"Jimmy has to remember that there always is choice – and that science applies only to what can be observed and measured, which, as Edison explained, amounted to only one millionth of one percent of all there is to know. In that millionth of one percent of all there is to know, the Word of God has been obscured completely.

"No one searches any more. They simply are content to drop anchor in the status quo as it has been handed down through the ages, choosing poorly to accept that they have no other choice than Lucifer's lies."

The famed gunfighter from the Old West cut in: "But, in order to discover the New World of total freedom, one must reel in the anchor of the closed mind and be willing to open it to the prospect of losing sight of the shore for a very long time. Only then will they see universes overlap and Columbus's ships on the horizon. That's why Jimmy was chosen – he has been searching for a long time. He searched for me in Glenwood Springs. And he hasn't stopped searching. He won't until he finds the Truth. Then, it will be up to him to describe what he sees once he makes the leap into the overlapping universes so everyone else can see the ships, too. And to experience what the freedom in the New World that was intended for them – and still is – really feels like.

"That's where Madison's Uncle John comes in, isn't it? He reinforced the fortune teller's message of parallel and overlapping universes." Doc Holliday thought for a moment. "I'm beginning to see a master plan at work here, formulated by the choices Jimmy and Sasha have made. They make their own choices, but God knows what they are going to choose, and the universe 'magically' connects them. They've chosen the journey that God knew they were going to choose ninety-seven years ago."

"It probably goes back a lot longer than that. But, you're right. Jimmy's mom and sister choosing to go see that psychic so many years ago, Jimmy and his mom going to the shopping mall for the Tony Hawk skateboard on his eleventh birthday...Madison making choices that put her at Berthoud Pass thirteen years ago, and her choice to call Jimmy after his video went viral because she had a gut feeling that reminded her of Berthoud Pass. Her Uncle John choosing to pursue nuclear physics. Then, there's just one degree of separation between her Uncle John and Jimmy for the 'missing link' message about quantum physics and parallel and overlapping universes to get to Jimmy. It all seems so random, but it's not."

"That's why Uncle John survived the radiation exposure at Los Alamos that would have killed 100 men in less than a week: he had a message to deliver that would confirm Madison's suspicions of other universes and give confidence to Jimmy and Sasha that they were headed in the right direction."

"Yes...which is in the exact opposite direction that their religious leaders have been herding everyone."

"So, you could say that Uncle John fulfilled his destiny?"

"Yes."

"Does that mean?"

"Yes."

"Madison will be so sad when she finds out."

* * *

The Southeast Denver Christian Bible Church was in full-on crisis mode. Jimmy Rivers was on fire, figuratively, if not literally, and the news media had arrived on the scene, whipping his flame into an absolute frenzy – just as the Santa Ana winds in southern California transform a wildfire into a raging inferno – devouring everything in its path, from the consciences of the misguided masses to the White House designs of the Partnership.

Satan had demanded the key players of the Partnership to make themselves available for a 4:00 p.m. conference call... or else. Dutifully, the Joaks called in from Jasper's panic room in Wichita, Al Dobson and Pat Bateman phoned in from Colorado Springs, and Annabelle Garton and Amon Smith made it to the church with fifteen minutes to spare. They all were dreading the call, but no one more than Jasper Joak. The man in the dark suit was conspicuous in his absence.

At 3:50, Satan's voice boomed over the loudspeaker. "Is everyone here?"

The moderator chimed in, "You're ten minutes early, sir, but everyone is here."

"Ten minutes early is late," Satan yelled, "especially when the proverbial shit has hit the fan!"

The moderator excused herself, and the Evil One railed, "Do you see why I told everyone to leave Jimmy alone?! This is an absolute catastrophe! The two low-lifes who set the fire already have been exterminated, and when I find out who put them up to it, they're going to wish they'd never been born."

"Sir, how do you know those two thugs from the Fundamental Truth Church didn't act on their own? I mean that group is pretty passionate about their opinions, and I don't think it would take much to push any of them over the edge and go rogue."

There was an awkward silence on the line. Then, Satan fumed, "Jasper, leave the thinking to me." Another awkward silence. "Moving on," the Evilest One finally continued, "we need to cover our bases on the fire. The Cardinal and Simon did a good job of sowing Doubt, Leon has watered those seeds of Doubt extensively on his social media platform, and we will reap the benefits of what they have planted and tended to.

"Ralph, I liked the way you threw those conspiracy theories into the mix. They really will muddle their thinking. Along with the 'fake' news theme you put out there – if a lie is repeated a hundred times, it is accepted as the truth because no one has the inclination to challenge it. They just choose to accept it. I should know, right?

"Right!" the members of the Partnership sang out in unison.

"So, let's keep it up. We can create a modern-day Tower of Babel in which confusion reigns, and no one can understand anything Jimmy is saying. The only thing they will know for sure is that they need the Partnership in the White House for their own good."

Satan chortled, "It's so funny, the Tower of Babel. They think God was responsible for it. Well, give the Devil his due – that was me! I created the confusion, I created the Doubt, I made it so no one could understand each other!

"His children are so gullible! They won't question anything that comes from one of their own religious leaders, particularly one who tells them not to mess with tradition. Those are OUR traditions they're not messing with, thanks to Caiaphas, and all the others, with a shout-out to our own Cardinal Phelps and Father Simon.

"So, they fear God. I created the fear!" Satan boasted. "He is portrayed in the Old Testament as the ultimate boogeyman – step out of line and He will strike you down. They are so stupid! Jimmy is right, damn it. God is not a killer. I am! And Doubt is my weapon.

"What happened to Adam and Eve when they chose to believe me and doubt the One who never would lie to them? They died. That was me, not God!

"And fear. What is fear? It is doubt of a positive outcome." Satan allowed himself another sinister guffaw. "They never even questioned it when we inserted 'fear' into their own divine liturgy. They're told to 'fear God' – they could have used a hundred different adjectives to get the meaning of 'reverence' across, but they chose 'fear!'" And 'fear,' to them, means only one thing – to be afraid, to doubt! That's the key that lets me into the Paradise He created for them – a Paradise that's still there but they can't see because of all the poor choices they've made that have pulled the wool over their eyes."

Satan paused and shook his head. "Then, God sent His Son to

save them from themselves and to set the record straight by clearing away all the Doubt I had planted in their minds, Doubt that had grown into an impenetrable forest through which they couldn't see because they chose not to believe the Son of God! How crazy is that?!"

"It is a tribute to your incredible chicanery that they've chosen not to believe the Ones who never would lie to them," Cardinal Phelps praised.

"Thank you, thank you," Satan acknowledged, "but I couldn't have done it without you to reinforce the Doubt. And I still need you," he grumbled, turning sullen, again. "Along comes this kid, Jimmy Rivers, and, suddenly, we're on the defensive, and my Tower of Babel is leaning, like that tower in Pisa, and it's about to fall down.

"Well, I am sick and tired of being on the defensive," he bellowed. "We're going on offense, going to get really offensive. We have to defend our Tower, and the best defense is a good offense."

Satan had waved the rally flag in front of his charges, and they responded in spontaneous, boisterous applause. They finally had something to cheer about after five days behind the eight-ball, and they let the Devil know he had their unanimous support.

After reveling in their enthusiasm, Satan continued, "First, now that the cat's out of the bag, so to speak, we're taking the gloves off against this kid. No more acting presidential – we're going full-on junkyard dog!

"Achilles was the greatest Greek warrior, but his unprotected heel made him vulnerable. This kid has an unprotected heel, too, and we're going after it tonight!

"Second, Fire Chief Orlando McDaniel is going to tell everyone that while it's early in his investigation, he's found remnants of a secret passageway that the kid used to escape the fire."

Annabelle Garton from the Blessed Unity spoke out, "How are you going to do that, sir? I know Chief McDaniel – he's as honest as the day is long. If he doesn't find evidence of a secret way out of the fire, there's no way he'd say otherwise."

"Miss Garton, how well do you know the fire chief?" Satan inquired, eager to play the ace up his sleeve.

"Very well."

"Well, then, you'll also know that twelve years ago, he had, um, an 'indiscretion' with a woman named Leticia Carter that produced an illegitimate son, Abraham Isaac Carter."

A deafening silence filled the room. Satan paused for effect to let the news of Fire Chief McDaniel's adultery sink in. Then, he said sarcastically, "Given that you know the fire chief so well, Miss Garton, do you think he will choose to play ball with me, or to subject his wife and five children – not to mention his mistress and their lovechild – to the most public humiliation?"

Annabelle hesitated for a moment, then admitted, albeit sadly, "Play ball with you."

"I would tend to agree," Satan bragged. "You know, we don't have to prove anything. We just have to create a reasonable – or even unreasonable – doubt that will muddle their thinking and get them to blink…and, they will sink back into their self-made prisons. And there's no one better at muddling thinking than our own mouthpiece, Leon Tusk!

Hearing the praise lavished on him by his mentor, Tusk quickly leapt to his feet, extended his right arm in a perfect Nazi salute, and shouted, "Heil Satan!"

"And third," Satan trumpeted, "we will reveal the mother of all distractions: the announcement of Andy Theus as the Senator's running mate.

"Ralph, do you think you can get the vice-presidential nominee here in an about an hour from now so we can talk about how the press conference will go down?"

"I'm sure of it."

"Sir, this is Amon Smith from the Community of Light. Can you tell us more about the boy's Achilles Heel?"

"I could, but then I'd have to kill you," Satan teased in a rare moment of levity.

Except, no one was laughing – they weren't sure if he was kidding or not, but no one wanted to try him.

Satan was evasive. "All I can say at this time, Amon, is that everything we are doing is for the greater good. Isn't that right, Senator?"

A sullen Senator Fenimore nodded his head. "Yes, it is."

"Good!" Satan exclaimed. "Oh, and one more thing," he added, singling out the elder Joak brother. "Jasper, I never said the culprits who set fire to the kid's house were from the Fundamental Truth Church."

8

No one had paid any attention to the young man with the Yankees baseball cap pulled down low on his head. In the parking garage of the Crawford Hotel, Jimmy and his parents followed Robert to the elevator, waiting until the door closed behind them to exchange polite pleasantries. An experienced bell captain, Robert knew the importance of discretion and did not ask about the fire. When the elevator stopped on the third floor, he handed the Rivers family the card keys to Room 331, and instructed them to take a left out of the elevator. They all thanked him, he wished them well, and they proceeded down the hallway.

A tasteful nameplate in gold letters adorned Room 331 and told them they had arrived at the Crawford Suite. George pressed the key against the key reader on the door, a green light illuminated, and he opened the door…and they stood in the doorway, mouths agape, unable to process the opulence that beckoned, which, at the same time, seemed off limits.

George was the first to test the water, stepping inside cautiously as if any sudden movement would make the vision disappear. He peeked inside at the 16-foot ceilings and windows from the original structure of Union Station and urged the others to come in and see for themselves – the stylish seating area with the brown leather pullout couch, the full dining room beneath the elegant chandelier, the bedroom with the four poster, king-size bed, clawfoot tub in the bathroom, and the fully-stocked kitchen and bar.

Jimmy raced past his father. "Dibs on the shower!" and he went straight to the bathroom.

George turned to Celeste. "Now, would be as good a time as any to ask him about the fortune teller."

His wife agreed, but demurred, "OK, but you go first."

Seven minutes later, Jimmy strolled out of the bathroom, fully cleansed, with a bath towel wrapped around his waist.

"Hi guys," he said casually, "so, how has your day been?"

"Just another day in the rich pageantry of life," his Dad grinned. "But, why don't you get dressed, your mother and I want to talk to you."

"Uh-oh," he groaned, feigning innocence, "what did I do, now? I wasn't playing with matches or sneaking a smoke, if that's what this is all about. I swear!"

Celeste still couldn't get over her son's perfect skin, unblemished by the flames. "Well, we're happy to hear that," she replied, as if that thought ever had occurred to them. "Actually, we want to talk to you about this fortune teller person you've mentioned."

Jimmy's heart skipped a beat. "You know about him?"

"Well, we know about a fortune teller, and we want to see if there might be any connection to your fortune teller."

"Oh my gosh, you guys," their son exhaled. "I've been wanting to..."

Before he could get another word out, an abrupt knock on the door startled them.

They all looked at each other uncertainly. Had the paparazzi found them?

George peered through the eyehole and breathed a sigh of relief. Madison and Sasha. He welcomed them in, then shut the door quickly behind them.

"Hello, Rivers family!" Madison greeted them airily. "Thanks for having us over!" Looking at Jimmy standing in front of them in a towel, she added, "I see you've already made yourself comfortable."

"Very comfortable," Sasha grinned approvingly, unable to hide her excitement at seeing her boyfriend's toned body adorned with only a towel. The two teenagers shared a sweet kiss on the lips.

"Madison, we can't thank you enough for this beautiful suite," Celeste gushed. "It must have cost a fortune!"

"Glad you like it! I love spending ABC's money," she laughed.

"We were just getting ready to sit down and have a chat about a fortune teller," George disclosed. "I'm sure Jimmy has mentioned him to you."

"Yes, he has, and count me in!" Madison enthused. She looked at Jimmy. "Do you want to put some clothes on, first?"

"Don't get dressed on my account!" Sasha blurted out. The words had escaped her mouth before she could stop them, and she turned bright red. "Omigod, I'm so sorry," she apologized, ducking her head in embarrassment.

Jimmy chuckled. "It's OK! If you were the one wearing the towel, I'd probably have said the same thing."

"That's not helping," she said sheepishly.

"Well, anyway," he announced to the others, "If you don't mind, I'm not in a hurry to get back into my clothes. They reek of smoke and sweat."

"So you haven't looked in the closets, yet?" Madison chimed in. "I had some clothes delivered for all of you."

Celeste hugged ABC's star reporter. "That was so sweet of you! When did you find the time?"

"Let's just say I'm a good multi-tasker – and I had a little help from my friends. And Cal, as curmudgeonly as he comes off, is really a pussycat. But don't you dare tell him I told you that!"

"How did you know our sizes," Jimmy asked.

"I'm pretty good at sizing up people," she said tongue-in-cheek.

While Jimmy excused himself to get dressed, the others took their seats in the parlor – George and Celeste on the couch, Madison and Sasha in the armchairs. Before they could discuss their next move, Jimmy popped back into the room.

"Ta-da!" he exclaimed, arms outstretched over his head, modeling his new clothes – dark blue True Religion jeans and a lime green polo shirt. "They're a perfect fit!"

"Of course, they are!" Madison crowed. "Was there any doubt?"

"Not in True Religion. Did you do that on purpose? Or was it a coincidence?"

"You know how I feel about coincidences," she winked. "It must be a sign that we're on the right track. But that was too quick. We didn't have a chance to talk about you behind your back!"

"Ugh. Guys have it so easy," Sasha sighed, having regained her composure.

"Well?" Jimmy asked, staring at his girlfriend and fishing for a compliment.

"I'm not saying another word!"

"Aww, come on," he prodded, taking one of the dining room chairs.

"Jimmy, leave the poor girl alone," Celeste interjected.

"OK, so the fortune teller," Madison redirected. "Before we begin, I want you to know that everything we talk about here will stay in this room. I have an idea how sensitive this information is, and I will not submit anything to Cal without your prior approval.

"Besides, I have a hunch that this involves me, too, more than just as a reporter. There simply are so many alleged coincidences. I think there's something going on here that's much bigger than all of us, some master plan that we're all a part of – or have been chosen for – for one reason or another, and I'm determined to find out what it is."

The mood in the room turned serious. "I completely agree," Jimmy affirmed.

"So, why don't you start," Madison suggested.

* * *

Alice Fenimore lugged the last of her groceries into her kitchen at 37 Skylark Lane. Chicken cutlets. Ham. Swiss cheese. Pasta. Asparagus. Garlic bread. Mixed greens. Eggs. Parmesan cheese. Hummus. Crackers. And enough Chardonnay for eight people, with a few extra bottles for herself for liquid courage. She hadn't even started prepping the chicken cordon bleu, and the heat already was too hot in the kitchen. But there was nowhere for her to go (giving rise to the extra bottles of wine).

As she mechanically went about unloading the groceries and laying them out for preparation, her mind was a thousand miles away, trying to process something that defied processing. She knew something was wrong. Very wrong! Roland was missing and the fact that he'd sent a letter of presumably incriminating evidence to the *Denver Post* about whoever he had been investigating did not bode well for him. Which meant Cooper probably was in danger, as well. Why, for God's sake, wouldn't her son pick up his cell phone or answer her texts? Had something happened to him, too? she worried.

She hadn't told her husband about Roland because the Senator was up to his eyeballs in alligators with the whole Jimmy Rivers thing and a campaign that was starting to unravel at the seams. Besides, she hadn't really had anything concrete to tell him...until now, that is. And Jimmy and that fire at his house – she hated to think it, but had someone from the Partnership set the fire to shut Jimmy up or, at the very least, send a message?

Speaking of messages, Jimmy's made so much sense. The church's and the Partnership's rebuttals sounded so hollow – and contrived. But Roland's envelope...he'd had it sent to the newspaper, and Sylvia had seen the newspaper's managing editor carrying it under his arm, trying to hide it – then, Hannah calls from her internship and tells her that the envelope was on Tom Farrell's desk at Joak Industries, unopened!

No matter how she looked it, danger was lurking around every corner. She didn't know where to turn or what to do. Sasha would know, she thought, but she had no way of reaching her since her daughter had forgotten her phone. One thing she did know, though, is that she would be putting Hannah in harm's way if she asked her niece to try and take the envelope. But Roland! And Cooper! Again, something was not right, and there was an envelope that had the answers. She picked up her phone and dialed Hannah's number. She would leave it up to her niece.

"Hi Auntie," Hannah whispered into her phone.

A new wave of anxiety swept over Alice. "Honey, are you ok?"

"Yes, I just don't want anyone to hear us."

Alice regretted what she was about to say, but that didn't stop her. "I hate to ask you this, and you have to promise to be honest with me if it would make you uncomfortable, but do you think you could take Roland's envelope and bring it to me?"

Hannah's voice perked up. "Oh, Auntie, I was hoping you'd ask me that! You know, Mr. Farrell's still not here. How could he miss what he doesn't know he had?"

"I would appreciate it so much, but I feel guilty putting you in this situation. There's something going on and I don't think it's on the up-and-up. It might be…"

Hannah cut her aunt off in mid-sentence. "I know. That's why I'm here, too, so I've already accepted the risk. I'll slip the envelope into my backpack when Annika's away from her desk, then I'll tell her that I'm not feeling well. I really want to do this!"

"You're a brave girl, Hannah McAuliffe!"

Hannah's eyes twinkled. "It's in my genes. Do you remember the story of my great Uncle Tony?"

"Yes, of course, I do. He was in charge of the 101st Airborne Division in Bastogne when the Battle of the Bulge broke out."

"Wow, good memory. They were surrounded by the Nazis in the dead of winter, low on ammo and supplies, and cut off from reinforcements. The Nazi commander knew it, too, and demanded their unconditional surrender or they would be completely annihilated."

"Right."

"And do you remember what he told the Nazi commander?"

"Yes," Alice recalled with a smile. "He said, 'Nuts!'"

"There's your answer. I'm a McAuliffe – it's in my genes. And I say 'nuts' to the danger, too!"

"Thank you, Hannah. Be safe. I love you."

⋆ ⋆ ⋆

At the District 1 police station at 1311 West 6th Avenue, Officers Mike McGregor and Houston Janney were finishing up their report on the body of Jackson Hill, found behind the 7-11 store near West 38th and Irving, when McGregor overheard a fellow officer mention the Fundamental Truth Church. "Hey Pete," he shouted above the din, "what about that church?"

Officer Pete Domenico sat three desks away from McGregor and shouted back, "Found a guy in his car with a GSW [gunshot wound] to the back of his head over at Sloan's Lake. He was wearing a Fundamental Truth Church t-shirt. Why?"

McGregor told his partner to keep writing, then walked over to Domenico's desk. "We've got a dead guy with a GSW to the back of the head wearing a Fundamental Truth Church t-shirt, too, not far from there at the 7-11 on 38th and Irving."

"Too much of a coincidence," Domenico stated the obvious.

"I know, right?"

"Any witnesses?"

"No. No one saw or heard anything. Sounds like a professional hit. Probably used a silencer. Any on your end?"

"No one heard anything, but some kids at the lake said they saw a man in a dark suit get out of the car. They remembered him because he looked so out of place."

"Anything else about this guy?

"Nah, you know kids. They weren't paying attention. All they noticed was the suit and that he just calmly walked away."

"Did they say which way?

"Yeah, now that you mentioned it, towards your 7-11. We should talk to the captain."

"Right. It sure sounds like this guy may have taken out both of our victims. But, first, I have to make a phone call."

"Maybe it was some sort of vendetta against that church. I've heard they're a bunch of crazies," he said as McGregor excused himself to make his call.

"Oh, and Pete," McGregor called out over his shoulder, "they're way beyond crazy!"

"What'd you find out, partner?" Janney asked before Mike punched in the number.

"The cases definitely are related. One perp took out both vics. It was a pro hit. I've got a hunch, though. I've got to call Madison," he said absent-mindedly, immediately regretting letting her name slip.

"Madison who?" Houston was quick on the uptake. "The reporter from ABC? You know her?"

"Yeah," Mike sighed, sorry that he had to reveal the details. "I met her years ago when she first was getting started. She was working that story on Berthoud Pass. I pulled her over for speeding here in Denver a few days later, and was about to write her up for not wearing a seatbelt, too, when she gave me a cockamamie reason why she wasn't. But I gave her props for creativity, so I let her off with a warning."

"Mike, that woman is smokin' hot! How well do you know her?"

McGregor noticed a hint of insinuation in his partner's voice. "I don't kiss and tell," he replied, dashing Houston's hopes for juicy gossip. "I will say she's a very determined, bold young woman. I think she sensed that I had more of an interest in her than just as a speeding motorist, so she told me why she was in Colorado and asked for my number in case she had any questions about the Berthoud Pass incident that I might be able to help her with.

"She's not the type of girl guys say 'no,' to – girls either, for that matter – so I gave it to her on the condition that she gave me her number in return. We exchanged phone numbers, and the rest is history. She'll call from time to time when she's in town. Almost always when she needs some information, though."

"She's in town, now. I saw her on TV covering that Jimmy Rivers story," Janney noted.

"I know. We've talked. But we haven't had a chance to get together."

"So, what's she like?"

McGregor thought about it for a minute. "Have you ever been to Prague?"

"No."

"Well, they have these pastries called trdelniks. Basically, they're this sweet, rolled dough wrapped around a spit, then roasted over charcoals, slathered with butter and topped with cinnamon and sugar. And, they're like nothing you've tasted before – something you might expect the gods to eat. They look and smell delicious – hard on the outside, but soft on the inside, and they're the best thing you've ever experienced. That's Madison."

"Sounds like someone is smitten."

"Everyone is. But don't let her looks deceive you. She's tenacious as hell. She'd cut your heart out for a story without giving it a second thought!"

* * *

Madison listened intently to Jimmy and Sasha replay the events of the last five days, taking notes and recording it all, and she couldn't help but feel a sense of vindication. She'd had a hunch about the Berthoud Pass incident thirteen years ago, and she hadn't given up. She had been teased, ridiculed, and eventually scorned for her blind pursuit of what no one else could see or fathom. A thought occurred to her as she was transcribing the teenagers' testimony, and she wrote it down in her notes to come back to later: "faith in story = faith in God."

She had one commandment when she was pursuing a story, given to her posthumously by Winston Churchill long before she was born: "Never, never, never, never, never give up." Only Cal had had her back, if only reluctantly. He'd just been promoted to executive producer of ABC News at the time of the Berthoud Pass incident, but the young intern had caught his eye. He'd seen in her his own drive and relentless, bordering on reckless, commitment to a story – to see it through to the end, no matter what, no matter where it took her. Seeking the truth was not a job, it was her "raison d'être," and the ultimate adventure. Everything else was secondary, although now, after thirteen years together, he had taken more of a paternal role in her life, and he was encouraging her to take the time to seek out a relationship of more than just a few days.

"Why?" she'd protested. "That's not who I am. This is who I am. This is how I get my kicks. It's the story that turns me on. End of story." And it was. Cal just shook his head, resigned to reaping the benefits of a reporter so singularly focused, and hoping she wouldn't burn out.

The possibility of burning out never was an option for Madison – as if the mere thought of it invited it. It was with a growing sense of pride that she was starting to put together the pieces of Jimmy's puzzle…and the fortune teller's. She was not a religious person, she simply was too pragmatic to waste time on what could not be seen; but, as she continued to take notes, the apparent symbiosis of what she had jotted down, "faith in story = faith in God," was not lost on her.

To her credit, her mind had not shut down in atheism, and it's a good thing, because after hearing everyone's account, she was able to recognize three unifying themes that bound all the pieces together. Kind of like putting all the outside pieces of a puzzle together to frame the puzzle, then filling in the middle. First, she noted that the fortune teller had said on a number of occasions, "Nothing is what it seems. The key is to see the world not as it is, but as it should be. Second, the so-called rules of man were not rules at all, simply observations, and they can be changed by changing one's point of view – ("changing universes?" she wrote down). And third, this story could go way back, all the way to the beginning of Time and to the ultimate struggle between Good and Evil.

The fortune teller had chosen Jimmy to carry "God's torch" because the boy had refused to accept the Church's version of the Great Flood – and the inevitability of Death. Quite possibly, the same fortune teller had told the teenage Celeste to deliver the message, "This is not the end," knowing that she would know when and to whom she would pass it along, even though it was years before she would meet the man who would become her husband.

But what was George's role, besides fathering their son? Random pieces don't fit neatly into puzzles. She jotted down another note to herself: "Big Bang not random…George?" Because her instincts told her that George couldn't have been connected randomly to the story.

At her first opportunity, she directed a question to the patriarch of the family: "Mr. Rivers, after hearing everyone's story, it's obvious to me that there is some sort of intelligent design thing going on here, and that no one is here by accident. I'm trying to put together the pieces of this intelligent design puzzle, and I just can't figure out how your piece fits in. But it has to. Any ideas?"

George thought for a moment, then his eyes widened in amazement. "Not until just now," he answered, barely able to conceal his excitement. "When you said 'intelligent design,' it's like a light came on. And everything suddenly became very clear."

All eyes were on Jimmy's father as he began to describe his revelation.

"Growing up, I was a huge fan of the rock group, Styx, and my favorite album of theirs was *The Grand Illusion*. This is going to sound disjointed, but bear with me and hear me out.

"I was sitting in an Orthodox Church I had gone to with a friend in September 1995. I remember that distinctly because that's when NATO had begun Operation Deliberate Force to try to stop the atrocities visited upon the Croats and Muslims by the Bosnian Serbs after the Serbs sought to enforce their ethnic cleansing mandate by massacring over 8,000 Muslim civilians in Srebrenica.

"This is all so vivid in my mind because I was 23 years old at the time and almost fanatically devoted to Christianity and, by default, to its leadership. But that's when I experienced a shocking mea culpa.

"You see, the Bosnian Serbs were Orthodox Christians, and one of the leaders of the Orthodox Church, a bishop no less, stood on the pulpit in church that day and assailed the United States and NATO for bombing what he called "our Orthodox brethren" to try to put an end to the ethnic cleansing. His sermon, if you want to call it that, rationalized that "our Serbian brothers only were doing to the Muslims what the Muslims had done to them a hundred years earlier!"

"You're kidding, right?" Madison interrupted. "A priest said that?"

"A bishop! He was stuck in the Old Testament "eye for an eye, tooth for a tooth' mentality, even after Jesus told us to turn the other cheek if our brother hits us – forget about the Ten Commandments, and Thou shall not kill!

"That's when I began to have serious reservations and distrust, not of the church, but of organized religion and of the very human and fallible leaders of the Church, who put their own agendas ahead of the Word of God.

"And now I see how they're connected. If you hadn't nudged me, I might never have made the connection. But maybe that's all part of the intelligent design, which really blows my mind. The name of the band, Styx, also is the name of the river in the underworld that separates the world of the living from the world of the dead. And *The Grand Illusion* is the band's seventh album which came out in '77...1977, that is. Seven is God's perfect number. God is telling me – telling us – that Death is a grand illusion!"

"And there it is!" Madison exclaimed. "The missing piece to the puzzle. One of the missing pieces, anyway. I knew you weren't randomly connected to the story! Subconsciously or not, you passed along your distrust of organized religion, and that's how a precocious five-year old boy asked "The Question' that started him on this journey that has brought us all together today."

Madison looked back though her notes. "That explains the trip to Glenwood Springs and the Doc Holliday connection...which led Jimmy and Sasha to the discovery of Spock mind melding with the Enterprise crew to eliminate all Doubt about the illusion of the perceived reality that bullets could harm them. Any doubt would have proven deadly. It's Doubt that kills. Which is consistent with Jimmy's fixation on Captain Kirk and changing the so-called rules, and on Jesus saying that nothing is impossible if you do not doubt – including, evidently, having bullets pass right through you without harming you."

George added, "That's also consistent with Jesus telling us that He has given us the authority to trample over serpents and scorpions and over all the power of the enemy, and nothing by any means ever shall harm us."

Madison was in awe at how these wildly disparate pieces of the puzzle were starting to fit together. "You know, I've made a career out of not believing in coincidences, and that's probably how I fit in. Six days ago, the Partnership was a shoo-in for the White House. Now, the Partnership is on the run. They're going to try to change the narrative, do something totally radical, very soon, you can be sure of that!

"As I've said, I'm not a religious person – yet, anyway – but from what I've heard in this room, I believe that you, Jimmy, have been chosen to stop something very sinister from happening, and…"

"Omigod!" Sasha shrieked. "I almost forgot, again. Jimmy, I saw dark suit man walking up the steps to my house this morning with Ralph and Father Simon!"

"What the hell!" Jimmy cried out.

"The same mystery man you think is following you?" Madison inquired.

"I know he's following us," Sasha corrected. "But, yes!"

"Wow," Jimmy gulped, "do you think your father is in danger?"

"I don't think so," Madison hypothesized. "Not if the dark-suited guy was with his campaign manager and his priest. But, it's very odd."

"And we've circled back to not being able to trust the leadership of the church," Celeste declared.

"This is turning out to be so much bigger than I imagined," Madison marveled under her breath. "I think we're just seeing the tip of the iceberg. My gut feeling is stronger than ever that the answer to all of this – the final missing piece of the puzzle of The Question you asked, Jimmy – is somewhere along Highway 40 near Berthoud Pass.

"But I've been there a hundred times, and I'm not any closer to seeing what it is. I need fresh eyes. Would the two of you consider coming to Berthoud Pass with me tonight?"

"Tonight?" Sasha winced.

"Things are just starting to go so fast, and I have a sneaking suspicion that, suddenly, we're running out of time. That man in the dark suit definitely is a game-changer."

"Sasha, we don't have school tomorrow," Jimmy reminded, hoping to overcome his girlfriend's hesitation. "We definitely could go!"

"Ugh. Mom's hosting a dinner party tonight at our house, and I promised her I'd be there to help out."

The caller ID illuminated on Madison's phone. She thought about not answering it, but a little voice in her head told her otherwise.

"I'm sorry, I have to take this call," and she excused herself to the other room.

9

"Hello, Annika," Tom Farrell greeted his receptionist, breezing into the downtown Denver offices of Joak Industries.

Annika Anderson had worked at Joak long enough to recognize her boss's perfunctory acknowledgement that said he had no time for small talk, but also that he was handcuffed to the dictates of professionalism and good manners.

"Hi, Mr. Farrell," she replied smartly.

"Any messages?"

There always were messages – he wanted to know if there were any calls that required his immediate attention, that were out of the ordinary, or that had come in from one of the Joak brothers.

"Mr. Stottlemeyer called. He seemed anxious for you to return his call."

She was good, Farrell thought to himself, taking a deep breath.

"Thank you!" Cursory had given way to sincerity. Annika noticed.

The phone was buzzing in his office before he got there.

"Yes, Annika?"

"I have Don Stottlemeyer on Line 1."

"OK, put him through. Thank you."

"Here he is."

"Don, I was getting ready to call you. I just got back to the office from a meeting."

The managing editor wasted no time. "Did you get the envelope? It's a bulky manila envelope addressed to the *Post*."

"I've got the mail right here. Hold on." The head of Human

Resources leafed through the pile of mail on his desk quickly – and then, a second time, more deliberately.

"There's nothing like that here," he said apprehensively. "When did you send it?"

"What do you mean it's not there?" came the exasperated response. "I sent it over this morning by courier. Your girl signed for it!"

"Don, let me put you on hold for a second." Tom buzzed his receptionist. "Annika, did a courier drop off an envelope this morning from the *Denver Post*?"

"Yes, sir. It should be on your desk with the rest of the mail."

"It's not here."

"Are you sure? I gave it to Hannah to put on your desk."

"Can you have her come to my office, please?"

"Sir, she wasn't feeling well. She went home sick."

Tom got back on the phone with the newspaperman. "Don, let me call you back."

He immediately dialed Hannah's cell phone. Three times. Each time, the call went straight to voicemail. The third time, he left a message. "Hannah, this is Tom Farrell. Please call me as soon as you get this."

He sat down in his high-backed chair and pondered the unthinkable. Could Hannah have taken the envelope? But why? She was just an 18-year old kid the Joaks had told him to hire because she was the Senator's niece. Had someone else been in his office?

The sound of his office phone's buzzer startled him. "Sir, I have Henry Joak on Line 2."

Tom picked up with a hint of trepidation. "Henry," he began, only to be cut off by the younger Joak's angry voice.

"Where in the hell is that envelope?"

"I'm not sure," he cringed.

"That envelope could ruin us, ruin everything!" Joak roared. "Don said he couriered it over to you and that Annika signed for it. So, what happened?"

"Annika said she gave all the mail, including the envelope, to

Hannah to put on my desk. But, it's not here."

"The Senator's niece?"

"Yes."

"And what did she say?"

"I haven't been able to talk to her, yet," he admitted, a slight tremor in his voice. "She went home sick."

"For God's sake, Tom, do the math!" Henry shouted. "She has the goddamned envelope!"

"Sir, maybe someone else…"

"And maybe pigs have wings!" he growled. "Of course, she has the envelope!"

"But, why?"

"How do I know why? She has it and we need to get it back. You have no idea what I'm dealing with right now. The contents of that envelope would be the final nail in our coffins."

"What do you want me to do?"

"Nothing. You've done enough already. I'll take care of it!"

Henry slammed down the phone in his brother's panic room, then quickly punched in Ralph Petiole's number.

"Henry, I can't talk right now," Ralph whispered into his phone. "We're about to go on air to announce Andy as the Senator's running mate."

"Is Samael there?" he inquired about the man in the dark suit.

"No. Why?"

"We've got a situation."

* * *

The name that had popped up on Madison's caller ID was "Mike Mmmmm' – as in Officer Mike McGregor of the Denver Police Department. She was excited to see his name, but she had no time for flirtatious banter. Nevertheless, she didn't want to reject his call.

"Hi, Mike!" she said brightly.

"What a day, huh?"

"Mike, I'm sorry, I really don't have time to talk to you right now."

"I know. Between the Berthoud Pass special, the interview with Jimmy, and the fire, you've got your hands full. But this is not a social call. Houston and I just found a guy shot in the back of the head, execution style, behind a 7-11 store in the Highlands. He was wearing a Fundamental Truth Church t-shirt. He's got all these newspaper clippings about high profile abortion doctors who've been killed. He even had one about Yitzhak Rabin's assassination."

"OK," the harried reporter uttered, wondering where he was going with this.

"So, we're back at the precinct, writing it up, and I hear a couple other officers talking about a guy they just found shot in the back of his head, execution style, in his car at Sloan's Lake. That's less than a mile away from where we found our guy – and their guy also was wearing a Fundamental Truth Church t-shirt."

"OK, that's weird," Madison allowed, her curiosity suddenly piqued.

"That's what I thought, too. We haven't established a connection between the two, yet, but I'm guessing that it wasn't a coincidence that they both were wearing the same t-shirts and were killed the same way. These were targeted hits, which means these guys weren't here for fun, they were here for business. And what's the business of The Fundamental Truth Church?

"Hate."

"And who do they hate?

"Progressives, liberals, homosexuals, Jews…"

"And who is getting all the press these days for tearing at the fabric of ultra-right wing conservative fundamentalism?"

Madison didn't have to have her hand held any longer. "Jimmy!"

"And what happened to Jimmy this morning?"

"The fire! Mike, you're a genius…I love you!" she gushed.

"For doing my job? I thought it was for my striking good looks," he teased.

"OK, Mr. Full of Himself…" She paused, the hint of a smile turning up the corners of her mouth. "Maybe that, too," she admitted, "but, why were they killed? And who killed them?"

"We're working on that. But I think it's safe to say they were hired to take Jimmy out, and I'm thinking they were killed because they failed. And whoever hired them didn't want any loose ends.

"Which is why I called you. To give you another angle for your story, and to warn you. The way these guys were killed points to a highly-organized and very professional criminal enterprise that doesn't tolerate sloppiness. You have to be careful, watch your back. I don't think they would hesitate to take you out, either. You remember what happened to that Russian reporter who was holding Putin's feet to the fire. What was her name?

"Anna Politkovskaya."

"Right. You might want to keep a lower profile. I have a very bad feeling about this."

Madison deflected his concern with the deftness of an Olympic fencer. "Awww, that's so sweet of you, to worry about me," she effused, "but you know that's not my style. I'm going to trust that your superior police work will keep me safe.

"And, I'm assuming that you're checking phone records to see who you might be able to connect these victims to?"

The policeman chuckled at his sometime-girlfriend's insouciance. "Of course, we are. You'll never change, will you…"

"You wouldn't want me to, would you?" she said with a gleam in her eye. "Anyway, before you go, because you do have some police work to do, were there any witnesses to either murder?"

"Not for our guy. But some kids hanging out at the lake said they saw a man in a dark suit getting out of the car who looked very out of place."

A chill went down the seasoned reporter's spine. "Thanks, Mike. I owe you!"

* * *

Madison stepped back into the parlor of the Crawford Suite to see George, Celeste, Jimmy, and Sasha staring at the TV.

George looked up. "You were right about the Partnership wanting to change the narrative. I got an alert on my phone that Senator Fenimore just announced Andy Theus as his running mate."

Madison checked her cell phone. Three missed calls from Cal while she was talking with Officer McGregor. "That's a good move," she remarked. "It switches gears completely."

"That's what the analysts are saying," Celeste confirmed. "They said it's a brilliant move at the end of a very tough week for the Partnership. That this announcement coming unconventionally at this time gets momentum squarely back on their side. Especially since rumors have Andy in the running for *Time* magazine's 'Person of the Year.'"

"The momentum won't last for long" Madison thought to herself.

George turned the TV off. "Anyway, you were saying you want to go to Berthoud Pass tonight?"

"Yes, but, there's an issue. That was my friend, Mike, from the Denver police force on the phone. Have you heard of The Fundamental Truth Church?"

"They're that hate group out of Kansas," Celeste answered. "They call themselves Christians, but that's like Satan calling himself an angel, and leaving off the 'fallen.'"

"Exactly. Well, Mike just told me that two members of that group were found murdered this afternoon not far from here. He thinks they might have been the ones who set fire to your house."

Madison turned to Jimmy, "Let's face it, Jimmy, yours is a very threatening message to just about everyone, but especially to these fanatics.

"And because it appears to have been a professional hit, Mike thinks they screwed up, somehow – maybe because Jimmy's still alive and talking – and they were killed by whoever hired them to clean up the mess they made."

George, Celeste, Jimmy, and Sasha sat in stunned silence as the reality of Madison's words sunk in.

"And that's not the worst of it," she continued. "One of the guys was killed in his car and witnesses said they saw a man in a dark suit getting out of it."

"The man who's been following us!" Sasha gasped, and her knees began to shake uncontrollably. "And my father," her voice trailed off.

Jimmy put his arm around his quivering girlfriend's shoulders, as the singularly-focused reporter forged ahead.

"I'm not sure your father knows what's going on with this guy, but Sasha, you can help us all by helping my friend to catch him. You said he's been at your house, so, obviously, your parents know who he is. When you go home to help your mom with dinner, ask her who he is."

"Wouldn't it be better if you sent your friend on the force over to the Fenimore's house to keep Sasha out of it?" George asked, playing the part of the concerned parent.

"I appreciate your concern, Mr. Rivers, but I think it would be a mistake to send the police over to the house. The Senator might not be involved, but the others at the dinner party could be, and we don't want to let them know we're on to them just yet. We want to catch them with the smoking gun, so to speak."

Madison turned to Sasha. "Are you okay with that, Sweetie?"

The reassurance of Jimmy's arm around her shoulders had helped her to regain her footing.

"I'm good, I got this," she assured them.

"This all just sounds so dangerous to me," Celeste worried.

"Mrs. Rivers," Madison explained, "this change in the narrative has bought us some time. The last thing in the world the Partnership wants is to have all the attention and momentum swing back to Jimmy. For all we know, those bastards from the FTC may have been killed for putting Jimmy and his thoughts even more into the limelight.

"Still, based on what Jimmy and Sasha have said, we have to assume that you're all being followed..."

"Everyone keeps telling us that," Jimmy agonized.

"Right, but, again, I don't think you're in imminent danger. The problem is that they might have followed Sasha to the hotel."

Sasha paled. "I'm so sorry. I didn't even notice."

"It's not your fault. You didn't know. But you're expected at your house for dinner tonight, so, if someone is watching the hotel, they're not going to follow you. They're going to wait for Jimmy, or Mr. and Mrs. Rivers, or me and my very conspicuous Lexus.

"So, Sasha, go home and help your mom with dinner and get us the name of the man in the dark suit.

"Mr. and Mrs. Rivers, I think it would be best if you stayed in the hotel room so they don't find out where you are. And, Jimmy, you and I are going on a field trip just as soon as I make another phone call."

Madison excused herself while Sasha exchanged hugs with each member of the Rivers family. She kissed Jimmy and set out on her appointed mission.

In the next room, Madison dialed her producer's number. "Hello, Cal, I need a car. And send Gina. Have I got a story for you!"

* * *

Henry Joak slammed down the phone in frustration.

"So, the Senator's niece has the envelope, I gather," his brother said calmly.

"It would appear that way."

"Damn it!" Jasper exploded. "I'm not going to let everything we've worked for be taken away by an amateur reporter!"

"Well, thanks to your imbecilic fire stunt, we're stuck in here for a while," Henry bristled, waving his arm around Jasper's fortified, bulletproof panic room. "What do you propose we do?"

"The way I see it, you have two choices…"

The brothers jumped at the sound of Satan's voice behind them, dripping in menace. They wheeled around to see a fearsome serpent, eyes blazing red, glaring at them.

"How did you get in?" Jasper stammered.

"You let me in," the serpent hissed. "Your insipid fear opened the door for me, and I slithered right in.

"Now, as I was saying, you have two choices. You can agree to sign over your company to Andy Theus at Safety First International, or I can arrange a meeting for you with Samael. Did you really think that I wouldn't find out about your friends from the FTC? And you made it so easy with your slip of the tongue – even after I let it be known in no uncertain terms that Jimmy Rivers was to be left alone, that I would take care of him, myself!"

Snarling, Satan continued, "Yet, you still chose to disobey me! "Have you seen all the publicity he's getting? So, pick your poison!"

"Can we at least have a minute to talk it over?" Henry pleaded.

"Absolutely not! What's to think about? Do you want to die or not? Make up your minds. Let me tell you, though, it won't be the quick and painless deaths those arsonists got. I will make sure it will be slow and very unpleasant. Nasty, even."

⋆ ⋆ ⋆

Samael, the man in the dark suit, was driving, two cars behind Hannah, undetected, when his phone rang.

"The Joaks have chosen to live," Satan informed the East European assassin. "Just get the envelope and kill the girl!"

10

Madison came out of the other room to find George and Celeste still watching the news and Jimmy sound asleep on the floor.

"Can you believe he's sleeping like a baby after everything he's gone through today?" his mother sighed.

"With everything he's been through this whole week!" Madison added. "Apparently, the Eveready bunny's battery eventually does run out."

George stared at his slumbering son with a father's sense of pride and a childlike sense of awe. "You just can't make this stuff up! I'm still having a hard time believing it. Do you really think you'll find answers on Berthoud Pass?"

"I can't explain it, I don't know what it is, but it's like a strong magnet that has been drawing me in for thirteen years, and the pull has gotten so strong over the past couple of days. I guess it's kind of like the Star of Bethlehem. The shepherds and the wise men all saw it and they knew they had to follow it, but they didn't know why until they got there."

"He's sleeping so peacefully," Celeste said softly, watching her son. "Can't we let him sleep a little longer?"

"Yes, but don't tell anyone. I have a reputation to protect.If it gets out that I let someone sleep while I was pursuing a story, it would ruin me," she smiled. "Actually, I'm having a car sent over, one that doesn't scream 'Madison Munro,' just in case someone is watching the hotel. Everyone knows my black Lexus. So, Cal has arranged for a woman who fits my general description to drop off a car here at the hotel.

"She'll bring us the keys, and we'll exchange clothes. Then, she'll take my keys, walk very conspicuously to where I parked, and drive far, far away in the opposite direction. Jimmy and I will wait a few minutes, then sneak off in her car, hopefully under the radar.

"But she won't be here for another hour, or so, and…"

The sound of her vibrating cell phone distracted the ABC News reporter. "Omigosh, I have to take this. It's Uncle John!"

"Uncle John!" she chirped into her phone. We just were talking about you!"

George and Celeste watched her indefatigable spirit sucked out of her in a matter of seconds, as she slumped into one of the armchairs, her atypical reticence broken up intermittently with "How?" and "When?" and, finally with, "Thank you. Keep me posted."

She ended the call, looking totally deflated. "My Uncle John just passed away."

⋆ ⋆ ⋆

Sasha was lost without her cell phone. Driving was her "down" time, when she could touch base with her friends, with Jimmy, with Hannah, and even with Cooper. Her brother was the hardest to get a hold of – except in the afternoon when she was driving home from school.

Thoughts of what Cooper was going through suddenly swirled through her head. He had to be so worried, and feeling so alone, even if his friends were with him to support him. His partner was missing! Had Roland turned up this morning? She had been preoccupied with the fire the whole day...until now. Jimmy was safe – well, for now – and her mind was free to roam around. She remembered her parents telling her about life without cell phones.

Life without cell phones? The ultimate oxymoron. She was dying without it. If Roland hadn't shown up, had he, in fact, sent a letter to the *Denver Post*? Who were these dangerous people and what could the letter possibly say? What had Roland gotten himself into? Would the letter turn out to be his obituary? She knew one thing for sure, as she pulled into the driveway at 37 Skylark Lane, next to her mother's car: she was determined never to forget her cell phone again!

"Mom, I'm home! I need my cell phone!" she shouted as she bounded into the kitchen and rolled up her sleeves to help in the dinner preparation. Alice was off to a good start – a large pot of water had begun to boil on the stove, the russet potatoes had been peeled and quartered, the mixed greens were in the bowl waiting to be dressed, the chicken cutlets were topped with ham and Swiss cheese, and the oven already was preheated to 400 degrees. The pasta, asparagus, and garlic bread also were laid out on the spacious counter, and that's where she spied her cell phone.

"Thank God!" Sasha exulted – to herself, though. Alice was nowhere to be found.

"Mom!" she shouted even louder, while quickly running through her messages. "Where are you?" The water on the stove is boiling!"

No answer.

"Mother!" she yelled, "what are you doing?"

She grabbed an apple from the counter to sustain her as she looked for her mom. From the base of the stairs, she heard sobs coming from upstairs and rushed to her parents' bedroom. Alice was writhing on the bed, crying her eyes out, and blubbering, "It's all my fault," over and over.

Sasha immediately kicked off her shoes, climbed into bed next to her mother and wrapped her arms around her tightly. "Mom, it's ok, I'm here. Take a few deep breaths and tell me what's the matter!"

But Alice was inconsolable. She just kept whining, "It's all my fault, it's all my fault."

"Mama, what's your fault?"

Alice barely could get the words out, she was heaving so violently. "Hannah was killed, Sasha," she wailed. "Someone shot her in the back of the head in her driveway. She was already dead by the time anyone got to her."

Sasha's body convulsed. She ran into the bathroom and bent over the commode, just in time to relieve herself of the contents in her stomach. She slumped on the tile floor, tears streaming down her face in total shock.

"It can't be true," she cried.

Somehow, Alice heard her daughter's heartbroken lament. "It is. Aunt Stephanie just called a few minutes ago while I was in the kitchen. And it's all my fault."

Sasha stumbled back to the bed and laid next to her grieving mother. "Why do you keep saying that?" trying in vain to make sense of the senseless.

"Because she found Roland's letter! And I told her to take it!"

That snapped Sasha out of her funk, if only for a few semi-lucid moments. "Wait, what? Where?"

"At Joak, of all places," Alice whimpered. "My friend, Sylvia, at the *Post* said she saw Don Stottlemeyer, the managing editor of the paper, nervously trying to hide it in the pile of mail he was carrying. Then, somehow, it ended up at Joak Industries, unopened.

"Hannah noticed it when she put the day's mail on her boss's desk. And she called me. Well, she called you, but you left your phone in my car, and I picked it up when I saw it was your cousin on the line. I was supposed to tell you to call her..."

Alice's voice trailed off, and she started crying, again. "It's all my fault!"

"Mom, stop saying that. You and I both know Hannah would have taken the letter even if you hadn't told her to."

"Still, I told her to take the letter and bring it to me! I just knew something bad had happened to Roland, and now she's dead because she took it. She was only 18 and had her whole life ahead of her!"

"Mom, try to stay calm. Just to make sure I got this straight, Sylvia saw that the editor of the *Denver Post* had Roland's envelope, but he never opened it and sent it to Joak Industries?"

"Yes."

"So, what happened to the envelope? Did Aunt Stephanie find it?"

"I asked her to look for it. She said there was no envelope in the car or in her backpack. She even looked in the trunk. Nothing."

"So whoever killed Hannah has Roland's letter. Have you told Daddy, yet?"

"I haven't had a chance. It's been such an awful day," Alice moaned.

"Mom, you have to call him and tell him!" Sasha insisted. "And there's no way we can have this dinner party tonight. I'll go turn off the stove and the oven."

Alice berated herself anew for having forgotten about the overheating kitchen appliances. Sasha helped her Mom to speed-dial the Senator's number. Then, she ran downstairs and dialed Jimmy's burner phone.

* * *

Leticia Carter and Isaac were just about to sit down to dinner when her phone rang. They had a strict "no cell phones during dinner" rule, but they hadn't said Grace, yet, and the name on the caller ID gave her pause. She decided to take the call.

"Hello, Orlando."

"Hi Leticia," Fire Chief Orlando McDaniels whispered into his phone.

"And to what do I owe the pleasure of this call?"

"Leticia, I don't have too much time, so I'll get right to the point." He hesitated.

She never had heard his voice so somber, even when they first found out she was pregnant with Isaac.

"What is it, Orlando? What's the matter? Is it about the fire? I couldn't believe what I saw on TV."

"That's just it," he lamented. "They don't want you to believe what you saw. What everyone saw. What I saw in front of my own eyes."

"I don't understand. Who's 'they?'"

The fire chief lowered his voice even more. "The Partnership of the Right!"

"Senator Fenimore?" she asked uncertainly.

"His campaign manager."

"What did he say?"

"He wants me to make a statement that we found traces of a secret passageway of some kind that the kid walked through to protect him from the fire. They want it to sound like a publicity stunt or something...you know, fake news to promote the news station."

"And, by the tone of your voice, I'm guessing there wasn't any such thing."

"No!" he whispered emphatically. "When I hear all these politicians clamoring about fake news, it tells me they've got something to hide."

"What do you think the Partnership is trying to hide?"

"I honestly don't know."

"So, what are you going to do? You're not going to let them tell you what to do are you? To lie for them? That's not like you."

"Leticia, they're threatening to expose us."

Silence.

"Are you there?" he asked, after an uncomfortable quiet.

"I'm here," she acknowledged, considering their options. "How could they possibly know?"

"I don't know! You've never said anything about us to anyone, have you?"

"Of course, not! And I know you haven't, either. You've got your wife and kids. I'm the vice-president of the parish council at church." She sighed. "I guess I knew this eventually would come out, somehow. I just hoped it would be a lot further down the road, when Isaac was older."

"Well, I haven't decided what to do, yet," the beleaguered fire chief confided.

"Oh, I think you have, Orlando. I know you better than that. And, I'll stand by whatever you say."

"They're going to scorn you at church," he worried. "And what about Isaac? He's completely innocent, but kids can be so cruel, especially when they mimic what they hear at home from their parents."

"Your kids are innocent, too, even though they're older. And your wife? How do you think Pam's going to react?"

"Yeah, I'm not sure we'd survive this. But, no matter how I look at it, I just can't let those bastards from the Partnership have their way. I'm sorry."

"Don't you apologize to me, Orlando McDaniels," Leticia replied, resolutely. "I wouldn't trade our son for anything. We were young. We weren't looking for anything. The situation got out of control, just like that river in Cleveland that spontaneously caught on fire. We're not bad people. We made a mistake. And Jesus understands we're not perfect. He stood in front of the men who were about to stone the prostitute to death and said, 'Let he who is without sin cast the first stone.' And not a single stone was thrown.

"And if people can't get past that, well, then, let them be judged for their sins as they would judge us."

"Isaac's a wonderful boy, don't get me wrong," the fire chief granted, "but I still can't believe I had such a moment of weakness. I hold myself up to the highest standards in every aspect of my life."

"Orlando, you have to stop beating yourself up! We both made a mistake. Don't let it define you. You know about David, right? The David who killed Goliath?"

"Yes. But what's he got to do with this?"

"Well, when he became King of Israel, he had an affair with Bathsheba, the wife of one of his soldiers, and he arranged to have her husband killed so he could marry her. She became queen, and they had a son, Solomon, who became one of the greatest kings of Israel.

"David eventually repented and asked for forgiveness, and God held him up as 'a man after my own heart.'

The dubious fire chief asked, "Do you really believe that?"

"Of course, I do! It's totally consistent with the story of the prodigal son. The glory of Christianity is the triumph of forgiveness."

"But, will Pam forgive me?"

"I can't answer that. From what you've told me about her, though, she's a good Christian woman, and I do believe that Good always wins out in the end."

"I cheated on my wife. That's a big deal. All the Partnership is asking me to do is to create a little doubt. It shouldn't be as big as cheating on Pam, but it just seems monumental. I've come to terms with my night of infidelity, I'm not sure I ever could with this."

Leticia thought about that for a moment. "I don't have all the answers, but maybe it's because our night together was not premeditated. It just happened. The situation spiraled out of control and we got lost in it.

"This is different. Doubt is the Devil's calling card. Evil is knocking at your door, and you have time to think about opening it or not. And I know you'd rather throw yourself on a grenade than consciously choose to open the door to Evil."

Her comment surprised him. "I can't believe you said that! I just had this conversation with another firefighter, and I said the same thing. We were talking about politicians, and I told him that no one is willing to throw themselves on a grenade for the good of the country!"

"You might have answered your own question," Leticia suggested. "And don't you worry about Isaac and me. I told you before that I believe that Good always wins in the end, but I can assure you, Evil will triumph if good men do nothing. And you're a good man, Orlando!"

"I hear you...loud and clear."

"Dinner's getting cold, but I'll tell you one more thing. If you do choose to throw yourself on that grenade, Isaac would love to meet his father."

⋆ ⋆ ⋆

Celeste instinctively put her arm around Madison's shoulders, and the stricken reporter leaned into her and silently cried, mourning the loss of her beloved uncle.

Then she stopped, abruptly, and straightened herself. "Omigod, I'm so sorry," she apologized, fetching a tissue to dab at her eyes. "I can't believe I'm crying. I never cry."

"Honey, your uncle just died," Celeste offered, soothingly.

"I know, I loved him dearly, but I never lose my shit, if you'll pardon the expression."

George cut in. "Madison, you're human."

"And I hate that about me!" she smiled meekly.

"Let's go into the other room and let Jimmy sleep until the car gets here," Celeste proposed. "Are you sure you still want to go to Berthoud Pass tonight?"

"Yes. Uncle John would hate it if I didn't follow up on a lead on his account."

"Come on, then, we want to hear more about your Uncle John," and they stepped into the spacious master bedroom and sat around the small coffee table by the window.

"He was a brilliant man," Madison began, "a nuclear physicist, one of the smartest people in the world. He worked in Los Alamos on the Manhattan Project with some of the world's most famous scientists, he lectured all over the world, and taught at Stanford for 40 years, but you'd never know it. He was so humble, kind, and loving.

"He told me that during the development of the atomic bombs there was an accident in which a container of radioactive material tipped over and was moments away from causing a devastating explosion. There was no time for caution. The others froze, but Uncle John didn't hesitate. He ran out of the radiation-secure observation room without any protective covering, and into the radioactively contaminated room to set the container upright – saving the others but sealing his own fate.

"He explained to me that exposure to radiation is measured in terms of how many people would die in a given amount of time and he was exposed to an amount that would kill a hundred people in a week's time, or something outrageous like that. The bottom line is that there is no way he should have survived – or survived without any lingering health effects. But he did. It was an absolute miracle. Which, as I think about it now, got me started on my path of not accepting anything at face value."

She shook her head. "He used up a hundred of his lives that day, and many more over the course of his lifetime, and lived to be 97."

"You speak so well of him," George said respectfully. "I'm sure he was very proud of you and moved on knowing you would be carrying his torch going forward. To Berthoud Pass tonight, even."

"Thank you, Mr. Rivers. I appreciate that. You know, speaking of Berthoud Pass, he was the one who confirmed in my mind what I'm calling the missing link that connects what happened on the Pass that night with what your son is going though now. Quantum mechanics and parallel universes – the kind that overlap."

As Madison began to describe what her uncle had told her about cutting edge physics and quantum mechanics, Jimmy was awakened by his vibrating burner phone.

"Hello?" he answered sleepily.

The sound of his girlfriend's frantic voice was like a bucket of cold water thrown in his face.

"Sasha, what's the matter?"

"Hannah's been killed!" she wailed.

Sasha might as well have stuck his finger in a light socket for the shock he felt. "What???" was all that he could manage.

"Jimmy listen," she prevailed through her tears, her voice choking. "Hannah was shot in the back of her head when she pulled into her driveway. She's dead!"

Jimmy was dumbfounded. Nothing registered. "Why?"

"Mom is hysterical. She keeps saying it's her fault Hannah got shot."

"How was it her fault?" he mumbled, still in utter disbelief.

Trying to get through to her disoriented boyfriend gave Sasha another brief window of clarity. "So, you know how I left my cell phone in Mom's car when she picked me up from the hospital? Well, Hannah tried to call me from her internship with Joak, and Mom answered the phone when she saw it was Hannah calling.

"Anyway, Hannah told Mom what she wanted to tell me – that she saw Roland's unopened letter to the *Denver Post* on Tom Farrell's desk.

"Wait, I don't understand."

"Jimmy, try to keep up!" Sasha pleaded, fighting to maintain her composure. "Mom's friend at the *Post* said she saw the editor trying to hide the envelope, but she saw Roland's name in the return address."

The cobwebs were beginning to clear from Jimmy's mind. "So, that means the Joaks – and probably the Partnership, too, control the newspaper." Jimmy became animated at his realization. "This isn't a theory, Sasha – it's a full-blown conspiracy! Do you think your dad knows?"

"I'm not sure. But, when Hannah asked my mom what she should do, mom told her to take the envelope and bring it to her. She was just so worried about Roland and Cooper. And Hannah took it!"

Now, fully engaged, Jimmy asserted, "These are very powerful people, Sasha, and I'm pretty sure they'll stop at nothing, not even murder, to get into the White House. Let me guess...the envelope wasn't found."

"It wasn't. Do you think it was the man in the dark suit?"

"Maybe. I wouldn't be surprised. Everyone has warned us that we're being followed, and he's been the one we've seen. Now, we know it's not to give us any good citizenship awards. We've got to be extra careful!"

"Jimmy, he was in our house!" Sasha fretted.

"Yeah, maybe you should come and spend the night with us at the hotel. I'm pretty sure the dinner party isn't going to happen."

"I can't, Jimmy. My Mom needs me. But I'm scared, and I feel awful about Hannah." Sasha couldn't hold back the tears any longer.

"I know. Let me talk to Madison and I'll call you back." Jimmy hung up and shook his head. The fortune teller was right, again, he thought to himself. Nothing is what it seems.

11

Across the street from the Fenimore house, at 38 Skylark Lane, neighbors Dan and Lori Larsen were on their way to Winter Park to celebrate their 15th wedding anniversary. Since Friday was a teacher's planning day, they were taking their children, David and Campbell, along, as well. Dan had come home early so he and his wife could enjoy some private time ahead of the long weekend in the mountains. They had basked in the afterglow a little too long, however, and had to scramble to get the car packed to pick up the kids from school in time to beat rush hour traffic.

They backed out of the garage, pressed the garage door remote, and sped down Skylark Lane without waiting to watch the door close completely. Had they not been in such a hurry, they might have seen a fortyish man with tousled black hair tinged with gray roll under the door before it closed. He gained access to the house from the unlocked door to the utility room and made his way to the front window. It was the perfect vantage point to monitor the activity at the Senator's house without being detected. The Cobra then dialed Ralph Petiole's number.

* * *

At the Southeast Denver Christian Bible Church, Senator Fenimore and his Partnership cabal finally had reason to celebrate after a hellish week of Jimmy Rivers. Andy Theus was the distraction the campaign desperately needed – the right man in the right place at the right time. No one noticed Ralph sneaking away to take a call.

"This is Ralph," he answered, away from the commotion.

"I'm in."

Those two words told Ralph all he needed to know. The Cobra – the world's most notorious hitman from the world's most notorious drug cartel – was in place, waiting to strike.

"Remember, top of the stairs, first bedroom on the right. Quick and painless."

There was a click on the other end of the line. Message received.

* * *

The Cobra watched his prey pull into the driveway across the street.

"Mom, I'm home!" Sasha announced as she bounced into the kitchen and rolled up her sleeves to help in the dinner preparation.

"Thanks for bringing my cell phone in! I can't believe I forgot it. It's awful to be disconnected," she declared, picking up her phone as lovingly as a young mother cradles her newborn baby.

Alice was on the phone and waved at her daughter.

"It's OK, I completely understand," Sasha heard her say. "We'll figure something else out. At least we know where it is. Thanks, again."

"What was that all about?" Sasha asked, checking her messages.

"Honey, look at me," her mother demanded. "That was Hannah. She called you when you left your cell phone in the car. I saw it was her, so I picked it up. She told me she saw Roland's letter on her boss' desk at Joak Industries. Just like Sylvia said, it was addressed to the *Denver Post*, and it hadn't been opened."

"Mom, that's great! I mean that the envelope has been found. But what was it doing on Tom Farrell's desk?"

"I don't know. I asked her to take it, if she had the chance, and bring it here."

"Mother, that's asking a lot! She could get in a lot of trouble."

"I know. I felt bad about it, but you know your cousin. Anyway, it's a moot point because she just told me that she never got the chance to take it."

"Something very weird is going on. How did that envelope wind up at Joak Industries?" Sasha wondered aloud. "And speaking of weird, who is that man in the dark suit who was at the house this morning?"

"How did you know he was here?"

Sasha was evasive. "I just do. So, who is he?"

"His name is Samael. He's connected to the Partnership somehow. I think he has something to do with security. He just started showing up last week. He really doesn't say much. He kinda gives me the creeps."

Sasha's cell phone began to vibrate. "Hold on, Mom, it's Hannah."

"Hi Hannah…"

Before she could get another word in, her cousin asked, "Did your Mom tell you about Roland's envelope?"

"Yes, and she feels badly that she asked you to take it."

"Sasha, I had it! I was putting it in my backpack when I saw a note that said, "Hannah, don't take Roland's envelope or you will die. I'll explain later." That note wasn't there when I left school because I put my homework there from class today.

"And do you want to hear the really freaky part? It was from Jimmy!

"I mean, that's Garden of Eden, forbidden fruit stuff all over again. And I chose to trust him. I didn't take a bite of the apple…I put the envelope back on Mr. Farrell's desk."

⋆ ⋆ ⋆

"Jimmy, Jimmy," Celeste gently shook her son awake. "The car is here."

"I'll drive!" he said instinctively, without a clue as to where he was.

George chuckled. "I think Madison's got that covered, son."

The sound of Madison's name supplied the clarity he needed. "Oh my God, Madison, I'm so sorry about your uncle."

A puzzled look crossed her face. "How'd you know? You were

sound asleep."

"I saw him. He told me to tell you not to worry about him, that he was in a very good place, and that he loves you."

* * *

"Samael!" the Prince's voice thundered. "He's done it, again! Freed another captive! TAKE HIM OUT!!!"

"But, sir...," the Bulgarian tried to protest.

"I don't care what I said before!" came the Evil One's loud retort. "The Joaks already screwed that up! I want him silenced!"

"Right away, sir."

* * *

Madison, still shaken at the news of her uncle's sudden death, stared at Jimmy in disbelief. So, did his parents. Nothing should have surprised the seasoned reporter, though, when it came to this 17-year old boy who, basically, in just 96 hours, had done more to upset the apple cart into which everyone uncritically had placed their core beliefs than anyone since the Son of God walked the face of the earth. But he had caught her completely off-guard in an uncharacteristically weak moment, and she defaulted to her reporter's instinct for corroboration.

"You saw my Uncle John," she challenged him.

"Yes.

"Just a few minutes ago," she continued.

"Yes."

"But, he died this afternoon. In California. We're sitting in the parlor of the Crawford Suite in downtown Denver, Colorado."

"Right."

The stubborn reporter would not give up. "You could have been pretending to be asleep when I got the news and overheard me tell your parents that he had passed; and you're trying to make me feel better."

"I could have. But, I didn't. And, no, I'm not trying to make you feel better. I'm just telling you what he told me."

The hint of a smile, knowing what he was about to say, turned up the corners of Jimmy's mouth. "He knows you so well. He said you'd need convincing. He told me when you were 15, you were living in Kalamazoo, Michigan, and he took you to a Jessica Simpson concert in Allegan, which was only about thirty minutes away."

Tears welled up in Madison's eyes, again, as she recalled the memory. She was confused. Terribly. Jimmy could have looked up where she grew up on the Internet, but there was no way he could have known about the Jessica Simpson concert.

"I had such a crush on her," she reminisced.

"Jessica Simpson? Really?" he teased, trying to lighten the mood.

It worked. "OK, don't judge me. I was fifteen and overrun with hormones," she protested, half-heartedly. "I'll never forget that concert – it was on September 8th, three days before 9/11, the day I knew what I wanted to do – no, had to do – for the rest of my life. I was so curious about the attack – I had to know the whole story, beginning, middle, and end. Well, I knew the end, but I needed to know the beginning and the middle, and how it all fit together."

A sudden knock on the door popped Madison's Memory Lane bubble, and she reverted spontaneously into survival mode, ushering the three Rivers into the adjoining bedroom and shutting the door. Then, she quietly made her way to the front door and peered through the peephole. It was Gina, her stand-in.

Breathing a huge sigh of relief, she opened the door to her dressed-down doppelganger, and invited George, Celeste, and Jimmy to come out of their hiding place to meet the woman who could have been her twin.

After pleasantries typical of a first-time introduction, George cut to the chase. "So, the two of you have done this before? And it's worked?"

Gina laughed. "Only a dozen times, or so, when Madison's fearless reporting has gotten her into situations where she needs two of her selves to get to the heart of a story. And, yes, it always has worked like a charm."

"Are you a reporter, too?" Celeste asked.

"Actually, I'm an actress, so I'm used to impersonating people. But Madison's my favorite because she's always wearing such nice clothes and shoes!"

"Now, if you'll excuse us," Madison interrupted, "we'll be right back. My room is just down the hall. Do not, I repeat, do not open the door for anyone!"

* * *

"Do you think he's the one?" the errant knight asked from God's side of the Wall.

A woman's voice replied, "Only one person knows the answer to your question."

"Help me with that," Don Quixote entreated. "Do we really have free will if our destiny is already written? You say that God already knows the choices Jimmy is going to make, so does Jimmy really have a choice?

"God has been called the "Author of Life," and as the author, doesn't he make the choices for His children? It's like playing chess against yourself – you're making all the moves."

"Do you think Cervantes knew all the choices you would make when he started writing your story? If it's a very well-defined character, then the character eventually will make his or her own choices, independent of the author, and will go off-script, so to speak. And the author simply will follow along, exchanging the creator's hat for the historian's pen.

"That's an oversimplification, of course. But the fact remains that even though God created His children in His image, and knows what choices they will make, He doesn't make them for them, and he doesn't intervene, pulling their strings as if they were no more than marionettes. Remember, Geppetto's true glory was not that he was a master puppeteer, but that Pinocchio was free to move about without strings.

"God knew that Adam and Eve would disobey Him, which would lead to their deaths, and even though He loved them unconditionally, He did not take away their free will. He has advised His children how to use their free will wisely, but they must choose to follow His advice.

"God does not play favorites. Adam and Eve weren't the only children He created in His image to live forever as masters of their universe. Our Father is the one true constant, and He will continue to create all His children in His image. And for all His children, He has provided the same breadcrumbs that will lead them back to Paradise and to their divine inheritance. So, each of His children has the same opportunity as Adam and Eve had to live forever as masters of their universe.

"Unfortunately, as Adam and Eve did, they all have chosen very poorly not to believe their Father in heaven, and their poor choices continue to lead them to the same fate as that of their first parents. And every subsequent generation has chosen equally as poorly to believe that Death is inevitable, not a choice.

"He knows how far each of His children will follow the breadcrumbs – how far each will get until they get distracted and blink, until they are not paying attention, until their open minds are shut down, until their ability to choose wisely has been compromised or impaired, until they get comfortable and drop anchor, or until they simply give up and choose the wide gate by accepting that they have no choice in the matter. Typically, that occurs when thoughts of mortality arise."

Don Quixote was trying fervently to keep up. "So, are you saying that Jimmy's mother getting killed was a breadcrumb?"

"If you're asking if God put Jimmy's mom on earth to be killed to help Jimmy along in his journey, absolutely not! Remember, God is not a killer. He does not believe in Death, nor did He create it. His children created Death through their poor choices.

"You also could ask if God put Judas on this earth to betray Jesus, which led to Jesus' arrest, "trial," crucifixion, and third-day Resurrection. In both cases, the answer is an emphatic and unequivocal

"NO!" Again, God's love for His children is unconditional and, for us, beyond comprehension. Creating Jimmy's mother just to be shot and killed in front of her 11-year old son, and putting Judas in this world just so he could betray Jesus – and hang himself afterwards in shame and guilt in order for Jesus to fulfill His destiny – is just too cruel to imagine and would not be consistent with His boundless love for all of His children.

"However, that does not mean that He didn't know what choices they would make that would lead to their deaths. I know this is difficult to wrap your mind around, but He loved them so much that, as much as it pained Him, He refused to interfere with their free will. If He had, where would He draw the line? He would end up putting all of His children back on His strings, reducing them to mindless puppets. How is a child expected to learn if a parent makes all of their choices for them?

"And as glasses either are half-full or half-empty, those two events turned out to be breadcrumbs leading back to Paradise for those who would choose wisely in their aftermath."

"It's the same Intelligent Design that created the universe via the Big Bang, as non-believers choose to call it. God, the Author of Life, 'wrote' this passion play with a beginning, middle, and end – but He allowed His children to choose their roles, even though He knew the choices they would make.

The errant knight's eyes were wide in amazement as he heard these words for the very first time.

The angel continued. "Cervantes gave you life, but he also chose for you in the end. When Jimmy was reading his account of your story for school, he had gotten tired of reading, mainly because he didn't like where the story was headed. So, he put the book aside and put on his favorite *Star Trek* episode, the one in which James Kirk realized that the test to ascend to the captain's chair of the USS Enterprise had been designed to be unsolvable, and that the actual solution was to choose to change the rules of the test.

"It was a form of man-made intelligent design. There was a beginning, a middle, and an end. The beginning was the design of the test. The middle was the competition to solve the test, and the end was the captaincy of the Enterprise for the one who solved the test. The difference between the man-made intelligent design and God's Intelligent Design is that no one knew who was going to figure out the captaincy test. But God knows all the roles and choices His players – His children – will make.

"Jimmy had left the book open on his bed, and you heard Kirk's words...and you, Señor Quixote, chose to change Cervantes' ending. The uninspired would protest, "That's impossible!" – and that's precisely why the human race is in the dire straits in which it finds itself. No one is paying attention. Except Jimmy. And you. Jesus said, "Nothing is impossible, if you have faith." He wasn't a kidder. And voilà...here you are!"

Don Quixote shook his head. He had made those choices the angel described, but he still was amazed. He wondered aloud, "Why didn't God just tell us all of this?"

"That's just it!" the angelic voice responded ardently. "He did. His children simply didn't believe Him – and they still don't believe Him – even though He never would lie to us. For the faithless, there is no substitute for putting fingers in the holes in Jesus' hands, or in the gash in His side.

"Despite what you may have heard, Thomas never doubted. In fact, it was he in whom Jesus privately confided that God's children must actively keep seeking until they discover the true meaning of His words and find their way back Home...only through the narrowest of gates. Along the way, Jesus said they will become disturbed because they will discover that they have been misled from the time that Adam and Eve chose not to believe God. Then they will become amazed, as you are, and rule their Eden as God provided. And, most importantly they never will taste Death.

"After all these years, however, it counter-intuitively is the dance with Death that ultimately forces one to choose – either to live, in which case, barriers are removed from the mind that prevent the embrace of one's divine inheritance, or to succumb to the barriers in the mind that prevent accessing God's authority over all things, including Death. But no one ever will discover that by sitting on the sidelines and being told how it is. They have to risk all that is known – which the scientist said correctly is only one millionth of one percent of all there is to know – by getting in the game and choosing wisely. As you did to vanquish windmill dragons and the Knight of the White Moon, and to be with your Dulcinea. There always is choice. The challenge of Life – of Life Eternal – boils down to the challenge of choosing wisely."

"But what about the prophecy of Saint John in the Revelation and the Second Coming? Doesn't the fact that Jesus has to come again to save God's children from themselves mean that they won't discover the true meaning of Jesus' words?"

"Goodness, Señor Quixote, you have been searching!" the angel smiled. "Yes, it does. But you must understand the difference between prophecy and prediction. A prediction means that a future event will happen, no matter what. A prophecy, on the other hand, suggests that the future event only will happen if an underlying factor doesn't change."

"So, you're saying that Jimmy could be the agent of change."

"Right. Make no mistake, though, the odds are stacked against him."

"The narrow gate."

"It couldn't be narrower. Minds have been shut down in acceptance since the beginning of time. No one has chosen to believe Him for over 2,000 years, and then there's the deception of planned obsolescence..."

"Wait," the knight interrupted. "Planned obsolescence? What does that mean?"

"Think about it. Can anyone afford to live forever? Cervantes didn't make you a rich man. Most everyone retires when they reach a certain age, say 65 or 70. What happens then? The "plan' is that the money will last until they die. Planned obsolescence. And don't get me started on life insurance or wills. Without giving it a second thought, God's children routinely are signing their lives away on the dotted lines of those policies and wills, in effect, agreeing to die. It's been said so many times – money is the root of all evil!"

A sudden realization jolted the Man of la Mancha. "Oh no! Safety First International. Andy Theus. He is the antichrist!"

"And more than likely, he'll be in the White House next year as the Senator's vice president."

"Not if Jimmy has any say about it!" the errant knight exclaimed.

"Yes, but will he have a say? The gate is getting narrower and narrower. Our Father's children are so set in their ways and in their beliefs. They've accepted their mortality. It would be next to impossible to get almost 8 billion people to change their beliefs."

"Not impossible, though! I mean with all the social media in the world, he could reach just about everyone in a very short amount of time. That's how his video went viral."

"True. However, he does have a glaring weakness that very well could cause him to blink and fall."

"You're talking about Sasha."

"Yes. Don't think that the enemy doesn't know it, too; and right now, she's helping her mother prepare to host a dinner in their house for the Devil's brigade."

12

Cal Everett discovered Gina Roberts seven years ago in New York City quite by accident. He just had exited the Credit Suisse office at 11 Madison Park, having met with CEO Travis Bigbee about his bank's donation of Trumbull's full-length portrait of Alexander Hamilton – commissioned in 1791 – to the permanent collection of the Metropolitan Museum of Art, when the unmistakable aroma of a Shake Shack burger reminded him that he had missed lunch.

He crossed Madison Avenue to the outdoor eatery in Madison Square Park and ordered a Smokehouse burger with extra cheese, hold the cherry peppers, and a fifty-fifty concoction of iced tea and lemonade. He scarfed them down in a New York minute, checked his watch, and hurried up 23rd Street to catch the subway to Times Square.

Halfway between Fifth and Sixth Avenues, he spotted a familiar face in one of the Pret-A-Manger outlets that dotted the Manhattan landscape, and he made a snap decision to surprise the woman. She didn't see him enter the store, so he snuck up on her from behind, put his hands over her eyes, and chirped, "Guess who!"

The woman didn't recognize Cal's voice, but played along, anyway, and guessed good-naturedly, "Leonardo DiCaprio. Really, Leo, you have to stop. People are going to talk!"

That's when Cal realized he'd made a terrible mistake. He immediately let go, the woman turned around and, seeing that it wasn't Leo or anyone else she recognized, asked, "Do I know you?"

"I'm so sorry," Cal stammered, his face beet-red in embarrassment. But even as he was tripping over his tongue trying to explain how he thought she was someone else, he couldn't help but notice the striking resemblance to his star reporter.

"Let me guess," she said with a smile, trying to ease the producer's agony. "Madison Munro."

"Yes!" he exclaimed.

"Please don't worry about it," she laughed. "I get that all the time. My name is Gina Roberts."

Somewhat relieved, Cal shook Gina's hand. "I'm Madison's producer, Cal Everett. Again, I'm so sorry. I never do things like that. I'm always afraid it'll backfire on me. And sure enough…"

"Again, no worries, Cal. But you really should change your mindset. When you worry about something going wrong, for sure it's going to go wrong! And besides, I'm a firm believer in serendipity, and I believe there's a reason the universe decided it was time for our paths to cross. And whenever the universe speaks, we should listen."

To say that Gina's charm was disarming would have been an understatement of the highest order. A second ago, Cal was horrified at his case of mistaken identity. Now, he was intrigued. "Well, I told you I'm a producer for ABC News. How about you?"

"I'm an actress...acting like I'm happy to be a hostess at Eleven Madison Park. I came here five years ago from North Platte, Nebraska, to see my name in lights on Broadway. It's not that I'm not an overnight success story, it's just that I've had to keep redefining "overnight,"' she grinned.

"I just passed your restaurant. I had a meeting at Credit Suisse."

"Yep, that's it. Listen, I'd love to stay and chat about our 'meet cute,' but I'm going to be late for work."

"At least let me buy you your salad," Cal insisted.

If flirting had been an Olympic event, Gina would have won a gold medal. "Why, sir, are you offering me a free lunch?" she asked with a twinkle in her eye.

"I guess I am," Cal said hesitantly.

"Well, my daddy says there's no such thing as a free lunch. Are you sure there are no strings attached?"

"No strings."

"Awww," Gina mock-pouted.

Was this girl really flirting with me? Cal wondered. It had been years since he had enjoyed such a playful back-and-forth with a young woman, and he definitely was out of practice. He didn't have a coy comeback. In fact, he didn't have any comeback at all.

Sensing his discomfort, Gina continued, bailing him out for the second time in five minutes. "Anyway, let me give you my card, and you give me one of yours, and when one of us figures out what the universe had in mind for us, we'll let the other one know."

They exchanged business cards...and Cal called Gina three weeks later. He had an idea to use Gina as a stand-in for Madison, and offered to pay her $500 a day, plus expenses. Essentially, it was an offer a struggling actress in New York City couldn't refuse. And she hadn't. In truth, she would have done it for free, but she never told him that.

That's how Gina Roberts came to be standing next to Madison in the hallway of The Crawford Hotel, outside of the Crawford Suite, wearing Madison's crisp, white Alexis stand collar poplin blouse, Veronica Beard tan skirt, Jimmy Choo green stilettos, and mirrored Moschino sunglasses, topped off with Madison's signature, navy blue New York Yankees baseball cap. Cal had had a hunch and sent her a plane ticket to Denver the night before. Just in case...

The first time she had stood in for Madison, Gina asked her about the Yankees cap. Madison told her she and Yankees great, Derek Jeter, had gone to the same high school in Kalamazoo and she was a huge fan.

The cap was de rigueur every time she'd been called upon to help Madison out.

For her part, Madison was wearing Gina's ripped Pac-Sun blue jeans, black, cropped AC/DC t-shirt, and black high-top Cons. This time, Gina had brought along a Red Sox cap to complete the ruse, but Madison had balked.

"No way!" she exclaimed.

"But no one ever would expect you to be wearing a Red Sox

cap."

"A person has to draw the line somewhere. I'd rather die."

"You might, as I understand it."

Madison smirked. She grabbed the cap reluctantly and knocked on the door.

George peeked through the peephole and did a double-take. He opened the door to two Madisons – the cloned actress, completely unrecognizable as herself in Madison's high-end outfit, and the star reporter, whose elevated profile was knocked down several notches, dressed down as she was in Gina's clothes.

The "twins' stepped into the room and George quickly closed the door behind them. "Celeste, Jimmy," he called out to his family hiding in the other room. "Come on out. You're not going to believe this!"

Jimmy emerged, looked first at Madison, then at Gina. Or was it the other way around. "Wow!" was all he could manage.

For her part, Celeste smiled in amazement. "With those sunglasses on, Gina, I'm not sure even Madison's parents would be able to tell that you were not their daughter."

The two women high-fived each other, after which Madison explained the sequence of events about to transpire.

"Gina is going to walk into the lobby very conspicuously, calling as much attention to herself as women can without being obvious, and she'll proceed out the front door, where she'll stop to send a text to us, giving whoever may be following her plenty of time to see "me."

"Then, she'll walk to the Coohills parking garage, and drive my Lexus in the exact opposite direction that Jimmy and I will be headed."

Gina took over, "I'll make a few turns in succession to make sure that a stalker has taken the bait, and I'll try to get a license plate. Then, I'll call Madison to confirm that her coast is clear, hopefully give her a license number so she can call her friend on the force, and I'll start driving to the airport."

"We'll give Gina a few minutes to put some distance between

us," Madison added, "then we'll leave in her car and make our way to Berthoud Pass. I'm sure…"

Jimmy never heard the end of Madison's explanation – his burner phone buzzed and the caller ID said "Sasha." He excused himself to go into the other room.

"Omigosh, Sasha!" he effused, "I've missed you so much ever since you walked out the door! I really wish you were here and going with us."

"I feel the same way," she answered in a hushed tone. "I have to keep my voice down. I'm in the kitchen with Mom.

"But, Jimmy, listen, did you put a note in Hannah's backpack telling her not to take Roland's letter? Because somehow his letter ended up on Tom Farrell's desk."

"I did."

Sasha was confused. "But, why? You know how much we wanted to get our hands on that envelope. It probably would have explained what's going on!"

"Sasha! Because Hannah took the envelope and the man in the dark suit killed her to get it back!"

"That can't be," his girlfriend protested. "I just talked to Hannah!"

"Exactly. When you got home, your mom told you that Hannah had been killed, and she was blaming herself for telling her to take the envelope. And you called and told me."

"Omigod, Jimmy!" Sasha suddenly realized. "You did it, again! Just like with your mom."

"Except this time, it wasn't a dream! I could see Don Quixote's overlapping universe in which Time doesn't exist and I chose it. I went back to when Hannah stowed her backpack in the employees' closet at Joak and put my note in it.

"So, do you want to hear the really freaky part of it?"

"As if this isn't freaky enough?"

"I know, right? This time, though, I was aware of what was going on in "our' universe while I was in Don Quixote's. While I was moving around in his universe, it's like everything and everyone in our universe was frozen. I saw Hannah and I saw the receptionist, but they couldn't see me. I noticed the clock on the wall and that the second-hand was between the same ticks the whole time I was there.

"I could have traveled around the world in Don Quixote's overlapping universe in the blink of an eye in this universe, and no one would have been the wiser! It's like I'm invisible, or something, moving faster than the speed of light."

"This is blowing my mind!"

"Isn't that what Jesus told Thomas would happen? We'd be troubled and then amazed the more we kept seeking?

"Sasha, that's how we got back from Glenwood Springs so quickly when it should have taken us six hours with all the traffic and the jackknifed semi on I-70! And that's how I escaped the fire completely untouched by the flames. I was 100% focused on what I wanted to happen – getting you home in time for your dad's interview, and surviving the fire – that I subconsciously chose the universe in which those things were possible. Really, though, it was an overlapping universe in which everything was possible, and nothing was impossible."

"Jimmy," Sasha said softly, "you really know how to show a girl a good time! I just wish there wasn't all this other drama."

"Sasha, don't you get it? If it weren't for all this other drama, we never would have gotten to where we are now! It's like all the things that have happened over the past five days are breadcrumbs leading to...well, I'm not sure where, yet. But I'm sure we're about to find out!"

"Well, at least to Berthoud Pass," his girlfriend noted.

"Yeah. We'll be leaving in a few minutes, as soon as we're sure we've ditched that creep in the dark suit, if he's even out there. But, do you know what? Even he is a breadcrumb!"

"Oh, Jimmy, that reminds me," Sasha cut in abruptly. "Mom says his name is Samael and he has an eastern European accent. Be sure to tell Madison."

"Good one! I will for sure, as soon as we hang up. One more thing, though. Now that we know Roland did send a letter, someone should tell Cooper."

"Right! That's so sweet of you to think of him with all this other stuff going on."

"I mean things are slowing down so much, it's like I can see everything."

"Can you see how much I love you?" Sasha purred.

"Yes, in all of the universes! I love you, too. Chat soon."

⋆ ⋆ ⋆

"Hey, Partner," Officer Mike McGregor called out to fellow officer Houston Janney. "Check this out."

Janney picked up his burly frame and ambled over to his partner's desk. McGregor handed him his cell phone. "Madison just sent me this text."

It read, "Man in dark suit's name is Samael. Eastern European accent. Connected to POTR."

"POTR?" Janney inquired.

"Partnership of the Right."

"What the hell! Our perp is tied to Senator Fenimore's campaign?"

"Could be," McGregor mused as he typed furiously on his keyboard. "Kind of makes sense, though. I mean you've got the ultra-right conservative religion of the Partnership and the extreme fundamentalist, right-wing fanaticism of the Fundamental Truth Church. It wouldn't be too much of a stretch to connect those dots."

"Eastern European," Janney thought aloud. "Have you checked with Interpol?"

"As we speak. I'm in the database right now." And he typed in the keywords, "Samael' and "Eastern Europe' into the search mechanism. The name "Samael Petrov' appeared.

The two officers read his profile: "Samael Petrov, aka "Yiyo." Hitman for hire. Born April 20, 1970, in Sofia, Bulgaria. Parents deceased, no living relatives; Right-hand man of Dragomir Dobrev, aka "The Grey Wolf," head of a clandestine group of ex-mercenary soldiers called "The Cleaners," loyal to no country, only to the highest bidder. Suspected in at least seventeen assassinations around the world, including those of Bulgarian investigative journalist Boris Aleksandrov and rival crime boss Stefan Angelov."

"Holy shit!" McGregor blurted out. "If this is our guy, and it sure looks like he could be, this just went from bad to nightmare in nothing flat!"

He quickly dialed Madison's number. "Come on, Madison, pick up!" he exhorted.

No answer.

He tried again. Still no answer. Finally, he resorted to an urgent text: "Samael Petrov, hired assassin, extremely dangerous, worst of worst. Playing with fire. Do not engage. REPEAT, DO NOT ENGAGE! Call me asap!"

* * *

Leticia Carter was in the kitchen cleaning up after dinner, when she heard her son shriek from the family room, "NO!!!"

"What happened, Isaac?"

"It's a stupid special report."

She made it to the family room in time to see a familiar face on tv fielding questions from reporters in front of Denver's Fire Station #7.

"Chief McDaniels, there has been a lot of speculation about how Jimmy Rivers walked out of his burning house completely untouched by a fire that you deemed too dangerous for your firefighters to enter. Was there some sort of secret passageway that protected him from the flames? Was it a publicity stunt to bring even more attention to his video?"

Leticia Carter, Annabelle Garton, the Partnership of the Right, the citizens of Denver, and reporters from around the world drew in their collective breath as embattled Fire Chief Orlando McDaniels considered his options up until the very last moment. He stood rigidly straight, squared his shoulders, and stared straight into the phalanx of cameras in front of him.

"I can say, categorically, to all the conspiracy theorists out there, that there is not one shred of evidence to suggest that Jimmy Rivers walking out of that blazing inferno that totally had engulfed his house was anything other than a miracle. There are some things that just can't be explained. The Bible is full of them. And this is another one."

Leticia didn't hear another word of his interview.

"Oh my God," she murmured to herself. "Good for you, Orlando!"

* * *

Gina Roberts, dressed as Madison, just had left the Crawford Suite on her decoy mission when Madison's phone buzzed with Officer McGregor's urgent text about the man in the dark suit.

Bulgarian mob?! she thought to herself. What the hell!

"Guys," she told the Rivers clan, "I'm going to need a minute."

While she deftly texted a message to her producer, George, Celeste, and Jimmy sat around the coffee table trying to process the day's incredible events...and to anticipate what lay ahead.

Madison thought about calling Mike back, but what would that do? He would tell her to "stand down," in effect, that she was playing with fire, and he'd insist that she "play it safe."

What is it with everyone? she contemplated. Playing it safe is the ultimate contradiction. She recalled how she first had met her Officer Mike. He had pulled her over for speeding – again! – and he'd asked her why she hadn't been wearing her seatbelt. He was about to give her a citation for that offense, as well, when she'd turned the tables on him. "Do you really want to know?"

"Yes," he'd replied, more to indulge her than anything else.

"OK, remember, you asked. It's because wearing a seatbelt is against my spiritual beliefs. Why do people wear seat belts?" she'd asked rhetorically. "In case they get in an accident. So, their overriding focus is on getting in an accident and needing protection –

and that invites the negative outcome they are worried about. And I don't want any part of that! You might call me a conscientious objector.

"I understand the illusion of safety they provide and why most people choose to buy into it. It's just that I don't."

That had caught Officer McGregor, who thought he'd heard it all, completely off-guard. He bemusedly shook his head and handed her license back to her. "Just slow down," he'd told her, without giving her any tickets. He started to walk back to his squad car, but she'd sensed an opportunity for a connection in the Denver Police Department in case she ever needed it, and before he'd taken three steps, she called after him and they exchanged numbers. And the enamored patrolman phoned her that same evening.

Madison giggled to herself at the memory – and at his warning about playing with fire. Didn't he know that she was with the firewalker, the one whom fire could not touch? Besides, she didn't want anyone or anything slowing her down and keeping her from her self-appointed date with destiny. Especially not when she was so close to connecting the dots of two almost supernatural events occurring thirteen years apart.

The sound of Celeste's voice speaking to her family interrupted her nostalgia. "I want to talk about the elephant in the room while we're waiting to hear back from Gina. Someone just tried to kill Jimmy and burned down our house. There's been this mysterious man in a dark suit following Jimmy and Sasha practically everywhere they go. We're hiding out in a hotel room. Gina is trying to throw off whoever might be following Madison in order to get to Jimmy. While all this is going on, you want to take Jimmy to Berthoud Pass tonight? Shouldn't we slow down a bit?"

Obviously, slowing down never had been part of Madison's DNA. She had one speed: pedal to the metal, coming in hot!

"Celeste," the reporter calmly rejoined the conversation, "I understand your concern. But I have been working this story for thirteen years, and every instinct in my body is screaming at me to take Jimmy to Berthoud Pass as soon as possible. I've always trusted this sixth sense of mine – it's never let me down."

It was at that precise moment that Madison decided not to tell George and Celeste about the Bulgarian mob connection.

"Well, what if you invited your friend, Mike, to tag along," George interjected.

"To tell you the truth, speaking of trust, I really don't know who I can trust right now. It's not that I don't trust Mike – I just don't trust the people around him. Think about the Partnership. It's kind of like the Brotherhood of the Bell, a secret cabal made up of the titans of industry, religious leaders, and politicians with one overriding, common goal: control.

"Similarly, there's really no telling how far the long arm of the Partnership extends, and for all his good intentions, Mike would slow us down. He's not spontaneous. He's a plodder. I can't have a plodder right now."

George shifted gears. "OK, while we're waiting for Gina's call, can you please tell us why you think Jimmy is connected to what happened on Berthoud Pass thirteen years ago, when he was only four years old?"

"Well, the age thing shouldn't surprise," Madison tittered. "Didn't he ask The Question – why did God, who is not a killer, send the flood to kill all the sinners in the world in Noah's time, but then send His Son to save all the sinners in the world the next time around? – when he was only five years old?"

The reminder of their precocious child's audaciousness seemed to take the tension in his parents' countenance down a notch.

"OK. Where to start?" Madison paused for a moment to reflect, then began, "I know what I saw that night on Berthoud Pass. I saw a man in a minivan purposely drive off a cliff to rescue a young girl whose car had been swept off the road by an avalanche moments before. I'll never forget the look in that man's eyes. Fiery. No fear. No doubt. No disbelief, as he flew off the road into the darkness.

"The young girl, Rachel, talked afterwards of a flying car and being dropped off at her home. If I hadn't seen it with my own two eyes, I never would have believed it.

"There was no explanation. The police investigation lasted a couple of weeks, but nothing added up – and since no crime had been committed, they just accepted that Rachel had been through a traumatic experience that left gaping holes in her story that never would be answered. They couldn't afford to spend any more time investigating what might have been a miracle.

"Of course, there were the conspiracy theorists, the Area 51-ers and the Rapturists, who had their own explanations, but, eventually, everyone pretty much lost interest, and they dropped anchor in acceptance...that flying cars probably were the result of a severe trauma that brought on a hallucinogenic experience, that wild animals probably dragged the man's body away, that the earth somehow swallowed up the remains of the minivan, and that, somehow, a young girl in deep shock made her way back to her home. Think Ted Kennedy and Chappaquiddick.

"But that didn't work for me. I never have taken anything at face value, and I always, always have trusted my instincts; and they were gnawing at me. That's the problem with most people. Their choice is to drop anchor in acceptance. Dropping anchor means you're not going forward. No progress. Just stagnation.

"I kept going back to the passion in that man's eyes. Not a shred of doubt as he flew off that cliff in his minivan. It's like he knew the ending before the end of the story, because he was the author and he was writing it as he went along. One writer who came to talk to our class in elementary school said that the 8-1/2 by 11 blank sheet of paper represented total freedom to him – as the author, he could be God. He could create a world of his own choosing and characters who could do whatever he wanted them to do. If he wanted them to fly, they could fly. I never forgot that.

"Then, I asked myself what was so unbelievable about what I had seen? Was it that a minivan could fly? Was it that a man could be so reckless and so confident at the same time? Old or not, what did age have to do with it, anyway? It occurred to me that we all are prisoners of our preconceived notions. We just accept things as truth that we can't explain, and we walk away judging the book by its cover.

"But what if we choose to dig deeper into those books, to open our minds and break out of our prisons? Do you know what lies beyond those prison walls? The freedom of possibilities. Of unlimited possibilities.

"And, suddenly, there's an explanation. Edison said that we only know one-millionth of one percent of all there is to know. That's why Einstein said imagination is more important than knowledge – because knowledge is so limiting. It takes imagination and faith to go beyond the limits of knowledge, beyond the one-millionth of one percent."

Madison was on a roll, and the Rivers family sat mesmerized by her fervor. There was no stopping her now.

"When you free yourself from the shackles of blind acceptance, then your mind is free to explore the seemingly unseemly. So, faith. When I freed my mind to consider that nothing is what it seemed to be, it unlocked all the preternatural thoughts from my subconscious soul and boom: I remembered a story from my own Sunday School about Peter walking on water, defying gravity while he was 100% focused on Jesus telling him to step out of the boat and walk towards Him on the water. Talk about a leap of faith! Peter couldn't swim – and, yet, he had complete faith that when he stepped out of the boat, he would be able to walk on top of the water because the Son of God, through Whom he passionately believed all things were possible, was telling him he could do it.

"That was my 'Eureka!' moment. It had been done before! Gravity is not so much a law as it is an explanation for what can be seen and measured in this realm of one-millionth of one percent. And I imagined that Peter had that same look in his eyes as the man in the minivan. They both had chosen to open their minds, and their jail cells, to the freedom of all possibilities beyond the prison walls of acceptance.

"When Jimmy related to me that his mysterious fortune teller told him to see the world not as it was, but as it should be, I finally had the link that tied him to what I had witnessed on Berthoud Pass.

The pieces of the puzzle were starting to come together. The solution lay beyond knowledge, beyond what was known. The answer was twofold: imagination and faith.

"Peter walking on water was just one of the miracles in the Bible. And what are miracles? Things that cannot be explained. So, I went to the source, looking for more clues. I found that after all of His miracle healings, Jesus never said, "I have healed you." It always was, "Your faith has healed you."

"To say that I was consumed by the Berthoud Pass incident would be a huge understatement, but I had faith, and I never blinked. To his credit, Cal humored me. I'm pretty sure he's not where I've gotten to in terms of faith, but, as a reporter and producer, he has had 'gut feelings' that required the suspension of disbelief, and the courage of his conviction to pursue. So, he's always given me the benefit of the doubt. He says I remind him of himself, but I had to do most of my investigation on my own time.

"I interviewed everyone who I thought might have had a possible connection to the story: Rachel, Sarah, and the rest of the kids traveling with Dirk that night, their families, gas station attendants, restaurant workers, convenience store operators, priests, theologians. I scoured the countryside along Highway 40 from Empire to Kremmling looking for anything that might help to fill in the blanks.

"But something was missing. For thirteen years. Until I saw that video of Jimmy in his civics class questioning the contradictory platforms of the Partnership of the Right – how they could be pro-life and, at the same time, support tough-on-crime capital punishment – but, more importantly, how God was pro-choice rather than pro-life, which was completely antithetical to the POTR's platform and raison d'être...and something clicked. Then, when I heard him say nothing was what it seemed, my instinct, suddenly, was on highest alert. I had to dig deeper.

"After the interview...well, you know how when people meet the person they're supposed to spend the rest of their lives with, they almost always say they 'just knew' that he or she was 'the one' right away?

"After thirteen years of 'dating' the Berthoud Pass story, so to speak, my subconscious mind had put together an ideal of 'the one' for me, based on what I liked and didn't like about all the clues I investigated. The only thing missing was the actual link, itself.

"When you finally cross paths with 'the one,' because the universe will bring you together, your subconscious instantly recognizes your partner for life – or, in this case, my missing link – and gives you a swift kick in the ass, even before you're aware of it.

"That's the way it was with Jimmy. The video piqued my curiosity, I got the interview, and I was hooked. I just knew. The pieces of the puzzle were starting to come together: an enigmatic, Pied Piper fortune teller leading Jimmy along with his 'see-the-world-as-it-should-be-not-as-it-is' tune, Jimmy's obsession with Captain Kirk changing the rules, the fortune teller's mantra that the rules of man are not rules at all, but observations that can be changed by changing one's mindset. And, then, there's Malachi..."

The sound of Madison's buzzing cell phone shocked the Rivers family out of Madison's hypnotic spell as unnervingly as the 1979 penny had broken the trance that had enabled Richard Collier to travel 68 years back in time to 1912 in the movie, "Somewhere in Time."

It was Gina. Story time was over. Destiny beckoned.

13

"Cooper, it's me. I have news about Roland. Please call me back."

That should do the trick, Sasha told herself. Sure enough, her phone began to vibrate seconds after she hung up. The caller ID said "Bro."

Before she could get a word in, Cooper warned – well, advised sternly – "You better have something, Sis!"

"Hello to you, too," she said, slightly off-put. She quickly apologized. "I'm sorry. I know this is hard on you, but you have to know it's hard on all of us."

"The Senator, too?" he asked, cynically.

"He's got his own issues," Sasha defended their father, but she knew it fell on deaf ears. "Anyway, I do have news, it's just not great news."

"Tell me."

"Roland did send a letter. Or, someone sent it for him, anyway."

"Omigod," her brother fretted. "So, we know he's in trouble. Did he send it to the *Post*?"

"Yes."

"OK, what'd it say?"

"We haven't seen it."

"You haven't seen it? So, how do you know it was sent to the newspaper?"

"Mom's friend, Sylvia, who works in the mail room, saw it."

"OK, can't we tell her how urgent this is that we see it?"

"It's not there, anymore. She saw the managing editor take the letter. Actually, he was trying to hide it from her...and then it wound up at Joak Industries."

"Joak Industries?" he repeated, incredulously. "How do you know that?"

"Hannah saw it there."

"Hannah, our cousin?"

"Yes. She got an internship there, and she saw an envelope with Roland's name in the return address, made out to the *Denver Post*, on her boss's desk. It hadn't been opened."

"Sasha, what in the hell is going on?" Cooper demanded, clearly agitated. "How did the Joaks get it? And, why them?"

"We don't know!" his sister tried to explain, "Hannah was convinced something shady was going on with the Joaks. That's why she got the internship there. She was working on her senior capstone project, trying to get into Northwestern.

"So," Sasha continued, "did Roland tell you anything about what he was working on? Anything that might have involved the Joaks?"

"No. I told you. He wanted to protect me. He said it was for my own good."

"Well, the Joaks are pretty powerful people. It sounds like Roland could have been doing a story on them, and maybe he hit a nerve."

The reality of what his sister was insinuating began to dawn on Cooper. There was an uncomfortable silence as his and his partner's life together began to flash before his eyes.

"Cooper, are you there," Sasha asked, finally.

"So, you think he's dead," he muttered morosely.

"I didn't say that. We don't know anything for sure. There are so many other possibilities."

"None of them great, though," Cooper moaned. "Does Dad know?"

"Not, yet. He's got so much going on with the campaign, we didn't want to bother him with this until we knew more. We were hoping Roland would show up with one of his classic 'you're-not-going-to-believe-this' explanations."

"Yeah, I've been watching the news. Kudos to your boyfriend, by the way. I mean, really, who knew Jimmy had it in him. He always was so quiet in public settings. Taking on the Partnership. Walking out of that fire like he was Superman. And all of those deep thoughts. It's always the quiet ones – still waters do run deep."

"That's a long story, Cooper, too long for now; and I'll tell you what, Roland would love it. But, thank you, he's so special to me. First things first, though. Getting back to your own special person, Mom and Dad are hosting a dinner tonight in about an hour, and guess who'll be here."

"The Joaks?" he offered, his pulse quickening.

"No, unfortunately, but the next best thing. Don Stottlemeyer and his wife, among others. We can ask him about Roland's envelope in front of everyone at the table."

"Who else will be there?"

"Ugh. The usual. The Partnership people."

"Ha!" Cooper enthused, poking his head out from his shell of sadness for a brief moment. "Can you imagine the look on the Senator's face when those fools find out that his carefully crafted Stepford family isn't so perfect? And I finally can come out of this damn closet."

Sasha came to their father's defense, yet again. "Cooper, don't be so hard on Dad…"

"You mean the Senator, don't you?"

"He's still our dad. I mean, I've seen the excruciating pressure he's been under this past week. And he's got that jerk, Ralph, pulling all his strings like he's a mindless puppet. I don't trust the rest of the Partnership, either. They have these rosy titles, but I think they're more thorns than rose.

"Deep down, though, he's still our father, and he'd go to the wall for all of us...even his gay son. If it came to a choice between the Partnership and his family, I'm sure he'd choose us, no questions asked."

Cooper frowned. "I'm not so sure about that, Sis, but I guess we'll see at dinner tonight."

Sasha's mood brightened. "So you'll come?"

"Yeah, I called the police to file the missing persons report, but they said they had to wait 24 hours to launch a full investigation... you know, in case Roland showed up. I realized I didn't have much information to give them. Now, there's this letter, though, and I'll get to ask Mr. Stottlemeyer directly why he sent it to the Joaks without even opening it. I'm sure the police will want to know, too.

"Besides, I haven't been able to eat much these last couple of days. I'm assuming Mom is making her world-famous chicken cordon bleu?"

"How did you know?" Sasha teased.

Cooper laughed, allowing himself a moment of levity. "See you soon, Sis!"

Meanwhile, across the street, The Cobra kept a watchful eye on the Fenimore house, waiting for his moment to strike. Sasha couldn't have been more misguided about her father's ultimate loyalty. After rushing to his defense twice in her conversation with her brother, she had no idea that the Senator had green-lighted her assassination.

* * *

No one paid any attention to the young woman in the ripped PacSun blue jeans, the black, cropped AC/DC t-shirt, and the black high-top Converse tennis shoes, her face partially shielded by a Boston Red Sox cap, and her eyes hidden by $9.99 drugstore sunglasses with mirrored silver lenses, as she and her "beau," a young man with a New York Yankees baseball cap pulled down low over his face, stepped into a reconditioned 1995 green Subaru Impreza with a "Green Hornet' bumper sticker on the back parked in the Crawford Hotel garage.

As soon as Madison fired up "The Hornet," and eased out of the parking space, she offhandedly mentioned to Jimmy, "I didn't want to tell you this in front of your parents, but your friend in the dark suit is a hitman for a secret group of mercenary soldiers turned assassins."

"What?" Jimmy gasped.

"I know. I've got to call Mike and get the deets."

While Madison speed-dialed Officer McGregor, Jimmy texted Sasha: "Samael is an assassin, per Madison. Call me when everyone leaves. And be careful! xoxoxo."

⋆ ⋆ ⋆

At the same time, about fifteen miles away, a woman's phone buzzed in a white Audi. Petya checked the caller ID. "Tova e Samael," she said in Bulgarian. ["It's Samael."].

"Slozhi go na visokogovoritelya' ["Put it on speaker'], the driver instructed.

"Zdraveĭte?" ["Hello?"].

Samael wasted no time with pleasantries. "Imash li momicheto?" ["Do you have the girl?"].

"Da." ["Yes"], Todor replied.

"Kŭde si?" ["Where are you?"].

"Nasochva se na iztok po I-70." ["Heading east on I-70"].

"Tova e stranno, siguren li si, che toven e tya?" ["That's strange, are you sure it's her?"].

"Da. Tova e neĭnata kola." ["Yes, it's her car"], Todor affirmed.

"I neĭnite drekhi' ["And her clothes"], Petya added, wistfully.

"Snimal li si ya?" ["Did you take a picture of her?"], Samael asked.

"Da." ["Yes."]

"Izprati mi ya." ["Send it to me"].

Petya sent the photo, and Samael checked his phone.

"OK, da, tova e tya. E momcheto s neya?" ["OK, yes, that's her. Is the boy with her?"].

"Ne go vizhdam' ["I don't see him"], Petya replied.

"Toĭ ne beshes neya, kogato tya napusna khotela' ["He wasn't with her when she left the hotel"], Todor added.

"Nyama nachin tya da go ostavi sled sebe si!" ["There is no way she would leave him behind!"] Samael insisted.

"Tya otiva na letishteto' ["She is going to the airport'], Todor cut in.

Samael thought for a moment. "OK, Imam novi porŭchki' ["OK, I have new orders'}, he told his Bulgarian comrades. "Shte poema ottuk." ["I will take over from here"].

"Shtom me vidite, obŭrnete se, kogato mozhete, i se vŭrnete v kŭshtata. shte ti se obadya po-kŭsno' ["As soon as you see me, turn around when you can and return to the house. I'll call you later"].

Gina was surprised, a few minutes later when she watched the white Audi with the man and woman who had been following her since she left the hotel turn off on Tower Road.

"Oh no," she worried aloud, "did they figure out I wasn't Madison?" She was afraid it hadn't been enough time for them to get out of Denver unnoticed.

She called Madison and put her phone on speaker.

Madison picked up immediately. "What's up, Gina?"

"I'm not sure. A man and a woman have been following me since I left the hotel, but they just turned off on Tower Road. Do you think they figured out I wasn't you?"

"Hmmm, that is strange. And you're still headed to the airport?"

"Yes."

"Were you able to make out their license plate?"

"Yes. Colorado plates, POR 013."

"That's a campaign car," Jimmy spoke up. "Sasha told me the Partnership has a whole fleet of white Audis with the prefix "POR.""

"Gina, was it a white Audi?" Madison sought to confirm.

"Yes, how did you know?"

"You never should underestimate me," the reporter laughed.

"I never have, but still, you never cease to amaze. Anyway, what should I do now?"

"We're about to get on I-70 off of 6th, and I haven't seen anyone tailing us, so we should be good."

"Oops, wait a minute," Gina hesitated. "That's odd."

"What is it?"

"Now, there's another white Audi behind me, but I can't quite make out the license plate."

"So, pull off onto the shoulder and let it pass you. I'll hold."

Gina put on her turn signal and eased Madison's black Lexus onto the right shoulder. But the white Audi never passed her.

"Shit, Madison, he pulled up right behind me."

"Did you see the license plate?"

"POR 666. He's getting out of the car!"

Madison's heart skipped a beat. The sign of the beast. It couldn't have been a coincidence. She didn't believe in them. Her pulse raced.

"Is he wearing a dark suit?"

"Yes! How did you know that?" Gina's voice trembled. "You're starting to scare me."

"Gina, drive!" Madison shouted. "Fast! Get the hell out of there!"

14

"Help me with my zipper, honey," Tina Stottlemeyer asked her husband. Being the wife of the managing editor of a major city newspaper wasn't nearly as glamorous as one might think, and Tina, seventeen years her husband's junior, was going to take advantage of every opportunity to dress up, even if just for a casual dinner party with friends.

"Tina, we're only going over to the Fenimores," Don protested mildly as he zipped up his wife's black, admiral crepe sheath dress.

"I know, but we hardly go out anymore, and I wanted to look nice."

"Well, I don't understand why these dress designers put zippers in the back. How do they expect women to zip them up themselves?"

Tina Stottlemeyer whirled around to look her husband in the eyes. "Don, women are perfectly capable of zipping up back zippers. Once we learn to fasten our bras from behind, the zippers are a piece of cake. It's just that asking our partners for help is a flirty thing to do. And, you never complain when you're unzipping me. Come on, what's the matter?"

"I'm sorry," he sighed, taking a deep breath. "Work has been so stressful these past few days, and I'm being asked to do some things I thought I'd never do."

He paused and tried to recapture the moment. "You look very nice, by the way!"

"Thank you," Tina beamed, even though she had had to fish for the compliment. Then, dutifully, she asked, "Do you want to talk about what's going on at work?"

"No, I'd rather focus on my beautiful wife," he insisted, and he leaned in for a kiss to wipe away all his troubles.

When they came up for air, Tina's face was flushed with desire and Don began to unzip her dress.

"Honey, we can't," she pouted. "All this," she grandly swept her arm from head to toe, "well, let's just say Rome wasn't built in a day.

"But," she continued coyly, giving him a playful squeeze, "maybe you'll want to help me out of my dress when we get back."

She gave her deflated husband a sexy little kiss on the lips to seal the deal, then retired to the bathroom to touch up her makeup and reapply her lipstick.

"It'll be really good to see Alice, again," she called out. "I miss her – we haven't seen each other in such a long time."

"I suppose running for President does have an effect on one's social life," Don answered, doing some repair work of his own. It would have been such bad form to show up for dinner with his wife's lipstick smeared all over his face.

"You know, the next time we're invited for dinner, we could be dining at the White House!" Tina exclaimed.

Not if the Partnership doesn't come up with an answer for Jimmy Rivers, her husband groused to himself, stripped of his randy intention.

* * *

Sylvia Brown had been troubled by her encounter with the *Post*'s managing editor in the mail room that morning, but the fire at the Rivers' house had distracted her for the balance of the day. On her way home from work, however, her misgivings resurfaced, and they had intensified.

She had caught Don Stottlemeyer in an outright lie – with her own two eyes, she had seen him trying to hide a large envelope that had Roland's name on it. Then, his denials. He had denied speaking with Leticia Carter, remanding her to the category of the nameless and faceless crazies who bombard the paper every day with their conspiracy theories and other ghost stories – and, yet, Leticia told her that he had called her last night, following up on the letter.

Then there was his morally casual attitude. He'd had an affair with one of the paper's young reporters, Tina Gallagher, on the eve of his silver anniversary with first wife, Sharon, while Tina was engaged to fellow reporter, Jack Thompson. There had been rumors of the affair for months, which he vehemently had denied...until he left Sharon, and Tina broke off her engagement. They married three months later. That was seven years ago – it had been so messy and tawdry, and some of the awkwardness remained to this day, which explained her uneasiness. Was he up to his old tricks, again? she wondered.

Except this time, she had a sense of something far more sinister. If Roland Thomas was being held captive somewhere, or had been killed, for an investigative story on some powerful people he had been working on, and Don was involved in the cover-up, then potential witnesses who could corroborate the existence of the letter also would be in the scope of those same powerful people – Leticia and her son, Isaac. Her disquiet escalated even more when she was gobsmacked by the realization that she, too, would be in those nefarious crosshairs.

Sylvia turned left off of Kalamath Street onto Fourth Street, then left on Inca Street in the gentrified Baker neighborhood a mile south of downtown Denver and counted her lucky stars to have found a parking spot in front of her bungalow at 456 Inca. She ran inside, making sure to lock the door behind her, and immediately dialed Leticia Carter's number.

"Hello?" Leticia answered.

"Leticia, this is Sylvia Brown from the *Denver Post*. We spoke earlier about a letter your son was paid to send to the newspaper."

"Yes, Sylvia, I remember you. Thank you for calling back. Did you find the letter?"

"We did, and that's one of the reasons why I'm calling. We have reason to believe that you and Isaac might be in danger."

"Danger?" Leticia shrieked. "I told that boy he shouldn't have gotten involved. Stranger danger. I don't care how badly we needed the money!"

"Look, I really can't explain right now, just be extra careful and aware. Make sure your doors and windows are locked, and, if you can, lay low this weekend. Whatever you do, don't let Isaac out of your sight! Hopefully, this all will be sorted out in a day or two'

"Sweet Jesus!" she cried out. "Isaac, come in here, please!"

Then, she asked Sylvia, "You said that warning us was one of the reasons you were calling...what was the other one?"

The eleven-year-old bounded into the kitchen. "What is it, Mama? The game's still on."

"Did I just hear Isaac?" Sylvia inquired.

"Yes." Turning to her son, she tried to remain calm: "Wait one second, Isaac."

"Leticia, this is very important. Can you ask Isaac if there was anything else he remembered about the day that Roland gave him the envelope? Anything that didn't seem normal, or that seemed out-of-the-ordinary?"

"Hold on."

Sylvia heard mother and son discussing what else he might have seen that day, but she couldn't make out their words.

After a few minutes, Leticia got back on the line. "He said he remembered a man in a dark suit he'd never seen before who kind of scared him."

* * *

"What do you mean you lost her?" Satan yelled.

"Sir, she made me," Samael explained. "I don't know how. I switched off with Todor and Petya, no problem, then she pulled off onto the side of the road. It was the highway. I had no choice – I had to stop behind her. So, I thought to pretend to offer assistance and got out of my car and waved as I started to walk towards her. And that's when she sped away."

"And?" the Satan asked impatiently.

"Sir, she's a smart woman. If she thought she was in danger, she had plenty of time to get my license plate and call it in. I had to ditch the car. I reported it stolen – and then I stole a car out of the long-term parking lot near the airport. I found one with the engine still warm, so it won't be called in until long after I'm finished with it. I paid the parking fee with a prepaid Visa card, so it won't be traced back to me."

"But, as far as anyone knows, you haven't done anything wrong! You are in charge of security for the Partnership of the Right."

"Yet, I have. And she has street cred and connections. Probably some friends on the police force, too. I couldn't take the chance of someone putting the pieces together. Think of how it would have looked for the Partnership.

"Remember, they stopped Tim McVeigh because of a broken taillight – and that gave them time to figure out he was the Oklahoma City Bomber."

Satan turned over his king. He had been checkmated and conceded, "You're right. I'm just so frustrated! I haven't felt this powerless since I fought Michael and was banished from heaven. This kid could be the death of me."

"Sir, with all due respect, we'll get him, and sooner rather than later. He's too high profile. Someone will see him, and we'll be there. The Cobra is our insurance policy. He's in place.

"When he kills Sasha, Jimmy will come running, even faster than Sonny did in *The Godfather* when Carlo beat up his sister. And we'll be waiting, just like Barzini's hitmen at the toll booth."

"That was a movie, Samael, damn it!"

"No, it is human nature, sir – art imitating life."

"Ah, yes, human nature...the tendency to choose badly," Satan allowed himself a moment of satisfaction. Then, he asked, "Where are you now?"

"Watching Pena Boulevard, in case the reporter hasn't left the airport, yet."

"Just so you know, Samael, I'm not happy you let her give you the slip, but I do admire your resourcefulness. Stand by. I'll call back in a few minutes."

⋆ ⋆ ⋆

Madison picked up her phone almost before it started buzzing.

"Gina, are you alright?" she asked, anxiously.

"Yes. Sorry it took me a few to call you back. I had to improvise a bit on the run which didn't lend to making phone calls."

"Thank God! What happened?"

She giggled, "Well, you know I'm an actress and I've gotten used to incorporating my director's cues into my performances on the fly, so when you basically yelled at me to 'get the hell out of there,' I didn't have to be told twice. I floored it and never looked back.

"I figured that guy following me wasn't trying to get an autograph, so I sped up to 90 mph hoping a traffic cop would pull me over. Of course, they're never there when you need them, and always there when you don't.

"I said I never looked back, but as I approached the terminal, I did look back and I didn't see him. That kind of unnerved me more than if I had seen him because I thought he was going to ambush me somewhere else along the way. At least when you can see someone, you don't have to worry about them popping up from out of nowhere.

"So, I parked your car in the East Garage on the third level in Row J. I went into the terminal, bought a change of clothes, and now I'm riding the light rail back to Union Station."

"Look at you, Gina!" Madison cheered. "All that improv training paid off. If you ever get tired of acting, I'm sure there's a place for you in a different theater – the theater of the clandestine!

"Anyway, when I got off the phone with you, I called my friend Mike on the force and explained what happened. I gave him the license plate, and he told me that the Partnership had called right after you called me and reported the car as stolen."

"The Partnership," Gina wondered aloud. "So, this guy either stole the car or works for the Partnership."

Madison applauded, "You're good!"

"I know how stories are put together, and I'm always on the

lookout for plot points."

"Well, this plot actually sickens because he does work for the Partnership – and he's a fugitive hitman from Bulgaria!"

"No shit!" Gina remarked, her knees starting to shake at the news.

"No shit!" Madison echoed.

"Well, that was close. Do you think that counts as one of my nine lives?"

"Nah, but if you do see him again…"

"Don't worry, I won't ask him to put suntan lotion on my back," she said bravely, but any reporter of Madison's caliber would have detected her fake bravado. "Actually, I called Cal and he told me he'd meet me at Union Station."

"Wait, what? Cal's in town? He never leaves New York!"

"It was a spur of the moment thing. He said he had a gut feeling about needing to be in Denver."

Cal always had been in her corner on her Berthoud Pass suspicions – who was she kidding, he always was in her corner – and any newsperson worth his or her salt would be starting to connect the dots between Berthoud Pass, the Partnership, and Jimmy Rivers. The picture that was emerging was shaping up to be the story of the year, or of the decade, even. Still, Madison had an inkling that the instinct to which he was referring was equal parts basic and primal.

"By the way," Gina inquired, offhandedly, "is Cal married?"

That question confirmed Madison's intuition that there had been some extracurricular flirting going on between the actress and the publisher – and that he had another reason for coming to Denver.

"He was about to be. His fiancée was killed by a drunk driver the day they were supposed to get married. It was 2:00 in the morning and she was taking her dress to a friend for some last-minute alterations. That was 20 years ago. He's been married to his work ever since and hasn't allowed himself to get close to anyone. As I said, I can't remember him leaving New York since I've known him, which is why I was kinda surprised he was here in Denver."

"Omigosh, that's awful!"

"The worst," Madison agreed. "He's always telling me I need balance in my life, that I need to get a personal life away from the office. I think he figured it's time he followed his own advice."

That's when the ABC news reporter went off-script: "He's fair game, Gina. In case you're interested." And she smiled.

* * *

By the time the Senator and his troupe arrived at his 37 Skylark Lane address, they were in foul moods. They just had heard Fire Chief McDaniels' report that the fire at the Rivers' house definitely would be classified "highly suspicious, pending further investigation," but that there was no sign it had been staged, replete with an escape route or tunnel, or any other secret passageway that Jimmy could have used to avoid the firestorm that had gutted their house. Then, he'd lobbed a grenade right back at the Partnership, lecturing them that the Bible was full of occurrences that couldn't be explained.

The group settled in around the coffee table in the living room. Alice and Sasha brought in the hors d'oeuvres – hummus and pita, brie and crackers with a sour cherry fruit jelly, and carrots and celery with ranch dressing – while the Senator attended to the drinks. Cardinal Phelps was having a Maker's Mark on the rocks, Ralph Petiole asked for a rum and coke, Don Stottlemeyer opted for an old-fashioned; he made dirty martinis for Father Simon and himself, and poured glasses of Chardonnay for Tina and Alice. Sasha had a tonic water with lime.

After a short period of small talk, Alice maneuvered to ask Don about Roland's letter, but she worried about not having had a chance to talk with her husband about it beforehand, and she ultimately demurred. Unfortunately, however, she unwittingly stepped into another minefield.

"Can you believe this day?" she asked innocently. "Just when you think you've seen everything, there's Jimmy Rivers walking out of that hellfire that had been his house, completely untouched by the flames. Sasha saw him in the hospital – tell them, Sweetheart."

Sasha relished the opportunity to talk up her boyfriend in front of the Partnership. "It was amazing!" she confirmed. "He was amazing! Not a single burn mark, not a single singed hair. Like Fire Chief McDaniels said, it truly was a miracle!"

It was the word "miracle" that tripped the wire and triggered an explosive outburst from Cardinal Phelps, an emotional blast that startled the other guests.

"Goddamn it!" he screamed. "I've heard just about all I want to hear about this so-called miracle. It's nothing more than fake news!"

"But, your Eminence," Tina objected, "we all saw it with our own eyes!"

Father Simon leapt to his superior's defense. "Tina, you've heard of the rapper, Tupac Shakur?"

"Of course, Father."

"He was shot and killed in Las Vegas in 1996. And, yet, he made an appearance at the Coachella concert in 2008. I was there, and I saw him with my own eyes, along with everyone else."

"Excuse me, Father Simon," Sasha cut in, her cheeks flushed in anger. "Are you saying that wasn't Jimmy walking out of his burning house, but a hologram of Jimmy? With all due respect, that's absurd! You may have been at Coachella, but you weren't there today."

"Sasha!" the Senator interrupted. "That's enough!"

"It's ok, Bill," the priest assured. "It's been a very emotional day for your daughter, believing her boyfriend might be dead, then thinking she saw him walking out of the fire she thought had killed him."

"I didn't think anything. I know what I saw. And what do you believe, Father?" Sasha asked, fire in her eyes. "Last Sunday, you told us in church that Jesus didn't really mean it when He said nothing was impossible for a person who has the faith of a mustard seed.

"Do you remember what happened in the Garden of Eden? Who it was that told Adam and Eve not to believe what..."

"Sasha!" Alice intervened, quickly grabbing her daughter's arm before she could finish and ushering her to the kitchen. "We need to get dinner on the table."

15

"I never get tired of this view," Madison marveled as they crested the hill on I-70 and the Buffalo Herd Overlook spread out before them in all its majesty.

She looked over at Jimmy – his eyes were wide open, but his mind was going faster than the car's 80 mph, taking him far, far away from the westbound lanes of the Interstate.

"Jimmy!" Madison urged.

The insistence in Madison's voice snapped him out of his daydream. "What is it? What'd I miss?" he asked nervously.

"Look around. This amazing vista!"

Jimmy ignored the scenery, needing to unburden himself. "Madison, I have to talk to you about something."

"This sounds serious. But what could be more serious than the last few days?"

"Well, you know Sasha has an older brother, Cooper, who's going to school in Boulder."

"Right."

Jimmy hesitated, wrestling with whether or not he should betray a confidence.

"Go on," Madison encouraged.

"OK, but I'm telling you this in the strictest confidence and only for context."

"Cooper's gay," she threw out, taking the words out of Jimmy's mouth.

"You knew?"

"I guessed, based on your level of discomfort and what it would mean for the Senator."

"The only thing I'm uncomfortable about is that I believe he deserves to be able to come out on his own terms, and that he should be the one to tell everyone...and there's a good chance that won't happen."

"But, he can't," the veteran reporter interjected. "The political and social climate fostered by the Partnership isn't nearly as forgiving as it was for the Cheneys' daughter, Mary. They've flipped the switch and created a divisive, homophobic hysteria that has no place at the table for a gay Cooper Fenimore to sit."

"It's funny you should say that. I think Cooper's going to be at his parents' dinner party tonight."

"Why would he take a chance? If the Partnership finds out that he's gay, it would be ruinous for his father's political career. Not to mention for their designs on the White House!"

"That's really what I wanted to talk to you about. The only "partnership" he cares about is his own partner, Roland Thomas. Roland is a freelance journalist looking to make a name for himself with an investigative report on some very powerful and dangerous people. He wouldn't give Cooper any details as a way of protecting him.

"Anyway, Roland never came back home on Tuesday, and he never called, which is very odd because he usually was obsessively compulsive about touching base with Cooper throughout the day. And before he left Tuesday morning, he'd told Cooper to call the police if he hadn't returned by nightfall."

"Jimmy, this isn't sounding so good for Roland."

"It gets better, or worse, I don't know. Roland was fastidious to a fault about details and about covering his bases. If he thought he was in danger, we – Sasha, her mom, and I – were sure that he would have made arrangements for whatever incriminating evidence he had gathered to be delivered to a newspaper.

"So, Sasha's mom called her friend who works in the mail room of the *Denver Post* and asked her to keep an eye out for an envelope or package addressed to the newspaper with Roland's name in the return address. Again, Roland was OCD about things like that. Besides, I'm sure he would have wanted to get the letter back if there was a problem with the delivery.

Sure enough, the envelope showed up at the *Post*, but it was intercepted by the managing editor before her friend could get it.

"Don Stottlemeyer," Madison groaned. "What a sleezeball! He had an affair with one of his interns, or junior reporters, whatever you want to call her – a girl I went to school with – divorced his wife and married my friend. He's got to be at least 25 years older than her."

"Tina Gallagher."

Madison cast a sideways glance at Jimmy. "That's right," she confirmed with a puzzled look on her face. "How did you know that?"

"I go to school with her sister, Lisa. She's like the queen bee of the school, and she has it in for Sasha because she thinks Sasha stole her boyfriend. So, she keeps trying to get back at Sasha through me."

"Ugh, what a small world! High school drama with all those raging teenage hormones. It's the worst," she recalled, shuddering at the memory. "Nothing has changed since I was in school. But go on…"

"So, Roland's letter ended up, unopened, on Tom Farrell's desk. He's the…"

"...HR guy for Joak Industries," Madison finished his sentence. "And there's your answer. Roland was investigating the Joaks, he got too close, and they canceled his ticket."

Jimmy was aghast. "You don't think he still might be alive?"

"Not based on what you've told me. Sorry to be so clinical."

So many coincidences and dots to connect, she thought to herself.

Then, as a bolt out of the blue, she pounded the steering wheel and exclaimed, "Holy Shit!"

"What is it?" Jimmy asked, taken aback by her outburst.

"My friend, Mike, on the police force, called me earlier about a gut feeling he was having. Two men from the Fundamental Truth Church, were found murdered this afternoon. They both were killed by a bullet to the back of the head. Obviously, a professional hit."

Jimmy's skin went cold. That's how Hannah had been killed before he left the note in her backpack.

"Samael, the man in the dark suit," he whispered under his breath.

"Yes!" Madison agreed, emphatically. "That ties the Partnership into your house fire! This whole thing, whatever it is, with the Joak brothers – they're from Kansas and that's where their world headquarters is. Their radical right, ultra-conservative fundamentalist religious beliefs line up perfectly with those of the FTC.

"Tell me the Wichita-based Joaks are not connected to Titus Corbin's cult of haters in Topeka! And who has money to burn for the Partnership? The Joaks. And who is the biggest threat to the Partnership getting into the White House next year? You are, Jimmy!"

"I have to call Cal!"

Jimmy just had witnessed the full force of the Madison Munro juggernaut. It was at once impressive and terrifying. He was glad she was on his side!

* * *

Across the street from the Fenimore house, The Cobra waited patiently as his time drew nearer. He watched the Senator's guests arrive for the dinner party while helping himself to some of the food and drink in the Larsen's refrigerator. He'd been pleasantly surprised to find a six-pack of Dos Equis beer and was reaching for his third bottle when his phone started to vibrate.

Only three people had the number to his burner cell – and the caller ID ruled out Ralph Petiole and Jasper Joak.

"Yes, Sir?" he picked up.

"Are you good to go?" Satan asked. "We have no margin for error on this one."

"As long as the Senator does what he's supposed to do."

"Ralph will make sure. He's at the Senator's house right now."

"Then, we're good."

"One more thing," the Evilest One continued.

"Yes?"

"I want the girl to suffer like Miki did."

"But, Ralph told me you promised the Senator to make sure it was quick and painless."

"How long have we worked together? Almost 50 years?" the Devil asked, benignly. Then, he bellowed, "I am Satan, the Father of Lies! I don't keep promises! I want Jimmy to know that his girlfriend suffered before she died. That really will mess him up. I need to send a message, loud and clear.

"That reminds me...before you finally kill her, I want her to know that her father approved of everything you did to her!"

⋆ ⋆ ⋆

"Hypocrites!" Sasha spat out. "They're all evil!"

"Keep your voice down," her mother ordered, "they'll hear you!"

"I don't care if they hear me," Sasha protested. "They should know that we're on to them and they can't hide behind their veil of secrecy anymore."

"Honey," Alice tried to soothe her daughter's ruffled feathers. "I think you've fallen under Jimmy's spell and might be overreacting because of what happened today. They may not be perfect, but they're helping your father get into the White House next year."

"Jimmy's spell? Mom, you're no better than they are if that's what you really think! I know you've listened to his words, but have you heard what he's saying? He's exposing their hypocrisy!

"And they may be helping Daddy get elected, but at what price? Are you saying the end justifies the means? Because, Mom, Samael is an assassin for some eastern European group of hitmen! Is he a means to the end, too?"

"That can't be true. Where are you getting your information?"

"When you told me his name, I called Madison, and she called a friend of hers at the police department. They did a search on Interpol, and that's what came up!"

That was the straw that broke the camel's back – of Alice's unquestioning support of her husband, that is. "That's it! That does it!" she exclaimed in frustration. "Something is very wrong here, and it has been for a while. I can't keep my head in the sand any longer."

Sasha desperately needed her mom's assurance that her father was not complicit in the Partnership's below-board activities. "Do you think Daddy knows about Samael?"

"I don't know. I just don't know what to think any more," Alice lamented.

"Well, do you think we should tell him about Roland before Cooper gets here?"

"Oh no! I forgot Cooper was coming! Yes, we should tell him. We can't let him get blindsided like that in front of everyone.

"Sweetie, go check on everyone's drinks and ask your father to come see me in the kitchen."

Through his binoculars, The Cobra watched as Sasha re-entered the family room and the Senator excused himself.

"Alice, what is it?" he asked brusquely. "This is not a good time."

Alice braced herself. "I haven't had a chance to tell you Cooper's coming for dinner."

"What?" he groaned, in utter disbelief. "With everyone from the Partnership here? You know how they feel about homosexuality! Absolutely not! What were you thinking?"

"There's more," his wife winced. "Roland is missing."

That sent the Senator over the edge. "I can't deal with this right now!" he said through clenched teeth. "Call Cooper and tell him it's not a good night for dinner."

"But, Bill…"

"That's final!" he hissed. Without another word, the Senator left to rejoin his guests.

Alice never before had seen this side of her husband, and she, too, wondered if he was hiding something unsavory about the Partnership and his campaign.

* * *

As they approached Floyd Hill, Jimmy turned down the radio to continue a conversation that had begun in the Crawford Suite.

"We were interrupted when you were telling us why you're so convinced that I'm somehow connected to what happened on Berthoud Pass thirteen years ago."

"Right," Madison replied, checking her blind spot to change lanes. "So, where did we leave off?"

"At Malachi."

"Oh, yes," she remembered, on Jimmy's prompt. "As I was saying, in order to process and try to make sense of that man driving his minivan off the cliff, I had to free my mind from the limits of the one-millionth of one percent of all there is to know and march into the universe of what could not be observed or measured.

"Now, the prospect of a car defying gravity was pretty miraculous, and, as I told your parents, I recalled the story of Peter walking on water from when I was in Sunday School, and all of a sudden, a precedent was staring at me right in my eyes. So, I decided to plumb the Bible from beginning to end to see if there might be any clues that would help me to understand what I had seen.

"It was a fascinating read from the perspective of searching for clues. Malachi is the last book of the Old Testament. The first book, Genesis, begins with the fantastic account of God creating the world and everything in it, and with His union with His children in the Garden. By the time of Malachi, God's children had separated from their Father and gotten completely lost – their choice – and they desperately needed a Savior to shine a light on the way back to Paradise.

"'Malachi' means 'my messenger,' and he foretells the coming of a Savior, the Son of God. Now, tell me if this sounds familiar. In Chapter 2 Verses 7-8, Malachi calls out the priesthood: 'You have turned away from the Way; you have caused many to stumble by your instruction.'"

Jimmy marveled, "That kinda sounds like me, and my parents."

"Exactly! That's what I thought. Malachi is all about correcting the lax religious and social behavior of the Israelites – but, especially of the priests. They were missing the mark, and what's another term for "missing the mark?""

"Sin!" Jimmy answered triumphantly.

"Right, again," Madison enthused. "Stay with me, here. You know the Christmas carol, "God Rest Ye Merry Gentlemen," don't you?"

Jimmy responded in song: "God rest ye merry gentlemen, let nothing you dismay / For Christ, our Savior, was born this Christmas day / To save us all from Satan's power when we'd gone astray / Oh, tidings of comfort and joy / Comfort and joy..."

Madison stopped him there. "So, that pretty much sums up Malachi. The priests led the people the wrong way – away from God, instead of towards Him – and they became vulnerable to Satan's temptation. Not his power, mind you, because he'd been stripped of his authority when he was banished from heaven."

"OK," Jimmy intoned uncertainly. "But there has to be more."

"Oh, there is," Madison reveled. "The book concludes by promising that Elijah would return prior to the coming of the Savior."

"Which he did, already, during the Transfiguration of Jesus."

"Yes. But look where we are now. Once again, God's children seem to be hopelessly lost, having been led the wrong way by our religious leaders – away from our Father and vulnerable to Satan's temptation – and they can't seem to find their own way out of the darkness."

It finally dawned on Jimmy what Madison was getting at. "Are you talking about the Second Coming?" he asked, incredulously.

"Jimmy, I'm saying that this all has happened before. Everything!"

"And you're saying that I'm Malachi?"

"No, Jimmy. Malachi was a messenger. The way I have it, your role is much bigger than that of a messenger. What is the purpose of a messenger? To report..."

"So, you're Malachi," he pressed, impatiently.

"Jimmy, I'm just trying to make sense of an extraordinary, almost otherworldly, event I witnessed thirteen years ago. And a sixth sense that won't let it go. The more I've searched, the more familiar everything is becoming.

"I don't necessarily believe in past lives, but I don't disbelieve in them, either. My mind is completely open to whatever comes along, and something was missing. And then I saw your video, and something clicked. I just knew you were one of the missing pieces to the puzzle.

"It was like déjà vu. I don't know how else to explain it. Everything is just so familiar – like I've lived this life before."

"As Malachi?"

"I don't know. But, maybe his spirit is within me. Have you heard of the book, *The Boy Who Knew Too Much*?"

Jimmy shook his head.

"It's the true story about a boy, Christian Haupt, who might be the reincarnation of Lou Gehrig."

"Of course, you'd know that being such a Yankees fan," Jimmy needled.

"Guilty, as charged. But that's not the point. The point is that this kid, from the age of two, knew things about Lou Gehrig that no one other than Lou could have known. And, at that age, where would he have heard the things he was talking about? Or, read about them?

"It's a fascinating story, and it opened my mind to the possibility of reincarnation. When that barrier of impossibility was removed, that's when I really began to connect the dots. Maybe I'm the "Girl Who Knew Too Much!"

"Then, when you told me about the fortune teller, that was another one of the missing pieces that fit perfectly into the puzzle."

"How so?" Jimmy inquired, 100% intrigued. He had so many of his own questions and thoughts about the enigmatic seer.

"What do you know about Elijah?"

"Not too much beyond what we've already talked about," Jimmy admitted. "From what you're suggesting, though, and from what Malachi said, if history is repeating, and we're about to witness the

Second Coming, then, theoretically, Elijah will precede Him."

"You catch on quickly," Madison smiled. "But here's the other thing – Elijah never died. He was transported to heaven by a chariot of fire."

Jimmy indeed was a quick study. "Oh my God," he whispered aloud. "A flying chariot..."

Goosebumps formed on Jimmy's arms as he began to conceive the inconceivable. But the fortune teller had told him he was the man driving the minivan! And he made a mental note to ask the seer to clarify his account the next time he saw him.

"There's more," Madison added. "After the incident, I knocked on hundreds of doors, checked out all the restaurants, gas stations, motels, fast food outlets, and convenience stores trying to get a line on the man. I got literally nothing, beyond what the kids told me. It's like he was a ghost.

"However, I had a very interesting conversation with a woman named Fern, who owned the KC Cabins in Hot Sulphur Springs. We chatted for a couple of hours – not about the man and the minivan, but you could tell she didn't get a lot of visitors and she was just excited to have someone to talk to.

"When I asked her how she stayed in business in such a sleepy town in the middle of nowhere, she told me about the hunters in the wintertime and the Greeks in the summertime. The Greeks explained to her that the mountains reminded them of their homeland, and, on the weekends, they would drive up from Denver to enjoy the mineral baths the town offered. They liked to stay at the cabins because the price was right and they had kitchenettes so they could cook their own food. She had enough cabins and an open area that could accommodate most of them and allow them to congregate and to eat their meals in a common space.

"Then, Fern told me that on one particular weekend in the early 1950s, two of the Greek families and their priest whose name she never forgot, Father Diacandrew, were picnicking on a hill above the town when Father Diacandrew noticed an unusual cloud formation. He called it a cloud oracle – a sign that God was telling him to build a Greek church on that spot.

"Over the course of the next two years, five Greek families would come up pretty much every weekend and they built the church, fulfilling the command of the heavenly oracle."

Jimmy's brow furrowed. "I guess I'm not seeing what that has to do with us."

Madison had set him up. "Here's the kicker – the voice that Father Diacandrew heard telling him to build a Greek church on that hill overlooking Hot Sulphur Springs also told him to name it Prophet Elias...which is Greek for Elijah!"

* * *

The Bulgarian hitman's phone vibrated five minutes after he had hung up with Satan.

"Have you seen her?" the Evilest One asked.

"No, Sir, I'm afraid she could be anywhere by now."

"Where are Todor and Petya?"

"I sent them to the safehouse to await further instructions."

"They need to go back and stake out the hotel. I don't know what business she had at the airport, but there's no way she left without the boy. She'll have to come back at some point.

"As for you, this damn reporter might be laying low right now, but it's not in her DNA. She paints only with broad, bold strokes and she's not one to let the grass grow under her feet. She is determined to make the connection between the boy and Berthoud Pass, but she would need to do that under the radar, and what better time than now, when she's given you the slip and no one knows where she and the boy are?

"She's got that damned sixth sense, almost like she's plugged into some mystical outlet – and even though there's no way she could know that The Cobra is across the street from the Senator's house right now, waiting for the lights to go out to kill the girl, I'm sure she has a sense of the urgency, that Death is about to catch up with this Jimmy Rivers."

"So you want me to go to Berthoud Pass?" Samael interpolated.

"Yes! You've proven how resourceful you can be. The kid probably is the most recognizable person in the world right now. And the reporter is no shrinking violet, either. Ask around. Do what you have to. Just find them!"

"If they're there."

"I'm almost sure of it. I've alerted all my sources to keep an eye out for them. They'll be seen eventually. I'll keep you posted."

Samael ended the call and set his GPS for Winter Park, just on the other side of Berthoud Pass.

Todor and Petya were only five minutes from Union Station when Samael called them with their new instructions.

Fifteen minutes later, the Bulgarians at the gate never blinked when a middle-aged man and his younger companion, dressed in a denim miniskirt, a French-tucked and collared light-blue, button down shirt and black loafers, her face partially hidden by a Colorado Rockies baseball cap pulled down low on her head, passed by them on their way to the reception area of the Crawford Hotel.

Neither Cal nor Gina noticed Todor and Petya, either.

16

Sitting around the dinner table in the dining room at the Fenimore house, everyone was on their best behavior after the earlier brouhaha over Jimmy's "miracle." The Senator sat at the head of the table, and to his immediate left sat Father Simon, followed by Ralph and Sasha. Cardinal Phelps was to the Senator's immediate right, then Don Stottlemeyer, and his wife, Tina. Alice was at the end of the table, across from her husband.

Still bristling over her arguments with Cardinal Phelps and Father Simon, Sasha fumed that the dinner party was the last place she wanted to be. Making matters worse, she was seated next to a man who gave her the creeps and across from her nemesis' older sister. She stared at her plate, her mind seventy miles away, wishing she was with Jimmy on Berthoud Pass.

Each of the guests, in turn, complimented Alice's culinary skills, heaping praise on her chicken cordon bleu before settling in on semi-private conversations among themselves. The Senator, Ralph, Cardinal Phelps, and Father Simon had moved on from Fire Chief McDaniels' bombshell announcement and focused on a self-congratulatory, pat-on-the-back discussion of a William Fenimore/Andy Theus ticket, while Tina and Alice withdrew into their sisterhood.

Sasha was oblivious to all the conversations floating around the room. She had hit the wall – physically, mentally, and emotionally drained from everything that had happened during the day. Her head was spinning, her thoughts were swirling, and she felt faint. She was about to excuse herself when a sudden commotion plucked her from her dizziness.

"Cooper!" Alice cheered, seeing her son standing in the foyer and momentarily forgetting the Senator's most strenuous objection to his invitation.

Sasha jumped up to greet her brother with a warm embrace, while the Senator stared at his wife in disbelief.

Alice welcomed her son with a motherly kiss on the cheek, then hurried into the kitchen to set a place at the table for him. Cooper went around the table shaking hands and introducing himself, when necessary. When he shook hands with his father, the Senator leaned in closely and whispered in his ear, "Don't embarrass me."

By the time he finished making his rounds, Cooper took his place between his mom and sister – and promptly dove right into the chicken cordon bleu as if he hadn't eaten in two days. Which he hadn't.

The Senator grimaced when Cardinal Phelps, who had been the Fenimore's parish priest before his elevation within the hierarchy of the Church, opened the door he'd hoped would remain shut.

"So, how have you been, Cooper?" the prelate asked. "It's been such a long time. Tell me something interesting about yourself."

"I've been fine, Sir..."

Alice quickly whispered in her son's ear.

And Cooper corrected himself. "Sorry, I've been fine, Your Eminence."

The cardinal smiled in appreciation of Cooper's decorum. "And, what's interesting?"

Cooper hesitated, taking note of the Senator's stern glare boring a hole into his soul.

Sensing the uncomfortably tense dynamic between father and son, Sasha picked up her brother's baton. "Your Eminence, if I may, what are your thoughts on homosexuality?"

The question caught the cardinal by surprise and discomfited the others.

Regrouping, Cardinal Phelps pontificated, "Well, the Bible is quite clear on the subject."

"Is it, though?" Sasha challenged.

Alice gently kicked her daughter's leg under the table, as the cardinal defaulted to his stock theology: "Genesis and Leviticus state unequivocally that homosexuality is an abomination – and that those who commit the abomination will be put to death and endure eternal fire."

Sasha had Cardinal Phelps right where she wanted him. "Those books were written by Moses, and we've already seen how he used fear to get the Israelites to follow God, because there's no way they could have understood His love.

"So, are you saying God will kill all of His children who are gay? When one of His Ten Commandments is, "Thou shalt not kill." After all, he didn't kill Lucifer when the former Angel of Light rebelled against Him."

"Sasha!" the Senator admonished. "That's enough!"

Cognizant of his previous outburst, the cardinal kept his composure this time around. "Bill, she is searching, and there's nothing wrong with that."

Turning back to Sasha, the cardinal continued, "You are correct in your assertion that much of what was written in the Old Testament was written in such a way as to advocate an agenda. Yet, even in the New Testament, after Jesus' time on earth, Paul's letter to the Romans is quite clear about the eternal penalty for homosexual relations."

"But, again, God is not a killer. He didn't kill Lucifer for his disobedience, and He didn't kill Adam and Eve for theirs."

"No, they brought death upon themselves by turning away from God."

"Exactly. Then, the fact that we all will die means that we've all turned away from God, not just gays. He sent His Son to save all of us sinners, which, presumably, would include the homosexuals that Paul said wouldn't be saved. Do you think Paul was a homophobe?"

Alice could sense the smoke coming out of the Senator's ears – not to mention out of those of the other Partnership members at the table – but she stopped kicking Sasha under the table. She was proud her daughter had the temerity to speak up for her brother in front of such an adversarial audience. For their part, the Stottlemeyers were transfixed by the back and forth between the neophyte and the veteran, with the neophyte more than holding her own – as if they were watching a rally between a young tennis player and Roger Federer, one of the greatest players ever to pick up a tennis racquet, and seeing the younger player getting the better of him.

The cardinal took a deep breath. "I can assure you that Paul was not a homophobe."

Sasha would not let up. "How can you be so sure? You weren't there, just like Father Simon wasn't there when Jimmy walked out of the fire. I was there, and I can tell you, most assuredly, that it was Jimmy and not a hologram.

"And let's not forget that Paul was a very fallible human being. He was Saul, one of the most feared persecutors of Christians in his day, before he was Paul. So, he had his issues, too. Really, the only ones we truly can trust are God and Jesus, and, just a few minutes ago, you were trying to tell us they didn't mean what they said."

Advantage Sasha.

The cardinal clearly was on the defensive, and when religious leaders are on the backs of their feet, they always retreat to their assumed higher learning, and Cardinal Phelps was no exception. "You have to go back and read the teachings of the church fathers before you can make such wild accusations."

"As if there hasn't been any inspired religious thinking in nearly 2,000 years! Besides, I'm not making wild accusations. How can you dispute that the only ones we truly can trust are God and His Son? Jesus said, "Believe in me and you will be saved." He didn't list any exceptions, nothing like, "If you're gay and believe in me, you won't be saved." So, how can Paul say that?"

There was no stopping Sasha. "Your Eminence, you just used the Lord's name in vain, a clear violation of one of the Ten Commandments. And, I'm sure, just like all of us, you've got plenty of other skeletons in your closet. Let me ask you, when all those self-righteous men were about to stone the prostitute to death, what did Jesus do? He stepped in front of them and said, "Only he who is without sin can cast the first stone." And not a single stone was cast.

"So, instead of judging, based on the word of an imperfect human being, you should ask yourself, "What would Jesus do?" and you should follow His example by stepping in front of anyone trying to stone another human being."

Game, set, match, Sasha.

The cardinal refused to lay any golden fiddles on the ground at Sasha's feet, but, instead sought to save face. "You're young, Sasha, and not well-versed in the ways of the world, yet. But I have appreciated our dialogue and the spirit in which your words were given."

Sasha politely refused the olive branch. "Your Eminence, didn't Jesus also tell us that if we were to enter the kingdom of heaven, we must enter as children?"

The Senator had had enough. "Can we please move on to another subject?" he pleaded, clearly exasperated.

Emboldened by his sister's tenacity, Cooper spoke up next. "I have a question for Mr. Stottlemeyer."

* * *

The Town of Berthoud Falls, ahead on the left – really, just a few scattered cabins tucked into the woods flanking both sides of Highway 40 – was like a shot of adrenaline to Madison's heart. It was the eastern gateway to Berthoud Pass and what loomed as the culmination of the past thirteen years of her life.

As excited as she was to see how everything fit together, however, the story would have to be put on hold for a few more hours, at least. Jimmy had fallen fast asleep, and she needed him wide awake and at his best when she took him to where the avalanche had swept Rachel's car off the edge of the road and over the cliff.

She turned left on Columbine, a poorly marked dirt road past a sprawling green building with a "Beware of the Dog' sign in the window that once was the town's General Store. Then, she turned right onto Pine Street – more of a path than a street – and parked the car in the tiny lot in front of the Lazy S Lodge so that it couldn't be seen from the highway. They may have fooled Samael at The Crawford, but having been fooled once, he wouldn't be fooled again. She was sure of it, and she wasn't about to take any chances.

There was only one problem with her hideout – no cell phone service. "Unbelievable!" she fumed. Reluctantly, she turned around and backtracked several miles until she heard the familiar ping of her phone connecting to a tower. Jimmy never moved a muscle.

Cal and Gina were in the throes of getting to know each other better when the buzzing of his cell phone interrupted their rhythm. The dutiful-to-a-fault producer reached for his phone on the nightstand, checked the caller ID, and untangled himself from his inamorata.

"This better be good," he said, trying to hide his breathlessness.

"Awww," Madison smirked, knowingly, "please tell Gina I'm sorry."

"How did you...this has nothing to do with Gina," he lied, but he was betrayed by the actress' inability to suppress a giggle. "Anyway, it's about time you called. I almost was worried about you."

"Yeah, I can tell you were worried sick," she replied, her voice dripping in sarcasm. "I'm glad Gina was there to hold your hand, so to speak."

"Alright, enough," he ordered, trying to pull rank. "We're both consenting adults and it's none of your business. What is your business is telling me what's going on with Jimmy and Berthoud Pass. What do you have for me?"

"This is going to take a minute. Do you want me to call back?"

Cal looked apologetically at Gina.

"It's ok, Madison," Gina insisted, good-naturedly, and loud enough for Madison to hear. "But you owe me, girl!"

"How about you keep the outfit and the Jimmy Choo's?"

"Done!" she squealed. "He's all yours."

"Are you girls finished, now?" the unamused newsman interposed.

"Actually, Cal, I'm just getting started," Madison gushed. "Have you heard of The Greatest Story Ever Told?"

"Of course, I have. It's the story of how I put up with this insane quest of yours for the past thirteen years!"

"Be serious."

"I am!" He paused. "OK, yes, it's the Bible."

"Right. So, get comfortable because I'm about to tell you the second greatest story ever told."

Over the course of the next thirty minutes, Madison explained to her wary producer in painstaking detail how she had arrived at her shocking conclusion. But Cal cut her off a moment before she got there.

"You've got to be kidding!" he exploded. "This is what I've been waiting thirteen years for? Jimmy Rivers is the vanguard of the Second Coming?! And you're this Malachi character, the messenger, warning us that Jesus is on His way?! Are you trying to make me the laughing stock of the industry and get me kicked to the curb? Hear me loud and clear, Madison – I will not become the Harold Camping of broadcast journalism!"

"Cal, just for a moment, consider the possibility that I might be right. You would be in the revered echelon of Woodward and Bernstein."

"They had Deep Throat telling them to follow the money!"

"And I have the fortune teller telling us to follow the Bible."

"It's just a fantastic coincidence!" The moment he heard those words leave his mouth, Cal Everett knew his loose lips had sunk his own ship. "OK, wait, Madison, that's not what I meant."

"And that's what the serpent told Adam and Eve about God's warning in the Garden, and that's what the religious leaders are saying today, and that's what the Partnership is saying…Cal, don't you get it? You know I don't believe in coincidences. It's the universe talking to us, and I'm choosing to listen. Nothing is what it seems."

The wizened, veteran newsman momentarily changed his tack to try to indulge his star reporter's perceived recklessness. "So, you're saying that this mysterious fortune teller is Elijah by virtue of the flying minivan, which you equate to the prophet's chariot of fire? And by the clues he's leaving for Jimmy?"

"So, who is Jimmy in this rapturous conjecture of yours?"

"Cal, it's not a conjecture. I'm convinced that it's the ultimate Truth! Remember, truth is stranger than fiction, and that all great truths start out as blasphemies!"

"That's not fair, throwing my favorite author in my face," Cal protested.

Madison smiled. She knew she was tipping the scale in her favor. Of course, she always did.

"Well," her producer pressed, "I'm waiting. Who is he?"

"I've connected all the dots, I've put all the pieces of the puzzle together, Cal." She hesitated, anticipating Cal's reaction. "Jimmy is the equivalent of John the Baptist."

The besieged producer took this one in stride, more or less. His star reporter, the same one who reminded him of himself in his younger years, had drained his reservoirs of shock and awe. "You know, this is sacrilegious. You're going to burn in hell for this."

Then, his curiosity got the better of him. "OK, humor me. How do you figure?"

Madison was ready for him. "John the Baptist was a rebel. He was a rabble-rouser. He didn't accept the norms of the day. In fact, he removed himself from them, and in exhorting people to follow him into the Jordan River, it was symbolic of casting aside one's old beliefs and starting fresh with new ones.

"Can you think of anyone who has raised more rabble in the past several days than Jimmy Rivers? His last name is "Rivers," too, for heaven's sake. Do you think that's a coincidence, too? He's got people's attention, and they're beginning to see that they're being led the wrong way. I think they're choosing to be baptized in the river, again, except this one isn't the Jordan – it's the Jimmy. Rivers.

"Alright, I'll play along. Who's Jesus?"

"Cal, you goofball, Jesus is the Son of God!"

"You know what I mean!" the exasperated newsman said, shaking his head. "You've identified everyone else, and if this truly is the Second Coming, who is the Jesus counterpart and where is He?"

"I'm pretty sure that Jimmy will fill that blank in tonight."

Cal Everett paused, considering everything Madison had told

him. He was standing on the precipice of the biggest decision of his professional career. He looked at Gina's fetching nakedness. She could have been Madison.

Finally, he decided that he had ridden the Madison Munro horse this far, he might as well go all the way. "OK, you win," he said, putting everything on the line. "Send me what you've got."

An elated Madison spouted, "Happy to do it, Cal!" Then, "Oh, and speaking of hell, I've got one more thing. Do you remember how Burke said, "The only thing necessary for the triumph of evil is for good men to do nothing?""

"Madison, I'm fifty years old. I'm not sure I can take much more of this. But, just for grins, which evil are you talking about?"

"The Partnership of the Right."

Cal sat straight up in bed. She had pushed one of his hot buttons, and she knew it.

"I'm listening."

Madison didn't pretend not to notice the alacrity in his voice. "I thought so," she declared triumphantly. Cal hated everything the Partnership stood for – and he was convinced there were significant skeletons aplenty in all of their closets. However, everyone connected with the unholy alliance of politics, plutocracy, and what passed for Christianity, had closed ranks and, to date, there had been no traitors in the mix.

There still weren't, but Madison proceeded to tell her editor about an intrepid, investigative journalist named Roland Thomas who had sent his detailed notes about purported improprieties at Joak Industries to the *Denver Post*, which, courtesy of Don Stottlemeyer at the newspaper, surreptitiously ended up on the desk of the head of Human Resources for the Joaks. She didn't have to mention how intertwined the Joak brothers were with the Partnership – Cal made that connection on his own.

He couldn't contain his elation. "Omigod, Madison, why didn't you lead with this?"

"Because I knew I wouldn't be able to get you to pay attention to the Berthoud Pass story."

Cal couldn't help but admire her playbook. "I've got to hand it to you. You worked me over like Muhammad Ali in his prime."

"But, remember, I'm on your side."

"That's just it. I'd hate to have you against me."

Madison seized her opportunity. "So, does this mean you're going to do something about Berthoud Pass, too, because I know you're going to pursue the Joak angle."

"Yes, and do you want to know why?"

"Because you love me?"

"No! It's because of Roland Thomas."

"You don't even know him or what might have been in his letter."

"Right, but I know the name, Rollo Tomasi."

Madison scoffed. "Who in the hell is Rollo Tomasi and what does he have to do with any of this?"

"Now, it's your turn to listen and learn from your elders," Cal gloated. "He has everything to do with all of this. Rollo Tomasi was the name of the man that was the key to exposing widespread corruption in the L.A. Police Department in the movie, *L.A. Confidential.* And it sure sounds a lot like Roland Thomas. You really have to watch more movies! They are art imitating life."

"Probably just a coincidence," Madison teased her producer.

"Or, just maybe it's a sign that the two stories are linked. Rollo Tomasi was killed by corrupt LA police officers to keep him from exposing their crimes - maybe your Roland Thomas was killed by the Partnership because he was about to open their closet doors, expose their skeletons, and air their dirty laundry right in front of the election. His death would clear the way, again, for Evil to take over the White House, and the driver's seat of the Free World – or so the Partnership would think!

"And what better time for the Son of God to come again."

Madison was vindicated...and impressed. "Hey, Cal, you're going to have to forgive all those nasty thoughts I had about you being over the hill and having lost your edge!"

Then, she couldn't resist. "Do me a favor. When you hang up

and lean over to pick up where you left off with Gina, pretend it's me lying next to you. I'm told we could be twins!"

"That is so gross!" he whined. "Just get me those notes asap. And thanks for ruining my life," he added, only half-jokingly.

Satisfied with herself, Madison hung up and returned to her refuge in the secluded parking lot of the Lazy S Lodge in Berthoud Falls. Wild horses couldn't have dragged Jimmy from his slumber.

17

"Donald Stottlemeyer, you are not going to 'out' Cooper Fenimore if you want me to stay with you," warned Tina, drawing a line in the sand while continuing their "discussion" from the car into their house. "That's something I feel very strongly about."

The clock in the Stottlemeyer's kitchen said 10:45, and the discussion that had begun the moment they left the Fenimore dinner party showed no sign of letting up.

Don was flustered and tongue-tied at the same time. "Tina," he stammered, "You're asking me to sit on one of the biggest "scoops' of my career! Halley's comet comes along more frequently than these types of opportunities do in a reporter's life!"

"That's just it, Don. It's sad that a person's sexuality has anything to do with the news, let alone the biggest story of your career!"

"But the Bible! And the Partnership..."

"Nope," she cut him off, curtly. "You don't get to moralize or sit in judgment of anyone else. How would you have liked it if someone had found out about our affair and chose to splash it in the news? Speaking of that, doesn't the Bible say something about sex outside of marriage?

"And what about that ridiculous lie you told about not having seen Roland's letter?"

"That wasn't a lie!" he protested, unconvincingly.

"Stop it right now! I've seen you in action, when Sharon caught us together in the newsroom, and I've noticed it ever since. You'd be a terrible poker player because you'd give away your hand every time. You can deny, deny, deny all you want, but a "tell' is a "tell!'"

That revelation took the wind out of her husband's sails. He knew he'd been busted, and it was pointless – and dangerous – to carry on the charade any longer. The chastened editor's tone quickly changed from defiant to apologetic.

"OK, I did intercept that letter and couriered it over to the Joaks. I should have known better than to try to lie to you. I'm sorry." In his next breath, he worried, "Do you think the others know?"

"I'm not sure they know you well enough. But your ex-wife surely did."

"Can we please leave Sharon out of this and move on? You made your point." Don desperately wanted to rekindle the aborted intimacy they had started while getting ready for the party.

Tina was having none of it. "Sure. Let's talk about blind ambition getting in the way of common sense."

Don sighed heavily. "What do you mean?"

"Obviously, that letter had some incriminating evidence against the Joaks, whatever it is."

"I suppose that's one way of looking at it."

"And I'm sure the Joaks pay you handsomely under the table to be their lackey."

"I'm not their lackey!" he objected.

"Please!" Tina scoffed, nearing the end of her rope. "Call it whatever you want. They pay you and you jump through whatever hoop they tell you to. A lackey by any other name still is a lackey."

"I've never heard you complain about the money I bring home!"

"I don't know what I was expecting," his trophy wife said with a hint of contempt in her voice. "You can't expect a tiger to change its stripes.

"Anyway, let's say you went ahead and scooped everyone else by outing Cooper Fenimore. Did you ever consider that you'd be biting the hand that feeds you?

"And what about the Partnership? You bring down the Joaks, and you bring them down, too. Those are some pretty powerful people, Don, and powerful people think they're above the law. Don't think that they wouldn't come after you.

"Even if they managed to distance themselves from the Joaks, the religious right has been speaking down to us from such a moral high ground, do you think Senator Fenimore's campaign could survive if his rabidly religious – in name only, mind you – followers find out about his son? You know, the acorn doesn't fall far from the tree and all that BS. They would take it to mean that if he can't even raise his own son 'right,' how could he possibly lead a country?"

"That's a stretch, and you know it," was all her defeated husband could muster.

"What I do know is that the ignorance of the American public, and their unwillingness to engage in any kind of meaningful, critical thinking, never should be underestimated."

"You're upset with me, aren't you?"

"What makes you say that?" his wife deadpanned. "More disappointed. I'm just...it's just that men get themselves in such predicaments by thinking with the wrong head and not considering the consequences of having sex without a condom, so to speak.

"I mean, look at Bill Fenimore. In his blind ambition to get into the White House, he's sold his soul to the Partnership. And look where it got him – a horrible shouting match with his kids at the dinner table in front of everyone. Then, Cooper storms out of the house, and Sasha runs to her room in tears. It was so incredibly awkward!

"I feel so sorry for Alice. She's in that horrible spot where she has to walk the most precarious line between being the so-called 'good wife,' dutifully standing by her man and holding his hand as he admits to some kind of infidelity, while, at the same time, providing their kids love, setting a good example, advocating for them, and otherwise filling in for an absentee father."

"Wow! I really struck a nerve, but I see your point," her husband said, throwing in the white towel and still hoping for what now would be "make up" sex. "I'll let Cooper come out on his own terms, although after what happened tonight, he might be standing on a soapbox tomorrow morning on 17th and Broadway shouting out to the whole world that he's gay."

"I wouldn't be surprised if he did," Tina agreed, "but I'd be ok with it because it would be his choice, not anyone else's."

The humbled newspaperman embraced his wife and nibbled on her ear. "Let's go to bed. We have some unfinished business to attend to."

Tina stared disdainfully at her husband. He looked so pathetic in that moment. "I just can't tonight," she balked, throwing ice water on his amorous intent. "Besides, I have this terrible feeling in the pit of my stomach."

Knowing what was good for him, Don switched seamlessly from Lothario to supportive spouse.

"Oh, no, I'm sorry. Do you think it was something you ate? The food was pretty rich."

"No, I don't think so. It's more of a feeling that something very bad is about to happen."

* * *

The Cobra checked his watch. It was 10:30 as the guests began to file out of the Fenimore house.

First to leave had been Cooper – he'd rushed out the front door about an hour earlier in a very agitated state, his mother on his heels, apparently pleading with him to stay, to no avail. He had peeled out of the driveway without the customary embrace between mother and son, and she dejectedly had returned to her guests.

Noting the time, Cardinal Phelps and Father Simon offered their appreciation for Alice's wizardry in the kitchen and were the next to leave, followed closely by the Stottlemeyers. The bananas foster had been a hit and finished off the evening on a high note after the disquiet wrought first by Sasha, in the defense of her brother, then by Cooper, in searching for answers to his partner's disappearance.

Ralph lingered in the doorway, engaged in what seemed to be a serious conversation with the Senator, who nodded periodically in acknowledgment of what his campaign manager was telling him. At one point, the Senator looked over towards the Larsen's living room window and solemnly nodded. He promised to signal The Cobra when the coast was clear with a single on-off flick of the family room light.

Even though he already had gone through the exercise of checking the firing mechanism of his Glock 17 that night – more out of boredom than anything else – the cartel assassin paid closer attention to one final inspection to ensure there would be no malfunctioning in the Senator's daughter's bedroom. He decided to dispense with the silencer-suppressor because he hadn't had the time to check its compatibility with the Jocketed Hollow Point (JHP) bullets he had selected to inflict maximum damage.

The hollow points had been a last-minute choice after Satan had instructed him to make the girl suffer before she died. The Cobra had a daughter of his own and the thought of torturing a young girl crossed the line, even for the world's most infamous killer. The JHPs would make it quick for his own conscience and messy enough to appease his boss. The report from the unsuppressed Glock would wake up the neighborhood, but before anyone realized what had happened, he would have vanished into thin air.

His weapon passed its final vetting with flying colors. The Cobra was coiled and ready to strike. The only question mark in his mind was the Senator. Would he actually go through with it? If their roles were reversed, the Los Hermanos cartel hitman wasn't sure that he could be so complicit in his own daughter's killing.

* * *

Bill Fenimore stood outside his daughter's door, his heart racing, his hands trembling, and his mind in absolute turmoil. At that moment, he didn't know if this would be the last time he would see her alive. He tried to focus on the greater good, and the story of Abraham and Isaac. Even though God's angel had stopped Abraham from plunging the knife into his only son's heart at the last minute, Abraham had been prepared to demonstrate that nothing came before the Lord. And, he wondered if Cardinal Phelps would issue a similar, eleventh hour stay of execution. In fact, he hoped with every ounce of his being that the prelate would. But, as he knocked gently on Sasha's door, he also recognized that the greater good often required the greatest sacrifice, incongruously reminding himself about the atomic bombs that ended World War II in the Pacific theater.

"Come in," invited his sleepy-voiced daughter.

"Hi Sweetheart," her father said softly, sitting down on the side of her bed. "I just wanted to say 'good night.'"

"I'm sorry, Daddy," Sasha managed. "I didn't mean to cause a scene at dinner. I hope I didn't put you in a bad spot."

"Don't worry about me," her father assured. "I'm glad you have such strong, well-thought-out opinions, and that you're not afraid to stand up for what you believe."

"Do you really mean that?"

"Yes! And I'm probably not as far away from your beliefs as you might think. It's just that sometimes," he explained, tears welling up in his eyes, "we have to make sacrifices for the greater good."

"I know. You've told us that. But, I just wonder," she asked pointedly, "the greater good according to whom? Who gets to decide what the greater good is?"

The Senator didn't like the direction their conversation was headed and chose not to pursue. "Well, it's late and we're both exhausted. I don't want to debate this with you right now. I just wanted to come in and tell you how much I love you and how proud I am of you and always will be."

Sasha opened her eyes a little wider, and through the dim light spilling in from the hallway, she could make out the tears in her father's eyes. She couldn't remember him ever being so melancholy.

"Daddy, what's the matter? Are you ok?"

"To be honest, Sweetie, no, I'm not. This campaign has drained me and taken quite a toll on all of us, and if I had it to do all over again, I'm not sure I would have chosen this path."

"It's never too late, Daddy," Sasha sought to reassure her stricken father.

"I'm afraid it might be, this time," he fretted, the tears starting to stream down his cheeks.

"Please don't worry, Daddy. I know I haven't made it easy on you, but I want you to know that I will be the perfect soldier for you as you carry on your campaign."

"I'm not sure either of us knows what that means. I'm so tired. But never forget how much I love you." Bill Fenimore stroked his daughter's hair. "You've had such a long day with everything that's happened. I haven't been much of a father for you, lately. Hopefully, one day you'll understand and you'll pray for me."

Sasha never heard her father asking her to pray for him – she had fallen fast asleep. He placed his hand on her shoulder and whispered, "Now, I lay thee down to sleep, I pray the Lord your soul to keep. If you should die before you wake," he choked back the tears, "I pray the Lord your soul to take."

Bill Fenimore kissed his daughter one last time on her forehead, stood up from her bed, wiped the tears from his cheeks, and walked out of the room, leaving her door slightly ajar. Alice already had cleaned up after the party, and when he peeked in on her in their bedroom, she, too, had closed her eyes to a most torturous day.

The Senator sighed heavily and lumbered wearily down the stairs to the back door. He hesitated, his entire life flashing before his eyes as he searched for an answer. Finally, he realized that it, indeed, was too late. He unlocked the back door, stumbled into the family room, and flicked the light switch on and off. And, with a heavy heart and the onerous burden of regret, he trudged back up the stairs to bed.

* * *

In the heavens above, the angels gathered around Michael to watch the drama unfolding below. As the archangel unsheathed his sword, one of the other angels immediately recognized King Arthur's Excalibur, and marveled, "So, the legend is true! Yours was the arm that rose and caught the sword when the mortally wounded king ordered Sir Bedivere to throw it into the lake!

"You brandished it three times as a kind of homage to the Trinity, and now that you are flashing it, again, does this mean we are about to witness the tumult of the Second Coming on earth?"

"No one knows the hour of the Day of Judgment, but one always must be prepared," the archangel counseled. "Remember the parable of the ten virgins who were awaiting the bridegroom. Five brought extra oil in their flasks in case he was delayed, while the other five rushed to meet him without stopping for extra oil.

"When the bridegroom was delayed until midnight, the bridesmaids who had brought the extra oil were able to follow Him to the wedding banquet, while the others missed out; and the Lord said, "Keep awake, for you know neither the day nor the hour."

"No one knows when the Son of God will come again, not even I, but the parable tells us always to be ready. Whether or not it's now, Excalibur's edges are razor-sharp and I'm ready for battle at any time."

Meanwhile, in the darkest corner of the Underworld, anxious demons were wondering the same thing – was the Son of God about to return to earth? "Sir," they asked Satan nervously, "You never told us He might come again!"

"It must have slipped my mind," Satan grumbled.

"I read about it in *The Great Divorce* by C.S. Lewis," one of the older demons volunteered. "I thought it was pure fiction, the product of a writer's imagination and a personal agenda. Now, I'm not so sure."

"It is only fiction!" Satan screamed. "Pure fantasy. Don't either of you believe a word that writer says." Before he could continue, his phone began to ring. "I have to take this call," he announced on checking the caller ID. "No one leaves until I get back and we can finish this conversation."

The moment the Evilest One disappeared, a nervous junior demon asked, "OK, he's gone. What did the book say?"

"Basically, that even here in hell, we'll get another chance to go to heaven, but we have to choose to turn away from the sins that got us here and ask for forgiveness."

"You mean all of us?" another demon wondered in awe.

"Well, we'll all have the opportunity. The writer says some of us will choose to repent and escape to this so-called "Promised Land," where there is no pain, sorrow, or suffering. He also writes that for the rest of us, our hearts will be too hardened to repent – that, even knowing what we'd be passing up, we would not be humble enough to let go of the anger of being sent here in the first place, to admit we were wrong and to say we're sorry."

"What do you think?" another of the junior demons asked.

"I don't know, but the longer I'm down here, the more unimpressed I am with our lot and with Satan. I mean look at us. We have no power, we have no authority. It gets old after a while. I mean all we can do to get our way is to lie and cheat and try to trick those who still do have authority to choose to use it against their brothers and sisters. And for what? Not to elevate us in any way, but to bring them down to our level. I think I'd like the chance to go up to their level, instead.

"But bringing down God's children is good enough for Satan. It's the only way he can get his revenge for being kicked out of heaven – by deceiving them into choosing poorly to turn away from Him. Just like he did with Adam and Eve."

"But aren't you mad at God, too, that you're here?"

"I'm upset, alright, but not at God. He didn't send me here, He didn't force me to make bad choices, and to turn away from Him. I did that all by myself, thanks to Satan's temptation. And, if I get a second chance, even down here, I've learned from my mistakes and I'll choose wisely this time, to turn back to God, like the prodigal son did."

The younger demons would not let up. "Why even think about it, though, when you're not sure what the writer is saying is true?"

"Because of Pascal's Wager. He was a mathematician and philosopher while he was on earth, and he applied the principles of gaming to the existence, or not, of God. Of course, for us, we already know, but while we were on earth, we weren't sure, or we didn't believe.

"Anyway, Pascal compared it to the flip of a coin: there's a 50-50 chance that He does or doesn't exist. He goes on to say that if you choose to believe in God and He does exist, then you'll receive infinite gain. If you choose to believe in God and He doesn't exist, then you'll have a minimal loss in terms of the pleasures and luxuries you would have sacrificed on living according to His will.

"If, however, you choose not to believe in God and He does exist, then you'll experience an infinite loss. And if you choose not to believe and He doesn't exist, then you'll have the relatively minimal gains you wouldn't have sacrificed on earth.

"So, basically, it boils down to a 50-50 chance either for a nominal loss and an infinite gain, or for a nominal gain and an infinite loss. How should a rational person wager?"

The junior demons didn't have to think long to come up with their answer – they agreed that they rather would take a chance on the infinite gain for a nominal loss, than on a chance for an infinite loss versus a nominal gain.

"Exactly. Again, it's a 50-50 chance between infinite gain and infinite loss. Any rational person would wager on infinite gain. But no one said Satan was rational."

The moment he heard his words aloud – about the Devil not being rational – the erudite, veteran demon gasped. They had triggered a sudden thought so inconceivable, so outlandish, so impossible that…"Oh, no," he murmured.

"What is it?" one of the junior demons asked anxiously.

"That's just it. Satan is not rational. He chose to challenge God, the Invincible One, in heaven. That was just plain stupid. It was irrational. And when he found out who had escaped his lair a few days ago, he flew off the handle. He didn't stop to wonder why someone who was as tight with God as the boy's mother apparently would not be in heaven after she died in the first place."

The younger demons sat in stunned silence. Their mentor was right – no one had considered what was right in front of their faces. They were so fearful of Satan that they had bought into his rage and fallen into line without question.

"That's how the obvious gets overlooked," the senior demon marveled. "Think about it. What if it's *The Great Divorce* in reverse?

What if she was part of a bigger plan and she had Abraham's trust in God? After all, six years in the context of eternity is shorter than the blink of an eye."

"But who would do that?" another of the junior demons shuddered.

"Right!" their mentor agreed. "Who would wheel a giant, wooden horse outside the gates of Troy as a gift to the Trojans? The Trojans weren't rational, either. They accepted the gift, opened the gates, and wheeled the hollow horse inside. Then, when they were sleeping, the soldiers inside the horse came out and unlocked the gates to let their fellow soldiers in, and the city was sacked. And the war was over.

"What if the boy's mother was a 'gift,' another Trojan Horse, since God knew her complete faith – and Satan has been asleep all this time?"

Satan's underlings were fortunate he was so engrossed in his phone conversation with The Cobra that he didn't hear a word they were saying.

* * *

"The Senator just sent the signal," The Cobra confirmed. "I'm going in."

Satan was adamant. "I can't tell you how imperative it is for all of us that you take the girl out just as I told you. It has to be horrific! I've tried everything and I can't get this kid to blink! Without overstating it, this is our only chance for survival! He has to blink, and fall, or we're dead. Sasha Fenimore's grisly death will serve that purpose – it will distract him.

"Then, when his guard is down, when his ability to make good choices is impaired, and he loses access to God's authority, Samael will be waiting for him. We'll finally be rid of his menace."

"I understand," he assured the Evil One. "Tune in to the news in about fifteen minutes."

The Cobra tucked his Glock into his back waistband underneath his shirt, destroyed his SIM card in the garbage disposal, and checked one last time to make sure the neighbors were asleep before leaving quietly out the back door. He crept along the side of the Larsen's house and waited behind the bushes for the approaching headlights of two cars to pass.

Dressed all in black, he was practically invisible as he crossed Skylark Lane under a moonless sky and made his way to the side of the Fenimore house. He slithered stealthily around to the back of the house and was about to try the handle to the back door when he suddenly hesitated. Was there an alarm?

They hadn't talked about an alarm! How could they have missed that detail? All the meticulous planning, and the simplest detail gets overlooked!

He didn't have the Senator's number, but even if he did, he couldn't call him at this hour to verify that an alarm had been turned off without raising suspicion. Hell, any call to the Senator immediately before his daughter was murdered would be suspicious. He wanted to abort, but then he'd have to deal with repercussions from Satan, which he decided would be a lot worse.

Gingerly, he placed his hand on the handle. His heart was pumping furiously in "fight or flight' anticipation of a blaring alarm – and flight was not an option. Holding his breath, he turned the knob and gently applied pressure to the door. To his utter relief, it yielded without a sound.

He was practically gasping for air as he carefully stepped inside and closed the door behind him, leaving it open a crack to facilitate his escape. He reached around his back for his gun and illuminated the flashlight on his phone. He had been well-schooled as to the floorplan of the Senator's house, and he stealthily made his way through the kitchen, around the corner into the hallway to the stairway leading to the upstairs bedrooms. One by one, he climbed the seventeen steps with cat-like cunning…and turned to the first doorway on the right at the top of the stairs.

There was a night-light in the room and he could see Sasha sleeping through her partially-closed door. He pushed it open ever so slowly, then stopped abruptly when it registered a complaint. He held his breath at the thought of being betrayed by a small squeak from one of the door's hinges, but Sasha didn't budge.

With another five muted steps, The Cobra was standing at the foot of the Senator's daughter's bed, training his Glock on a spot between her shoulder blades so the hollow point bullet could exact maximum damage to her internal organs.

Meanwhile, Bill Fenimore lay awake in bed, consumed in guilt and haunted by second thoughts. He had heard the tell-tale squeak of his daughter's door hinge, which told him that The Cobra was about to strike.

In a rare moment of clarity, he murmured under his breath, "Oh my God, oh my God, oh my God, what have I done?"

He wasn't Abraham, and neither was it God who told him, figuratively, to plunge a knife into his daughter's body. In one swift motion, he threw off the covers, reached for his cell phone, jumped to his feet, and yelled, "NO!"

Startled, Alice opened her eyes. "Bill, what is it? Did you have a bad..."

The thunderous report of a gunshot interrupted her question and answered it at the same time.

"That was a gunshot!" she shrieked, her body violently quaking. "It sounded like it came from Sasha's room!"

"I'm calling 9-1-1," her husband croaked, the horrible finality of what that gunshot meant dragging him under for the last time.

Instinctively, Alice lunged for their bedroom door. Bill tried to stop her while giving the information to the 9-1-1 operator.

"Alice, you can't go in there!" he shouted, throwing his arms around his wife's waist. "The police are on their way!"

Fueled by the adrenaline of her child in danger, Alice broke free of his grasp, throwing all caution to the wind and racing into the jaws of death.

In the next moment, the air was filled with her anguished, blood-curdling scream.

18

Cal Everett heard about the 9-1-1 call from the Fenimore house almost as soon as the police did. He and Gina were basking in the warm afterglow of an extended lovemaking session when the shrill ring of his ABC News cell phone slapped him in the face.

"Shit!" he exclaimed, trying to disentangle himself from his lover to silence the offending intruder.

"Don't answer it!" Gina pouted.

But Cal's singular focus on the news – which had sabotaged every one of his romantic interludes over the years – prevailed.

"I have to...it could be Madison!" he defended himself.

It wasn't, according to the caller ID, but he answered it anyway. The time was 11:47, and, typically, nothing good ever happens that late at night.

"Mr. Everett, this is Officer Mike McGregor of the Denver Police Department. I'm a friend of Madison's. She gave me this number in case..."

"Oh my God!" Cal interrupted, sitting bolt upright in bed. "Is she ok?"

"Sir, as far as I know, yes, but that's not why I'm calling. As I was saying, she gave me this number in case I couldn't get through to her.

"We just received a report of gunfire at Senator Fenimore's house."

"Oh no!" Cal mumbled.

"What is it?" Gina whispered into his other ear.

The anxious newsman waved her off. "Did anyone get shot?"

"I've told you all I know right now. I'm off duty, but I heard the call from dispatch. Listen, if you get a hold of Madison before I do, and she wants to head over there, tell her to ask for Officer Lester. Tell her to use my name."

"I'll probably get there before she does."

"Fine. You can do the same thing."

"Thank you, officer, I really appreciate it."

Cal hung up and immediately tapped in Madison's digits.

"Cal, talk to me" Gina insisted, "what's going on?"

"Shots were fired at the Fenimore house."

Gina gasped and instinctively covered her mouth with her hand.

"I know, right?"

His call went straight to voicemail. "Damn, she's probably out of service up there!"

He tossed his phone to Gina and dictated a text message as he threw on his clothes: "Gunshots at Fenimores. Call me asap."

In seconds flat, he was dressed, teeth brushed, and ready to go.

"Gina, I'm so sorry…"

"Hush," she cut him off. "I understand."

They kissed each other goodbye, as lovers do who don't know when they'll see each other, again.

Cal eventually retreated, apologizing, "I really have to go."

"I know," Gina said, "but wait a sec."

She reached in her purse to retrieve her pocket atomizer, and before Cal could object, she gave him two squirts.

"What was that for?" he recoiled.

"You smell like sex!"

"And now I smell like…"

"It's better this way, trust me' she insisted. "Now, go!"

Cal didn't need to be told twice. He raced out of The Crawford smelling of Clinique's "Happy' citrus-flavored scent, dialing and re-dialing Madison's number every few seconds. It hadn't taken long for his mind to go to the worst-case scenario: if whoever tried to kill Jimmy earlier in the day killed Sasha to get to him, then their lives were in imminent danger. If Sasha was the intended target, that is.

It made complete sense to him. To the best of his knowledge, the Senator hadn't antagonized anyone, recently – it was Jimmy who posed a threat to the "beloved" Partnership, and the POTR did have their extremist, gun-toting followers! Whoever sanctioned the hit – the Partnership, the Joaks, or whoever – obviously would stop at nothing to shut him up.

Cal's rental car screeched to a halt a block away from 37 Skylark Lane as police cruisers and police tape had completely cordoned off the area immediately surrounding the Fenimore house. He approached one of the officers securing the area and asked for Officer Lester.

"I'm Officer Lori Lester," replied the diminutive policewoman. "Are you Cal?"

"Yes, I am," he affirmed, unable to mask his surprise.

"Mike didn't tell you I was a woman, did he?"

"No, he didn't. I'm sorry. I just was expecting…"

"A 6'3," 260-pound Irish cop with a shock of red hair," she finished his sentence.

"Something like that," he said, sheepishly.

Lori Lester smirked, "Ha! I get that all the time. Anyway, come with me." She lifted the yellow police tape for Cal to follow her to the side of the house, where she stopped without warning so they could speak privately.

Officer Lester spoke in a barely audible whisper. "OK, first of all, this is off the record. As soon as the captain makes a public statement, you can run with it – but not a moment before. And I expect it will be a while before he speaks to the press."

"Why is that?"

"Because of the nature of the crime scene. Apparently, the Senator and his wife were asleep when they heard a gunshot coming from their daughter's room. The Senator called 9-1-1 and Mrs. Fenimore rushed to her daughter's room and screamed bloody murder."

Cal shuddered. "Sasha Fenimore is..."

"Missing. There is a dead body on the floor of her room, though, an unidentified man probably in his sixties.

Cal was taken aback by this unexpected turn of events. So much so that he thought he hadn't heard the officer correctly. "Wait, what?" he virtually shouted. "Sasha wasn't killed. And she's missing?"

"Mr. Everett, I'm going to have to ask you to keep your voice down. But, yes, Sasha is missing. We don't know if she's been kidnapped, or if she's even still alive."

"And the dead body?"

"Well, here's where it takes a 90-degree turn into the bizarre. One of our detectives is former Drug Enforcement Agency (DEA). Have you heard of The Cobra?"

"Are you talking about the Los Hermanos hitman?" he asked incredulously.

"Yes! Detective Cummings isn't 100% sure because the man hasn't been seen for so long, but he's pretty positive that's who it is. He didn't have any identification on him, so they're running his fingerprints as we speak."

Cal barely could keep up with the thoughts racing through his head. "But, if it's him, what's the connection to Senator Fenimore? It couldn't have been totally random. And who shot him? It would be hard to get the jump on the world's most feared assassin. And where's Sasha?"

"Right," the policewoman agreed. Cal hadn't realized he had been speaking out loud. "Now, do you see why it might take some time for the captain to make his statement? We don't want to divulge too much too soon and put other lives in jeopardy. But at least you can get a head start on the other news agencies.

"Mike tells me you work with Madison Munro."

"Yes, I'm her producer," Cal replied, trying to compose himself.

"Well, you tell her she has a huge fan in Officer Lori Lester. That girl really kicks ass!"

"I'll be sure to pass it on. Thanks so much for your help!" Cal turned to leave, then hesitated. "I have one more question for you, if you don't mind."

"Shoot."

"Was there any sign of forced entry?"

"No."

"So strange," Cal pondered aloud.

"We thought so, too," she agreed. "Now, can I ask you a question?"

"Of course."

"Is that 'Happy' you're wearing?"

* * *

It hit him like a ton of bricks as he drove to the ABC News affiliate in Capitol Hill. Cal just had briefed the local news team at the scene and was hurrying to get a jump on the other news stations when he had his "a-ha!" moment.

"Rollo Tomasi!" he shouted out loud in his car, finally making the connection. "That's got to be it!" In all the excitement, he had forgotten about explaining to Madison why he was willing to give her the benefit of the doubt as she continued to pursue her improbable theory that the Berthoud Pass incident might have been the advent of the Second Coming that was somehow linked to Jimmy Rivers and the POTR. In that moment, it dawned on him that the similarity between the name that had clued Sergeant Ed Exley into the fact that his captain on the Los Angeles police force was a crooked cop, and Roland Thomas couldn't have been a coincidence! The universe indeed was talking.

It all was so far-fetched, it had to be true, he reasoned. What if Roland Thomas secretly had been investigating some connection between the Joak brothers, the POTR, and the Los Hermanos drug cartel? And what if Jimmy Rivers was the forerunner of the Son of God's second mission to the planet? Then, came another blast of déjà vu for the harried newsman: from his own days in Sunday School, he remembered that Herod's step-daughter had convinced her step-father to have John the Baptist beheaded on her mother's behalf. If Jimmy was, as Madison surmised, the modern-day John the Baptist…

The parallels were striking. The Partnership was being threatened by Jimmy Rivers and needed to get rid of him. The Joaks and the Partnership were intimately connected – after all, money is the tie that binds – and potentially linked to The Cobra's cartel. It would have been too obvious to kill Jimmy – and, besides, they wouldn't want him getting any more free publicity than he already had. But, if they killed Sasha, Jimmy would be devastated. Beheaded. What about the fire, though. That didn't fit at all. Instead, it had backfired pretty spectacularly!

Suddenly, Cal had a truly sickening thought, one that shook him to the core. It upset him so much that he had to pull over on Speer Boulevard to consider the horrible possibility. Officer Lester had said there were no signs of forced entry, and that the Senator had chosen to call 9-1-1 before going to his daughter's aid. What father would take the time to make a phone call when his daughter was being attacked? Cal wondered. Every precious second would have counted towards her survival. He should have reacted as his wife had – unless...and that's when Cal's whole body began to shake. Had Senator Fenimore known in advance of a plot to kill his daughter in order to silence Jimmy Rivers? And to pave his way to the White House? Had he purposely left the back door unlocked for The Cobra to carry out the unspeakable?

He frantically needed to talk to Madison and run his suspicion by her. Her instincts were impeccable. He punched the "redial' button on his phone for the umpteenth time. Again, the call went straight to voicemail.

"Goddamn it, Madison!" he wailed. "Where are you when I need you?"

⋆ ⋆ ⋆

Cal Everett's star reporter still was in the tiny parking lot of the deserted Lazy S Lodge, hidden in the woods that engulfed the remote settlement generously dubbed the Town of Berthoud Falls, typing furiously away on her laptop while Jimmy slept off the chaos of the day.

Without Internet connection or cell phone service, she had no idea that the Los Hermanos' most notorious enforcer had been shot and killed in Sasha Fenimore's bedroom, and that Sasha had disappeared, and was feared to have been kidnapped, or killed, by whoever had killed The Cobra.

However, her forced solitude gave her the time to put together pieces of the puzzle that Cal was missing thanks to her sometime beau on the police force. The Joak brothers were the deep-pocketed benefactors of the Partnership of the Right, and they stood to gain millions – even billions – with Senator Fenimore in the White House. The Joaks were in Wichita, a stone's throw from Topeka and their brothers-in-arms, the parishioners of the Fundamental Truth Church.

It wasn't a stretch of the imagination by any means, to assume a link between the ultra-right Joaks and ultra-right fanaticism of the members of the The Fundamental Truth Church (a misnomer if ever there was one). Nor was it a stretch to think that two members of the radical church might take it upon themselves to do the Joaks and the Partnership a favor by offing Jimmy Rivers. Think Jack Ruby and Lee Harvey Oswald.

"It's clear that they were acting on their own because they both wound up with bullets to the back of the head," she read her words aloud.

Her typing couldn't keep up with the synapses in her brain firing on all cylinders. The two zealots from the FTC were killed because the Partnership and the Joaks couldn't afford the martyrdom of Jimmy Rivers. Besides, what if Jimmy pulled a Lazarus and came back from the dead? That would completely derail the POTR's aspirations for 1600 Pennsylvania Avenue. After all, he'd already very publicly survived an inferno at his house that morning.

Those two loose cannons, acting on their own, would have to be silenced in case they were apprehended – they could not be trusted not to spill the beans. Which meant that Sasha's life was in imminent danger! She had to wake Jimmy up and get to a place where she had cell phone service.

A gentle tapping on the back window changed all that.

⋆ ⋆ ⋆

Satan flew into an absolute rage when he heard the news, the likes of which his demons had not seen since the Son of God came down and destroyed the Gates of Hell and rescued all of God's children he had lured away, including Adam and Eve.

"How could he be so incompetent?!" he screamed into the phone. "The Cobra's dead and the girl is nowhere to be found! How could this happen?!"

"Maybe the girl beat him to the punch…"

"Right," Satan scowled in disgust. "Think of what you just said. A teenage girl beating the world's deadliest assassin to the punch! Somebody must have tipped them off."

"But who?"

"When I find out…," the Evilest One's voice trailed off as he savored his vengeful carnage. "But, right now," he continued with a sudden burst of heightened animus that shook his minions even more, "we have to find Sasha Fenimore before anyone else does!"

He turned to one of his senior demons. "Get me Samael!"

19

Through the darkness, Madison couldn't see who was tapping on the passenger side window in the back of her car. And she assumed the worst: the Bulgarian hitman aiming his gun at Jimmy's head.

In one swift motion, she tossed aside her laptop and turned the key in the ignition. Before she could press the gas pedal to the floorboard, however, she heard Jimmy rejoice, "Sasha!"

Her hand shaking with the surge of adrenaline flowing through her body, Madison breathed a huge sigh of relief and turned off the ignition as Jimmy scrambled out of the car to embrace his girlfriend. It was a shameless display of affection that Madison witnessed when she, too, got out of the car.

"Alright, you two, save some of that for me!" the grateful reporter demanded, as the three of them group-hugged. "Sasha, you scared the hell out of me!" And they all carried on as if someone just had survived an assassination attempt, although they still were blissfully unaware of what had transpired minutes ago at the Fenimore house in Denver.

A moment later, reality came crashing down on Madison. She broke away and looked around the parking lot.

"I hate to be a party pooper, but, Sasha, how did you get here? How did you know where to find us?" she asked, worried that Samael might not be far behind.

"You guys," she began, holding tightly onto Jimmy's hand, "It's been the most bizarre night!

"The dinner party was a total disaster. I got into it with Cardinal Phelps about homosexuality. Cooper got into it with Mr. Stottlemeyer about Roland's letter, and I had the strangest conversation with my Dad. He apologized for not being a good father and told me he was proud of me for my strong opinions, and I thought I heard him ask me to pray for him as I was falling asleep. It was a talk you'd have if you weren't going to see the other person, again – or, for a very long time, anyway.

"But I was too tired to make any sense of it. I fell into such a deep sleep! And I had another incredible dream – or, at least I thought it was a dream. Señor Quixote was in my room with a friend of the fortune teller's he introduced to me as 'Miki.' And Señor Quixote told me that we had to leave immediately. So I grabbed my phone, my headphones, and my speaker and we left. Miki stayed behind."

"Teenagers," Madison sighed.

"Omg, I met Miki in the dream I had while my house was on fire!" Jimmy exclaimed.

"Hold on!" Madison frowned incredulously. "Are you talking about Cervantes' Don Quixote de la Mancha?"

"Yes."

Jimmy suddenly realized he hadn't told the astonished reporter about the Dairy Queen encounter with the errant knight. He had been in such a hurry to tell her his story that he had focused only on the fortune teller's message – to go to Glenwood Springs in search of John Doe – not the messenger.

"But he's not real. He's a fictional character, the product of a writer's vivid imagination. I thought it was Jimmy's vivid imagination trying to work through an extremely complex and completely implausible series of events after he'd fallen asleep reading the book."

She turned to Jimmy. "I just assumed the fortune teller had kind of hypnotized you and planted that whole dream sequence about destroying "The Premise' in your mind since you already were reading about Don Quixote. It made sense. More sense, anyway, than what you described."

"Nope, he's real," Jimmy said calmly. "He was the one who delivered the fortune teller's message about Glenwood Springs when

Sasha and I got together at Dairy Queen last Sunday afternoon to talk about our shared dream, or whatever it was."

Sasha added, "And he was very pleased with himself for…"

"I get it," Madison insisted, getting up to speed, "Dairy Queen. DQ. Don Quixote."

"Right."

"OK, but who's Miki?"

"Another friend of the fortune teller," Jimmy answered.

"This might be the most unbelievable part of a most unbelievable story," sighed Madison.

Jimmy alibied, "Maybe not mentioning it before was my subconscious kicking in, not wanting to lose you. We have to remember that nothing is what it seems, and that we need to see the world not as it is, but as it should be."

"But…"

"Madison, you know how you found out about parallel universes? Well, there are alternate, overlapping universes out there, too, every one of them a function of what we choose to believe, or not to believe. They all are under God's 'anything-is-possible' umbrella.

"Everyone assumes Darwinism and the story of Creation are mutually exclusive. But I believe there is room for Darwin's theory of evolution within the story of Creation. Anthropologists have identified three very distinct types of Homo Sapiens that existed thousands of years ago. So, even if you ascribed two of them – the Neanderthals and another one – to evolution, there's still one left over that would be consistent with God having created us in His image.

"Even the species attributed to evolution were created by God because He created the organisms that eventually evolved into the Neanderthals. So, in one of the alternate, overlapping universes, God created Cervantes, who, through God's authority, created a fictional character who evolved into a living, breathing Don Quixote de la Mancha.

"You're going to have to choose to suspend your disbelief to embrace these other universes where everything – and I mean everything – is possible. The only limits are those that are self-imposed. Limits don't come from God. He is limitless. I know this is taking you far beyond the quantum physics your Uncle John was describing to you, but science eventually catches up to faith, as methods of observation and measurement continue to evolve."

Madison was dumbfounded as she stared directly into Sasha's soul. "So, you're saying that Don Quixote brought you here?"

"Yes. I think so, at least! On the back of his horse, Rocinante, and with Sancho Panza. Because when I woke up, we were here and he told me you and Jimmy were in this car."

"Where is he now?"

"He said he had to go, but that he'd see us soon. Then he and Sancho disappeared into thin air."

Madison had no choice but to buy into Sasha's explanation. There simply was no other way she could have gotten to Berthoud Falls, let alone find her way to the remote Lazy S Lodge parking lot. There had to have been some sort of divine intervention – the same kind she had been pursuing for thirteen years. And all roads pointed towards the fortune teller.

"Well, I'd say I'm about 90% of the way to believing you. I hope I get to meet Señor Quixote at some point. He's such a romantic! I remember reading about him in school. I would have loved to have been his Dulcinea," she rhapsodized. "But, what about Miki? Who is he? And where is he?"

Jimmy spoke up. "I don't know any more about him than what I've already told you. He knows the fortune teller and, apparently, he has what the fortune teller called 'special skills.'"

"Obviously, I don't know about that," Sasha continued, "and, again, he stayed behind."

Madison sighed. "I just spent about four hours writing this up for Cal, and I'm beginning to think I haven't even scratched the surface of what's going on here.

"What I do know for sure, though, is that I have to get to a place where I can connect to the Internet so I can send what I have to him." Turning to Sasha, "I also have this feeling that your life is in grave danger, especially after what you said about your conversation with your father.

"What I really need, though, is to talk to Cal. I could use another set of eyes on this, eyes that are somewhat removed and might be able to see more clearly."

Sasha jumped into the back seat next to Jimmy, and the three of them started up the road to Berthoud Pass. It was 1:00 in the morning.

* * *

Back at the Fenimore house, Detective Frank Cummings was trying to process myriad scenarios that might account for what looked like the world's most notorious hitman for the world's most ruthless drug cartel lying in a pool of his own blood in Sasha Fenimore's bedroom. He hadn't seen a recent photo of him in years, but he'd studied every molecule of the man's face during his stint with the DEA when he was pursuing the merciless drug kingpin.

It gave him chills to see that he had used his blood to scrawl the name "Miki' in the carpet next to where he laid, mortally wounded.

"It couldn't be," he argued with himself. DEA agent Ernesto Casimiro "Miki' Sanchez had been kidnapped, brutally tortured, and murdered by Ramon Quesada – aka, "The Cobra' – thirty-five years ago in Guadalajara, Mexico. He'd seen his battered corpse. He'd been to his funeral. He'd consoled his wife, Marina, and their three sons.

Yet, now, if the dead body in Sasha Fenimore's bedroom indeed belonged to RQ, as he was referred to by the DEA, was he expressing remorse in his dying breath or, incredibly, identifying his killer as the same man he had killed all those years before?

"Excuse me, Frank…" Those three words shook the lost-in-thought detective as if he had seen a ghost.

"I'm sorry, sir," his partner apologized. "I didn't mean to startle you."

"No worries, Eddie," he gulped, trying to regain his composure.

"I was just a thousand miles away in another universe. What do you have for me?"

"You were right!" he reported, unable to contain himself. "Forensics just confirmed that our dead guy is "The Cobra!""

"Unbelievable," he marveled in a barely audible whisper. He was trying to stay in the moment but felt himself losing the battle. "What in hell's name was he doing here? And who shot him? And where is Sasha?"

Then, in a moment of clarity, the addled detective switched gears. "How are the Fenimores? Are they cooperating?"

"Mrs. Fenimore is in shock. As for the Senator, his campaign manager is here and they're lawyering up."

"Lawyering up?" he repeated, dubiously. "That just irks me to no end! There's a dead body in their daughter's bedroom, their daughter is missing, and they're lawyering up?! Shades of JonBenet Ramsey! Her parents were more worried about covering their asses than about helping to find out who killed their daughter! That's just not natural. It sure casts the net of suspicion over the Fenimores' heads!"

Frank Cummings thought for a moment.

"There's no sign of forced entry?" he asked his partner.

"No."

The pensive detective shook his head. "I'm not liking where this is headed. See what you can find out from Mrs. Fenimore. Those damn lawyers already have put up a brick wall around the Senator."

"Well, he is running for President! You never know what he might say in the heat of the moment that he'd regret later, or that could be misconstrued by the press."

"Like a slip of the tongue that would connect him to The Cobra!" Frank paused as his mind began to explore the possibilities, leaving his partner hanging.

Then, "I'm sorry, Eddie, I'm going to need a few more minutes alone here."

Detective Eddie Devereaux had been with Frank Cummings long enough to know when to give him his space. Besides, he had his marching orders, and he went downstairs to try to talk to Alice Fenimore before the lawyers got to her, too.

Alone with the crime scene investigators who quietly went about their business of gathering evidence, the erstwhile DEA agent again contemplated the unthinkable. As so often happens when one opens oneself to explore possibilities outside the realm of reality, the mind, freed of its constraints, rarely disappoints in trying to attach rhyme to reason. Which is how Frank Cummings suddenly remembered The Passion of the Christ. It was so unanticipated, and so foreign because Frank was an avowed agnostic, and there is no way his mind would have fallen back on a Christian explanation.

Yet, importantly, agnostics confess to neither faith nor disbelief in God, which means their minds are left open to explore the possibilities of both theses. Maybe if he'd been an atheist, the film would not have entered his mind. The movie depicted in graphic detail Jesus' flogging at the hands of his sadistic Roman guards, such that His back was a bloody mess of pulverized flesh either ripped away from His body or hanging on by a thread. Then, came His crucifixion – being nailed to the cross – the crown of thorns, and the stab wound in His side…by the time He was laid to rest in the tomb, His body had been ripped to shreds.

It was the scene of His third-day resurrection that truly captivated, however. The rock sealing the tomb had been rolled away, and Jesus emerged, His body perfectly immaculate, almost glowing in its purity. Standing in Sasha Fenimore's bedroom with The Cobra lying dead on the floor and the forensics team doing their thing, Frank wrestled with his newly found freedom. Had Miki been resurrected as Jesus had been, his battered and tortured body restored to immaculate perfection in a universe called heaven? In order to stop The Cobra?

If so, was there the possibility of the two universes, heaven and earth, overlapping? Could Miki still be in the room, invisible because of his own – well, mankind's, actually – unevolved self? What the bleep do we know, anyway?

A water bottle abruptly fell off the nightstand next to Sasha's bed. Frank stared in the direction of the fallen vessel, freed of his agnosticism and open to all possibilities. He kept staring, searching for an answer. Gradually, he became aware of an image starting to come into focus. No one else seemed to notice what he was beginning to see, or his eyes widening in amazement, as the shape of the unblemished body of a man smiling at him took form: Ernesto Casimiro "Miki' Sanchez.

Miki winked at the trembling detective. And then he was gone.

* * *

"Omigod! Madison stop the car!" Jimmy shouted impulsively. Startled by Jimmy's sudden outburst, she pulled over at mile marker 237.10, the exact spot where Rachel's car had been swept off the road by the avalanche thirteen years earlier. Jimmy hopped out of the car.

Madison followed him, gratified and elated, at the same time, that her sixth sense had been confirmed – there was no way Jimmy could have known the exact spot of the avalanche. Sasha was right on their heels listening to The Weeknd's *After Hours* album on her headphones.

Jimmy peered over the edge into the void of the steep, darkened mountainside and tangled thicket that dropped off into oblivion just beyond the tops of his shoes. He looked back over his shoulder, adrenaline coursing through his veins.

"I see them!" he exclaimed.

The two women looked behind them and saw nothing but a mountain rising up from the road. They turned back to Jimmy. He clearly was in another world.

"Who do you see, Jimmy? Madison asked.

"I see you all! Dirk, Sarah, Jake, and you, Madison...and the minivan!" He paused. "Wait! The driver is getting out. It is the fortune teller! He's asking for a volunteer, but everyone's too afraid."

Neither Madison nor Sasha could have anticipated what happened next.

"I'll go!" Jimmy shouted across Highway 40, and as he ran across the highway, he disappeared in front of their very eyes. Vanished without a trace, leaving them completely bewildered. In another universe, Jimmy ran to the passenger side of the minivan and opened the door only to find the passenger seat occupied.

Time stood still as the fortune teller introduced his young charge to his aged passenger. "Jimmy, I want you to meet Elijah."

"We have been waiting to meet you for a very long time," the prophet smiled. "It is an honor." He motioned for Jimmy to come closer. Jimmy leaned in and Elijah whispered something into his ear. Then, Jimmy stepped back, and Elijah shut the door. Literally. Figuratively, however, he left the door wide open!

The fortune teller shouted at the others, "Get out of the way!" and floored the gas pedal, and the minivan lurched forward, accelerating along Rachel's tire tracks to the avalanche's path over the edge of the road.

The moment the minivan flew off the road, Jimmy returned from his alternate universe and saw Madison and Sasha staring at him in utter disbelief.

"Did you see that?" he asked excitedly.

Stunned at his inexplicable disappearance, the women were stirred even more by his sudden reappearance.

Sasha ran over to her boyfriend. "Jimmy, where did you go?" she asked, her voice faltering. "Were you dreaming, again?"

"What do you mean?"

"She means you disappeared," Madison responded. "You said you saw all of us, and the fortune teller getting out of the minivan… and you ran across the road, and then, poof! You were gone."

Jimmy was flabbergasted. "It wasn't a dream!" he insisted. "It was so real. I was there! I mean, I was here when Rachel's car was swept off the road, but no one could see me except the fortune teller. And the old man!"

"No way," Madison objected. "There really was an older man? I didn't see anyone else in the minivan, and I don't miss details like that."

Madison wasn't quite ready to buy into Jimmy's "vision" – those were details he could have gotten from a number of sources. "Tell me the number on my license plate," she demanded.

He didn't have to think about it. "No number. It said M-DOG."

The doubting reporter was astounded. "There's no way you could have known that."

"Wow!" Sasha shuddered.

"Anyway, the fortune teller was there, Madison. And the old man. I saw them! I talked to them, and they saw me and they heard me. The old man knew my name. Maybe you weren't ready to see him at the time."

The reporter considered the possibility. Especially after what she and Sasha just had witnessed.

"OK, I can accept that," she conceded. "And the old man? Did you find out who he was?"

"Yes. The fortune teller introduced us." Jimmy hesitated. "Are you ready for this? It was Elijah!"

A chill went down Madison's spine. Her breath was shallow. "Oh my God, it is happening again," she muttered to herself.

Sasha held on to Jimmy's hand for dear life. "What did he say?"

"He said he'd been waiting for a long time to meet me. Then, he said, 'Go to my church. They're expecting you.'"

Part Seven

It began to dawn on Madison in the darkest hours of Thursday morning that she was sitting on the second greatest story ever told and there wasn't a damn thing she could do about it.

"Come on!" she implored the teenagers, her frustration near a boiling point. "We have to get to a place where there is cell phone and Internet service."

They quickly piled back into the car and started the rest of the way up the mountain.

"So, where's Elijah's church?" Sasha wondered, nestled snugly in Jimmy's arms in the back seat.

Madison was quick to respond. "There's a Prophet Elias Church in Hot Sulphur Springs, another 45 minutes from here. I remember it from when I was trying to find out anything I could about the old man."

Jimmy squeezed Sasha's shoulder lightly and looked into her eyes. "So, if you thought the last six days were a wild ride, wait "til you hear this!" He proceeded to tell his girlfriend about Malachi, Elijah, John the Baptist, and the cloud oracle – and about Madison's theory about how they all fit together: the Second Coming!

"Jimmy, I'm scared," Sasha shivered. "I can't believe this is really happening!"

Madison pounded the dashboard. "Still no service! Can you both now see why I'm so stressed? My instincts have been right all along! Everything is falling into place. Jimmy is the missing link. I knew it the moment I saw his video that went viral. Something just clicked.

"I also knew I had to bring Jimmy here to Berthoud Pass. I never told him where the avalanche was, but he told me to stop at the exact spot it swept Rachel's car off the road! How can you explain that?

"Then what just happened – the whole disappearance thing and somehow going back to the time of the incident. And my license plate! Universes do overlap! And I can't get a hold of Cal!

"It makes so much sense! I am Malachi, the messenger. Elijah preceded the Son of God the first time, and he was here, again, preceding Him, again. He's back for the second time, I'm sure of it! The fortune teller has been leading you to Him.

"You, Jimmy, are the rebel, the agent of change. People followed John the Baptist into the Jordan River to show they had changed their minds. Today, they are casting aside the treasonous words of the misguided and false prophets to dive into another river – or Rivers – to embrace the true Word of God.

"The imposters tried to kill you today, as they beheaded John the Baptist. And, they're still trying to kill you. Somewhere out there, there's a Bulgarian hitman trying to finish the job. And I still can't get a damn signal!"

She took her frustration out on the dashboard a second time, even more forcefully than the first – and whether or not it was the impact of her hand against the dash, the yellow gas light indicator illuminated, signaling they were dangerously low on gas...in a sparsely populated area of the Rocky Mountains in the middle of the night.

"Just great!" Madison frowned. "Sasha, do me a favor. Check your cell phone for a 24-hour gas station on Highway 40 near Winter Park. This is a state highway. There has to be one open somewhere."

"Madison, remember, no service."

"Crap! What's the matter with me..."

"Wait a second," Sasha rejoiced. "I just got a signal!"

"Finally!" the impatient newswoman exhaled. She checked her cell phone – 15 missed calls from Cal. "Uh-oh, something's happening."

No sooner had Madison uttered those words than a news alert popped up on Sasha's phone and she cried out in anguish. "There's been a shooting at my house!" her voice quivered.

Jimmy hugged his frightened girlfriend closer while Madison pushed the redial button on her phone.

"Madison!" Cal roared. "I've been..."

The anxious newswoman cut him off. "Cal, what happened at the Fenimore house? Are the Senator and his wife ok?"

"Yes."

She looked over her shoulder to reassure Sasha. "Honey, your parents are fine."

"Wait! Did I hear you talking to Sasha?" Her producer was incredulous. "The police think she's been kidnapped. How did you..."

"Yes, she's with Jimmy and me. I'll explain in a minute. But, Cal, you can't tell anyone where we are right now. I think we're in the middle of a huge conspiracy and I really don't know who can be trusted. And that goes for the Senator...and maybe his wife."

"Well, expand your net a little bit, because whatever conspiracy you're talking about just got bigger."

"What do you mean?"

"Guess who was killed in Sasha Fenimore's bedroom."

"Cal, I don't have time for games!"

"This can go no further than your ears right now." He hesitated, then confided, "The Cobra."

"What?" Madison shrieked in disbelief. "The drug cartel hitman?"

"Yes."

"Who killed him?"

"No one knows."

"This keeps getting crazier and crazier! I can't think about that now, though. But, Cal, can you see how all of my hunches for the past thirteen years have been confirmed? I've got them all written up and I'll send them to you as soon as I find a gas station. Everything is happening so fast. I don't have time to stop twice. Hold on a sec..."

Madison turned back to the youngest Fenimore. "Sasha, I need you to keep it together. Your parents are ok. I need you to find me a 24-hour gas station."

That tiny job was just the tonic to take the young girl's mind off the nightmare unfolding at her house. Wiping the tears from her face and typing with the dexterity only teenagers have, she found one within seconds.

"There's a 7-11 in Granby that's open all night. It's about 20 miles away."

Although he'd only been on hold for a few moments, the beleaguered producer was beyond agitated by the time his protégée got back on the line.

"Cal, calm down," Jimmy and Sasha heard "the messenger' say. "Look for my email in about twenty minutes. I know it's late, but stop the press! This is a story for the ages!"

"You keep saying that, but…"

Madison hung up before Cal could finish his sentence and immediately focused on Sasha. "How are you doing, Sweetie?"

"Better," she answered with a forced smile. "But why would this drug person want to hurt my dad?"

"I have an idea, but right now, you probably should call your parents. The police think you've been kidnapped." She turned around to look Sasha in the eyes. "Sweetie, this is important – you can tell them you're with Jimmy and me, but you absolutely can't tell them where we are right now. Just tell them that you're safe and that you'll call back later."

"I understand," she agreed, and dialed her mother's number. The call went straight to voicemail. Then, she tried her father's number.

The Senator, seeing his daughter's name pop up on the caller ID, picked up on the first ring.

"Sasha!" he blurted out. "Oh my God, are you ok?"

"Yes, Daddy," she assured him. "I'm with Jimmy and Madison. I just heard the news! How are you and Mom?"

The Senator never heard her question. He was distracted by Ralph Petiole motioning for him not to divulge any information. His exasperated campaign manager mouthed, "Ask where she is?"

"Honey, where are you?"

Madison listened closely as Sasha assured her father that she was safe and would call back soon. She checked the rear-view mirror to see Jimmy's protective arm around his girlfriend's shoulder, still holding her closely.

What she didn't see in the rear-view mirror, however, was a car following them at a distance with its headlights turned off…driven by a Bulgarian assassin. As it turned out, no one was safe.

★ ★ ★

"Samael!" Satan bellowed, finally getting through to his hired thug. "Where have you been? I told you to keep your cell phone with you at all times!"

"Sir," he answered calmly. "The service is very sketchy up here."

Unable to contain his anger, Satan yelled, "Everything is wrong! The Cobra royally f - - ked up!"

"What do you mean?"

"Somehow, he got himself killed in the girl's bedroom!"

There's a reason for the expression, "cold-blooded killer' – Samael never batted an eye. "And the girl?" he asked, dispassionately.

"Missing!"

"It doesn't matter," he replied, evenly.

"What do you mean it doesn't matter?" Satan wailed, about to go out of his mind.

"I'm following the reporter and the boy as we speak." Through the darkness, the assassin couldn't see Sasha cradled in Jimmy's arms in the back seat.

Satan let out a huge sigh of relief. "Thank goodness! Where are you?"

"Just leaving Winter Park, headed north."

"I knew it!" the Evilest One proclaimed loudly. Then he had a second thought. "But, wait…headed north? They're going the wrong way – the Pass is behind them!

"What are they doing?" he wondered aloud, his voice drenched in exasperation.

The notorious assassin patiently awaited his marching orders, unperturbed by Satan's tirade. This was not his first rodeo.

After giving it a moment's thought, Satan returned to the line. "I don't care. Just take them both out, now!" he demanded.

"Understood. At my first opportunity."

"NOW!" Satan shrieked.

"Sir, there's a state patrolman just ahead of them."

"Unbelievable!" the fallen angel howled. "At this hour? How

many lives does that boy have?! As soon as you can, then, kill them both. We can't have any witnesses!"

"Consider it done," Samael said calmly.

"I'm not considering anything 'done' until you call me and tell me they're dead!"

"As you wish." And the Bulgarian assassin ended the call.

* * *

The Senator's wife wasn't the only one in shock at the Fenimore house. When Detective Devereaux reentered Sasha's bedroom, he found his partner standing motionless next to The Cobra's body, staring blankly in the direction of a water bottle on the floor next to Sasha's bed.

"Frank?" he asked.

No response.

"Frank?" he asked again, more deliberately, waving his hand in front of his partner's face. Still, no response. Together for nearly seven years, Eddie Devereaux never had seen his partner so engrossed, so lost in thought.

He put his hand on his shoulder and gave him a gentle nudge. "Frank!"

Frank Cummings jumped as he came back to reality. This reality, that is.

"Sorry," Eddie apologized. "I did it, again."

"Don't apologize," Frank said under his breath, trying to shake the images from his head. "I must have drifted off."

"To where?"

"Don't ask. You wouldn't want to know. Anyway," he regrouped, "what did you find out from Mrs. Fenimore?"

"When I told her there was no sign of forced entry, she said that was impossible because the Senator was obsessive about checking all the doors at night and setting the alarm."

"Of all nights for him to forget! That's almost too much of a coincidence to be random. But what could connect him to the Los

Hermanos cartel?"

"I asked if she suspected her daughter of being into drugs, but she insisted that there have been no changes in her behavior, she's a straight-A student, and her friends are solid. The only wild card has been her relationship with Jimmy Rivers."

Detective Cummings shook his head in amazement. "What is it with this kid? A week ago, he's a nobody. Now, everyone knows his name and it keeps popping up everywhere! If this is the universe talking to us, I need some clarity. Because nothing is adding up."

"Here's a thought," Detective Devereaux volunteered. "What if Sasha unlocked the door and turned off the alarm after her dad went to bed so Jimmy could sneak in and sleep with her?"

"Well, that would explain the lack of forced entry and why the alarm wasn't activated, but what about this guy?" he countered, tapping the dead body with his foot. "And why would Jimmy have a gun? Even if he had been awake and had the gun in his hand when The Cobra snuck into the room, he'd have been scared shitless and probably wouldn't have been able to hit the broadside of a barn before The Cobra put a bullet through his heart. How could he have gotten the jump on a trained killer? It just doesn't make sense."

"Yeah, I suppose," Eddie agreed. "But, hey," he perked up, "you were pretty deep in thought when I came in the room. What were you thinking about?"

"Nothing, really," he said dismissively, even though the sight of Miki's image still troubled him. He paused. "Eddie, do you believe in ghosts?"

"Talk about random!" his partner laughed. "To be honest, I don't not believe in ghosts, but I do believe in paranormal activity. Why do you ask?"

"What if The Cobra was trying to identify his killer when he wrote "Miki?""

"You mean the DEA agent he kidnapped and killed all those years ago?"

"Yes! I know it sounds crazy, but I could have sworn I saw him over there by the girl's bed just before you walked back in – and he winked at me!"

"Partner, it's been a long day, and I think your mind is playing tricks on you. Let's stick to the facts."

"You're right. Just the facts. Mrs. Fenimore pretty much ruled out a connection between Sasha and the cartel, so it has to be the Senator."

"I'll buy that," Eddie concurred. "Drug cartels are not above going after the families of those who have screwed them. It sends a pretty brutal message."

"Yes, but that implies some kind of relationship between the frontrunner for the White House and the Los Hermanos cartel."

"Well, we have to start somewhere, and that's as good a place as any."

"OK, so are you aware of any antidrug cartel legislation the Senator was trying to sponsor, or any extradition of cartel members he was pursuing?

"No, and I follow that stuff pretty closely."

"Even if there was that connection, it still doesn't answer who killed The Cobra...or explain what happened to Sasha."

"Maybe it was your ghost who killed him," Detective Devereaux offered, semi-seriously. "And Sasha's afraid of ghosts and ran out of the house."

"No way! She would have run to her parents' room; and even if she had run away, she wouldn't have gotten very far and would have been in touch by now."

"So, are you saying she was kidnapped?"

"I'm not saying anything, other than the fact that the Senator has chosen to lawyer up instead of trying to help us find out what happened to his daughter is very inculpatory. Nothing is what it seems."

* * *

Sasha had calmed down considerably by the time they drove through Tabernash on the way to Granby. She was laying in Jimmy's lap, which brought her a measure of comfort, but she was frustrated she couldn't speak with her mom. Her dad had assured her that her mother hadn't been harmed and was being treated for shock, but his bedside manner left a lot to be desired.

The Senator had ended their conversation abruptly, without even telling her that he loved her – but she wrote that off to the stress of the night's events. She knew that despicable man, Ralph Petiole, was hovering and pulling all his strings. That thought bothered her the most – that her father was nothing more than Ralph Petiole's puppet.

The car was silent for several minutes as they each caught their breath and tried to work through what had happened and to come up with a plausible explanation. Sasha was the first to break the ice. "Do you think this has any connection to Roland?"

Madison was quick to respond. "Yes and no. Roland disappeared before Jimmy's video went viral. I think he may have found a connection between the Los Hermanos cartel and the Joaks, and the cartel had him killed. End of story, except for the letter.

"Then came Jimmy's fifteen minutes of fame, the threat to the Partnership, the man in the dark suit, and the fire. Jimmy is the common denominator."

"Why does that matter?" Jimmy wondered aloud.

"Because The Cobra wasn't going after Sasha's father!"

Sasha was confused. "I'm not following you."

"OK. Let's assume the Partnership is working with the cartel," Madison explained, "and Roland is about to expose them. The cartel sends The Cobra to take care of the problem. He's already here in the state, and the Partnership has another problem: you, Jimmy. But, they can't find you. I didn't have a chance to tell you this before, but The Cobra was killed in your room, Sasha. I think you were his target as a way to get to Jimmy."

The naïve teenagers were astonished as Madison expounded her theory. "Jimmy, ever since your video went viral, you've exposed the fraud and the hypocrisy of the so-called True Believers, the Partnership and its unholy alliance between the church, the state, and the ultra-right rich.

"They tried to kill you this morning in the fire, but that was a phenomenal miscalculation that got you even more publicity at the Partnership's expense. Afterwards, when I hid you, I basically put a target on Sasha's back.

"One more thing. There was no sign of forced entry into your house, Sasha."

"That can't be right," she disputed. "Before he goes to bed, my dad always checks the doors to make sure they're locked, and he always sets the alarm."

The realization of what Madison seemed to be insinuating began to creep up on Sasha, and Jimmy felt his girlfriend's body starting to tense up, again. "Are you saying my father was in on a plot to have me killed?"

"I'm not saying that at all," Madison lied, trying to reassure the Senator's daughter. "Maybe in all the excitement, he just forgot to check the doors and the Cobra found a way to disable the alarm."

Sasha wasn't buying Madison's excuse for her father, however. "That would explain why my dad was acting so weird and saying all those strange things." She was disconsolate. "I think I'm going to be sick!"

"Hold on, Sasha!" Jimmy tried to soothe his girlfriend by stroking her hair. "I see the 7-11 up ahead on the right. We can get out of the car and get some fresh air when Madison gases up."

"Rats!" Madison spat out, unexpectedly.

"What's the matter?"

"That patrol car we've been following for the last thirty minutes or so just pulled into the 7-11."

Jimmy was stymied. "And that's a bad thing because?"

"Because there's probably an APB out on Sasha, and we can't take the chance of him recognizing her. Or us, for that matter. At this point, I don't know who we can trust, especially since we've seen how long the tentacles of the Partnership really are, and the lengths to which they'll go to shut you up...permanently."

Madison veered right into the deserted parking lot of the Wrangler Tire and Tune Shop, about a block away from the 7-11, and quickly turned off the headlights – and the ignition, to preserve what little gas she had left. Jimmy rolled down his window to get some fresh air into the car, and Sasha sat up to drink in its cool refreshment, which seemed to settle her nerves and her stomach.

They all had their eyes riveted on the patrol car ahead of them at the 7-11 store. Not one of them noticed a man in a dark suit silently approaching their car with a silencer affixed to his gun.

When he was only a few strides from the back of the 1995 Subaru with the Green Hornet sticker on the bumper, the Bulgarian assassin stepped on a twig which, in the absence of any other noise, sounded like a sonic boom to Jimmy. He looked over his shoulder in the direction of the broken twig and saw the gunman starting to take aim.

In one swift motion, he flung the back door open, hopped out of the car, and yelled, “Samael!”

Hearing his name caught the hitman by surprise, and he hesitated for one instant – which is all the time Jimmy needed to act: “In the name of our Lord and Savior Jesus Christ, I command you to drop the gun!”

Sasha screamed, and reflexively, Madison flew over the top of the seat to shield the younger girl's body with her own in the back seat – just as Jimmy's mother had shielded his body at the mall six years before.

Madison braced herself for a fusillade of bullets to tear into her at any moment – which never came.

Samael felt his body overtaken by a sudden paralysis...and the gun fell harmlessly from his hand. He just stood there, frozen, unable to move a muscle, as Madison and Sasha cautiously peeked over the back seat and out the back window.

They watched in awe as Jimmy looked Evil squarely in the eye and issued his second command – on the Son of God's authority: “Samael, walk over to that policeman at the 7-11, tell him who you are, and that you're turning yourself in for the murders of two men this afternoon in Denver. You are not to say a word about us.”

Unconvinced that the Bulgarian assassin was powerless to resist, and wasn't going to snap out of his hypnotic state, pick up his weapon and end their lives on the spot, Madison and Sasha didn't venture from the perceived safety of the back seat, keeping their heads just high enough to peer over the dash and to see Samael approach the patrolman in the convenience store parking lot, say a few words to him, then obediently put his hands behind his back to be handcuffed.

The arrested hitman slid into the back seat of the patrol car without resistance, the officer climbed into the driver's seat, turned on his flashing lights, and made a right-hand turn out of the parking en route to the county jail in Hot Sulphur Springs.

Madison got out of car, walked over to Jimmy, and stared at him in disbelief. "Who are you?"

Sasha raced over to her boyfriend, threw her arms around him, and answered brightly, "He's my hero!" before giving him a kiss the likes of which a bride gives her groom when the officiant pronounces them "husband and wife."

Madison finally had to clear her throat for the teenagers to break off their smooch. "Sorry," they both said, sheepishly.

"It's ok. I'd be locking lips with my boyfriend, too, if he just had saved my life." She paused. "But, what just happened? This story keeps getting more and more incredible!"

Jimmy smiled. "You should know. It's what you've been saying all along – all of this has happened before. Do you remember the story in Matthew about Jesus casting out the demon who was causing a boy to suffer seizures? That was after His disciples had tried and failed. The disciples asked Him afterwards why they hadn't been able to drive the evil spirit out themselves.

"Jesus told them it was because they weren't 100% sure they could do it. They still had lingering doubts. Then, He asked them how long He would have to be with them before they had the faith of a mustard seed."

Jimmy paused. "I was 100% sure."

At that moment, a gratified reporter thought of her producer –

how he had believed in her and had been in her corner for thirteen years with only her hunch to go on – and she wanted to celebrate with him and toast his unwavering support.

"It certainly fits," she agreed. "This whole narrative fits. But the story isn't finished. It's nowhere near finished. There are so many moving parts. Right now, though, we have to gas up and I have to get you to the church on time!"

They climbed back into the car, Madison pulled up to the pump and handed Jimmy her credit card. "Will you do the honors? I have to get this to Cal while we still have service!"

Jimmy got out and Sasha bounced out after him, a portable speaker and her cell phone in her hand. He put the credit card in the slot, withdrew it quickly, selected unleaded gas, inserted the nozzle into the gas tank, and pressed the lever on the handle until it clicked and began to fill automatically.

Sasha put her hand on his shoulder. "Jimmy, after all that, I need to dance. It's the only way for me to unwind. Dance with me."

She placed the speaker on top of the car and pressed "play" on her playlist. And the air was filled with the unmistakable sounds of the hauntingly evocative chords of The Weeknd's *Blinding Lights*.

Sasha raised her arms and began to move rhythmically in perfect sync to the pulsating beat. Jimmy tried to keep up, but he was completely taken by the seduction of her dance and the lyrics, especially the part about someone – in this case, his girlfriend – drowning in the night and he being the only one she trusted. And he was inescapably blinded by Sasha's light and her sensuous sway, at once entreating, eloquent, and erotic…

When the song ended, Sasha pushed "stop" on her playlist, and the silence left a deafening void. Jimmy was enthralled, but speechless. Sasha sidled up to him and laid her head on his shoulder.

Madison had caught the last minute of her dance after sending her report to Cal and was just as beguiled as Jimmy. The woman who bought ink by the gallon for a living only could muster a stupefied, "Wow!"

She reveled in the moment with the spellbound lovers, and then brought them back to earth. "OK, you two, it's time to go!"

Jimmy replaced the gas nozzle in its holster, Sasha retrieved her portable speaker and phone, the teenagers returned to their cozy place in the back seat, and Madison turned back on to Highway 40 for the last ten miles to Hot Sulphur Springs. Every nerve ending in her body was tingling with excitement to see how the story – her thirteen-year odyssey – would end.

For Jimmy and Sasha, the tale was just beginning.

⋆ ⋆ ⋆

By the time the three travelers reached Hot Sulphur Springs, and Madison turned left on Hemlock Street to traverse the dirt roads to the white Prophet Elias church at the top of the hill, it was nearly 3:00 in the morning. Ninety-six miles away, Cal Everett furiously was getting Madison's report ready to air, Detective Frank Cummings still was trying to figure out if he had seen a ghost, and Senator Fenimore's campaign manager, Ralph Petiole, was in damage control.

At the top of the steps leading to the entrance of the church, the intrepid reporter and the teenagers found a man, conservatively dressed and who looked like an accountant, waiting for them.

The fortune teller smiled at Jimmy. "I see Elijah delivered my message."

He greeted Sasha warmly. "You have been so brave. Never underestimate your role in helping Jimmy to get to this place. Remember, you were the catalyst when you asked him to the Sadie Hawkins dance at your school."

"It was that purple velour curtain," Sasha grinned, and she kissed the fortune teller, first on his right cheek, then on his left.

The fortune teller turned to Madison. "Madison Munro," he addressed her by name, despite never having been introduced. "In thirteen years, you never blinked. You tenaciously pursued the story, the connection, staying focused and open-minded. So, your mind was free to see the signs – what you variously called instinct, or hunches, or sixth sense – and you paid attention.

"You never would have seen them had your focus shifted and your mind wandered. It is a pleasure to make your acquaintance. That which you are seeking is at hand. And, as it has been all along, the way it ends depends on Jimmy and on the choices he makes going forward. You are, indeed, the Messenger!"

"And you are the one I saw drive the minivan over the cliff!" she rhapsodized, elated at finally being able to put to bed who was at the wheel of the flying car thirteen years ago.

"Yes."

"And Elijah was with you?" she asked, wanting to confirm Jimmy's account.

"Yes, again. He was riding shotgun, as you say."

"But why did you stop and ask for help from the others?"

"That was for your benefit – and it was a test, not unlike Captain Kirk's, to illustrate a point. And no one passed. Why can a person easily walk across a two-by-four piece of wood when it is lying on the ground, but they can't even take a single step if it is suspended 2,000 feet above the ground?"

The fortune teller didn't wait for the star reporter's response. "Because their focus has shifted away from something that is the easiest thing for them to do onto Doubt and the fear of falling. Obviously, it made an impression. Look where it brought us. Jimmy received Elijah's message, and here we are at his church."

Madison nodded her head. "You know me so well, and, yet, you don't even know me. I knew I had the beginning of an extraordinary story, and I desperately needed the middle and the end. There's a saying here that the Texas Rangers always get their man. Well, I always get my story – beginning, middle, and end – no matter how long it takes. I never ever, ever, ever, ever give up."

"Of course, we knew that."

The fortune teller turned back to Jimmy. "This is your moment. From here, you will proceed alone, to embrace it or not. This church, to which you have been led, is your moment of Truth. If you choose to step inside, life as you know it will change forever. How it changes is up to you."

Jimmy tightened his grip on his girlfriend's hand. "What about Sasha? Will that change, too?"

"Without a doubt."

Sasha felt Jimmy's resolve suddenly wobble. It was her cue to speak.

Looking him in the eyes, she insisted, "Jimmy don't! Hesitate, is what I mean. I can't speak for you, but I can speak for me, and I can tell you that I'll be here when you walk out of this church, and I'll always be here for you, no matter what you choose.

"I can't tell you what to do – and I wouldn't want to – but after all you've been through, and that we've been through, to get here...I think we have to trust the universe, and trust God as Abraham did with Isaac."

She paused to let her words sink in. Then she continued, emphatically, "Jimmy, I've been paying attention. It looks more and more like whoever has been trying to stop you from going forward tried to get to you through me. More than losing you, I wouldn't want to give them the satisfaction that you stopped searching because of me."

Madison put her arm around Sasha's waist. She whispered in her ear, "You are the bravest of the brave, truly!"

There really was no question in Jimmy's mind what he had to do, but hearing Sasha's words fortified his resolve. He hugged both women, then nodded at the fortune teller as if to say, "Let's roll!"

The fortune teller opened the oversized, brown wooden door to the church. They all were greeted by the warm sight of the rustic nave and the hand-hewn pews on either side of the red-carpeted aisle leading up to the solea, and the icon screen alit with candles in red vases at the foot of the icons and in red votive holders hanging over them. The altar doors were closed, but they still could see the figure of Jesus crucified on the cross beyond them.

Jimmy solemnly stepped into the narthex. It was a figurative step onto the two-by-four suspended 2,000 feet above the ground. He never looked back. And the fortune teller closed the door behind him.

* * *

"Now what?" Madison asked after Jimmy had disappeared inside the church.

"We wait," the fortune teller replied evenly.

The exhilarated reporter couldn't contain herself any longer. "Is this the Second Coming?" she blurted out.

The fortune teller said simply, "Everything soon will be revealed to you."

"Is he going to be alright?" Sasha fretted.

"He has discovered the true meaning of Jesus' words. He never will taste death."

"Literally?" Madison asked.

"Literally."

"What about us?"

"That will depend on the choices you make."

Madison was in hot pursuit. "How have our religious leaders gotten this all wrong? Throughout time!"

"For whatever reason – laziness, personal agendas, fear – they have chosen very poorly to sit at the table of acceptance set by Lucifer, or as you know him, by Satan. The laymen, unwilling to expend the time or effort required of the narrow gate to examine critically what they are being taught, instead have chosen and continue to choose the easier and wider gate of acceptance where that which is difficult routinely is written off to impossibility. And the course of history is set. But you must heed the motto of the U.S. armed forces: 'The difficult, we do immediately. The impossible takes a little longer.'

"The issue, of course, is when trusted authorities turn out to be liars or charlatans – the religious authorities to whom you referred, however well-intentioned they may or may not be. This is the problem with tradition: when a religion, or any body of knowledge, is based on false traditions, they are protected, intentionally or not, by the masses choosing not to rock the boat, and choosing to keep the company only of others who share the same false beliefs. The brave souls who have the temerity to challenge those false beliefs are casually dismissed as fanatics or heretics who are doomed to hell.

"Skewed epistemologies come from a lack of contact with these brave souls and, thus, from a lack of untainted truths. It is a herd mentality, and the human herd has chosen to follow their misguided leaders off the cliff since the beginning of time."

"Except Jimmy," Sasha interjected.

"Yes," the fortune teller said with satisfaction. "Except Jimmy. It was 'The Question' he asked as a mere child that set him apart from the herd, the purported men of God, and everyone else who have been blinded through the ages by their choices to accept the word of the evilest liar this world ever has known and his minions."

"He asked his Sunday School teacher why God killed all the sinners during Noah's time, but then later changed His mind and chose to save all the sinners when He sent His Son to atone for their sins," Sasha recalled.

"Precisely," the fortune teller said, emphatically. "He refused to accept his mother's death. Our religious leaders teach us that death is a part of life, but that's antithetical. Their explanation that we have to die to the things of this world is a contrived play on words to justify dropping anchor. It also is a convenience in their ministerial responsibilities.

"Tell me, ladies, which path you would choose to go Home? The easy, well-traveled one taught by your religious leaders that accepts death as the stairway to heaven, or the arduous, less-traveled one advocated by the Son of God along which the true interpretation of His words can be found so that we never taste death?

"Because that is the challenge of choice and the crisis of belief in a nutshell. Da Vinci put it another way. He said, "An artist's studio should be a small space because small rooms discipline the mind and large ones weaken it." Why? A spectacularly appointed, large room comes with many distractions compared to Spartan, smaller dwellings.

"Of course, large rooms are more comfortable. Yet, comfort is the enemy of discovery. It is discomfort that leads to New Worlds.

And to the disturbance that what has been taught since Adam and Eve is wrong. As Thomas noted in his conversation with Jesus, once we become disturbed, amazement is not far behind – amazement at what it truly means to have been created in the image of God...to live forever ruling over the All, on His authority, and never tasting death.

"It always has been troublesome to me that everyone simply dismisses the fact that Adam and Eve were created to live forever in Paradise by our Creator for Whom nothing is impossible. Do they think He changed His mind and stopped creating His children in His image? It is the same issue Jimmy noticed as a five-year-old, and that's how he got here. He wasn't chosen for this journey; he chose it by asking The Question.

"The fact that no one has lived forever is not proof that it's impossible, only that it hasn't been done, yet, because God's children continue to choose very poorly to trust the serpent – who never can be trusted to tell the Truth – over Him, the only one who can be trusted always to tell the Truth. That's what I mean by crisis of belief. Adam and Eve didn't believe God, and they died. And, ever since, *while His children claim to believe in Him, they still don't believe Him*. And they die.

"The serpent in the Garden telling Adam and Eve not to believe God today is disguised in ecclesiastical garments, and he's still telling God's children not to believe Him – that we are born to die, that living forever is impossible. Really, nothing has changed – it still is the serpent in the Garden telling Adam and Eve that God didn't really mean what He said when He warned them they would die if they ate the forbidden fruit.

"Sasha, this is the conversation you had with Father Simon earlier this evening, is it not?"

Sasha was stunned. "How could you know that?"

The fortune teller ignored her question and continued. "Have you thought to ask yourselves why God would not want His children to know what is evil? It is because to know evil, they would have to welcome the Evil One into their lives. And you can see where that has gotten them!

"Ultimately, though, the forbidden fruit is revealed to be not believing God, which puts the disbelievers on the side of the fence away from God where Death exists. Adam and Eve didn't believe God, ate the forbidden fruit, and they died. To this day, God's children still are choosing to eat the forbidden fruit, and they still are dying. They are choosing the word of the fallible over the Word of the Infallible.

"If only they recognized that living forever or dying always has been a choice, and that they still can choose to repent as the prodigal son did. God instantaneously would welcome them back Home with a great feast, and they would reclaim their divine inheritance of having been created in the image of their Father, and rule over the All without ever tasting Death."

In her wildest dreams, Madison could not have imagined that her sixth sense would have led to her standing in the company of Senator Fenimore's daughter and an enigmatic fortune teller at 3:30 in the morning outside the tiny Prophet Elias church in Hot Sulphur Springs, Colorado – built on that exact spot because of a cloud oracle witnessed by an enlightened Greek priest and two Greek immigrant families seventy years before – awaiting a 17 year-old prodigy to seize his moment.

Her preoccupation was interrupted by an unfamiliar voice from behind; "Sometimes a feeling is all we humans have to go on."

Both women wheeled around to see a man wearing a long-sleeved gold turtleneck with a Starfleet insignia on the left breast-pocket.

"Captain!" Sasha squealed. "Jimmy's going to be so glad to see you!"

Madison was astounded to see the legendary USS Enterprise captain and the others gathering behind them…with horses. "Wait, what's happening here?"

"And Señor Quixote, and Sancho, and Doc," Sasha enthused. She rushed down the steps to embrace the Man of La Mancha. "You saved my life!"

"At your service, Miss Sasha," the errant knight blushed. "But, you'll have to thank Miki, as well, and the fortune teller."

Despite everything she had seen over the past several days, the skeptical reporter had to pinch herself to make sure she still was in the present. "This can't be real!"

She hadn't realized she had registered her guardedness out loud.

"It depends on your perception of reality," responded the bemused Starfleet captain.

"Do I have a choice?"

"Of course you do. There always is choice. Never forget that. Your reality is the one you choose from all the overlapping universes."

As her story took another fantastic twist, Madison sighed, "No one is ever going to believe this."

"Your Uncle John did. And the most important thing is that you believe because once you stop, this all goes away. When your Uncle John first told you about parallel universes, you were on the outside looking in. Now, you're on the inside looking out, and who better to help you explore these different universes than yours truly?"

"Excuse me, Captain," Sasha apologized, as she grabbed the star-struck reporter's hand. "I want to introduce Madison to the rest of the gang."

One by one, the riders alighted from their respective mounts: Don Quixote from Rocinante, Sancho Panza from his donkey, Dapple, and Doc Holliday from his sturdy mare, Big Nose Kate.

Don Quixote bowed grandiloquently and kissed Madison's hand. "Enchanted!"

Sancho Panza clumsily imitated his master.

Doc Holliday tipped his hat with a hearty, "Howdy, Ma'am!" Then, he added, "You'll be riding with me."

"Where are we going?"

"Where no one has gone before, I expect."

The feel of the strong hands of one of the Old West's most famous personalities around her waist and boosting her into his saddle was not unpleasant, Madison realized with a rush.

From atop his powerful steed, Enterprise, the Captain led a

magnificent white horse over to Sasha and helped her into the saddle. "This is your horse."

"What about Jimmy?"

"That will be up to him."

Madison was enjoying a flirtatious moment with her renowned cowboy when her cell phone rudely cut in. It was Cal.

"Cal, I can't really talk right now," she almost giggled as Doc playfully blew in her ear.

"Are you kidding me?" her exasperated producer shouted. "Why not?"

"You wouldn't believe me if I told you."

"Madison, stop fooling around. I need the rest of the story!"

"You have to trust me when I say this, Cal, but we're all holding our horses, literally, and you have to hold yours, too."

"Who all? And what horses are you talking about?"

Madison hung up, then texted, "Talk later." And she turned off her phone.

* * *

The moment the front door to the Prophet Elias church closed behind him, Jimmy felt an otherworldly presence about him, and he noticed that the inside of the tiny chapel seemed to be bathed in an ethereal, almost heavenly, light.

A white-haired priest emerged from behind the icon screen and opened the altar doors. The grandfatherly clergyman beckoned him forward and met him halfway at the fourth row of pews.

Touching his right thumb to his ring finger, the priest moved his hand vertically then horizontally in the sign of the cross, blessing Jimmy before introducing himself .

"Demetrios, I am Father Meletios Diacandrew. I am humbled to welcome you to the Prophet Elias Greek Orthodox Church. We have been waiting to meet you for a very long time."

"Father Diacandrew?" Jimmy gawked, reverently, recalling the name from his conversation with Madison. "You were the one who saw the Cloud Oracle!"

"Yes, my son."

"That was almost seventy years ago. If you don't mind me saying, you don't look that old."

"Surely, you must know by now that time is a man-made construct, and that nothing is what it seems."

Jimmy chuckled. "I'm starting to get that idea. But this is all so new to me. I mean seven days ago, my life was so different."

"Your life was different, yes, but not you," the priest noted, wisely. "The Colorado River runs through Hot Sulphur Springs below. The water is new, but the river is old. As the river, your circumstances are new, but you are the same five-year old child who asked "The Question' twelve years ago."

Jimmy allowed Father Diacandrew's words to percolate in his mind. Finally, he asked, "Have you ever wondered why you were chosen to see the Cloud Oracle?"

The kindly priest smiled, "Of course, I did. And I prayed on it. Our Father answered that He hadn't chosen me, that they were my choices I had made of my own free will that put me in this place seventy years ago to witness the oracle and to understand what it meant.

"It is the same with you. You were not chosen. You made your own choices and you have chosen wisely. And, yet, you still are troubled and you still are searching. I know you have many more questions, but come forward with me. There are others who want to meet you and who better can answer them."

Jimmy followed the priest to the front of the nave.

"Wait here," the cleric told him, indicating the first pew on the left side of the aisle, directly in front of the icon depicting the Virgin Mary holding her Son. "Remember, you were not summoned here. You are here as a result of all the choices you've made in your life. The water is new, but the river is old."

With those words, Father Diacandrew climbed the three steps up to the altar and disappeared behind the icon screen, leaving Jimmy to contemplate the road ahead. He became aware of the incense burning in the altar - filling the warm air with an intoxicating aroma that served not to dull the senses, but to elevate them into a type of super-consciousness lifting him out of the temporal, while, at the same time, keeping his feet on the ground.

His head was spinning, as if he'd been drugged – but the Truth was this drug, and suddenly, the Son of God stepped out from behind the icon screen in all His radiance, cutting through Jimmy's haze. The dove of peace sat on His right shoulder, and, from out of nowhere, a deep voice boomed, "This is my Son, with Whom I am well pleased."

Jimmy immediately fell to his knees, but Jesus bade him to his feet. "I would wash your feet as you would wash mine," He said, humbly. And the Son of God invited the trembling boy to sit with Him in the first pew.

Jesus tried to put Jimmy at ease. "When my disciples couldn't cast out the demon from the child, I asked them how long I had to be with them before they found the true interpretation of my words. You have given the answer: nearly two thousand years."

Jimmy still couldn't untie his tongue.

"Jimmy," Jesus continued, "you've come such a long way to lose your voice. You have two, very powerful women waiting for you outside. What would they have you ask Me?"

The mention of Sasha and Madison snapped Jimmy from his awestruck daze. "I'm sorry, Lord, but I'm overwhelmed."

"Don't apologize, and please don't be intimidated. It is a lot to take in, I know. I have been in your shoes. However, as Father Diacandrew said, you are here because of your choices, and those choices originated from 'The Question.' Should we start there?"

That opened the floodgates. "OK, I don't believe our Father killed all those people during the Great Flood. Or, did He?"

Jesus studied Jimmy closely and smiled. "You are on the right path. It is as you say – our Father is not a killer. Those who died chose poorly not to believe Noah delivering His warning. You see, it wasn't raining when Noah built the ark, and they chose to ridicule him, instead.

"It is the same as it was with your first parents. They also chose poorly not to believe our Father and, rather, to doubt His warning, which led to their eventual deaths, as well.

"The account was written, however, in such a way as to encourage our brothers and sisters, born of hundreds and hundreds of years of slavery and ignorance, to change their course. And, given that context, Fear comes before Love, not only in the alphabet, but also in convincing those who have been subjected to such tortures to choose to shed their yokes of tyranny and to change their ways.

"Our Father knew He would be sending Me here the first time to correct the message and to save His children from their sins until one of them discovered what it meant to have been created in His image.

"Can you hear what I am saying?"

"I think so. This is the Second Coming?

"I am here a second time, yes, fulfilling part of the prophecy of Saint John. The rest is up to you."

"I'm not sure I understand."

"It is of the covenant between our Father and His children that I said that nothing would be impossible for whoever had the faith of a mustard seed. My Father's part of the covenant, or alliance, if you will, is to provide access to His authority over all things. His children's part of the covenant is to provide the conduit through which His authority would flow. And that conduit is called faith.

"There have been others who came before you whose faith was of such a magnitude as to access the authority of our Father, and they were able to accomplish what you call 'miracles:' the blind man having his vision restored after I rubbed clay on them, the paralyzed man picking up his pallet and carrying it home, the Roman soldier healing his beloved servant of an ailment that otherwise would have killed him…

"After each so-called miracle, I went to great lengths to assure those who had been healed that I wasn't responsible for them being able to overcome their afflictions. To each, I said, 'Your faith has healed you.'

"But Lucifer sent his gusts of wind and, eventually, they all blinked and fell into the water as did Peter."

"No one believes you entirely," Jimmy lamented.

"Well, almost no one," Jesus winked. "The lack of faith is testament to Lucifer's nefariousness, and to our brothers and sisters exercising their free will poorly, choosing not to believe, or putting personal agendas ahead of our Father and His will. It is why our Father didn't want His children to know evil. Nothing must come before Him. In effect, His children are putting their belief in Death ahead of their belief in Our Father and Me and in what We have told them.

"Be assured, His will continues to be to create children in His image to live forever as masters of their universe, on His authority."

Jesus smiled warmly. "It is so refreshing to speak with you. We've been anticipating this meeting for a very long time! Truly, it is absurd to think that our Father, for Whom all things are possible, and whose love for His children is uncompromising and eternal, would create them to die. The whole paradigm of being born to die is a thing of man, not a thing of God. It is a sin because it misses the mark. It separates His children from their Father. Death in this world awaits those who are separated from Him.

"It is one of the greatest sins because, to the undiscerning human mind, Death is accepted as sacrosanct and inviolable. It has been perpetuated through the ages through blind acceptance, a lethal choice to believe in impossibilities rather than to believe Me. It breaks the covenant – the conduit through which our Father's authority flows – thereby separating His children from Him and from His authority and their divine inheritance, and Death becomes a self-fulfilling prophecy."

Jimmy nodded. He was hearing the Truth for the very first time and it was indescribable. He felt an extraordinary lightness of being – the original freedom from all limits. The Truth, indeed, had set him free. It was the purest joy he'd ever experienced.

Then, he backtracked. Something was unclear. "You said "We...""

Jesus replied, "Yes?"

"You said, "We've been anticipating this meeting for a very long time.""

"Ah, you noticed," the Son of God acknowledged.

All of a sudden, the sweet-smelling incense that had filled the Prophet Elias chapel began to swirl and cluster in front of them, spinning faster and faster until gradually manifesting in an other-worldly, heavenly form.

At once, Jimmy knew he was in the presence of God and bowed his head in reverence.

"Hello, Jimmy." God greeted him compassionately.

"Hello, Father," Jimmy replied in awe, his gaze fixed on the ground two feet in front of him.

"Please be at ease," the Supreme Being insisted. "It is I who am gratified finally to meet you!"

His comment caught Jimmy completely unprepared. He looked up.

"Yes," God explained. "I have known all along the difficult choices you would make of your own volition. You have chosen wisely the path through the narrowest gate that no one before you ever has traveled. As the poet has written, it has made all the difference. You are a young man after my own heart, and I wanted to meet you in this world. As it would for any parent, it gives me great pleasure," He said with a glimmer in His eyes.

"Can I ask you a question," Jimmy stammered.

"You mean another one?" his Father teased, good-naturedly.

"Yes," he answered bashfully, "another one."

"Please!"

"Why me? I mean, why did You choose me for all of this."

"My son, it is as Father Diacandrew said. You are here as a result of your own choices. As you have testified, I never would seek to impose My will on any of My children. That's the way I intended it from the very beginning. To do otherwise would be to control you, to pull all your strings. Your freedom had to be complete, otherwise, where would I stop?

"I warned My first children not to take a bite of the apple from the Tree of Knowledge of Good and Evil. Even though I knew they would choose to disobey Me, and in doing so, they would die, I didn't stop them. I love all of My children – past, present, and future – too much for that. My intervention would have had eternal consequences. No one ever would be standing where you are now. My image is not that of a puppeteer."

"And You still create us that way – in Your image, to live forever as rulers over the All."

"Of course, I do."

"So, we are not born with the original sin of Adam and Eve."

"That would be contrary to My insistence of free will for all My children. The progeny of Adam and Eve did not choose to disobey Me in the Garden, so why should they be burdened with the consequences of their first parents' poor choices? Instead, they have inherited their tendency to sin.

"No, Jimmy, I have not changed, nor have I changed My mind. I am, to put it in your vernacular, an equal opportunity Creator. Every one of My children comes into this world as My first children did, with the same opportunities, and challenges, to live eternally and to rule over the All. The problem is in the translation. You have said, rightly, that I am not a killer. But my warning to Adam and Eve has been translated as a threat. And that's how it has been passed down through the ages – that I will kill those who disobey Me. Nothing could be further from the Truth.

"If it is difficult for you to comprehend this Love I have for My children, think of how much harder it was for My less evolved children. They understood only the crack of the whip. And so, in order for them to follow Me, I am portrayed as a vindictive, angry God who will strike down those who disobey Me.

"Moreover, the belief that a poor choice brought Death into this world, against which there is no recourse, suggests that I am an impotent Authority. My Son told the parable of the prodigal son. Again, they are the choices of the children that make all the difference. No one until you has chosen the path of the narrow gate that My Son told them would lead the way back Home. I do have authority over all things including Death. On My authority, My Son raised his friend Lazarus from the dead after he'd passed away four days prior.

"And then, in turn, My Son came back to this world three days after choosing to sacrifice His life to enter Lucifer's lair in order to free My children imprisoned by their choices. It is important that you understand Lucifer has no authority whatsoever. He is the jailer, yes, but My children have the key to their jail cells. They just don't know it, that they have a choice, that they have the key. And then there is the exacerbating wordplay by those who claim to believe in Me, but who don't believe Me that keeps the wool pulled over their eyes, and they are led further away from Me, instead of back Home to Me.

"If, as these theologians and religious leaders claim, there has to be Death to this world to enter the kingdom of heaven, then why would I intend to send My Son here a second time?"

Jimmy was mystified. How had he overlooked something so obvious? he chastised himself. Then, he gave himself the benefit of the doubt, deciding he would have gotten there, eventually.

God continued, and He was adamant. "Let me make this perfectly clear. Adam and Eve brought Death into their own world, not into anyone else's. That Death is perceived to be inevitable is the result of choosing poorly to believe Lucifer's lies that there is no choice.

"As I said, I don't play favorites. Living eternally or dying is as much of a choice for all My children as it was for Adam and Eve. There you have it, again, straight from My mouth: Death is a choice, as it always has been, and My children are choosing very poorly to believe in and accept its inevitability ahead of their belief in what I have told them.

"Now, getting back to 'The Question' you asked in Sunday School when you were very young – of course you were right. I don't kill my children when they disobey Me. What kind of a loving God, a parent to all, would do such a thing? Instead, what did I do when it became apparent that My children were lost in the darkness and unable to find their way back Home? I sent them a Light! My Son. To save them from themselves, in effect, from the poor choices they were making. This is not what an angry or vindictive God would do. A loving God forgives, and that's why it is said that the glory of Christianity is the triumph of forgiveness.

"Taking it a step further, this means that Adam's and Eve's most grievous choice was not to take a bite of the forbidden fruit, but to choose not to repent and ask for forgiveness. They would have been forgiven instantly, as was the prodigal son, and their return to Paradise would have been celebrated with a great feast.

"But I couldn't make that choice for them, either. It was incumbent on them to choose to turn back to Me. Otherwise, I would have been pulling their strings and taking away their free will. Make no mistake. I suffer the greatest pain every time one of My children succumbs to Lucifer's temptation, just as Death pains everyone in this world who loses a loved one.

"Yet, knowing that I will be reunited with My children, through My Son's sacrifice, is a salve that comforts and heals. It is this moment that has justified My love. It is why I wanted to meet you in this world."

Jimmy was completely overwhelmed by what he was hearing, and His Father sought to comfort him.

"My son, there are no insignificant choices. As you have seen, a single, unexamined choice can change the course of human history. I knew that loving My children so much as to give them free will came with great risks – sin, in other words, or making poor choices that missed the mark. But compared to the puppet alternative, it was a risk worth taking.

"Be that as it may, there always has been a 'get out of jail free' card, if you will. It is the most important choice – the choice to ask for forgiveness when one has sinned. Because all sins will be forgiven, no questions asked. Instantaneously. Just as they were for the prodigal son. No probation. No purgatory.

"You asked 'The Question' when you were five years old. Which means you've known for practically your entire life that there was something wrong with the world as it was presented to you – and that it started with the dogma of the church and with its protagonists. It was like a splinter in your mind that kept festering until the fortune teller came into your life."

Jimmy jumped at the opening. "That was You, wasn't it?"

"Was it? Did I send him to you, or did you choose to enter his tent at the carnival?"

"The carnival!" Jimmy exclaimed. "Was that real? Did my Mom really get killed?"

"As real as you chose for it to be. It was your subconscious trying to work around that splinter. And the riddle of Sasha. You see, even before Madison made you aware of overlapping universes, your subconscious was choosing the universe that solved those issues, and the one that became your reality.

"That's why free will is not negotiable. There always must be choice, and, through it, there can be the purest freedom!"

At that moment, Jimmy began to feel overwhelmed by the incense that had invaded his senses. He felt lightheaded, as if he was being lifted out of his body into a level of awareness that transcended his reality and tapped into the "ether," the essence of the universe. It was a flow of electromagnetic waves that permeated all matter and space which he had plugged into – a type of adrenaline made up of equal parts "nothing is impossible," and, "you have to see the world not as it is, but as it should be" – that pulsated through his veins.

He was flying...until, suddenly, he froze and came back to earth. The final destination of his journey had been revealed to him. He knew where he had to go, what he had to do, and what rules he needed to break to become captain of his own "enterprise." The realization was as a slap in the face of cold seawater across the bow of his ship that brought him back to the current reality inside the Prophet Elias Greek Orthodox Church.

"Oh my God!" he whispered in awe. But God wasn't there anymore. Nor was Jesus. Or Father Diacandrew. He was alone, but he wasn't. He felt the authenticity of those depicted on the icon screen who had come before him, and as he made eye contact with each of them, one by one, from left to right, it was as if they each knew what he was about to do and were giving him their blessing: Saint George, Archangel Michael, Prophet Elias, the Virgin Mary, Jesus, John the Baptist, Archangel Gabriel, and Saint Demetrios.

He paused. Demetrios. That was what the elderly priest had called him. What a coincidence! Or not.

A voice from behind startled him. "This is your moment, Jimmy. You must seize it," the fortune teller insisted. "Your time has come. They're waiting."

"Thank you," he replied solemnly. "For everything."

"No, Jimmy, thank you. You are the one, and only one, who refused to stop seeking. You have found the true interpretation of His words. You were disturbed, and now you are amazed. You must embrace your destiny."

"But, first…"

"Yes, I know. Let's go."

Jimmy was not prepared for what he saw when he opened the chapel door and stepped outside. Standing in front of him at the bottom of the stairs, were four powerful horses: one white, one red, one black, and one pale. And sitting atop those sturdy animals were the people most responsible for his journey: Sasha, on the white horse; Don Quixote and Sancho Panza, on the red horse; the Captain, on the black horse; and Doc Holliday and Madison, on the pale horse.

He was mesmerized by the show of support, and he felt himself trembling. Not from fear, but from the extra adrenaline occasioned by his "posse" ready to follow him wherever he led, no questions asked.

He walked down the steps to the pale horse on his right. "Doc, I can't thank you enough for being here."

The storied dentist-cum-gambler-cum-gunfighter tipped his hat. "This huckleberry has your back!"

Turning to Madison, he said, "Thank you for bringing me here." He paused. "I know why I'm here, but I can't tell you how this going to end."

"That's why I'm here, Jimmy. I have to know the ending. I've waited thirteen years for it. Probably my whole life, actually. Cal's going to pull his hair out when I tell him I'm sitting on a horse behind Doc Holliday, forget about whatever comes next!"

Jimmy made his way to the black horse. "Captain, it is such an honor to meet you. Your choice to change the rules to solve the captain's test truly inspired me."

"And I have been inspired by you, Jimmy. I'm ready to follow you to where no man has gone before," he winked.

Jimmy moved on to the red horse. "Señor Quixote, you helped me to destroy 'The Premise' and bring my mother back to life. They've called you 'mad' for tilting at windmills. Well, I'll tell you this – there's not enough madness in this world!"

The errant knight sat a little taller in his saddle. "Thou hast seen nothing yet!" he proclaimed grandiosely. "Do you still have it?"

The Man of La Mancha was referring to the medallion depicting a knight sitting high atop his steed, his lance at the ready, that his father had given him and that he, in turn, had bequeathed to Jimmy before they had tilted at Carrasco and at "The Premise."

The teenager reached inside his shirt and pulled out the medallion at the end of a thin gold chain. "I have worn it since you gave it to me and, as you promised, it has brought me nothing but good luck! Thank you."

The knight bowed extravagantly. "At your service!"

Finally, he turned to his soulmate sitting atop the white horse. Tears welled in his eyes as he searched for words that seemed so inadequate.

"Sasha, you saved my life. I was drowning in self-pity, yet, somehow, you saw through it and reached out to me and invited me to the Sadie Hawkins dance. But instead of going to the dance, you took me to the carnival. And that kiss...And the fortune teller..." Jimmy choked up.

Tears streamed down Sasha's cheeks. "Jimmy, I'll say it again, you really know how to show a girl a good time! I love you, I'll always love you. And I'll follow you to the ends of the earth!"

That was all Jimmy needed to hear. Wiping the tears from his eyes, he hopped onto the saddle in front of Sasha, and they sealed their devotion to one another with a kiss as sweet as the mythological music Orpheus played that melted the coldest hearts of Hades and Persephone, and moved them to grant the release of his beloved Eurydice from their underworld prison.

Jimmy leaned back and wiped the tears from Sasha's face. He grinned. "To the ends of the earth, huh? Well, then, hold on! We're going further than that!"

Sasha wrapped her arms tightly around Jimmy's waist as he dug his heels into the sides of the robust white horse. The mighty stallion got the message – it reared up on its hind legs, and Jimmy called out to the rest of them, "We ride!"

And ride, they did! On the seventh day, at full gallop, never was there a more magnificent seven, as they passed through the Berthoud Pass portal, through centuries, and eons, eschewing every windmill along the way, with a single destination in mind.

How long did they ride? Hours? Days? Weeks? Months? Years? No one ever will know as they bore deeper and deeper into the realm where Time did not exist.

When Uriel appeared on the horizon, the indefatigable stallions kicked into hyper-speed. As the riders approached the six-winged seraphim, the angel laid down his flaming sword, giving his blessing to the mission that had been laid out for Jimmy from the very beginning.

Charging forward, they began to discern the improbable shape of what appeared to be a human form in the distance. Improbable, because they hadn't seen anything even remotely resembling a human being since they took off from the Prophet Elias Church.

And, suddenly, Jimmy called out at the top of his lungs, "EVE! NO!"

Startled to hear a voice that clearly was not Adam's, the woman, about to take a bite of an apple, hesitated. She pulled back from the fruit to see what the commotion was all about, and who had called out her name.

The serpent who had been tempting the woman to partake of the forbidden fruit, panicked, and redoubled his efforts to get her to stray as the riders approached.

Doc Holliday pulled out a rifle from underneath his greatcoat and took aim with the pale horse at full gallop. And he pulled the trigger.

None of the seven could know if William Tell again would be called upon to replicate his celebrated marksmanship – or if he even would be born again, for that matter – but the famed archer from the world left behind, renowned for shooting an apple off the top of his young son's head, would have been proud to have seen the dentist's shot finding a similar mark.

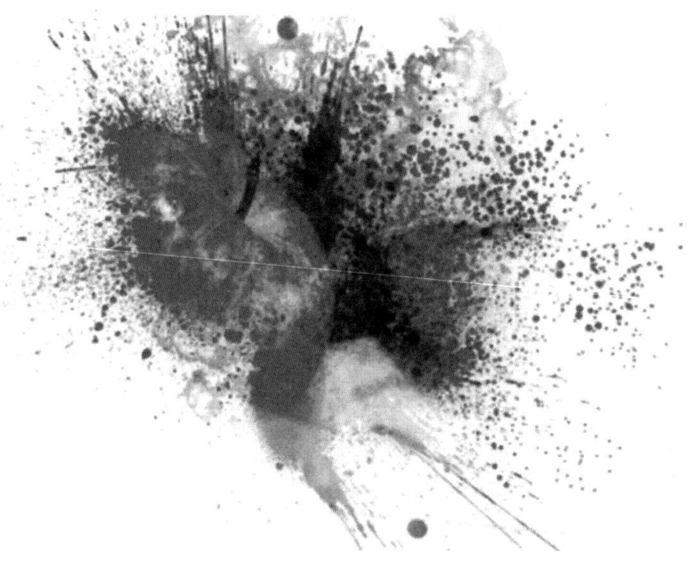

And humanity got a second chance.

Acknowledgments

The expression, "It takes a village to raise a child," also applies to writing and publishing a book. The writing is the "easy" part, especially when the characters take over and the writer simply follows along, taking notes and providing an accounting of the choices they make and of the journey that results which oftentimes – as in this case – deviate from what the writer originally had in mind. But, when the characters are well-defined and the writer trusts them, they will choose their own path and everyone, the writer included, will be better off for it.

"Easy" was put in quotation marks because the writer has to figure out a way to remove himself from his own reality and insert himself into his characters' reality. And when the writer is married and has three beautiful daughters, he has to remove himself from the lives of his wife and children for hours at a time – hundreds of hours, in fact. So, first of all, I want to acknowledge the love/patience, and support of my wife, Doria, and my daughters Elleni, Cassiane, and Mariah for allowing me the time to pursue my passion.

The difficult part comes later: the business part of writing. It is a daunting task that can destroy dreams and egos. For the un-agented writer, who has yet to achieve the notoriety of a Stephen King or a JK Rowling, the odds of finding an agent or publisher willing even to talk to him seemingly are longer than those of winning a lottery. This is the part where hopes are dashed and self-esteem takes a hit that many times is unrecoverable.

This is where daughter Mariah comes in. As a kindergarten teacher, her school year ends towards the end of May. Three years ago, her summer employment was weeks away and she needed something to do in the interim – almost at the exact time that my manuscript was ready to be peddled. A light went off in my head – I could slough off the dreaded business aspect to her and pay her $500 to search the Internet for agents and/or publishers who might be interested in working with me. I had no expectations. There literally are hundreds, if not thousands, of these agents/publishers to prospect, and I told her of the long odds involved. Yet, armed with a few key words, nimble fingers, and a Millennial mindset, she dove headlong into the project. I told her she didn't have to treat it like a full-time job, that she just could multitask late at night when she was watching tv, listening to music, or talking on the phone with friends. That age group can multitask like no other.

A week went by with nary a word – and I knew she was running into the same brick wall that had been my experience for my first book, *How To Lift Cars Off Your Face And Other Tips For Living Forever.* But, on the tenth day, she called me at work and I could discern the excitement in her voice when she gushed, "Dad, I think I found one!"

Of course, I was skeptical, but I played along, not wanting to rain on her parade while it lasted. She directed me to the website of the Black Spring Press. When I read, "...the identity and the vision of the press was declared instantly, as celebrating outsider, underground, outlaw, radical, and avant-garde voices and styles, unafraid of exploring taboo subjects and expressing the truths about human lives," I was at once dumbfounded, shocked, and excited. It was as if the publisher was speaking to me directly. "Omigod, Mariah, you might be right!"

Never had I been so hopeful in sending out a query – it was the same feeling one gets when, for the first time, they meet the person they are going to marry. I kind of knew this was "the one." And when I received an email a few days later from Todd Swift, the publishing director of the Black Spring Press, saying that he was interested in my manuscript, my whole body began to shake.

There followed several emails back and forth, and a phone conversation – and we came to terms. The next thing I knew, I was on a plane to the United Kingdom to meet my publisher! Needless to say, my nerves were on high alert on my way to meet Todd at the Maida Vale Underground station, but he immediately put me at ease with his kindness, his humility, his intuition, and, yes, his unkempt brilliance not unlike Philip Henslowe, in the movie, *Shakespeare in Love*. We ended up spending hours together, and I knew straight away that he "got" me and that I was right where I needed to be. So, a million thanks, Todd, for your trust and your friendship, and for taking a chance on this outsider, underground, outlaw, radical, and avant-garde writer, unafraid of exploring taboo subjects and expressing the truths about human lives!

Then came Cate Myddleton – does the name sound familiar? This Cate's surname comes with a hyphen: Myddleton-Evans, and she is my editor. To say that I feared working with any editor would be an understatement of the highest order. As all writers do, I had bared my soul writing this book, and I was afraid a complete stranger might find fault not only with my work, but also with my soul, coldly dissecting both and telling me they were faulty in one regard or another – and filling my pages with red editing marks, heartlessly cutting and slashing, and rearranging my words until there hardly was any resemblance to the original manuscript.

Nothing could have been further from the truth. Kate Middleton might be the Princess of Wales, but Cate Myddleton-Evans is my lovely Princess of Editing. In tackling my book, I found her to be compassionate and sensitive with a keen eye for detail and a rapier-like intellect that enhanced, rather than detracted from, my effort. Thank-you, Cate – I cannot begin to describe the depth of my appreciation!

Last, but certainly not least, I would like to thank you, the reader, for taking a chance to read my book. I hope it was as spiritual and thrilling for you to read as it was for me to write it. God bless.

To continue the conversation, or to find out more, I can be reached at: www.tomcladiswrites.com